Christma... love and ... blend toge... those who... missing a m... hard to think what might be at the top of their Christmas lists…

A Child's Christmas Wish

Three heart-warming stories of families formed during the festive season

A Child's Christmas Wish

featuring

Snowbound Baby
by Susan Meier

Meet Me Under the Mistletoe
by Julianna Morris

Stranded with Santa
by Janet Tronstad

*M&B™ and M&B™ with the Rose Device
are trademarks of the publisher.
Harlequin Mills & Boon Limited, Eton House,
18-24 Paradise Road, Richmond, Surrey TW9 1SR*

A CHILD'S CHRISTMAS WISH
© by Harlequin Books S.A. 2007

Snowbound Baby © Susan Meier 2005
Meet Me Under the Mistletoe © Julianna Morris 2005
Stranded with Santa © Janet Tronstad 2002

ISBN: 978 0 263 86599 8

009-1207

*Harlequin Mills & Boon policy is to use papers that are
natural, renewable and recyclable products and made from
wood grown in sustainable forests. The logging and
manufacturing processes conform to the legal environmental
regulations of the country of origin.*

*Printed and bound in Spain
by Litografia Rosés S.A., Barcelona*

SNOWBOUND BABY

Susan Meier

Snowbound Holiday Punch

2 tsp whole cloves
1 tsp allspice
4 sticks cinnamon
1/2 cup sugar
2 1/2 cups water
1 cup frozen lemonade
1 cup frozen orange juice
2 pints cranberry juice
1 1/2 quarts iced water

Combine spices, sugar and 2 1/2 cups water in saucepan. Simmer 10 minutes, strain and cool. Combine lemonade, orange juice and cranberry juice and add to spice mixture. Just before serving, add iced water. Pour over ice in punch bowl for serving.

Ginger ale can be substituted for iced water.

SUSAN MEIER

is one of eleven children, and though she's yet to write a book about a big family, many of her books explore the dynamics of "unusual" family situations, such as large work "families," bosses who behave like overprotective fathers, or "sister" bonds created between friends. Because she has more than twenty nieces and nephews, children also are always popping up in her stories. Many of the funny scenes in her books are based on experiences raising her own children or interacting with her nieces and nephews.

She was born and raised in western Pennsylvania and continues to live in Pennsylvania.

Chapter One

"Son of a…"

Cooper Bryant cut off his curse, needing all of his mental and physical energy to maneuver his eighteen-wheeler around a Toyota that was stuck in the middle of the snow-covered mountain road. Passing the car, he peered down, ready to make a gesture to let the driver know exactly how he felt about people who blocked the way. But he saw the stranded motorist was a young woman. And she had a baby in the back seat.

Shoot!

Well, he couldn't stop to help. Ironically, the shortcut that he'd cajoled from the turnpike tollbooth attendant hadn't allowed him to outrun the storm, but had, instead, slowed him down. The twisting, winding route up the Western Pennsylvania mountain couldn't be taken with any kind of speed. The curves all seemed to hug the edge of the world. And once a semi lost speed climbing a steep slope, it was impossible to get it back. If Cooper stopped now, his truck would stay exactly where it was until the state plowed away the snow.

He made it another couple hundred feet, but his wheels began hesitating. Cooper knew his truck wasn't going to reach the top. Unlike the driver in the Toyota who had simply parked where her car had stopped, he eased his vehicle onto the first shoulder he found that had more than six inches of space between his truck and a cliff, and cut the engine.

He didn't like wasting precious hours like this— however, lost time was better than a wreck. He didn't have one of the elaborate, expensive trucks with sleeping quarters, but he'd passed several hunting cabins. One of them, if not all of them, probably had a woodstove. He had two sandwiches, a thermos of coffee, soap, towels, a blanket and a shaving kit. He could be comfortable for the night, and rested when he got back on the road tomorrow.

Hoisting his backpack of supplies, Cooper jumped out of the cab and into the crystallized white snow. He had switched his trademark cowboy boots for thick work boots at the truck stop off the turnpike exit, but he still had his black Stetson and denim jacket. Unfortunately, they weren't much against the bite of the unforgiving mountain wind. Cooper was an Arkansas boy, born and bred, but he'd transplanted himself to Texas where he and a buddy had bought a ranch. For the past three years he'd been saving the money he made driving truck to increase the herd and he'd been everywhere from Oregon to Florida. He'd experienced cold, wind, even snow…but not like this.

He tucked himself more tightly inside his jacket as he made his way down the hill. Only about twenty feet from his truck he saw a cabin. Small, with chipping white paint and a sagging roof, the structure was nonetheless good enough for the night. He was about to turn down the snow-covered lane when he remembered the young woman in the Toyota.

And her baby.

Shoot!

He sighed. He wasn't much on company. Ever. His beliefs were so far out of sync with those of the general population that every time he opened his mouth he seemed to get into an argument. In his reckless youth, that had led to some nasty bar fights. Even his own brothers had said he was always making trouble and kicked him out of their lives eight years ago.

Determined to keep his world peaceful, he wasn't somebody who went looking for human contact. So, fate should have known better than to throw a stranded woman in his path. He might be able to help her find shelter, but he wasn't about to play gin rummy until the snowplow came through. If she was a chatterbox who needed constant entertainment, she'd get on his nerves and he'd probably end up making her cry.

Yeah, this was going to be peachy.

Still, he started walking to her car. He didn't get too far

before he realized it was at least two football fields away. If he went down the mountain to offer the woman the opportunity to share a cabin, he wouldn't simply be going the length of two football fields to get her. He would have to walk those two football fields back up again.

Shoot.

He didn't want to let a mama and baby freeze to death, but she should have known better than to travel on a day like this.

Cooper continued down the mountain anyway. Slipping and sliding as the powerful wind pushed him along the steep slope, he traveled the distance in what he knew had to be record time. In only a few minutes, he rounded a curve and saw the Toyota. It was now covered with snow, and he could see no sign of exhaust coming out the back. Cooper guessed the driver was either gone or she'd quit running her motor to save gas for the long night. Though he knew having her along would be nothing but irritation to his already frayed nerves, he couldn't stop a surge of male ego. If she was still in that car, she would be really glad to see him.

With the wind urging him on, he half ran the rest of the way, almost losing his balance twice on the icy incline. When he reached the car, he tapped on the driver's side window. The snow-covered glass began a very slow descent, but it stopped after about four inches. Then the barrel of a gun greeted him.

Cooper jumped back. *What the hell!*

"Get lost," the young woman yelled. "I don't have any

money and I'm not willing to share my car with you. I have a baby."

"I don't want to share your car. My truck's parked just up the road." Cooper paused long enough to curse under his breath because his heart was jumping like a jackrabbit. Only an idiot used a gun so carelessly. "Look, I passed three hunting cabins on my walk down the hill. I saw you on my way up but couldn't stop. If you want, you can spend the night in a cabin with me, and I'll take care of the wood-stove. If you don't, that's cool, too."

He waited for a response but got none. Fool woman! Just like a mare he'd bought two years ago. Didn't have a whit of common sense.

He gave her another thirty seconds. Still nothing.

"Suit yourself," he called, then turned and began re-climbing the hill, the howling wind nearly blowing him down again. He knew it couldn't be any warmer than ten degrees. When the sun set even that scant heat would disappear. With the wind chill it would be so far below zero the number would be irrelevant. Anyone without proper shelter would freeze to death. Even if that kid had a blanket—*four* blankets—she and her baby would freeze to death.

Shoot!

He let the wind blow him back down to her car, then tapped on the window and jumped out of the way as the glass lowered, just in case she aimed the barrel of the gun at him again.

"It's going to be below zero tonight. You are not going to survive in that car."

"We'll be fine."

"No, you won't!" Getting angry now, he tried her door but it was locked. "If you didn't have a baby, I wouldn't give a flying fig about you freezing to death. But you've got a kid. You have to be reasonable."

"I am reasonable." She sighed and rolled down the window. Cooper couldn't help noticing her blond hair, clear pink skin and cornflower blue eyes. "Look, I called a friend. Any minute now I'll be rescued."

At that Cooper laughed. "Rescued? Haven't you heard the weather?"

Her pretty eyes narrowed. "Yes and no. I heard about a snowstorm, but it's always snowing here. I live on the other side of this mountain. I'm so used to the snow I hardly pay attention."

"Well, you should have paid attention because this is a blizzard." He drew in a quick breath and his lungs rebelled at the cold. "The temperatures are falling faster than normal. They're predicting two feet of snow. If your friend is smart, he'll stay home."

Waiting for her reply, he blew on his hands. Even with gloves his fingers were going numb.

When she said nothing, his patience suddenly evaporated and he yelled, "Come out in thirty seconds or I'll break your car window to save your kid."

He swore he heard her sigh with disgust, but decided it had to be the wind. Then she kicked open her door and pushed herself out. A blast of air caught her pale hair and fanned it away from her head.

More concerned with getting them safely to shelter, he barely noticed the pretty feathery locks. "Where's your hat?"

She turned and her blue eyes pinned him with an exasperated look. "It's in the car."

"Good, put it on and let's get the hell going. It's cold."

She said, "Right," then bent and reached inside her vehicle. Her red leather jacket only came to her waist and when she stretched he got a full view of the enticing curve of her bottom.

Cooper quickly turned away. Since she had a baby, the woman was obviously married, and staring at her behind, no matter how nicely rounded, was inappropriate.

The wind kicked up. From the back of her car, the woman pulled out a white plastic contraption lined with pink and navy blue plaid padding. She set it on the driver's seat, then reached into the back again and extracted a baby wearing a pink snowsuit and wrapped in a pink blanket. She sat the kid in the padding of the white plastic thing. When she looped a handle from beneath and snapped it into place, Cooper guessed the contraption was some kind of baby carrier.

"I should take her," Cooper said, assuming the baby was a girl because of all the pink.

"I'll carry her," the woman disagreed, leaving the baby on the front seat of her car so she could dig out an enormous diaper bag. Pink plaid to match the travel seat, it was stuffed to capacity and looked more like a trash can with a strap. "You take this."

She shoved the two-ton diaper bag into Cooper's arms just as a gust of wind hit him and he nearly fell backward. But he didn't. He didn't fall. He didn't curse. He didn't even yelp. Instead he saw the nice, quiet evening he could have had blow away on a frigid blast of air.

He nodded up the hill. "The cabins are this way."

He turned to begin the upward trek, but she caught his arm with her glove-covered fingers.

Everything inside of Cooper stilled. It had been so long since anybody had dared to touch him—except in a fight— that his hands automatically curled into fists. But before he instinctively took a punch, he looked into her round blue eyes and a tingling sensation exploded in his gut. Now he understood why she mistrusted him. She was gorgeous and he was about to spend the night with her.

With her body shielding the open car door and Daphne from the wind, Zoe Montgomery stared at the man in front of her, pretending her shivers were from cold, not from fear. She shouldn't have touched him. Until she'd touched him he'd seemed like a grumpy Kola bear. Now he looked like an angry panther. His green eyes glittered, his hands were fisted and his body was stiff, poised and ready to strike.

Tall and lean, with a black Stetson pulled low over his eyes, her rescuer was definitely all male, but he also had an air of trouble. For all she knew he could be an escaped convict. Well, actually, he'd said he drove a truck and she'd seen an eighteen-wheeler pass her about ten minutes after her car had simply stopped. But truckers weren't always reputable. Some were hellions who took advantage of roaming the country doing all kinds of crazy things and this guy obviously had a hair trigger.

Still, not all truckers were bad. Some were Good Samaritans. Touchy though he was, this man could be one of those who saw it as his responsibility to help anyone on the road when problems hit.

Also, her options were limited. Whoever he was, he was right. If her car hadn't died because it was old, but because it couldn't handle the snow on the mountain, then LuAnn— her rescuer—wasn't getting up here, either. And if the temperature was about to plummet, Zoe knew she and Daphne would freeze to death in the car.

She wasn't sure she was any safer in a cabin with a stranger, but technically she didn't have to "stay" with him. There were lots of hunting cabins on this mountain. Many of them were in clusters. He could sleep in one. She and Daphne could sleep in another.

She took a silent, life-sustaining breath. Not only was that a safe plan, but also it was a smart plan. He didn't look like the kind of guy who wanted anyone invading his space, and she didn't need anyone helping her. When her ex-husband had discovered Zoe was pregnant and left her, she'd gotten a crash course in taking care of herself. Brad had moved on so quickly, he hadn't bothered divorcing her. She'd had to divorce him. And even though there was a court order filed for child support, Brad didn't honor it.

Zoe knew some men saw responsibility as a frightening trap, but more than that, she'd learned the value of standing on her own two feet and she wasn't letting anybody steal her independence away from her. She liked taking care of herself. This trucker didn't want her around and she didn't want him around. Separate cabins worked.

She pulled her fingers off his forearm and smiled slightly to take the sting out of her forwardness of touching him. "Or we could go down the mountain *with* the wind rather than against it. I live around here, remember? This part of the mountain is used almost exclusively for hunting. We're bound to find more cabins on the way down. In fact, we'll probably find clusters of cabins," she added, preparing him for the fact that they would stay in different shelters, if he hadn't already decided that himself.

He grunted as he hoisted the diaper bag on his shoulder where it settled beside his backpack. Then he turned and began walking down the hill.

Zoe grabbed Daphne's baby carrier from the front seat of the car, slammed the door, and followed him. The wind picked up. Swirling along the ground, it gathered fallen snow and propelled icy crystals upward, causing them to slap against Zoe's face. She pulled Daphne's blanket loosely over her head to shield her from the blasts, then lifted the carrier to chest height and slanted it toward her to provide even more protection for her baby.

"By the way, I'm Zoe Montgomery," she shouted to be heard above the wind. "And this is my daughter, Daphne."

For several seconds the trucker said nothing and Zoe worried that he wouldn't tell her his name. Not that she really *needed* to know his name, but if he wouldn't tell it, there could be a reason. Which took her back to her concern that he might be a criminal. Or worse, he could be a sex offender who had unspeakable plans for her. His not telling her his name was not a good sign.

Adrenaline pumped into her bloodstream and she remembered the gun in her jacket pocket. As a single mother, who lived alone on the edge of a small town that was too close to the turnpike, she frequently carried. Her cousins had shown her everything she needed to know about guns when they'd taught her to hunt, so she wasn't an amateur. And she also wasn't a hothead. She wouldn't arbitrarily shoot this trucker, but if he tried anything she wouldn't hesitate to defend herself and her daughter.

But right now, because they weren't too far from her car, simply running back to her vehicle and locking herself in was much smarter than shooting somebody.

She was formulating her plan of how to most effectively bolt when he said, "I'm Cooper Bryant."

So grateful she nearly collapsed with relief, Zoe said, "Well, it's nice to meet you, Cooper Bryant."

But Cooper Bryant said nothing. Either he didn't agree that it was nice to meet her or he wasn't the kind of guy to make small talk. Fine. She'd already figured out he was a loner. She respected that. He would probably jump for joy when she told him she preferred her own cabin and was perfectly capable of keeping a fire going all night.

They struggled another ten feet down the mountain. With every step they took, the temperature seemed to fall. The inside of Zoe's nose began to freeze. She huddled the baby carrier closer to her chest, protecting Daphne. She didn't need a thermometer to know it was much colder than it was even ten minutes ago. This storm was worse than any she'd ever seen.

The stranger beside her tapped her arm. Rather than try to speak above the wind that now roared through the trees and hollows, he pointed to the left. Cuddling Daphne's carrier against her, Zoe squinted, trying to make out what he apparently saw, but the only things in her line of vision were the black trunks of barren trees and swirling white snow. Visibility was down to about three feet. And that was another problem. If the wind and snow took away their ability to see, they could easily get lost in the woods.

She shook her head, indicating she saw nothing, and he caught her arm and hauled her across the road and up the slope into the woods.

Clinging to the baby carrier, which bounced precariously because of the trucker's hold on her arm, Zoe barely kept up with him. Fear churned through her at the way he was dragging her as if she were a kidnap victim. In her head she said every prayer she knew, hoping she hadn't gotten herself and her baby into terrible trouble, as the stranger propelled her through the woods, almost toppling her when he turned her to walk into the oncoming wind again. She gasped for breath, and righted herself, tightening her hold on Daphne. But as she did, she suddenly saw what he must have seen—what had motivated him to shove her through the forest.

A *house!*

Even if they had to spend the night, they would have a bathroom, food…and be among people! She wouldn't be alone with him!

Trying to run in the deep snow while hugging a bulky baby carrier, Zoe nearly fell twice. But her escort was running, too. She'd never felt the temperature fall so quickly and knew they had to get to shelter *now* or die.

With her boots clumped with snow, she stumbled on the front porch steps. When Cooper Bryant reached the top, he turned and grabbed the baby carrier from her hands, hauling it to his side before he caught Zoe's hand and pulled her up, too.

Still holding Daphne's seat, he ran across the plank porch to the door and pounded. Huddling into her insubstantial leather jacket and shivering violently, Zoe noticed there were no lights on in the house. A new fear tumbled through her. If there was no one home, they were in big trouble. God only knew how far they would have to go to the next shelter. And even if they did easily find another building, there was no guarantee it would have a stove. And if they found a cabin with a stove, there was no guarantee it would have wood.

If this house didn't pan out, there was a very good possibility she and Daphne would die.

"Here!"

Cooper Bryant shoved Daphne's baby carrier at Zoe and she caught it in trembling hands, again clutching Daphne close to her to protect her from the freezing wind. Cooper Bryant reached into his back pocket and retrieved his wallet. Just as quickly, he pulled out a credit card. Before Zoe realized what he was doing, he was sliding the card into the space between the doorknob and wood frame.

"You can't!"

He peered at her from beneath his Stetson. His green eyes glittered with annoyance. The angles and planes of his face were drawn in stern lines. Yelling to be heard above the roar of the wind through the trees, he said, "In case you haven't noticed, we don't have a choice."

He shimmied the card a few times, jiggling the doorknob as he did. The wind howled. Frigid air pricked at Zoe's cheeks. The lock on the door gave and Cooper shoved against the wood closure, opening it.

He grabbed Daphne's seat and Zoe's arm, propelling both Zoe and her baby into the house before him. Still holding Daphne, he slammed the door closed and for ten seconds or so they stood in the entryway of the simple two-story frame house, just breathing.

When it sunk in that they were out of the cold and safe, Zoe reached for Daphne, taking the handle of her baby carrier from Cooper Bryant's hand. They might be out of danger from the elements, but the ease with which this man had gotten them into a locked house increased her fears about him. Worse, she couldn't send him out into the cold to look for another shelter. Visibility was so bad now that he might not get back to the road.

"You're very good with a lock."

He returned the credit card to his wallet. "I knew this probably wouldn't be much of a lock."

She swallowed. "Really?"

He sighed. "I'm not a criminal. It's just that this house is so far out in the woods I'm surprised the owner bothers with locks at all. I'm from a very small town in Arkansas where locks are more or less for show, so people frequently forget their keys. Everybody in Porter's good with a credit card."

Cooper reached for the light switch. At his touch, the entryway lit. "Hey, we're in luck. If the electricity is on, that means there's likely a furnace and maybe even food in the fridge." He walked down the corridor and flipped a second switch, turning on another light and revealing the square corner of a bed in the room at the end of the hall.

"And here's a thermostat. It's set at fifty-five—just enough to keep the pipes from freezing. The person who owns this place obviously planned to be away awhile." He shifted the knob of the gadget to the left and the sound of a furnace rumbling to life came up from the basement.

Zoe glanced around nervously. "I don't feel right about this."

"You'd rather freeze to death?"

"No. But this is somebody's *home*."

Cooper tossed Daphne's diaper bag to the floor along with his backpack before he removed his jacket, revealing a red plaid work shirt and nice-fitting jeans.

Zoe blinked. She'd already noticed that he was handsome, but in the silence of the foyer she was suddenly taking note of other things. For one, he was older. He had the air of experience that made a man sexy. Add that to his

dark, dangerous, mysterious personality and he was one seductive guy.

She swallowed. Luckily, that was exactly the opposite of
the kind of man she wanted. She was no longer "into" sexy
guys.

Once he'd hooked his coat on a peg, he glanced around.
"I don't think this is somebody's home. From the setting
on the furnace and the dust on that TV," he said, pointing
into a sitting room off to their left, "it looks more like a
weekend retreat."

"It still belongs to somebody."

"Who would probably welcome us to spend the night in
his house rather than freeze to death." He grabbed his
backpack and slung it over his shoulder, then like a boss accustomed to giving orders, or a chauvinist who thought all
women were pea-brains, he nudged Zoe to look down the
hall. "There's your bedroom. You can have the one on the
first floor to be closer to the kitchen since you have a kid.
I'm going upstairs."

She tried to pretend she didn't notice his high-handed-
ness and smiled graciously. "Don't you want to wait until
I fix us something to eat?"

He patted the backpack. "I have a thermos of coffee and
two sandwiches. No need for us to even speak another
word."

Though Zoe had planned for them to separate, something
about his tone confused her. She hadn't asked for his help.
He had volunteered it, yet he was acting as if she was an
unwanted thorn in his side. "You're leaving?"

"Think of it as me giving you your privacy. I don't need to entertain you just because I rescued you."

There was that tone again, the one that said having her around was a huge inconvenience. She couldn't argue that he hadn't rescued her. Not realizing the severity of the storm, she would have waited for LuAnn until it was too dark to find shelter. So, technically, he had rescued her. But she'd certainly never asked him to entertain her.

"No one said you had to. In fact, I was going to suggest you find a different cabin once we were settled."

"Right," Cooper scoffed, starting up the steps.

Zoe knew she should have let him go, but she hated that she'd never gotten the chance to prove to her ex-husband that she wasn't a wimp, that she wouldn't have smothered him, that he could have stayed with her if he'd just given her a chance. She wasn't letting another man on the face of this earth believe she was a clingy female. She was defending herself. "I did intend to take care of myself."

Cooper stopped walking and sighed. "Oh, come on. A woman who looks like you doesn't ever have to worry about taking care of herself."

Zoe felt her eyes widen at the insult. "I'm a single mother. I have to know how to handle anything that comes along."

"And that's why you called somebody—a man, no doubt—and were waiting in your car."

"LuAnn would be insulted to hear you call her a man." Zoe drew a quick, bolstering breath. "I didn't realize the storm was as bad as it was or I would have looked for shelter, not called someone to come and get me."

He shook his head, and didn't even try to hide his smirk. "Right."

She gaped at him. "What kind of experience do you have with women anyway?"

"Enough to know that the really good-looking ones take advantage of their assets."

This time her mouth fell open. "As if good-looking men are any better! I married a good-looking man and he left me alone to have his baby. While I was fighting morning sickness and wondering how I'd pay the bills, he used *his* assets to very quickly replace me, as if to prove to me he didn't need me. So don't stand there like the pot calling the kettle black."

Clearly exasperated with her, he said, "Look, I'm—"

Zoe didn't want to hear what he had to say. The best way to prove she could handle any problem that came along would simply be to do it. To hell with him and his opinion. "Save your piddly explanation for someone who cares. You and your thermos of coffee can go upstairs. I want a good man, not just a good-looking man. You and *your assets* aren't needed down here."

Chapter Two

At the top of the steps Cooper found two bedrooms. He peered into the first, which had two single beds, then looked into the second and found a queen-sized bed with a thick comforter.

If the huge bed hadn't won him over, the thought of being wrapped in a comforter would have. His toes had long ago frozen. He didn't think the inside of his nose would ever be the same and he was sure his Arkansas-transplanted-to-Texas bones now had ice chips for marrow.

He tossed his backpack on the dusty dresser and sat on the bed to pull off his work boots and rub his feet. Though he had ratcheted up the furnace, the house wouldn't be warm for a while, if it truly heated up at all in the face of the biting wind. He massaged his sock-covered feet, trying to increase circulation, but in the quiet of the bedroom, he could hear Zoe Montgomery's movements below him.

Guilt tapped him on the shoulder, but he ignored it. He hadn't come upstairs because he liked to be alone. That was just a perk. He'd left to show her she was perfectly safe with him. She was a pretty girl with a face and figure that could set any man to drooling, and her physical appearance probably caused most men to make at least one pass at her. That was the best explanation for why she was skeptical of help from a man. Undoubtedly lots of the men who had offered her assistance in the past had counted upon something in return—most likely sex.

But Cooper wasn't interested. Well, he *was* interested if she was looking for a quick roll in the hay. But he was just about positive she wasn't. She'd admitted in her parting shot that her marriage had failed, so she was available. But she'd also said she wanted a good man, not merely a good-looking man, and when a woman said that it usually meant she was seeking a commitment. Rolls in the hay were not commitment-based. The way Cooper had it figured, she was one of those women who was searching for that special man who could make her trust again.

And Cooper was not anybody's special man so it was best to nip that fairy tale in the bud. God only knew how long they would be stranded together. Having felt the sting of the cold and seen the rapid rate of the snowfall, he was beginning to understand the biggest difference between a "storm" and a "blizzard" was that storms were a nuisance and blizzards were deadly. Smart people stayed indoors for the duration of a blizzard.

On top of that, as a trucker, Cooper had enough experience with highways and departments of transportation to realize that rarely traveled, two-lane roads used for shortcuts weren't the first to be cleared. He and Zoe were stuck in this house for the next twenty-four hours—at least. His actual guess was that they were here for the weekend. He didn't anticipate getting back to his truck before Monday morning.

But as long as he and Zoe had minimal contact, that might not be a problem. It was December twelfth. Though his brothers had bought the mortgage to his ranch and given him until Christmas to pay it off, he still had thirteen days. It would take him three to deliver his load and only another two to drive his certified check to Arkansas and put it in the hands of his brothers' lawyer. He had absolutely no intention of placing the check in Ty's hands, as he had been instructed in the letter advising him his brothers were calling in his debt. No court in the land would side with them if they tried to take his ranch just because he'd given the check to the lawyer, rather than directly to his brother.

Thirteen days was plenty of time. Technically, he had eight days of wiggle room. The storm wouldn't last eight days. The department of transportation crews wouldn't forget this road for eight days. There was no reason to be concerned about being stranded for a day or two. Particularly since he already had the check in hand.

Thinking about the check made him reach for his

backpack. His partner wasn't involved in his family's feud, so Cooper had taken it upon himself to find the money for the balance of the mortgage. He'd cashed in his savings account and IRA, and had been forced to use the herd money, but he had almost every dime. All he needed was the pay from this delivery to add to the certified check. Then his brothers couldn't hurt him anymore. He'd never again be so stupid as to give them an opportunity like a mortgage to find him.

He unlatched the closure of the backpack, lifted the lid and slid his hand inside to get the white envelope containing the check he'd had prepared at the bank. When his fingers found only two sandwiches, a coffee Thermos and a Twix bar, his heart stopped and he dumped the contents of his backpack on the bed.

But as everything came tumbling out, he remembered he had put the check in the safe in his truck. A new kind of panic tightened his chest. But he reminded himself the truck was locked. Hell, the safe was locked and it was hidden, camouflaged as the seat back. On top of that, conditions outside weren't fit for man or beast. Nobody was going anywhere near his truck. His money was fine. There was absolutely no reason to freak out.

He sighed. He might not freak out, but he sure as hell couldn't feel comfortable about leaving a check worth hundreds of thousands of dollars in an abandoned vehicle. Still, since there was nothing he could do about that until morning, there was no sense dwelling on it.

After eating his sandwiches and returning the candy bar

to his backpack, he lay down on the bed and angled his Stetson over his eyes, but from downstairs he heard the baby cry. The sound got louder and louder until little Daphne was screaming, sounding like she was testing out her lungs.

Cooper squeezed his eyes shut. Great. As if it wasn't bad enough he had a constant niggle of doubt about whether his check was safe, he was stuck with an oversensitive woman and a crying baby. If he had any tolerance for cold at all, he'd go back to his truck, get his money and find another cabin.

But he couldn't handle the cold and it was getting dark, too dangerous to go outside even for a few minutes. He took a breath, pretending he couldn't hear the crying baby or the soothing voice of her mom and that he truly believed no one would steal his money, but he knew it would be a long, long night.

When Cooper opened his eyes again, muted light was edging into his bedroom through the dusty blinds on the window, and he bounced up in bed. He'd chosen this room for the thick comforter, but had drifted to sleep on top of the covers and spent the night without it.

He couldn't believe he'd fallen into such a deep slumber that he hadn't heard a screaming baby. Positive that something had happened—like maybe the storm had stopped and his roomie had gotten curious about what he had in his truck—Cooper rolled out of bed, bounded down the stairs and made the sharp left into the kitchen.

Zoe stood at the sink, washing dishes. Without turning around she said, "Don't worry. I didn't run out to your truck and plunder for valuables. The baby's just asleep."

He stiffened. The clock on the stove said seven-fifteen. It had only been light for about twenty minutes. If she'd gone to his truck, she'd still be shivering. His check was safe.

But her reply reminded him that she was one incredibly defensive lady. He couldn't even give her her privacy the night before without her jumping him about his motives. She might be among the world's most beautiful women but she was pricklier than a cactus and suspicious as hell. And if he didn't say something, he would alert her that there really was something of value in his truck.

"I wasn't worried."

"Sure you were. That's the only explanation for why you ran down the stairs like your feet were on fire." She paused, then added, "Unless there's no bathroom upstairs."

Confused, Cooper said, "I didn't see a bathroom."

"Well, there's a bathroom in the bedroom I'm using. It's the only one I found. This is a really old house. I'm guessing it was built before indoor plumbing because the bathroom was built in the corner of the bedroom."

Cooper suddenly understood what she was talking about. He'd been so focused on making sure she hadn't gone to his truck that he'd forgotten nature's call. He said, "Thanks," and left the room.

Glad for a few seconds to collect himself before he faced Madam Cactus again, Cooper conceded that he had all but told her he had something important in his truck. That meant at some point he would have to brave the storm, get his check and pin it in his underwear for safekeeping because he was absolutely positive that was one place she wouldn't look.

But after he stepped into her bedroom he forgot all about the check, the temperatures and even nature's call. He could smell her. He didn't know if she had special soap or shampoo or maybe perfume that she carried in her purse, but the room already smelled intimately of something light and tropical. Oceans and coconut oil. Suntan lotion.

His mind jumped to a hot beach and Zoe in a bikini and he squeezed his eyes shut. But he forced them open again. He was not attracted to her…well, he was attracted, but he knew he shouldn't be and he wasn't giving in to this… this…base instinct.

So, he held his breath as he quietly slid around the bed and into the small bathroom, which—just as she said—was built in the corner of the bedroom. He left as quickly as he could but as soon as he walked into the kitchen, the scent found him again because she was wearing it. As she stood at the sink, with her back to him, his gaze slid down the sleek locks of her pretty yellow hair, down her slim back, along the dip of her waist to her perfectly rounded backside, show-cased in tight jeans.

Turning from the sink, she said, "There's bacon on the table."

Her silky blond hair curved around her cheeks and chin and then fell in lazy curls to a point somewhere between her collarbone and her breasts. When his gaze reached the bottom of the very last curl, he had to fight his eyes to move upward again.

"You found bacon?"

If Zoe noticed the way he had ogled her, she didn't let on. "There's plenty of food in the cupboards. Even meat and bread in the freezer."

After her reaction to being in someone's house the night before, that cheerful observation surprised him. "You looked around?"

She sighed. "I have a baby. I have to care for her. I had to see what was available and what wasn't. Besides, I've been up since five. Daphne went back to sleep but I couldn't, so I explored. You were right when you guessed this was a weekend retreat. But it's not for hunters. I think it belongs to a family. Though there's a poker table in the corner of the great room, the games in the cupboard are actually kids' games like 'Candyland' and 'Yahtzee.'"

She dried her hands on a dish towel and walked past him. Not giving him a chance to comment on her discovery, she said, "If you don't like bacon, there's sausage in the freezer. Make anything you want. I intend to leave cash on the table to pay for everything we use."

With that she walked out of the room and into the bedroom. She closed the door, effectively shutting him out the way he had shut her out the night before.

He shook his head in wonder, not sure if he was more surprised by her sense of responsibility or by the fact that she clearly wanted nothing to do with him.

Well, whatever. She couldn't have missed the way he'd

taken inventory as if *she* were the breakfast buffet, so he didn't fault her for wanting to get away from him. He should be happy she'd removed the temptation of her fabulous face and figure. More than that, he should be absolutely joyful that she was making reparation for the bacon and bread. If she couldn't take a couple of food items without a conscience flare-up, he didn't have to worry that she would run to his truck and steal his money.

He grabbed two slices of bread, piled bacon on one and used the other for a lid, making himself a sandwich, and walked to the sink where he looked out the window at the storm.

He didn't even bother trying to stifle his groan. He could actually see the wind because it was picking up the icy snow pellets and tossing them around, as if the falling snow wasn't creating enough havoc on its own. That certainly proved there was no need for him to brave the elements to get his check. If there was anybody outside, they weren't plundering trucks. They were racing for shelter. As long as the wind wailed and the snow fell, his money was safe.

He ambled into the great room. A sofa and chair sat in front of the fireplace along the back wall. He saw the poker table Zoe had mentioned in the far corner. But he was more interested in the television.

He walked over, fell into one of the chairs in front of the TV and grabbed the remote from the end table. He pushed the power button and the screen came to life.

He almost hooted with joy. Not just entertainment, but satellite TV! In a few flicks of the remote he found sports, movies, reruns of old sitcoms. With something to do other than snipe at each other, he and Zoe could be in the same room.

Not that he wanted to be in the same room with her. He didn't. He simply didn't want to force her to stay behind a closed door with nothing to do, as if she were in prison.

But he also didn't want to give her the wrong impression about the two of them spending time together. If he invited her into the great room now, with the promise of television, it wouldn't appear he had changed his mind from the night before and now wanted to chitchat. His invitation would be to watch TV.

He bounced up from his seat. Sandwich in his left hand, he tapped on her bedroom door with his right. "Hey, the television works. If you want to come out and watch TV that would be cool. I wouldn't mind that."

"Thanks, but I'm going to take a shower."

Shower?

Instantly a vision of Zoe naked popped into his head. He could see her glorious yellow hair cascading around her. Her perfect pink skin. Her shining blue eyes. Her nice round…

He squeezed his eyes shut. He would like to blame that quick mental image on her for saying the word shower. But he knew hormones or maybe his gender were at fault. Still, smart men didn't chase after every good-looking woman they saw. They reminded themselves they were adults and also reminded themselves of all the reasons they couldn't act like sex-crazed teenagers. Lord knows, he'd fought this battle before. He'd simply used logic and proper behavior. And this time around he had plenty of ammo.

First, he didn't want anything to do with this woman. Second, she sure as hell didn't want anything to do with him. And third, he had TV. There was absolutely no reason to stand outside her bedroom door salivating.

He said, "Okay. Great," then could have kicked himself because the way he'd said it he sounded as if he thought the idea of her taking a shower was great. Well, too late to fix that. Time to retreat and hope for the best.

He nearly ran back to the great room, shoving the remainder of his sandwich into his mouth before he picked up the remote. He clicked through the unfamiliar stations until he found the Weather Channel then wished he hadn't.

Staring at the map of the United States, he moaned in frustration. The storm that had stranded them had stalled over the mountain. The forecaster happily expected it to move on by the next morning. But *he* could be happy about that because he wasn't stranded with a woman he didn't know and her baby. The weatherman also didn't have a check representing every cent he had in the safe of his abandoned truck!

A half hour later, Zoe came into the great room dressed in brown pants and a soft-looking red sweater, holding a happy Daphne. Though Cooper didn't really want to make small talk, the obvious observation came out before he could stop it.

"Looks like you're the same size as the woman of the house."

"I wouldn't know. There are no clothes in the closet. I keep an extra pair of pants and a sweater in the diaper bag because babies are messy and sometimes I end up needing changing as much as Daphne."

She turned toward the kitchen and Cooper's gaze took in every inch of her perfect body. A million visions and images popped into his head. Once again he blamed his hormones. Once again he knew logic and proper behavior would keep him in line. He forced his gaze upward away from her backside, but when he did he saw the way her pale curls contrasted with her sexy red sweater and a whole bunch of other images sprang to his mind.

He rubbed his hand along his nape. Did the woman own any color except red? Sure, she looked great in red, but that was the problem. She looked too damned great. Too damned sexy.

Taking himself back to logic and proper behavior again, he reminded himself that even if she found him as attractive as he found her, they couldn't sleep together. They were stranded for two days. If it were only for the afternoon, a fling wouldn't be out of the question. But two days didn't work. If he seduced her, sex wouldn't last two days. Eventually, they'd stop and she'd want to talk and then they'd know too much about each other. And then it wouldn't be a fling. It would be the beginning of a relationship.

His stomach knotted. No way.

"I'm afraid I have some bad news."

"Storm's getting worse," Zoe said, turning to face him, and Cooper's stomach plummeted.

She was darned gorgeous. He couldn't believe any man was capable of speech around her, let alone capable of leaving her once he married her. Then he realized she had to be a shrew for her husband to have left her. So far her behavior around him sort of hinted to that. Even the way she always had to be one step ahead of him was an indication that she needed to be right.

No man liked that kind of one-upmanship in a woman. Hell, no man liked that in another man.

He drew a quick breath. "Well, excuse me for trying to help."

Zoe had been on her way to the kitchen again to take one of Daphne's bottles out of the fridge where she had stored them the night before, but his comment stopped her. She wasn't sure why he thought she was simpleminded or stupid, but she knew from their conversation the night before that he worried that she would be a burden. She'd thought she'd already put that doubt to bed, but apparently he was still skeptical.

"I found the TV, too," she added.

"I was just trying to tell you about the storm."

There was that tone again. As if she were an idiot. This guy might be the sexiest man on the face of the earth with his whipcord-lean body very nicely showcased in his worn workshirt and perfect-fitting jeans. Add his silky-looking black hair, and she couldn't pretend that she didn't notice his physical attributes. But he also had chauvinist written all over him and she simply wasn't putting up with it.

"Here's the deal, Bryant," she said, deliberately using his last name to keep them on totally impersonal terms, so he could stop treating her as if she were a ninny. "I have a child. I don't just pay my own way. I also pay hers because my ex doesn't believe in child support. No matter how many court orders get issued, if he runs fast enough he can always evade them. So, I work. I take care of a household. I can fix a faucet. I can fix a tire. I can make a fire. I can turn on a TV."

"Very funny."

"No. It's not funny. It's not one damned bit funny that I have to tell you I'm a capable adult because you clearly think I'm some kind of spoiled princess or something. I'd like to get that squared away so we can move on."

"We can move on."

"Great. Because if we're stuck here for the weekend I don't intend to be the only one cooking and doing the dishes."

"That's fine by me because, just like you, I work and take care of my own house…and run a ranch." He smiled tightly. "I guess you could say I have you beat."

She turned to go into the kitchen again. "You won't have me beat until you also add in caring for a child."

He followed her. "Last year, three of my cows had calves."

She slammed the refrigerator closed. "Did you have to get up with them at two in the morning?"

"Once. And I'm painfully familiar with colic."

"Well, good for you. You're the first man I consider myself equal to."

His eyes narrowed as if he knew she'd insulted him—or somebody—but he couldn't figure out how. Zoe took Daphne and her bottle into the great room. She settled on the rocking chair and fed the baby one of the five bottles of formula she had prepared the night before. Even if they could leave tomorrow, and she knew they couldn't, Daphne would be out of bottles before that. Zoe would have to again prepare formula from the faucet water and there was no guarantee that wouldn't eventually upset Daphne's system.

Preoccupied with the baby, Zoe didn't notice that an uncomfortable silence had settled over the small house or that Cooper Bryant was pacing until Daphne had fallen asleep and Zoe rose from the rocker to take the baby into the bedroom. Even then, she didn't say anything. It was not her problem that Cooper Bryant was pacing the room, obviously bored.

She laid Daphne in the center of the double bed and began to arrange the pillows around her. But, on second thought, she pushed the bed against the wall, giving Daphne two sides of protection. It wasn't the best situation in the world, but they were stranded. As long as Zoe checked on the baby every few minutes, Daphne should be fine.

Satisfied, Zoe ambled into the great room. She wasn't much for TV, but she had seen a deck of cards. It had been a while since she'd played solitaire. Entertaining herself that way would be fun. In fact, it was a great deal of fun to be away from her house that always needed to be cleaned, the mountain of bills she couldn't pay and the notice that told her her house was going up for sheriff's sale because no one had paid the taxes.

She entered the great room and found Cooper Bryant staring out the French doors behind the poker table. If it weren't for *him,* this weekend away from reality might actually be a nice break.

He didn't turn from staring at the mounting snow, which Zoe had earlier watched just as he was doing right now. She was sure the look of disbelief on his face probably mirrored the one she'd worn staring at the sight.

Approaching the poker table, Zoe said nothing. She opened the top drawer of a cabinet, found the cards, pulled a chair away from the table and sat. The only sound in the room was the noise the cards made as they slid against each other when she shuffled.

"I'm not much of a card player."

"Great. I was going to play solitaire."

He turned. Crossing his arms on his chest he said, "Okay. I *get* it. I get it big-time. You are not a helpless female who needs someone to take care of her."

She began to lay out the cards. "Thanks for recognizing the obvious."

He scowled and Zoe dropped the cards and studied him for a second before she said, "Look, I know you'd rather be alone. Frankly, so would I. But since we aren't, the alternative for us is to form some kind of a truce."

"A truce?"

"Sure. We agree to share chores. We agree to be civil.

And we declare each other off-limits romantically. That way, we can talk pleasantly without worrying that one or the other is getting any ideas."

Because what she said made sense, Cooper almost agreed until a tantalizing thought entered his head. Whether she knew it or not she had just backhandedly admitted that she found him attractive, too. They were stuck together. They were both attracted. Neither one of them wanted a relationship with the other.

This weekend could be a lot of fun if he could figure out a way to convince her that they should take advantage of their two days away from real life by having a bit of no-strings-attached sex.

But before he could come up with a way to form the suggestion, Daphne cried and Zoe was off her chair and in the bedroom like a bolt of lightning. Cooper realized *that* was the reason he and Zoe couldn't have no-strings-attached sex. Women with babies had a guaranteed, built-in defense mechanism. Every time things heated up, Daphne would probably start crying.

Zoe came out of the bedroom carrying Daphne. The baby looked tired, but not sleepy, and though Cooper knew little to nothing about kids, he didn't think this was a good sign. Zoe didn't say a word. She simply walked back to the table, sat on the chair, put the baby on her lap, and continued her solitaire game.

Cooper turned to look at the snow again. "I think a truce is a good idea."

"Okay. Great. Now we can be civil."

He nodded and relaxed a little, but not completely. He may no longer fear that she wanted something from him, but that didn't stop his sexual attraction. Because he was a responsible adult he would curb it, but controlling it required being wise about distance and proximity, and also being careful about the conversational topics he chose.

Luckily, the weather was always safe. "I've never seen snow fall like this before."

"I have. A few times." She paused, then said, "Daphne, honey, don't grab the cards."

Cooper faced the table again. Zoe held the baby on her lap with one arm and used the other hand to grasp Daphne's little fingers to keep them away from the cards.

She smiled up at him. "Would it be out of line for me to ask you to put that red seven on that black eight?"

He glanced down, saw the play she mentioned, and shifted the seven of hearts to the eight of spades.

"Thanks."

"You're welcome." He almost turned again to the window, but courtesy wouldn't let him. "Want the red four on the black five?"

"What red four?"

"This one," he said, taking the card from its spot on the board and placing it on the five.

"Oh. Didn't see that. Thanks."

He took a seat across the table, grabbed the card stack, and asked, "Do you play one card at a time or three?"

"Three."

"Do you shuffle them or play them in order?"

She gave him a horrified look. "I play them in order. Anything else is trying to beat the odds! I play fair."

He stifled a smile. This woman had some set of morals. "Okay. Whatever." He counted off three cards and placed them face up so she could see her play options.

She sighed. "That card goes nowhere. Try again."

He counted off the next three cards and slapped them on the table.

"Oh, an ace!" She glanced at him. "You know where that goes."

He stifled another smile at her enthusiasm and put the ace of spades at the top of her play area. He jutted his chin toward the cards on the table. "Want that two of spades up here?"

She nodded, but said nothing else as she examined the board. Daphne screeched, trying to pull her hand free of Zoe's.

"If I let your hand go," Zoe said to her baby, "will you promise not to touch the cards?"

Daphne only screeched again.

"I'm not sure I'd take that as a yes," Cooper cautioned and the little girl grinned toothlessly at him. She was an adorable kid. Her eyes were big and blue, like her mom's, and her hair was so light it sometimes looked white.

"I agree. But I can't sit here holding her hand all morning. It's probably driving her crazy." She released Daphne's hand and the little girl instantly pounded it on the table.

Cooper began sliding the cards in play away from

Daphne and closer to himself. He was surprised that he only had to move them three inches to get them out of her reach.

Zoe smiled her thanks.

Cooper's heart did a somersault. It was so damned unfair to be alone in a cabin with a woman this good-looking and not be able to even *try* to seduce her.

"You're a natural at handling babies."

He cleared his throat. "Like I said, I did have those three calves last year."

She laughed. Cooper counted out three more cards and set them on the growing stack.

"Put that red nine on the black ten."

He did as she asked.

"Black eight on the red nine," she said with a nod toward the card. He made the move.

Studying the board, looking for additional plays, she said, "So, you own a ranch."

He realized he'd set himself up for the question since his ranch was the only thing he'd spoken about and the only conversational opening she had. But the last thing he wanted to talk about was the ranch. It only reminded him that he was forking out his herd money because his brothers hated him.

Unfortunately, he couldn't ignore her when they'd finally found a way to be amiable. "Yeah. I own a ranch."

"And you drive a truck?"

"Yeah."

"So who watches the calves while you're away?"

"They're not exactly like Daphne. I don't have to put them in day care."

She nodded. "So you just leave everything alone, jump in your truck and go?"

"No. It's not that easy, either."

Daphne patted Zoe's face and screeched. Zoe caught her hand. "Would you mind…" She sighed. "No. Forget it. I'll do it."

"Do what?"

"Get a rattle from her diaper bag," Zoe said, but she rose and began walking toward the bedroom where he knew she had stashed the baby's things. When she returned, Daphne was chewing on something that looked like a blue plastic pretzel.

"I could have gotten that."

Zoe shook her head. "Right."

"Are you back to showing me how strong you are?"

She glanced at him. "I don't know. Are you going to tell me who babysits your cows?"

"You're basing how you react to me on the fact that I didn't tell you I have a partner?"

"I'm basing how I treat you on how you treat me. You'll help with my card game because you're bored, but you won't tell me about your life—even the insignificant fact that you have a partner—because you don't trust me. And since you don't trust me, that makes you suspicious. People are typically suspicious of other people because they aren't trustworthy themselves…. So…" She shrugged. "I didn't think it wise to let you rummage through my stuff."

He stared at her. "Are you kidding me? You think I'm some kind of criminal because I won't tell you about myself?"

She shrugged. "No, I just don't think you're trustworthy."

"I'm one of the most trustworthy people on the face of the earth!"

"Yeah. Right. That's why you're so suspicious."

"I'm *not* suspicious. I'm simply not much of a people person."

She didn't answer, only stared at him until he couldn't take it anymore and said, "What?"

"I'm waiting for you to tell me why you're not a people person."

He laughed. "Why should I?"

"Oh, come on. We're here in the middle of a snowstorm. Nine chances out of ten when we get out of here Monday, we'll never see each other again. This is like a fantasy or something. It's our one chance to pour our hearts out to a member of the opposite sex and get some answers."

He stared at her. "*That* is your *fantasy.*"

She was silent for a minute, then she said, "Well, I never actually thought of it as a fantasy, per se. But I have thought that just once I would like to sit a man down and ask him some pointed questions so I can figure out what the hell makes your gender tick."

"Well, honey, I've got a fantasy, too. And it also involves being stranded with a member of the opposite sex. And we communicate, too. Except we don't talk. We communicate on that extraspecial level that doesn't require talking. You know what I'm saying?"

Her eyes narrowed. "You want me to have sex with you?"

He smiled.

"A stranger?" she said, horrified.

"Women." He laughed and shook his head. "Look, honey, it's every bit as preposterous for me to pour my heart out to someone I don't know as it is for you to have sex with someone you don't know." He shoved his chair away from the table and started toward the kitchen. "I'm going to make another pot of coffee," he said, but he stopped suddenly because something she'd said had finally penetrated his thick brain. They really wouldn't see each other after the snowplow went through. Monday morning when they parted company, it would be as if they had never met. He could tell her every damned tidbit and morsel about his life and it wouldn't matter.

In fact, it was beginning to sound like a nice compromise. And why shouldn't it? She wanted to talk. He wanted to spend the weekend engaged in a more pleasurable pursuit.

They could both get what they wanted.

He faced her. "You know what? I really would like for you to think about my offer. No. Let's call it a proposition. If you agree to spend Daphne's next nap having no-strings-attached sex with me, I'll talk your ear off. I'll tell you absolutely everything you want to know." He stopped and grinned. "And here's a teaser. I haven't spoken with my brothers in eight years. They recently bought the mortgage to my ranch and they are foreclosing."

Zoe blinked at him.

"The story behind all this is rich and juicy…" He smiled again. "Curious?"

Chapter Three

God help her, she *was* curious. But not curious enough to have sex with a stranger. That was simply a ridiculous suggestion, even if she had experienced a zing of sexual awareness when he'd said it.

Not because he was good-looking. Physical attractiveness might be part of the reason she reacted to Cooper Bryant, but it was the ease with which he slid them into a negotiation for what he wanted that caused her blood to heat in her veins. He had no compunction about going after what he wanted. He wanted her. He said it. He negotiated for it. After months of focusing only on caring for her baby, having a man behave so boldly was a stark reminder that she had more facets to her personality than simply being a mother. She was also a woman. No matter how outrageous his suggestion, it was still flattering.

She shivered and decided she'd simply been without male attention for too long and told herself to stop thinking with her hormones. Particularly since she suspected he'd been either trying to shut her up or joking when he'd made his suggestion. Except she didn't think he'd been kidding about his family. The words had come out too quickly for him to make them up on the spur of the moment. She would bet her last fifty cents there really was a story there.

And she intended to get it. Not so much because she was nosy as bored. Plus, his mentioning his family might have been a subconscious clue that he *needed* to talk. Otherwise, he wouldn't have brought them up. Because she didn't think it was possible for anybody to be trapped with another person for two days and not talk, she knew she could get this story out of him. In fact, she decided to make it a game. Having a purpose to the long, empty hours that stretched ahead of them was a much better way to pass the time than playing cards.

She considered for a second that initiating any kind of cat-and-mouse game with him might be dangerous. His additional life experience probably made him quicker, sharper than she was. Worse, if he hadn't been joking when he'd made his suggestion, he'd very clearly told her what he wanted in exchange for his story. If she wasn't careful, she might find herself in *his* trap.

Nah. He wasn't *that* clever. And she was a lot smarter than people believed a blonde could be. She would know if she was getting herself in over her head and she would simply drop back.

While Cooper made the coffee, Zoe fed Daphne the remains of her bottle and the little girl fell asleep. Though Zoe's daughter typically didn't take a nap after every bottle, today Daphne seemed listless and cranky. Zoe gently set the sleeping baby in the middle of the bed and Daphne didn't stir. Curious, Zoe sat beside her. After a close inspection, she noticed the Daphne's cheeks were a brighter pink than usual. She placed her palm on the baby's forehead and realized she had a fever.

Having been a mother for six months, Zoe didn't panic. She had a thermometer and a bottle of pain reliever/fever reducer in her diaper bag. She would use one to find out if she needed the other. She rose from the bed and rummaged through the baby things until she found both and set them on the dresser for easy access when Daphne woke up.

Then she stood by the bed, not quite sure what to do.

There weren't many options in a house in the woods during a storm. With Daphne asleep, Zoe's only choice was to go out to the great room. But then she would be tempted to talk to Cooper and that wasn't a good idea. She didn't want to talk too much or too soon. He would recognize she was digging and he would clam up. Or, worse, remind her of his proposition. If getting him to open up was going to be the big weekend challenge that kept her from dying of boredom, she had to be smart about it.

At the same time, she couldn't stay in the bedroom as if she were afraid of him. That could make him believe he had the upper hand and every time he wanted something, all he would have to do would be suggest they sleep together. The trick to getting Cooper's family secret would be balance. Casualness. She had to project an attitude that said she was comfortable with him but not overly interested. Eventually, out of sheer boredom he would reveal a bit here and a piece there, and pretty soon, he would have confided his whole sordid tale.

That sounded like the perfect way to handle her challenge, so Zoe cast one more glance at sleeping Daphne. The baby appeared peaceful, but she wouldn't be asleep forever. When she awakened, probably achy and miserable if she had caught a virus, Daphne would be whiny and weepy and Zoe would have to dedicate her full attention to her.

Best to get into the great room now while she had some time and start making friends so she could get Cooper Bryant's story.

With one last peek at Daphne, Zoe left the bedroom and strolled into the great room. Cooper had pushed the two TV chairs out of the way and replaced them with the sofa where he currently lay watching television.

"What's on?"

"Basketball." He gave her a pained look that somehow made him look extremely masculine and sexy. "You're not going to ask me to change channels, are you?"

Telling herself to stop noticing how sexy he was, she glanced at the screen. Sports. She'd simply never found a way to get interested in them. But she wasn't the type of person to begrudge another of his pleasure. Besides, letting him have this favor was a great way to begin showing him she was kind and trustworthy—somebody he could talk to.

She smiled at Cooper, as one friend smiled at another. "No, you watch. I'm fine. I can play solitaire."

Without acknowledging her warm expression in any way, Cooper settled into the sofa and glued his gaze to the screen. He didn't so much as grunt a thanks.

Well, whatever. Part of gaining his trust was not pushing for an answer when he didn't believe any was required. She had to show him she accepted him as he was so he would feel comfortable telling her his big juicy life secret.

She sat at the poker table and saw that her original solitaire game hadn't been disturbed. She resumed play and within three or four moves realized that the game was lost. She gathered the cards and started again. Within a few plays, though, that game was lost, too. So she gathered, dealt and started again. Another loser. Another deal. Another loss. Deal. Loss. Deal. Loss.

She squeezed her eyes shut. She didn't mind being unlucky, but being unlucky while bored could drive anyone insane.

She glanced longingly at the television, then at Cooper. Were his eyes closed?

She slowly rose from the poker table and walked to the head of the sofa. Peering down, she confirmed that his eyes were tightly shut and realized he wasn't *watching* the game. He was *sleeping through* the game.

Unfortunately, he was also holding the remote. On his stomach. Right about belt level.

After all the reactions she'd been having to him since he'd made his preposterous proposition, she wasn't sure touching him in any way, shape or form was wise. But the man *was* sleeping and she wanted the TV.

Studying the perfect male specimen stretched out before her, Zoe got another of those zings of attraction. He was solid man. Somebody who worked for his muscles, didn't just work out. In his jeans and plaid shirt he was nothing but pure, unadulterated man. He was so gorgeous *any* woman would have reactions to him.

Which meant she was perfectly normal, and she shouldn't be making a big deal out of simply taking the remote from his hand. Because it wasn't a big deal. He was attractive and she noticed. So what? It wasn't as if the remote was on his upper thigh. It was on his stomach. No big deal.

Slowly, quietly, she reached down, loosely gripped the top of the remote and began sliding it from his hold. But before it was even halfway out, his free hand came up and clamped around her wrist.

Without opening his eyes he said, "If you're taking me up on my proposition, I want to be awake for that. Actually, I think I *need* to be awake for that."

Heart racing, Zoe snatched her wrist from his grasp and jumped back. "I wasn't taking you up on your proposition! I want the remote."

"You said I could watch television."

"Yeah, but then you fell asleep…" Damn it! Her heart wouldn't slow down. Her limbs were trembling. He'd just about scared her lungs into collapsing.

"I wasn't asleep. I was listening to the game."

"Right," she scoffed.

"I really was," he said, then gave her the exact score.

Because basketball was a game where points could be added in a matter of seconds, she knew he wasn't lying and, chastising herself for having any kind of attraction to such an idiot, she went back to the poker table. Before she sat, however, she heard Daphne stir so she changed direction and went to check on her.

As Zoe entered the bedroom, Daphne opened her eyes and Zoe saw they were glassy. Combining the look in Daphne's eyes with her now bright red cheeks could have been enough to confirm that she had a fever, but wanting to be safe rather than sorry, Zoe took the thermometer to check Daphne's exact temperature. Sure enough, it was above normal. Not high enough to worry, but high enough to warrant medicine.

After setting the thermometer on the dresser again, Zoe reached down to lift the baby from the center of the double bed and turned toward the door. Grabbing the medicine with her free hand, she headed for the kitchen. Apparently dazed from her virus, Daphne didn't even whimper until Zoe slid the teaspoon of liquid medicine on her tongue, then her lips trembled and she opened her mouth to protest and a red stream of fever reducer poured from each corner.

"It's okay, Daphne. You're going to be fine." Zoe used the teaspoon to gather the medicine from the baby's chin and force it back into her mouth, but by this time Daphne was crying in earnest and the liquid came sputtering out again.

It took three tries, but eventually Zoe was satisfied with the amount of medicine Daphne had swallowed and she cuddled the baby against her chest, rocking her back and forth.

"It's okay, sweetie. Mommy knows you don't feel well. Just give the medicine a few minutes and you'll go to sleep again."

Daphne cried harder. Zoe began pacing the kitchen, rocking, cooing soothing words. But nothing helped and before Zoe could prevent it, Daphne began to scream.

Cooper sat up on the couch. "Are you beating her?"

Zoe sighed. "No." She paused, considering whether or not she should tell him her daughter had caught a virus—which meant he had been exposed to a virus—and decided she might as well. In these close quarters, there would be very few secrets from him.

"Daphne must have caught a virus at day care."

Cooper looked at Zoe for a few seconds as she stood in the hall between the kitchen and the great room, rocking the sobbing infant.

"So this is what I have to look forward to for the next few days?"

"No, only a couple of hours," Zoe guessed. "If it's a twenty-four-hour bug she may have had symptoms I didn't notice last night." She drew a quick breath. "So, she could be over this in twelve hours or so."

Cooper frowned and said, "If you're worried about me, don't. I've made the best of worse situations before." Then he lay down on the sofa again.

"I'm not worried about you. I'm worried about her."

He sat up again. "Don't worry about her, either. My mom always taught me that you shouldn't borrow trouble. Do you have a thermometer in that trash can of yours?"

"Yes. I already took her temp. It was a little high."

"Does she feel like she's burning up?"

"No. She's hot but she's not burning up."

He smiled patiently. "Okay, then. Your thermometer's probably right. She has a temperature, but it's not too high. No borrowing trouble."

As he said the last, Zoe noticed that Daphne was no longer crying. Her eyelids were droopy, her cheeks still bore two round red spots and she gave her mother a pitiful look.

"Mommy's going to take you to bed," Zoe said as she carried Daphne to the bedroom. She laid her among the pillows but instead of leaving her, Zoe lay down, too. She rubbed the baby's arms, smoothed her hair, whispered soothing words. In twenty minutes, probably the time it took for the fever reducer to kick in, Daphne was sleeping again.

Though Zoe rose from the bed, she couldn't seem to pull herself out of the bedroom. She knew Cooper was correct. Daphne's fever wasn't so high that her life was in danger, but Zoe didn't want to leave her just in case. Because there was no chair in the room, she sat on the floor and propped her back against the wall. She sat, staring straight ahead and listened to the sounds of Daphne breathing.

Twenty minutes later Cooper appeared at the bedroom door. "What's up?"

"Nothing. She's sleeping."

"Game's not over, but it's getting dull, so if you'd like to watch TV, I'll find something else to do."

From her position on the floor, Zoe smiled up at him. "No. I'm fine. I need to be here, just in case."

Cooper turned to leave, but his face pinched with a pained expression and he stopped halfway and sighed. "My mother used to do the same thing."

"Sit in your bedroom when you were sick?"

"I don't remember her doing it for me, but I remember she did it for my baby brother, Seth. So, I assume she did it for all of us."

"That's right. You said you have brothers."

He hesitated. "Two."

"I'm an only child." She paused. "It must have been fun to have siblings."

"Don't try to slide me into a conversation thinking I'll spill my guts about my family. You know the deal on getting my story."

She laughed. "I wasn't trying to get your story."

"Good, because I would have made a great spy. I don't tell anyone anything."

"Except in return for sex."

"Everybody's got his price."

She laughed again and Cooper left the room. But he felt guilty and he didn't know why. He hadn't made Zoe's kid sick. But he didn't have a clue how to help, either. And for some reason known only to God, he felt he should be doing something.

Seeing that it was close to noon, he decided to make lunch. As a fresh pot of coffee brewed, he threw together some sandwiches using one of several cans of tuna he found in a lower cabinet. He took two sandwiches and a cup of coffee to the bedroom.

"Here."

She glanced up and Cooper's heart turned over in his chest. Her eyes were such a soft shade of blue that they could zap the strength of any mere mortal man. But this was the first time he'd really looked at her face and seen something more appealing than just attractiveness. He saw strength, grit, determination. All the stuff that when used in the right way, at the right time, could make a woman incredibly good in bed.

His gut tightened and if he had had a free hand he would have slapped himself upside of the head. What was he doing thinking about her like that? It was one thing to proposition her. It was quite another to torture himself.

He shoved the plate and cup at her.

She shook her head. "I'm not hungry."

"Well, eat to keep from getting bored then."

"That's how people get fat."

She wouldn't take the dish. He couldn't seem to get himself out of the room unless she did. Damn attraction! Damn woman!

"All right," he said and lowered himself to the floor. "Here's the deal. I'm not much of a people person. I shouldn't give a darn about you, but for some reason I cannot fathom, it's driving me nuts having you in here."

Zoe studied him for a second, then shrugged. "I don't see why. You would have let me sit at the poker table with nothing to do. How's it different to have me in here?"

He scowled at her perceptiveness. "I don't know." He picked up a sandwich and took a bite. If she wasn't going to eat the damned sandwiches, he would. And once they were gone he wouldn't have any more reason to stay.

Zoe was quiet for another few seconds, then from the look on her face Cooper could tell she'd drawn some kind of conclusion. He wasn't a bit surprised when she said, "I think I know why it drives you nuts to have me in here." Apparently having changed her mind about the sandwiches, she lifted the second one from the plate. "When I was in the great room, you knew what I was doing. While I'm in here, you don't. You don't like to be left out."

He supposed it was because he'd just mentioned Seth's name, but in his head Cooper heard his younger brother say the same words eight years ago. *You don't like to be left out. You have to know everything. Even when you know as well as Ty knows that having you involved is going to cause trouble. It would be such a relief if you would just leave!*

As if it were yesterday, emotion rushed through Cooper. Fear. Pain. Pride. Anger. He remembered Seth had stormed out of the bedroom and Cooper had decided to oblige him and leave. He had packed in less time than most people took to change clothes and was gone before Seth could have second thoughts about what he'd said or Ty could realize his middle brother was heading out of town.

Not that he thought either of them would have stopped

him, but at the time he had needed that sliver of doubt. He'd
needed to believe they cared enough not to allow him to go
and that he could only get out of town if no one knew he was
going.

"I'm actually better on my own." He rose to leave, but
Zoe gaped at him as if he were crazy.

"How can anybody be better off on their own? When I
turned eighteen my parents divorced. I don't know how I
missed it, but they were only staying together for me. *Me.*"
She shook her head and looked at the ceiling. "Anyway,
they got divorced and my mom moved to California where
she hoped to get into movies and actually married an actor
who does a lot of bit parts. My dad moved to Florida, where
he fishes. The parents who were so careful to make sure I
had a family left me totally without one, as if eighteen was
some sort of magic number that made it okay."

Cooper said, "That's rough," but he didn't sit again.
Instead, he turned to the door. "If your coffee's cold there's
a whole pot out here to refresh it with."

Zoe smiled ruefully and he knew she hadn't missed his
not-too-subtle escape from their personal conversation. But
he didn't care. His family was the last thing he wanted to
think about. Unless she wanted to take him up on his proposition; then he would keep his end of the bargain and dredge
up memories of how he and his brothers didn't get along.
But Cooper didn't think she would sleep with him, so her
virtue and his sanity were safe.

Zoe stayed in the bedroom another twenty minutes and
though Cooper tried to watch TV, there was nothing inter-

esting being shown. He walked to the French doors and stared at the falling snow for a few minutes. Paced for a few more. Turned off the coffeepot. Rinsed it out. Wiped down the countertop. Watched it snow some more.

Finally, he skulked over to the bedroom again. "Still asleep?"

"She whimpered a few times. I sung her back to sleep."

"I didn't hear you sing."

"Do you think I'm going to sing loud enough for you to hear?"

He grinned. "Is your voice that bad?"

"No. But baby songs aren't exactly top ten. I sing about bunnies and cats and puffy clouds that talk."

"Now, see. There might be some entertainment in that. Sing a bunny song."

She shook her head. "No."

"Sing about the puffy clouds then."

"No! I will not entertain you. Go watch TV."

Once again Cooper felt himself tumble back through time, and as if he were ten he heard his father say, *Go watch TV.* How many times had his parents said that? They'd regularly shoo him and his brothers to the television or to the store…anywhere so they could have peace and quiet. And Ty, Cooper and Seth would run outside and have a ball, probably making enough noise to wake the dead.

But Zoe hadn't had siblings. When her parents had said, "Go watch TV," she had been alone.

And she was alone now. Except for this baby. It was no wonder she was so protective of her.

"So what happened with your husband?"

She peered up, studied him for a few seconds, then sighed. "He left when I discovered I was pregnant."

"He didn't want kids?"

"He wanted to be successful first."

Cooper understood wanting to succeed. In his best day-dreams he didn't as much as say hello to either of his brothers until he had proven himself. Which was why they were foreclosing on his ranch. For as much as he wanted to prove they were wrong—he wasn't a no-account trou-blemaker who would never amount to anything—they were determined to prove they were right. But as God was his witness, he would win that battle. He would prove himself.

She sighed. "I'm guessing you understand that, since you didn't say something sympathetic when I told you why he left."

Cooper licked his suddenly dry lips, then said the only thing he could say. "I can't understand someone leaving his own child. But I do understand him wanting to achieve success. Sorry."

"It's all right. I know men and women are different. All I have to do is look at my parents to see that. She's in California drinking green tea and taking vitamins and my dad's in Florida swilling beer and wearing the same clothes for three days."

Cooper laughed. "Oh, come on."

"It's true. He's not much on laundry and he claims fish have no sense of smell."

"So you talk with him by phone?"

"When I can afford it." She paused. "He doesn't call me."

Inwardly, Cooper groaned. Zoe Montgomery was pretty, sweet and the most devoted mother he'd ever seen, yet she'd been treated abysmally. If he didn't at least dole out one line of commiseration, he would be no better than the mother, father and husband who had left her.

"Men aren't much for talking."

She laughed quietly. "No kidding."

He took a breath, deciding this would be a nice time to leave the room, but before he could she said, "So what are your parents like?"

"My parents were nice," he said, "but they were killed in an automobile accident."

Clearly mortified by her mistake, she gasped, "Oh, God! I'm so sorry."

"It's all right. It was years ago."

"And now your brothers are taking the family ranch and cheating you out of your share of the inheritance?"

He grimaced. "No. My brothers and I were raised in a tiny town in Arkansas. My parents owned a small construction company that came to us when they died. I bought the ranch in Texas a few years after I left home." He paused, then added, "Technically, I walked out on my share of the inheritance a long time ago. They didn't cheat me out of it."

She stared at him, obviously waiting for him to continue. He said nothing.

"You're really not going to tell me why, are you?"

"You know my price."

"Right."

"Besides, you've already gotten more out of me than most people." Without a pause, he changed the subject. "What do you want for supper?"

It took her a second to catch up, but finally she said, "Didn't we just eat lunch?"

"Not much to do here. Besides, if we want roast or something, the meat will need time to thaw and bake. There are potatoes in the one cupboard. I can make mashed or baked or just plain buttered." He paused, then said, "Anything tempting you?"

"No. But I just ate." She waved her hand in dismissal. "Go cook, Chef Boyardee. Make whatever you want. I'm not picky."

He turned to leave, but Zoe called after him, "Hey, and check the Weather Channel again."

He grimaced. He knew why she wanted him to check the Weather Channel. She wanted to leave. Maybe to get Daphne to a doctor. Or maybe because he wasn't any more entertaining than she was. Of course, he grudgingly admitted, she was somewhat interesting. She had a sad life and she sang idiotic songs to the baby her husband hadn't wanted.

All right. So he was a bit curious.

Only a few minutes after Cooper left, Zoe decided she needed to move, too. With her behind numb from sitting on the hard floor, she had to roll to her side to rise. Daphne hadn't awakened or whimpered, but now Zoe herself was feeling somewhat tired. She blamed the cold, the boredom and her fitful sleep from the night before. She lay beside the baby and after only a few minutes her eyelids began to droop. She reminded herself that it would be a hell of boredom to be up all night because she'd taken a nap, but couldn't seem to force her eyes to stay open.

What felt like hours later, a knock awakened her. Disoriented, she glanced around the dark room and realized it was after five because the sun had set. She looked at Daphne, who was awake but still listless.

Cooper knocked again. "Is everything okay in there?"

Zoe said, "Yeah. We'll be out in a minute." She pushed herself off the bed and found a lamp to light the room before she grabbed Daphne and made her way to the door.

When she opened it, Cooper was standing there. "Kid okay?"

A bit groggy from her nap, Zoe nodded. "She's still sick. I have the medicine on the counter out here. After I try to get her to eat something, I'll give her another dose and she'll go back to sleep." She paused, then said, "Would you mind getting her baby seat and bringing the diaper bag out so I can get a jar of food?"

He said sure and Zoe started to feel guilty that she had disliked him so much in the beginning. No matter what he said, he really wasn't as bad as he thought he was. Worse, she was also feeling a tad guilty that she still intended to pry his secret out of him. Of course, with Daphne sick, there might not be time for that. So, maybe there wasn't anything to feel guilty about.

He brought the baby seat to the kitchen. Zoe set it in the center of the table and strapped Daphne inside. Then she rummaged through the diaper bag for a jar of baby food. She chose apple, because it seemed to be the kind that would probably sit the easiest on the baby's stomach, opened it and got a spoon from the drawer by the sink.

Clearly bored to tears, Cooper Bryant had watched her every move. "That's all you do? Just open the jar and get a spoon?"

"Sometimes, if she's having a vegetable like strained carrots, I heat the food. But for applesauce, this is all I do." She spooned out a mouthful of food and put it to Daphne's lips. Daphne took the bite and swallowed it. Feeling victorious, Zoe scooped a second spoonful, but apparently the first hadn't set as well as Zoe had hoped and Daphne spat it out.

Zoe put the lid back on the jar and handed it to Cooper. "Put this in the refrigerator, would you?"

"That's it?"

"She's not hungry. She's got a virus. She probably can't even drink her formula. Once I give her some more medicine, I'm going to feed her a bottle of water and hope she goes back to sleep."

An hour later, Cooper tiptoed to Zoe's bedroom again and peeked inside. Not only had Daphne fallen asleep but Zoe had, too. He stretched into the room, reaching for the switch on the lamp and extinguished the light. Zoe may not want to go to bed at seven o'clock, but she was asleep so she might as well get some rest. She might be up the entire night if Daphne decided she was done sleeping.

When Cooper went to bed at ten, Zoe and Daphne hadn't stirred, but he heard them a few times in the course of the night. He couldn't really sleep, and when he did drift off he had odd dreams, mostly about his family. He didn't care to remember the good times and he sure as hell didn't want to relive the bad, so when his wristwatch said six, he rolled out of bed. He didn't know if Zoe had heated any of the dinner he'd prepared the day before, but because she had rocked a baby all night he decided she needed nourishment.

He slipped downstairs and into the kitchen where he put on a pot of coffee and began frying some sausages, knowing that would bring her out.

Two minutes later, just as he assumed, she walked out into the kitchen. Cooper turned from the stove. "Hey, good morning."

She mumbled, "Good morning."

Peeking at the baby, who appeared to be over her virus and actually looked bubbly and perky, he said, "Wow, look at Daphne. She's back to normal."

Zoe said, "Yeah, she's great," but her response was so subdued, Cooper peered at her. Her cheeks were flushed. Her eyes were glassy. Oh, Lord! Unease squeezed his stomach. "You're not sick, are you?"

She didn't answer. Instead, she walked to the stove. "What are you making that smells so awful?"

"Sausage."

She gave him a dismayed look. "Oh, no!" she said, then shoved Daphne at him. "I think I have to throw up."

Cooper just barely caught the baby before Zoe raced away. Holding Daphne at arm's distance, he stared at her. She stared back. "This will only take a minute," he told the baby, hoping he was correct.

She let out a yowl.

Cooper said, "Right," then waited. And waited. And waited.

Finally, realizing something might really be wrong, he carried Daphne into the bedroom, around the bed and to the corner bathroom. "Everything okay in there?" he called.

Zoe opened the door and came out. "No. Everything is not okay. I'm really sick."

A ripple of dread swept over Cooper. "What, exactly, does 'really sick' mean?"

"It means you'll have to care for Daphne today…at least for a few hours. It was only a twenty-four-hour bug. I felt myself getting sick last night. I'll be better by this time tomorrow."

"This time tomorrow!" His eyes widened with horror. His stomach plummeted. "I can't care for Daphne!"

"You have to," she said, then fell to the bed facedown, as if she didn't have the energy to get into bed like a normal person.

"You don't understand. I *can't!* I don't know how."

"I thought you had all kinds of experience with baby cows."

"They don't wear diapers."

She didn't even lift her head. "I'm sorry, Bryant. But you've got to do this. And you can. I didn't have anybody teach me how to care for her. My mother's in California, remember? I figured it all out myself. Except for special case scenarios like yesterday's virus, Daphne is actually fairly self-explanatory."

"You think she is, but…" He glanced at the bed. Zoe was out. He glanced at Daphne. She patted his cheek, then shifted her hand, grabbed at the stubble of whiskers on his chin and twisted.

"Ouch!"

Daphne laughed.

Cooper groaned. "Zoe?"

She didn't even move. Cooper almost fell to the bed in frustration. He did not know one thing about caring for a baby, but it looked as though he was about to learn.

Chapter Four

"Okay, how hard can this be?" Cooper said, using psychology on himself as he walked Daphne out to the kitchen again.

Hadn't he faced greater challenges?

Shoot, yes!

When he left Arkansas, he had about three hundred bucks. The only job experience he had was working for the family construction business with two brothers who didn't like him, so he couldn't name them on a résumé. Nonetheless, he found a company similar to the one he and his brothers had inherited when his parents had died, and he got a job as a laborer.

Because he really had been a construction worker and even had experience running the family company, he rose quickly through the ranks and not only saved lots of money, he also found a friend who wanted to be partners with him on a ranch. Once they bought the ranch, he easily got his commercial driver's license—CDL—and found a trucking company that would employ him when he needed quick cash. The ranch couldn't be depended on to make money, let alone provide instant funds when an unexpected bill came along. Driving truck didn't require him to be on the job at 9:00 a.m. every Monday and gave him long stretches of time off. It was perfect.

The system worked so well Cooper drove truck a lot. First, he did it to get the resources he and his partner needed for improvements to the existing outbuildings on the ranch. Then he began saving to increase the herd so that he could finally retire from trucking and ranch full-time. Instead, the cattle money was going to pay off the mortgage, but that was okay, because it would only take a few years driving truck to restore it again. And then he really would be on his own. The ranch would be his. The herd would be paid for. No bank…no *brother* would have any claim on him.

When he wanted to be, Cooper knew he was resourceful. And determined. And strong.

Surely to hell he could take care of one measly baby.

"Last night your mother opened some applesauce," he told Daphne, who screeched and slapped his cheek. "That's what you're having for breakfast."

She hooked her fingers in his nose and twisted.

"Ouch! Geez, kid," he said, catching her chubby little hand and holding it so she couldn't grab anything else on his face. "You could disfigure me at the rate you're going."

She laughed.

Cooper sighed. "Right."

Luckily the baby seat was still in the kitchen. Cooper buckled Daphne in and then retrieved the applesauce. He remembered his discussion with Zoe about feeding Daphne. He also recalled watching her slide the spoon into the baby's mouth. He could do this.

He pulled a chair up to the table and popped the lid off the short, stout jar. He stuck the spoon into the ground apples, pulled out a healthy portion and aimed it for Daphne's mouth.

Her eyes widened and her lips parted. Clearly, she was hungry. That was good.

He slid the spoon along her tongue, being careful not to shove it in too far or too fast. Daphne gulped the food. Unfortunately, before she swallowed, she grinned at him and applesauce came pouring out of her mouth.

"Shoot!" Remembering what he'd seen Zoe do the night before, Cooper caught the wayward applesauce with the spoon before it dripped off Daphne's chin and onto her chest. Because if that happened he would have to change her shirt and he absolutely, positively was not doing that.

"Come on, kid. Work with me here."

She laughed and patted her hands on her thighs.

"Okay. No yelping. I'm giving you another spoon of this stuff, so you need to calm down."

Having learned his lesson, Cooper judiciously measured the second helping—careful not to give her so much the residual rolled out. He cautiously slid it into her mouth and when she grinned with joy there was no surplus to dribble out. Most of it stayed on the back of her tongue where he'd put it.

He damned near whooped with excitement over his success. But not taking anything for granted, he didn't whoop until he fed her half the jar. After that she began to blow bubbles with it and Cooper had a theory. Anytime a woman started playing with her food, she was either on a diet, unhappy with the entrée or not really hungry. He chose number three and rose from his seat.

"Good job," he said, then winced when he realized that was exactly what he told his horse when they returned from mending fences. But, really, caring for Daphne was a lot like dealing with an animal. She couldn't speak. He was never really certain she understood what he said. And she didn't realize that things she thought were fun could wound him.

By the time he got the applesauce in the refrigerator, Daphne was no longer spitting or slapping her chubby palms on her equally chubby thighs. In fact, she appeared to be downright calm. So calm she looked to be in the mood for an after-breakfast nap.

Fine by him.

He opened the refrigerator again and took out the last of her bottles. That would have panicked him, but he had more important concerns. He wasn't entirely sure how this part went, but he suspected he couldn't simply hand her a bottle and tell her to go to sleep. In movies and on TV he had seen mothers feed bottles to babies while rocking them. Because that seemed like an excellent formula to get the kid back to sleep, he unbuckled her from her seat, plucked her out and headed for the rocker, bottle in hand.

With a sigh, and glad that absolutely none of his trucker co-workers could see him, he dropped to the rocker, arranged the kid across his lap, pillowed her head on his forearm and slid the bottle into her mouth. She began to suck. He began to rock. Too late, he realized he should have turned on the TV so he would have something to do while she drank her milk. But that ship had sailed. So he rocked back and forth, watching her suck down half the contents of her bottle and noticing that her eyelids quickly became droopy and began to drift shut.

He shook his head in amazement. This was so darned easy he really had to wonder why parents whined about caring for kids. When Daphne's eyes had been closed for about two minutes, Cooper knew he could lay her down. But, as he rose from the rocker, congratulating himself on the good mothering he had just done, he realized that Zoe was asleep in the room at the back of the hall. Not only was she sick, but she'd thrown herself sideways across the bed.

Well…okay. That ruled out Daphne's usual sleeping place. But no problem. He would take her upstairs.

He climbed the steps, intending to secure her on one of the two single beds in the room across from his, but they were too thin. If she rolled twice, she could fall off. So Daphne couldn't stay in the spare room.

He carried her into the bedroom he had been using, but he realized that though this bed was wider than the singles in the other room, it was too high. If she rolled off, she'd fall so far she'd probably be hurt.

So, the first bed was being wholly taken by her mother. The second beds were too thin. The third was too far off the ground. He sighed again. At some point even Goldilocks found a bed that was just right.

Daphne stirred in his arms with a whimper. He quickly began to rock her back to sleep. "Shhhhh," he crooned, then rolled his eyes heavenward. He was so glad there wasn't anybody around to witness this!

But Daphne didn't quiet down from the rocking or the crooning. Instead, she stretched, her eyes opened, her face puckered and she began to cry.

"Oh, no! No. No. No. Come on, kid! Remember, I'm not a pro. I need some…"

He stopped talking, then sniffed the air. Dear God!

"Oh, Daphne! Darn it, kid! I hadn't yet worked myself up to change a *wet* diaper. I can't handle what you cooked up down there!"

Daphne began to cry in earnest.

"Shhhhh," he soothed, then groaned when he got another whiff of what he knew was in her diaper. "Your mom owes me big-time," he said as he turned and jogged down the steps, holding Daphne about two feet away from himself.

Luckily he'd brought the diaper bag into the kitchen the night before. He grabbed it and pulled out a disposable diaper, but he suddenly realized there was nowhere to change her, so he turned and ran upstairs again, back to the room he was using with the bigger bed.

He laid her down and ripped open the front snaps of her one-piece pajamas. Not quite sure what to do then, he studied the situation and realized he would have to take her legs out of the pajamas to get her diaper off.

He did that. Then examined the diaper, noting the strips of tape on either side. With a resigned sigh, he yanked open both tape tabs and then groaned at what awaited him. Especially when he realized that he had left the diaper bag—and therefore the wet cloths—downstairs.

He didn't have any choice but to make the best of the situation and eventually got her cleaned up and a new diaper installed. By the time he slid her legs into the pajamas again, she was laughing.

"Oh, yeah, that was really funny."

She gooed delightedly.

He sighed and reminded himself he had not died. He had successfully completed the diaper change. And there was no point in being negative.

"All right. Let's go downstairs and find something on TV."

Daphne didn't argue, so Cooper grabbed her from the bed and jogged downstairs. He found the remote, turned on the television and settled on watching a rerun of a docudrama. Unfortunately, he couldn't lie on the couch with Daphne. That meant he was back to the rocker. But Daphne wasn't happy. She squiggled and squirmed as if she wanted to get down. And Cooper supposed she could. The great room was huge and there weren't a lot of things she could bump into if she rolled. The only problem was that he couldn't be sure it was clean.

So he jogged up the stairs again, Daphne on his arm, yanked the spread from his bed, and carried it to the great room. One-handed, he managed to open it on the floor. Then he placed Daphne in its center. On a stroke of genius, he ran to her diaper bag and found a few toys. He tossed them to the blanket beside her. She looked up at him and grinned.

He grinned back. Success again. He was no longer so cocky that he would criticize any parent. But he had figured out some fairly sticky problems. He knew he wasn't perfect but he thought he was pretty darned good at this.

Ultimately, Daphne played herself out. Without a word or help from Cooper, who had decided to watch television from a prone position on the sofa, she laid her head on the bedspread, made herself comfortable and fell asleep. Also played out from his morning, Cooper fell asleep, too.

Ten minutes later he heard a scream and launched off the couch as if someone had set off a starting gun. He immediately looked at the blanket where he'd left Daphne and much to his horror she was gone.

Luckily, she screamed again. Cooper pivoted in the direction of the noise.

"Oh, my God! Daphne!" he yelped, scrambling over to the section of the room from which her cries and frustrated screams and screeches were coming. She'd somehow gotten wedged between the television stand and a bookcase.

He caught her up in his arms. "How the heck did you do that?"

She sniffled and looked away.

"All right. It's probably a trade secret. I can respect that. Want some more milk?"

He figured that if he fed her more of her bottle she would take another nap. He wasn't sure how she had gotten herself wedged so far away from where he put her, but this time he simply wouldn't go to sleep. He would watch TV with one eye on her in case she decided to roll again.

She drank the remainder of the last bottle, dozed off, and continued sleeping when he laid her in the center of the blanket on the floor again. He sighed with relief and went back to his television show. But what seemed like only a few seconds later she was crying. This time he found her wedged between the two chairs.

He picked her up again. "Okay. Two times means you haven't learned some kind of lesson yet. I don't even know how you're getting where you're going, but I'm hoping being trapped twice taught you your lesson."

He sat her down on the blanket. She grabbed for a rattle. Cooper went back to TV.

This time when she howled, he found her on all fours backed into a corner and he suddenly saw what she was doing. "You can only crawl backward!"

She made a grunting noise while rocking on her knees as if trying to push through the wall behind her.

"You've got to come forward, kid."

She screeched with unhappiness.

Cooper stooped down and moved her right arm forward. "This way." He thought she would mimic the movement with her other arm and go forward. Instead she simply slid the arm he had moved back to its original position.

Given that she didn't appear to be a quick learner and he wasn't anybody's teacher, he scooped her from the floor again. Unfortunately, he caught the aroma of something he didn't like and he groaned. "Not again!"

She laughed.

In the bedroom he was using, he repeated the diaper ritual, but this time with all the necessary equipment. Clean and happy, Daphne again settled on the blanket to play, but she never did nap.

By the time evening rolled around, Cooper was exhausted and Daphne wasn't much better. She could play on the floor, but she couldn't sleep on the floor because the second she awakened, she crawled backward into some kind of trouble. But the bed situation on the second floor hadn't changed and Daphne's mother was still using the downstairs bed. Zoe had only come out once to check on things, but she'd been so weak and feverish she'd damned near fainted so Cooper had shooed her back to bed.

Worse, Daphne had drunk the remainder of the last bottle. There were empties on the counter by the sink, but there was no milk to fill them. The only thing Cooper could give her was water and that earned him a bop with the same bottle he had filled for her.

As nine o'clock quickly approached, Cooper rocked a very cranky baby with no idea where he'd put her down for the night and absolutely positive he couldn't hold her for one more second.

"All right," he told sobbing Daphne. "I can't do anything about the milk, but we're going on a quest for a bed for you. And this time, we're thinking outside the box."

He carried the baby upstairs again, not even glancing at the single beds or the bed he had been using because he already knew they were worthless. He scanned the room, reminding himself to think creatively, and then he saw a wicker laundry basket.

Small, but somewhat tall, the basket had the look of a crib or cradle of sorts. He slid it out of the corner, positive he could put in on the floor beside his bed and hear Daphne if she awakened. It seemed perfect. But by the time he lined it with a blanket there wasn't any room left for Daphne.

He glanced around the room again. With the wicker basket and the bed out of play, the only thing left in the room was a mirrored dresser. He frowned at it. He remembered reading a story in grade school about a poor family who had been forced to have their baby sleep in a dresser drawer.

He pulled one of the drawers from the empty dresser. It wasn't quite as tall as the basket, but it was much wider and longer. There was plenty of room for Daphne *and* a blanket. He lined it with a quiltlike blanket that acted as a makeshift mattress, laid her inside and gave her the bottle of water.

Sitting on the edge of his bed, he watched her drink enough to settle herself and ultimately fall asleep. Then he took the bottle and set it on the dresser, turned out the light and collapsed on the bed.

When Daphne woke at two, Cooper knew she wasn't going to let him get back to sleep. After no nap the day before, she had been too tired to protest the water, but with five hours of sleep behind her she wouldn't settle for second best. His only hope was to rock her until she drifted off but he had a sneaking suspicion that wasn't going to work.

He took the dresser drawer downstairs, settled Daphne inside and turned on the TV.

Zoe awakened the next morning feeling a bit stiff and sore, but no longer weak and dizzy. She rolled out of bed, tested her health by standing without holding onto anything and pronounced herself well. Then she remembered she'd abdicated Daphne's care to a perfect stranger and ran out of the bedroom.

In the great room, she skidded to a stop and her eyes widened at the scene that greeted her. A comforter had been spread across the center of the floor. On top of the comforter was a dresser drawer lined with a blanket. On top of the blanket was her sleeping baby. And atop her sleeping baby was the long arm of the rancher/trucker who was lying on the floor beside her.

Zoe couldn't tell if he was keeping an arm across Daphne as a sort of early warning system for when she awoke, or if it was a sign of affection. She only knew the scene was adorable.

She sat on the sofa, staring at sleeping Cooper Bryant. He was without a doubt the most complicated man she had ever met. He liked to be alone, yet he was too good to ignore her and too kindhearted to desert Daphne when she needed him. But, kind as he was, he didn't get along with his own brothers. It didn't make any sense.

Unless his brothers were real losers.

She took a deep breath, deciding that would be more acceptable if Cooper were married, proving there was at least somebody he got along with. Or maybe if he had a different job. Truckers were loners. Ranchers could be loners. Loners were usually difficult people.

Still, Cooper had said he had a partner. And he and his partner had a mortgage, which Cooper's brothers had bought in order to take his ranch away from him. And what else had he said? They already had his family inheritance. They got it by default when he left them.

Looking at Cooper, sleeping on the floor, one arm laid protectively across her baby, it appeared the whole fault of Cooper's troubles belonged with his brothers.

Except Cooper wasn't exactly Mr. Personality, and he could have driven his brothers to the point where they might have felt justified to ask him to leave.

Rising from the sofa and heading for the kitchen, she cursed under her breath. Damn it! Why was she so curious about him? Because he was so good-looking?

The question made her stop. She turned around to study him again. She studied his soft-looking black hair, the smooth lines of his handsome face, the solid build of his shoulders and back and his cute butt, and she sighed. His good looks should have turned her off. That was the rule she'd made when Brad had left. No more good-looking men. And she'd stuck to it, too. So, she wasn't continually thinking about Cooper Bryant because of his good looks. She also didn't feel sorry for him. She continued to be curious about him because of the way he treated *her*.

Chauvinist that he was, he nonetheless recognized her strength, but he didn't assume that because she was strong he could ignore her. They were sharing a house, so they really did "share." He hadn't fended for himself for breakfast, lunch and dinner. They had eaten together. When Daphne had been sick, and Zoe had sat on the bedroom floor watching over her, he might not have known how to make her child better, but he'd wanted to do something. She could see his desire to help in his expressions and in the way he couldn't simply ignore her.

In fact, having him stay and talk with her while Daphne slept had been odd for *her* to accept. She hadn't chosen to be a loner. She certainly didn't like being a loner. But she was. Just as Cooper's brothers had gotten his family inheritance by default, she had become a loner by default. She wasn't someone anybody catered to. She was someone people typically left alone. Hell, she was someone people *pushed* away!

"Be who you want to be," her mother had said, right before she'd hugged her only child and taken off in her SUV for California.

Her father had said, "In this world you have to be strong, princess, and I'm glad you are." Then he'd slammed the door on his U-Haul and twenty seconds later she was watching him drive out of her life.

"Pregnant?" her husband had said before he'd basically fallen to their sofa, staring at her as if he were trying to comprehend the word.

But as quickly as he'd fallen in disbelief, he'd risen. "You know what? You can handle this, babe, but I can't." He walked into their bedroom and, as if it were the logical thing to do, just started packing. "You're strong," he'd said. "But *I* can't do this."

He'd said a few other things, then he was gone, too. She'd tried to talk him out of it, of course. She'd scrambled after him as he'd strode to his car, giving him assurances that he could handle being a dad, but he'd kept shaking his head, arguing that he couldn't.

She'd hoped that after a day or two away, he would miss her. But he hadn't. And that had upset her more than his not wanting their baby because she knew that was the bottom line. If he had loved her, a pregnancy wouldn't have scared him off. But he hadn't loved her.

So he'd told her she was strong and left her.

Cooper Bryant was the first person who recognized her strength, accepted it and yet still stayed.

True, they were stranded together because two feet of snow had fallen on the mountain, and he couldn't leave. She frowned. He might be trapped with her, but he didn't have to talk to her and that was the point. Cooper could be ignoring her. Yet he wasn't. And since he wasn't a naturally nice person, the only explanation could be that he liked her.

She blinked. He liked her? Or he wanted to sleep with her?

He wanted to sleep with her. He'd already said it. Still, a man who wanted to sleep with her could ignore her child. Cooper Bryant had cared for Daphne.

In the kitchen, Zoe put coffee grounds into a filter and poured water into the reservoir of the coffeemaker, then tried to look out the window above the sink, but couldn't. Snow had crammed into the little squares of the screen, which the cabin owner hadn't removed from the summer, even though an entire fall had passed and winter had begun. They were now ten days away from Christmas. The holiday she had loved the most as a child. The holiday she missed the most as an adult. But at least now that she had Daphne she had a reason to put up a tree and buy presents.

The thought lifted her spirits. She didn't have a lot to spend on a celebration, but it didn't always take money to make a holiday happy. Not when there was a baby involved!

As the coffee dripped into the pot, she walked through the great room to the glass doors by the poker table and glanced out. There was definitely two feet of snow, but the sun was shining. The wind wasn't blowing. With Cooper and Daphne sleeping so soundly on the floor beside the TV, she couldn't turn it on to watch the Weather Channel, but she almost didn't have to. It wasn't snowing. The storm was over. They would be leaving today. The smart thing to do would be to shower and begin gathering her things while Daphne and her knight in shining armor slept.

When she reached the end of the great room and was about to enter the hall to her bedroom, she turned and looked at Cooper Bryant one more time. She wondered what his Christmas would be like. His parents had died and he was estranged from his brothers so she knew he didn't have a family tradition to attend. Did he celebrate with his partner? Did he celebrate at all? The thought that he would be as alone as she had been last Christmas squeezed her heart. With her husband gone, celebrating with the new woman in his life, and her parents both forgetting to phone, Zoe had experienced the worst day of her life. She could not imagine anybody would be that alone deliberately.

Would it be totally and completely inappropriate to invite him to her house for Christmas? She frowned, considering that. He lived in Texas. She lived in the mountains of Pennsylvania. It wasn't as if he could drive over the river and through the woods to get to her house.

Except…

She owed him. He had taken care of Daphne when she couldn't. And she still believed he needed somebody to talk to about his family. And she intended to have the best Christmas ever. Wouldn't it be nice to share that with him?

Of course it would. And if he was as alone as she believed he was, he might be willing to drive to Pennsylvania to avoid that long, lonely day. Heck, if he drove to Pennsylvania from Texas and then back again, even if he only spent one afternoon with her and Daphne, he could avoid the whole long, lonely holiday season!

Giving him the chance to sidestep that misery was the least she could do for the kindness he'd shown her.

Still, she didn't want to be pushy. Or invade his privacy.

But if he gave her one sign, one real, solid sign that he
didn't want to be alone for Christmas, she would ask him.
But it had to be his decision. *He* had to give her a sign.

Chapter Five

Cooper awakened to the scent of fresh coffee. Disoriented, he sat up. His back was so stiff with prickly pain that he wondered if he'd slept on a bed of nails, then he glanced around and almost groaned. He was still in the god-awful house in the woods he'd found to shelter Zoe, her baby and himself. He was on the floor, sleeping atop the comforter that he'd originally spread out for Daphne, but which had become the only place he could sleep while still keeping an eye on her. It was no damned wonder his back ached. Then Daphne slapped him across the nose with her empty bottle.

"Don't try to make up with me now."

Daphne screeched joyfully.

"Oh, you're up."

At the sound of Zoe's voice, Cooper twisted to face the

sofa, where she sat brushing her hair. Damp blond curls fell loosely past her shoulders. Her face had a freshly scrubbed look.

His first thought was that even right from a shower—with no makeup and wet hair—she was absolutely gorgeous. His second thought was that she was "up." Not just awake but full of energy.

"Daphne and I have already showered." She smiled prettily. "I like the drawer idea, by the way. That's why I put her back in after I cleaned her up. She can't really crawl, except backwards and she gets herself in all kinds of trouble. Putting her in the drawer is a nice way to keep her in the room with us without having to watch her every move."

Relief poured through Cooper. He was so damn glad she wasn't sick that he forgot his back hurt. He forgot the long night with the baby, who screamed nonstop because the only thing he could put in her bottle was water. He forgot he'd had fewer than two hours of actual sleep. All he could focus on was how damned wonderful Zoe looked. Awake! Alert! Not sick!

"I made coffee," she said, rising from the couch and casually padding in her sock-covered feet to the kitchen, where she extracted two mugs from the dish drainer beside the sink.

He scrambled off the floor and nearly ran to the kitchen.

Facing the coffeepot, she couldn't see that he had followed her and she called, "Would you like me to bring a cup into the great room for you?"

She should throw him a damned parade. She should pay for an X-ray of his face to see if her daughter's head butting, bottle slapping and skin grabbing had caused any real damage.

Holding two mugs of steaming coffee, she turned but stopped short when she saw he was right behind her. She smiled. "Are you that desperate for coffee?"

"I'm that desperate for help with your child." He took both mugs from her hands and set them on the counter before he clasped her shoulders and stared into her eyes. "You're really well?"

She laughed. "I feel terrific. Sorry about yesterday. I—"

She didn't get to finish her sentence because Cooper kissed her. He had never been so happy to see anyone well as he was to see Zoe up and about and capable of caring for her own baby. And he wanted to thank her simply for being alive, but when his lips pressed to hers, an odd thing happened. The absolute softness of her mouth caused him to forget all about appreciation and to head directly to the sexual place he'd been telling himself was off-limits unless Zoe gave him the go-ahead.

Falling headfirst into wonderland, his thoughts rolled to things like satin sheets, perfumed oils, bubble bath and wine, as his body tensed with anticipation. He deepened the kiss and let ripple upon ripple of pleasure pour through him.

Just as he was about to declare kissing her the definition of heaven, he realized he was *kissing* her. Not thanking her. Not kissing her for joy. But honest-to-God kissing her as if they were about to tumble into bed.

He jerked away, but that did nothing to lessen the flood of hormones replacing the blood in his arteries and veins. Dear God. Kissing her wasn't merely powerful. It was potent. She was soft. She smelled good. She fit against him. And everything in his body responded to that quickly, easily, naturally. Almost as if he didn't have any control.

But he did have control. He *always* had control.

His gaze jumped to catch hers and what he saw in her eyes shot conflicting reactions through him. She was not confused. She liked the kiss. If the gooey expression on her face was anything to go by, she liked *him*. If he kissed her again, as his hormones were voting he do, she wouldn't stop him. She might even let him take her to bed.

Though his body tensed and tightened and damned near took over for his mind, he managed to find a few functioning brain cells and focused on the other side of this deal. He might have been trying to get her into bed for the past two days, but he'd never expected her to take him up on it. The very fact that she "liked" him made him realize he couldn't take them down that road. She was not the kind of woman a man trifled with. She was the kind of woman a man settled down with. And Cooper was not the settling down kind. Hell, women should thank him for realizing that about himself and staying away from them.

But he didn't think Zoe was going to thank him. She had too many stars in her eyes.

Shoot!

He pulled his hands from her shoulders and stepped

away. "Okay, that was supposed to be a gee-I'm-glad-you're-better kiss. I'm sorry it got out of hand."

She stared at him for a few seconds as if she couldn't respond. Well, he certainly understood that. That kiss had rolled through him like a thunderstorm in Oklahoma. It was a miracle he could talk. It was a miracle he could think. But he had thought. Thank God. And because he had enough presence of mind to realize kissing the way they had been was wrong, he was getting them out of this before the ideas clearly rumbling through Zoe's brain went too far.

He grabbed his mug of coffee, downed it and turned toward the front door. "I have a change of clothes in my truck." He set the mug on the countertop. Zoe continued to stare at him. "A shower sounds like heaven now, but a change of clothes sounds better. Plus, I think it's time I checked on road conditions. The snow has stopped, but that doesn't mean the roads have been cleared."

Zoe found her voice. "You have a radio."

She said it as a fact, not a question, but he nodded anyway. "Yeah."

He didn't give her any more answer than that, and went in search of his boots. Once he had them on, he didn't reiterate his mission or even say goodbye. He simply headed for the door. Shoving his hands into the pockets of his lined denim jacket, he trudged through the two feet of snow to the driveway. Because it was dark when they'd arrived, he and Zoe hadn't seen the easier access to the house and had bounded up the front yard. In the daytime he not only saw the driveway and garage, he saw the path to the road.

Focused on getting to his truck, he refused to let himself think of anything but trekking through the snow. When he reached the road, he groaned. Sparkling with reflected sunlight, the white blanket on the highway and in the surrounding woods hadn't been touched by man or vehicle. No one had walked or driven on this road since the storm had started Friday night.

With a resigned breath, Cooper made the first line of footprints in the perfect snow. He would have thought it a shame to ruin something so beautiful since it was clear no one was leaving that day, but he had to get the hell away from Zoe.

Though he hadn't let himself venture anywhere near thoughts of Zoe, the kiss, her reaction, or even his reaction while he'd walked down the driveway, his subconscious hadn't let any of it go. Like a dog with a bone it gnawed at his brain, reminding him he was in trouble.

Zoe liked him. Maybe because he'd cared for her daughter, maybe because she was a dreamer, or maybe because of a combination of the two, she had gotten the mistaken impression that he was someone worth liking. But he knew he wasn't. Given half a chance, he would take advantage of her naive assumptions about him. If he played his cards right, spoke nicely, pretended to be the person she thought, she would let her guard down that night. He could make love to her for the rest of their stay and be gone two seconds after the snowplow went through—without a backward glance.

But she deserved better than that.

He pulled his Stetson down to block the blinding glare of the sun off the wind-packed snow. Of course, if he had misjudged her and she wasn't looking for a permanent re-lationship, he might be rejecting something really, really good.

Cooper kicked the snow. Hard. That was genuine wishful thinking. It was as ridiculous for him to even consider she wanted a one-night stand as it was for her to think he was some kind of knight in shining armor.

He trudged up the hill, gratefully unlocked the truck door and climbed into the cab. He nearly hugged the steering wheel because, to him, this vehicle meant freedom. Lots of days he was secretly glad he could get away from everything, head for the open road and just listen to country music stations from Texas to Canada. Having this job pre-vented arguments with his partner, saved him and his partner from growing tired of each other's company, gave his partner a chance to bring women to the ranch and gave Cooper a chance to find women in unexpected places.

And kept him from being with any one person so long that she got all the wrong ideas.

When Bonnie—a seemingly easygoing, undemanding woman he dated and might have actually considered settling down with—had dumped him five years ago, she'd said he all but ignored her and he knew it was true. He had thought she was the kind of woman who didn't care about all the touchy-feely stuff other women wanted. But, apparently she had. And he had missed the signals she had been tossing out for him to understand that. Most days he didn't think of anything but the obvious, which for him always had something to do with his own personal well-being. That was actually why he'd cared for Daphne. Not because he was *nice* but because it was common sense. If he didn't feed her and entertain her she would scream. He hated screaming. So he'd cared for the baby to make his own life more comfortable.

But how did a guy explain that to a woman with stars in her eyes?

He didn't.

He should leave. Right now. He was out the door. There hadn't been a scene. He hadn't made a promise he wouldn't keep. He hadn't even led Zoe on. She might be dreamy-eyed about the kiss and think about him for an hour or so. She might even sputter and spit a bit when she realized he wasn't coming back. But he wouldn't have hurt her. She'd forget him within a day or two of getting home.

Unfortunately, he could not get his truck up this mountain when there was at least two feet of snow on the road. He might be able to get down….

Damn! He knew that was too dangerous. Besides, it wouldn't be fair to Zoe simply to leave.

Yet, it also wouldn't be fair to Zoe to go back to that house with her having the wrong idea about that kiss.

On the other hand, if he didn't go back, she might not curse him and sputter about irresponsible men. She could worry that he had been hurt. And that wasn't fair. Worse, if he didn't go back and the furnace broke, she and Daphne might freeze. The kid was already out of milk. Water had kept her from killing him the night before, but if this road didn't get plowed in the next few days…

He sighed. When in the hell had his life gotten so complicated?

Friday afternoon. When his semi had lost its ability to go forward.

With another sigh, he raised a trucker on his radio and asked about road conditions. Things were bad. Twenty-four to thirty-six inches of snow had fallen. The state had begun to plow, but even the main arteries weren't open yet.

Cooper thanked the trucker and wished him well, then signed off and did what he knew he had to do. He pulled a duffel bag of spare clothes from the compartment behind his seat and tossed it in the space beside him, ready to take it with him when he went back to the house because he knew his conscience wouldn't let him leave Zoe and Daphne alone. Plus, now that the storm itself had subsided, he had to get his check. Nobody would be driving up the mountain, but anybody walking by could break into his truck and steal the one and only true valuable he had.

He leaned around and removed the cover that hid the safe, then fiddled with the lock. When it opened, he pulled out the white envelope containing the certified check. He wished he hadn't been forced to pay off the mortgage now, but he had no choice.

Just as he had no choice but to go back to that house. He couldn't strand Zoe. So he was stuck. And his libido was just going to have to play gin rummy or something until he could leave. He was sure the road would be cleared in another day or two. Forty-eight hours wasn't that long to control himself. Lord knows, he'd done it before.

That logic satisfied him until he returned to the house. Zoe stood in the hallway that separated the open great room from the kitchen. Her pretty yellow hair had dried and hung sexily around her, but her blue eyes were wide and round as if she hadn't expected him to return.

But as if she realized he really was standing in the foyer, she hadn't conjured him in her imagination, her entire face changed, relaxed, became filled with relief. And Cooper felt something inside him respond to that look. He didn't feel happy. He didn't feel glad to be back. What he felt was something more primal, more instinctive. It was almost a sense of duty that had clicked in. As if he had a mate's responsibility to this woman. Worse, that feeling of responsibility didn't fill him with fear or anger. It felt very natural.

That almost made him groan. First, he could not be responsible for someone he didn't really know. Second, he never put his name and the word "mate" in the same thought process with a woman. Something was terribly wrong here and he suddenly suspected he knew what it was. Because he'd cared for Daphne, his desire to seduce Zoe had come head-to-head with her motherhood. So to make seducing her acceptable, he was thinking like a mate. Not a husband…God forbid. But something more primitive. Because he wanted to be primitive with her. The way he wanted to make love to her was raw and natural, not nice or respectable.

The very fact that he couldn't stop thinking about this

should have scared him silly but he capped the hypothesis by realizing that by respecting Zoe, he was actually giving her the wrong idea. When he thought that he knew he'd finally gotten to the bottom line. Unless he wanted her hearts-and-flowers notions to take root, he had to stop being nice to her.

The easy way for him to get her to dislike and mistrust him the way she had originally would be to make a pass at her. Not implement some sweet seduction, but make a cool, calculated suggestion, as he had when he'd been willing to trade his story for sex. If he came on to her as his true I-only-want-sex self, their relationship would probably go back to normal. No thoughts of kisses or "having feelings."

Yeah, he was going back to behaving like his obnoxious self. No more of this letting her think he was Mr. Nice Guy.

He wasn't.

For Zoe, the rest of the morning and afternoon passed almost like a typical day at home. She made a fresh batch of formula, earning a groan from Cooper, who had apparently endured Daphne's temper the night before because he hadn't had anything but water to put in her bottle.

Then she found a washing machine in the basement, and though she had to hang her and Daphne's clothes on a line she strung in the great room, by the end of the afternoon they had something clean to wear.

Cooper watched replays of classic games on a sports channel and only grunted when she tried to make conversation. At first she thought he might be angry that he had been forced to care for Daphne the day before, but then she remembered the real reason he'd left her alone that morning. His thank-you kiss had turned into something he hadn't intended it to be. And his response wasn't the only unexpected reaction. She could all too easily recall the softness of his lips, the way he nibbled and nipped and finally given himself over to the incredible kiss. And when he'd fallen over the edge, she had, too. How could she help it? The man dripped sex appeal. He was gorgeous, street-smart, worldly. If she hadn't known that before he kissed her, she certainly knew it now.

Peeling potatoes to put around the roast she had baking, Zoe suppressed a shiver. No first kiss had ever stolen her breath the way his had. No kiss had ever reached into her soul with emotion the way his had. But Cooper Bryant was nothing like the man she envisioned herself with in her second time around romantically. She didn't want somebody so practiced in the ways of the world. She wanted an average guy. She didn't want someone brimming with sex appeal. She wanted a guy who wanted a family.

And Cooper had abandoned his family.

She stopped her thoughts and took another breath. He'd said his brothers had kicked him out of their lives, but it was fairly clear from the things he said and how he behaved that he kept himself out. He absolutely, positively, definitely was the wrong, wrong, wrong guy for her.

However…

She had asked for a sign that he might want an invitation to Christmas dinner and if that kiss wasn't a sign, she didn't know what was.

More than that, though, she didn't know everything about him. Heck, she hardly knew *anything* about him. There could be extenuating circumstances in his family situation. He might secretly long for everything she wanted and simply be unable to admit it because he was still hurting from his brothers' rejection....

Boy, was she ever reaching! Particularly since his behavior after the kiss had negated any sort of message she'd thought was in that kiss. He'd grabbed the first excuse to leave the house, and when he'd returned he hadn't spoken one word beyond his groanings about Daphne's formula. Not even to tell her about the road conditions. She'd assumed he hadn't heard anything good since he'd brought his duffel bag, showered and changed into clean clothes before settling on the sofa. So she hadn't asked and he hadn't volunteered.

He was clearly sorry he'd kissed her. But that was fine since he wasn't right for her. He was too old, too complicated. The last thing either one of them needed was to get involved with the other.

The best thing to do would be forget that kiss happened. And she would. Because that was the right thing to do. For both of them.

With the potatoes in the oven, she strolled into the great room again. Casually. Confidently. The same way she had Saturday morning before either one of them had even considered kissing. Positive this behavior would take them back to how they'd felt about each other before that kiss.

"You never told me if you raised anyone on your radio."

"I did."

She smiled. And he was right back to being as rude as he had been on Saturday morning. Thank God. "And what did this person say?"

"About what?"

"About the road conditions. Did you get any information?"

"Parts of the valley actually got thirty-six inches of snow."

She gasped.

"My thought exactly." He nestled into the sofa, as if to get back to his classic game. "So even the main arteries aren't open. My guess is we have another two days before anyone remembers there's a road on this mountain."

"Oh my God!"

"I couldn't have said it better myself."

He shifted his gaze to the television and Zoe knew the conversation was over. Fine. She'd endured a weekend of him already. She could do another two days.

She checked on Daphne, who continued to sleep soundly in the drawer on the floor of the bedroom, but when she walked into the hall again she realized she had absolutely nothing to do. Except straighten the kitchen. Though they continually tidied up their messes, it wouldn't hurt her to do a little extra cleaning. Maybe dust out a cupboard. Wipe down the refrigerator.

Because the owner of the house was a basically neat person—or family—arranging the cupboards and wiping out the refrigerator took only an hour. When Zoe was done, she paced behind the sofa so Cooper couldn't see her, but she was beginning to get annoyed with the way he hogged the television. She understood that he was angry with himself for kissing her, probably angry with himself for being nice to her, and even angry with himself for insisting she come along with him Friday afternoon to find shelter, but that didn't give him the right to make her miserable.

Luckily before she could say anything to him Daphne woke. Without taking her from the bedroom, Zoe changed her and played with her. When the timer on the stove rang, she came out, turned off the oven, fed Daphne some baby food, then served dinner for herself and Cooper. But rather than eat at the table, he fixed himself a plate and took it into the great room where he continued to watch TV. With Daphne in her travel seat, Zoe cleaned the kitchen. When that was done, she bathed the baby, put her in fresh pajamas, fed her a bottle and put her to sleep.

She almost lay down on her bed too, but she wasn't tired. And, damn it, she was bored and that stupid Cooper had hogged the one and only form of entertainment long enough.

She stormed into the great room. "Give me the remote!"

Drowsy, Cooper raised his gaze to meet Zoe's. He knew she was bored. He'd deliberately squandered the television. He'd not spoken. He'd eaten alone. All so she would realize he was an inconsiderate, selfish guy who wasn't going to change.

If he kissed her now, she'd probably slap his face.

He sat up on the sofa. "Sorry," he said a tad arrogantly, as if he were clueless to the fact that he'd been rude. He tossed the remote at her, then patted the sofa cushion beside him.

Looking as if she hadn't expected his easy acquiescence, Zoe cautiously caught the remote and even more cautiously sat. She hit a few buttons, bypassing the nightly news, two sitcoms and a movie in favor of an hour-long drama that she probably suspected they both would enjoy.

Even when she was mad at him she couldn't help being nice.

She was such a babe in the woods that Cooper almost felt guilty for what he was about to do, but not quite. He wanted to kill her infatuation. He didn't want her thinking he was something he wasn't. He didn't want her sympathy. He didn't want her affection. If she could make love without any of those, then he was her guy. If not, he wanted that out in the open, too, so she didn't accidentally tiptoe back to her crazy ideas about him.

As she became engrossed in the television show, he slowly raised his arm along the back of the sofa, resting it behind her. She appeared not to notice.

He inched closer. This time she shifted uneasily and glanced at him in her peripheral vision. Jerking his eyes in the direction of the television, he pretended not to see her looking at him. When she returned her attention to the show, he lifted his hand from the sofa back and gently dropped it on her shoulder.

For that she turned and stared at him. He frowned as if someone in the television show had done something confusing. When she glanced away, it was all he could do to hold back a smile. He'd never known that slowly making a pass at someone could be so amusing.

A commercial came on and neither one of them moved. He feigned being hypnotized by the screen. Zoe seemed as if she wasn't even breathing. When the show finally returned, and she relaxed enough to pay attention to the TV again, Cooper began playing with her hair.

Wow. Soft. And wonderfully springy. He glided his fingers through a curl and when he let it go, it rolled back. That made him smile. In fact, it completely stole his focus. This time when he slid his fingers through a thick lock, he watched them ripple through the strands, then watched her hair spring back into place.

"Your hair is amazing."

Cautious, she peeked at him. "It's naturally curly."

"Mine's straight," he said, then unwound a long lock to see it bounce back.

"Good for you."

He heard the slight quiver in her voice and realized that while he had become analytical, she was falling victim to the movement of his hand through her hair. The knowledge that she was responding sent a shiver of arousal through him and reminded him to get back to his mission. This seduction wasn't supposed to be successful. He was supposed to disgust her. He shifted another few inches closer, let his hand drift from her hair to her shoulder and down her arm.

"What are you doing?"

He should have known that a talker like her wouldn't just get angry and tell him to stop. Nope. She wanted a syllabus.

"I'm seducing you. Should I give you the steps or is the broad definition enough?"

She stared at him. "Are you—"

Nuts? he suspected she was about to ask, so he kissed her before she could say anything else.

Her lips were as soft as he remembered, her mouth as yielding. Once again, Cooper felt himself tumble to the edge of reason, but this time he didn't let himself plummet over the precipice. He could enjoy a kiss, be drawn into a kiss, nibble and suckle and twine his tongue with her in a kiss, but he absolutely refused to lose control.

That was his last coherent thought before reason totally deserted him. Overwhelmed by her softness and the sheer pleasure of kissing her, he couldn't think of anything else, until suddenly, she jerked away from him and jumped off the sofa.

"You're *not* seducing me!"

"Why? Because I ignored you this afternoon? Honey, what's going on between you and me has nothing to do with getting along, or making a commitment or even exchanging phone numbers. And right now your body's telling me you feel the same things I do. Do you want to do this or not?"

"You are so crude!"

"I'm certainly not hearts and flowers." There. It was out. The thing he'd wanted to deny all day. The thing he wanted her to understand. The thing he needed for both of them to get beyond, so they could make these next two days at least passable.

"Well, I'm a hearts and flowers kind of girl."

"Hey, I didn't say I wouldn't be romantic."

"I don't want romance. I want love."

With that, she turned and left the room. Cooper heard her door slam and he reached for the remote, satisfied that any romantic notions she'd entertained had been killed.

But halfway to changing the channel, he realized he felt like scum. He tamped down the guilt by reminding himself that the air had needed clearing between them. But then he heard an odd sound. A click.

He rose from the sofa to see if he could determine the sound's origin and realized it had come from Zoe's bedroom. Specifically her bedroom door. He heard the click again. It was a key. Because the house was old, the bedrooms needed keys to lock them. Cooper hadn't thought to look for his, but apparently Zoe had found hers.

And she'd locked her door.

A foreign sensation gripped him. He felt creepy. She'd just told him she didn't trust him.

And she shouldn't. Her not trusting him shouldn't bother him. He'd set out to make sure she knew what kind of man he was and clearly she now understood.

So why the hell did he care? And why the hell wouldn't this feeling of being a slime go away?

Chapter Six

Zoe stiffened when Cooper walked into the kitchen the following morning. Still fuming over his attempted seduction, she had spent the past hour tiptoeing around him while he had done exactly as he'd pleased, as if he didn't have a worry in the world.

She frowned. Damn it, he'd done that on purpose! He hadn't wanted to sleep with her the night before. He'd made the blatant pass at her to make a hundred percent sure she mistrusted him, as she had in the beginning, before his caring for Dáphne had proved he wasn't such a bad guy. And before he'd kissed her in a way that made her toes curl.

He wanted her to remember he wasn't the kind of guy she could put any kind of faith in, so he'd simply reverted to the plan he'd been using all along to get her to keep her distance. After he'd behaved like an inconsiderate lout all day, he'd reminded her that the only thing he really wanted from her was a little physical fun.

And just as he'd expected, she'd run.

It made her so mad she longed to pop him. But she wouldn't. She was a nice girl.

And he counted on that, too.

He walked to the cabinet beside the sink, and Zoe fought the urge to inhale the fresh scent of his aftershave, then cursed herself for being attracted to such a hardheaded, argumentative pain in the butt. She couldn't understand why her hormones weren't getting the message that she shouldn't be interested in him, but they weren't. Anytime he got close to her, as he was now, a yearning billowed through her. Still, he was so gosh darn good looking, any woman would be attracted to him. Plus, he was experienced, funny and sexy. Physically perfect.

Listing his good qualities actually brought Zoe back to planet Earth and she shifted away from him. Dressed as she was, she felt like a dirt ball. Though she'd washed her clothes the day before, yesterday afternoon Daphne had spit baby food all over her. She was rumpled and grimy. He was clean, organized, in control. Even if she decided to break her rule not to get involved with another overly good-looking man, this particular hottie was way out of her league.

Of course, they weren't really on a level playing field. She had exactly two outfits she was rotating. As a trucker, he was accustomed to living out of a duffel bag. She wasn't even sure he had a house. On the other hand, she had a house, but it was partially empty because of her parents' scavenging when they'd moved. Worse, her house was on the verge of being taken away. Her parents hadn't paid the taxes for years, and neither had thought to tell her that a few years ago when the amount was small enough she might have managed to squeeze it out of her own budget. But several years worth was too much for her to pay. This time next year *she* could be living out of a duffel bag.

Maybe she and Cooper weren't so different after all?

Without a word, Cooper grabbed a mug and poured himself a cup of coffee. Surreptitiously, Zoe watched him spoon in nondairy creamer. He wouldn't say good morning. He probably didn't feel he had to. He had made his wishes clear the night before. They were two ships passing in the night. If he wanted anything from her it was sex. If she wanted anything from him the price was sex. His life boiled down to basic needs, as if he intended to walk through without making a footprint. The way he lived allowed him to be in control and relatively content. And she couldn't help wondering if his philosophy wasn't right. After all, wanting more than just the basics only seemed to leave her wanting.

He made a sandwich with bread she'd taken from the freezer—the second loaf they were using—and bacon she had fried. The cost of this little retreat was mounting and that was beginning to trouble Zoe, too. At first, the money she'd intended to leave for the supplies they used was cash she had earmarked for that weekend anyway. A few dollars for gas. A few dollars for food. But now she was forced to dip into the money she was saving for Christmas gifts for Daphne.

And, damn it, that caused a lump to form in her throat. She barely had twenty bucks to spend on her baby. The gifts she could afford would have been nothing but tokens and trinkets. But at least Daphne would have presents under the tree. Now that she and Cooper were eating more bacon than she would use in a year, more coffee than she would drink in a month, and more bread than she'd eat in two weeks, she wouldn't even be able to buy those little things.

Angry, hurt, tired of life tossing her to the ground and stomping on her, Zoe felt her chest tighten, but she swallowed hard and forced air into her lungs. She wasn't a person who fell victim to self-pity. She also wasn't a quitter....

Still, she knew she couldn't possibly be on the right track with her life, or everything wouldn't be going miserably wrong. Her parents had left. Her marriage had failed. She was losing her house. Maybe it was time to realize the common denominator in all these problems was *her*.

She turned away from the kitchen sink and glanced at Cooper, who sat on the sofa in front of the TV, eating his bacon sandwich, mindlessly staring at the morning news. He'd had every bit as many problems as she had. His parents had died young. His brothers had kicked him out of their lives. Yet he hadn't merely survived, he was happy.

Why? Because he'd built a life that couldn't hurt him. True, it was somewhat empty of people, but he was fine. She kept trying to build a life that was full of people, and she consistently got hurt.

She dried her hands on a dishtowel, then leaned against the counter. Facing the prospect of a Christmas without gifts, without cards, without calls from family, Zoe considered that it was time to face reality. Maybe that was why she had been stranded in the woods with Cooper Bryant. Maybe fate wanted her to see that some people were destined to be alone, and he had entered her life to show her how she should be living, and the kinds of decisions she should be making so she would stop getting hurt.

Still braced against the counter, she crossed her arms on her chest. It seemed logical. God knew Cooper was certainly keeping the upper hand with her. She was the one walking on eggshells, while he controlled the TV and basically did what he wanted. Did she need any more proof that his way of doing things was better?

No. She didn't. But before she would give up her long-held dream of having a family, belonging somewhere, being important to someone, she wanted to know if he really was happy. If his life truly worked for him or if he was just a good actor. And the only way to know if he was genuinely happy was to hear his entire story.

And the only way to hear his story was... Well, she knew his price.

So, before she made any deals with him, she wanted to get some idea whether her theory was correct. And she had a good test for that, too. She marched into the great room before she lost her courage and stopped in front of the sofa, where he sat, legs extended.

She kicked his feet. "Don't you ever think of things like

maybe I don't have the cash to pay for everything we're using?"

He didn't even glance up from the television. "I wasn't going to let you pay for everything. I can see that Daphne has her own food and you and I aren't exactly eating an equal amount." He picked up the remote and switched channels. "My thirty bucks would have been right beside your twenty on the table with the note."

"This is going to be more than fifty bucks altogether."

"How much do you think, then?"

"Eighty."

"Plus whatever else we use until the snowplow goes through."

She relaxed somewhat. "Yeah."

"Okay, then. You pay $30 and I'll pay $50."

Well, that was it. Test one. She'd confronted him and he'd hardly reacted, just spit logic back at her. He really was calm. He really didn't stress. He clearly didn't obsess. In lots of ways he made her feel just shy of insane. And that was another thing she was tired of. Always feeling she was nuts, crazy, bonkers because she was reaching for something she would never quite catch.

She drew a breath and blew it out slowly. "Okay, you know what? Things have sort of happened in my head over the past day and I've decided I want to know your family story."

Slowly, as if he couldn't believe what he had just heard, he lifted his gaze until he caught hers. His green eyes glittered. "You know my price."

"Yeah, but, you know, I've never been one to pay full price for anything."

He tilted his head in question. "I'm not sure what you intend to negotiate."

"Well, you put your story out as if it's a big deal. And I've discovered I have a few reasons for wanting to know it. Those reasons have nothing to do with you. I'm doing this because I think I could learn some things from you. But the problem is you could be exaggerating."

He laughed. "Not hardly. My story is good."

"Or," she said, talking over him as if he weren't speaking, "your story could be worthless to me."

His eyes narrowed as he studied her. "What do you think you're going to learn? I'm not Gandhi."

"No, but you are calm. You take life as it comes. The only time I've seen you yell was when you had to convince me to find shelter with you. That means you have a sense of decency and responsibility. But the other things that have happened, well, you seemed to take them in stride. Even caring for Daphne."

He shrugged. "Living life any other way than mine makes it too hard."

"My point exactly. So I want to know how you got where you are to see if it makes sense for me to do the same things."

"And once I tell you my story, we go to bed?"

She took a step back. "Well, that takes us to negotiating again. Like I said, your story may not contain the elements I need to help me."

He shook his head. "Sex is a winner-take-all proposition, Zoe. I tell you the story. We make love. Or we make love and I tell you the story. I don't see any other way to do it."

"Strip poker."

As if he couldn't contain it, a laugh burst from Cooper. "Are you kidding me?"

"Nope." She turned her back on him and walked to the poker table. Suddenly, after six years without support or comfort from her parents and an entire year of missing a husband who really hadn't been worth the time or the effort, she felt very, very calm. "Here's the deal. If I win the hand, you tell me a piece of your story. If you win the hand, I take off a piece of clothing. If I'm naked before your whole story is out, we make love and you finish your story."

But when she pivoted to grab the cards from the credenza and found he was right behind her, her calmness vanished. She always reacted when he was near, but having him so close after propositioning him brought home the reality of what she was suggesting and her breath hitched. He was tall, strong and clearly experienced. She'd been attracted to him from the beginning and if her luck didn't hold there was a good possibility she'd be following through on that attraction. Her nerve endings jumped in anticipation.

"And if my story is finished before you're naked?"

"Then you lose," she said, sliding away from him, forcing herself to be confident again. Exceptional card skills gave her the advantage. If his story was an ego-driven piece of drivel that didn't help her to understand life, she wouldn't hesitate to tell him that. But she didn't think it would be.

He had a past every bit as demoralizing as hers and she had a feeling his story would illustrate how he'd risen above it. And she needed to hear that.

"That's why you're so confident. You're sure you're going to win."

She grinned, took a seat across the table from where he stood and began to shuffle the cards. "The same cousins who taught me to shoot a gun taught me to play poker."

"And where are these guys? Should I be worried that you'll call them tomorrow morning and they'll ride up on snowmobiles and beat the living tar out of me?"

She laughed. "No. In case you haven't noticed, there's no cell phone service here. So I can't call anybody. Besides, one cousin moved to Washington, D.C."

"Lobbying against gun control, no doubt," Cooper said as he pulled out a chair and sat.

"The other got married. He's busy with his family."

Cooper tilted his head as if something struck him as odd, so Zoe wasn't surprised when he said, "You told me your parents left you. But what about your aunts and uncles?"

"What about them?"

"Didn't they kind of take over for your parents?"

"No."

"No?"

She sighed. "Look, I'm not a talker when I play cards. So if you think you're going to distract me with chitchat, forget it."

"But you expect me to talk."

"*After* you lose a hand and before we start the next hand."

"You're a prickly little thing about poker." He paused, then glanced up at her. "Unless *you* have something to hide."

She sighed again, disgusted that he wouldn't take her at face value. "My aunts and uncles are busy with their own families. After my parents left I tried to integrate, but there wasn't a whole heck of a lot of room. There are four kids in the one family, six in the other. So I remained an outsider. But that wasn't such a bad thing. Seeing their family inter-actions, the closeness, gave me the example of what an ideal family is supposed to be." She took a breath. And maybe that was another problem. Maybe she'd modeled her hopes after families that were the exception to the rule, not the rule.

"But I've been miserable trying to make that system work for me. If I hadn't had that dream of creating the picture-perfect family, if I had stayed single, gone to school, or maybe looked for the *right* guy instead of settling for someone who dazzled me, my life would be different now."

"But you wouldn't have Daphne."

She conceded that with a slight smile. "Yeah. You're right. She's the one good thing that came out of that marriage. But otherwise, the marriage was a huge mistake. My whole life since my parents left has been a series of wrong choices. You, on the other hand, might not be Chuckles the Clown, but you're content. Sometimes that's all we can hope for. That's why I want to hear your story."

With that, she began dealing. "Five-card stud. Nothing

wild. Since there are only two of us, let's make it a three-card draw."

"All day? Don't I get a chance to call the game?"

"Five-card stud is pure."

"I still want the chance to call my game."

"Fine. You deal next. You call the game."

"Great."

Cooper picked up his cards and had to work to keep his expression blank when he saw he had two aces. Grinning like a fool was not appropriate in poker. Especially not when the prize was such a good one. He'd never been given such a wonderful opportunity, and already luck was with him. He couldn't help wondering what piece of clothing she would take off first. Her sweater seemed the obvious place to start.

His collar suddenly felt tight and his nerves began to crackle. He couldn't believe Zoe had caved about sleeping with him, but technically she wasn't caving. She didn't know he was a skilled poker player, so she thought she could win. Still, he understood why she was taking this risk. She was a bundle of emotion and unless she got a poker face for life, people would always take advantage of her. Hadn't he quickly honed in on her weakness and kept the upper hand through their entire stay? The woman needed to toughen up. And it would be his pleasure to help her.

"Draw?"

He lifted his gaze from his cards and caught hers with a steely-eyed look designed to confuse her. "Gimme all three."

She dealt his cards and his serious look crumbled when his eyes nearly fell out of their sockets. He got another ace. Somebody up there really, really liked him. If his luck held, this game would be over in about four hands. Sweater, jeans, bra and panties. His stomach clenched. Four hands seemed like an eternity.

"Since we're not betting, show your cards," she said.

Maintaining as solemn an expression as possible, Cooper set down three aces.

He saw her blink then draw a breath, but otherwise remain calm as she said, "Beats my two kings."

Confidence flooded him. This would be like taking candy from a baby, and he would use her poor choice of poker when he explained his life. He never took a bet he didn't know with absolutely certainty he could win. She'd underestimated him, or overestimated herself. In challenging him to cards, she'd set herself up to lose.

"And I think you owe me a sweater."

"Not yet, cowboy. The first hand gets a sock."

He gaped at her. "Socks? Three aces gets me your socks?"

"I said *sock*."

His eyes widened even further and his mouth fell open. "One damned sock?"

"Well, it seems to me that you probably have a really long story. No sense rushing things."

He studied her for a second, giving her points for keeping control. He hadn't thought she had that in her, but since she'd thrown him into the role of her teacher, he couldn't just let her walk all over him.

"Okay. Fine. If you're insecure about your poker skills, we'll play your way."

"We'll play my way because it's my game. I'm not insecure," she said and proved it by beating him the next hand.

She rested her elbow on the table and after a few seconds of studying him said, "I'd like to hear about your parents."

"I had no say in the sock decision. You get no say in what I tell you. And what I consider to be equal to a sock is this— I have two brothers."

"I already knew that."

"I'd already seen your right foot."

She sighed. "Give me the cards."

She beat him again and this time he told her about the family construction company. When he beat her, she gave him her second sock. Her ankle bracelet came after her third loss.

"What? Are you going to give me polish chips off your toenails if you lose again?"

She only harrumphed, but she didn't lose again. He did. She was craftier than he gave her credit for, and he worried that the little girl who'd come to him for help dealing with life was about to outwit him. Concluding he was somehow missing an important element about this game, something obvious she was doing to best him, he nonetheless told her that Ty had been old enough to become fifteen-year-old Seth's guardian when their parents were killed.

At the next loss, he admitted that Ty had put him through college.

At the next, he regaled her with a story of how Seth had been a hot commodity with the ladies.

She laughed. "So your younger brother is a sex symbol?"

"We all had our moments with the ladies."

He saw her swallow and was gratified that—at least—she wasn't totally unaffected by him. But none of that would matter if he didn't figure out how she was winning.

She beat him again the next hand and Cooper's head was spinning. Just as she'd said, five-card stud was pure, especially when there was no betting involved so neither one could bluff. Unless she was pulling cards from the bottom of the deck, out-and-out cheating, she had the best luck he'd ever seen.

"I want to know about your moments with the ladies."

"I think my moments with the ladies are irrelevant."

She caught his gaze. "Tell me anyway."

He sighed. "Okay, you won the hand and I'm out of stupid, equal-to-socks things to tell you anyway, so I'm going to give you the equivalent of my shirt."

Her eyes brightened and she leaned across the table eagerly. Cooper's chest tightened. She was so darned beautiful that he knew her ex had to be a total dimwit to leave her. And so darned fresh-faced and enthusiastic, he began to wonder if sleeping with her would be as easy and uncomplicated as he kept all his other liaisons. He hadn't wanted to get to know her. She'd slipped past his defenses. He hadn't wanted to talk to her, yet he was now halfway through his entire life story. He *had* wanted to sleep with her. She was gambling him out of it.

Still he'd promised her something good, so he said, "I once dated the same woman for five years."

Her eyes widened in disbelief. "Are you kidding?"

"Nope. Not kidding." But he was feeling odd. This part of his life story did not paint him in a good light. "Same woman. We weren't in love. Not the passionate, icky, sticky kind that you feel when you're eighteen."

She nodded.

"But...well, I think you need to win another hand to hear the rest."

She groaned. "That's not a shirt's worth!"

"Okay, consider it my wristwatch." He handed the cards to her. "Deal."

Clearly frustrated, she dealt the cards. Cooper didn't think he had a very good hand, but much to his surprise he had better cards than she did.

She passed her wristwatch across the table.

"Very funny."

"Give me something substantial in your next loss and I promise you will get something substantial in mine."

Her statement brought him back to the fact that all he had to do was get her naked and this stupid game would end. He either had to beat her more often, or he had to step up his story so she'd be compelled to remove her more important garments.

He was almost gratified to lose since that gave him the opportunity to tell her something good—and something good should net him, at the very least, her sweater the next time she lost.

"Okay," he said, working to word his next revelation in such a way that it would have value. "My girlfriend called it quits because she told me I'm not very thoughtful. But I think of myself first because that's how I stay on top of things. I might lose a woman here or there, but I don't make any major life mistakes."

Zoe studied him. "Let me get this straight. Your girlfriend put up with you for five years, suddenly called you inconsiderate and left?"

"I'd missed a lot of birthdays. She'd given me a lot of second chances."

"Wow. It sounds like it crushed you."

He shrugged and picked up the cards. "Zoe, that's the whole point. I never let myself invest so much that I get hurt. Life taught me that lesson right off the bat. I lost my parents. I fought almost constantly with my brothers until they asked me to get the hell out of their lives. Losing my parents hurt because I loved them. Losing my brothers hurt because I had trusted them. And they didn't trust me. In fact, they distrusted me so much it was easier for them to lose me than put up with me."

With that Zoe fell silent. And Cooper was damned glad because the god-awful odd feeling was back in the pit of his stomach. He'd never suspected his sparse love life was entwined with losing his family and, frankly, he could have gone the rest of his days without knowing.

Without saying a word, he dealt, looked at his cards, tossed two, and motioned to her to tell him how many she wanted.

"All three."

He dealt her three cards, then gave himself two. Two kings to go with his three sevens. If this wasn't perfect timing, he didn't know what was. Now that the real truth about his life was out, he was determined to start winning so they could move on. To the bedroom.

"Only the strong survive," he said, then caught her gaze and flipped over his hand, revealing his full house. "I intend to survive and I want your sweater."

She turned over her hand. Four nines.

He stared at her. "How the hell do you do that?"

"Once I warm up, I'm lucky at cards." She shrugged. "Lucky at cards. Unlucky at love."

Though he had been gathering the deck, what she said stopped him, and he suddenly knew why she wanted to hear about his life. "You don't want my story. You want to know how to live like me."

"I believe I told you that."

"No, you made it sound as if you wanted my life philosophy but you don't want the generic facts. You want to know my decisions. You want to *copy* my life."

She said nothing, only looked across the table at him.

"Zoe, I'm on the road, have no kids, and have a partner who can back me up…. You *can't* make the decisions I've made."

"Are you saying a girl can't live like that? Because if you are, you should know that I beat my male cousins at cards. I was also a better marksman. And I got better scores on the SATs."

But she hadn't gone to college, likely because her parents deserted her. He and Zoe were comparing apples to oranges. Sure, they had similar pasts in that they had both lost their parents and neither one of them had fit into the life that was left after their parents were gone. But the real reason he lived his life the way he did wasn't a decision—it was an admission that he was untrustworthy. She was about the most trustworthy person he had ever met. There was no reason for her to live like he did. If she copied his life, she would essentially go from being good and reliable to being a relationship schlep like him. He felt like a heel for giving her the idea.

"What do you do for a living?"

She shook her head. "Nice try. But you lost the hand. So you're the one who's supposed to be talking."

He drew a frustrated breath. She had a baby. She needed to be soft and sweet and honorable. This was all wrong. Even having an afternoon fling with her suddenly seemed horribly, horribly wrong.

He swore he heard his hormones groan, but he knew it was true and he knew he had to stop this right now. "My fight with my brothers began over a woman."

One of her eyebrows rose. "Really?"

"My brother Ty, the oldest, was engaged. His fiancée ran around on him all the time, but I didn't tell him until she hit on me."

"Holy cow!" Her eyes widened in disbelief and Cooper realized he had a quick way to end this game, the conversation, even their bet.

"You want to hear about some more cows? My brother had already taken the family business much further than my parents ever dreamed. Anita was a gold digger. Ty had money and she wanted it."

Her eyes widened to the size of saucers. "Your family had money?"

"Ty made Bryant Construction into Bryant Development. He's probably worth a billion dollars right now."

"You left *billions of dollars?*"

"No, when I left we were only millionaires."

"You're a millionaire?"

He shook his head. "No. I washed my hands of it."

"Are you insane?" She rose from the poker table with her eyes flashing fire. "Every month I wonder whether or not I'm going to have enough money to pay my utilities. This fall, I got a notice from the county that my parents haven't been paying the taxes on my house. I'm going to lose it soon because after so many years of unpaid taxes the county can sell a piece of real estate right out from under anybody living there."

"Money isn't everything."

His quiet statement seemed to bring her back to earth and she shook her head and sat again. He had expected her to storm out of the room. Instead she grabbed the cards. The game was still on.

Anger ripped through Cooper. Under normal circumstances hearing that someone was about to lose her house would have made him think the involved person was a nitwit who couldn't keep up with life. But having felt the sting of betrayal after reading the letter from his brothers' attorney, he knew that sometimes some people really were innocent victims.

This woman was about as innocent as they came and he would *not* be the one to ruin her.

"Why don't *you* pay the taxes?"

Calm again, she shuffled the cards. "I didn't realize they were going unpaid. I was eighteen when my parents left. Which means six years have gone by. When I got the notice that the taxes were so far behind, I called my dad, and found out he had paid for a few years but he'd felt it was my mother's responsibility to pay for a few years."

"And your mother?"

"My mother was busy. She couldn't believe I had called her. She said that since she didn't live in the house, she had no reason to be responsible for the taxes and hung up the phone."

"Oh."

"Don't," she said, holding up her hand to stop the flow of sympathy he could feel ebbing from himself and which she undoubtedly could feel as well. "After I got off the phone, I realized she was right. I'm twenty-four years old. I shouldn't be calling my mommy to bail me out. Since I'm the one living at the house those taxes are my responsibility."

She drew a quick breath. "Unfortunately, with the penalties and interest that have accrued, I owe so much I can't even get a loan for the amount. But even if I could, I couldn't afford the loan payments. I'm a clerk at a grocery store. The only thing that has made it possible for me to live on my own and support a child is that I have a house and haven't had to pay rent." She paused and sighed. "But we're talking about me again."

"And I told you something equal to your win." Not sure what else to do, Cooper ran his hand along the back of his neck. "If you want more info you need to beat me again."

She dealt. He lost. He was beginning to believe she really was cursed to being lucky at cards, unlucky at love.

"Frankly, Zoe, I'm out of things to tell you."

She looked him in the eye. "Tell me how to do it. Tell me how to stay sane, how to get the attitude that I should only look out for myself, how to resist the temptation to try one more time to get somebody to love me."

He couldn't handle the sadness in her pretty blue eyes, so he focused on the other point of her question. "Is that how you see me? As somebody who only looks out for himself?"

"Isn't that how you see yourself?"

Yes and no. He looked out for himself because he was strong, able, independent. Somebody avoiding pain. Not somebody intent on hurting people. Not somebody who was selfish. She saw him as selfish.

He cleared his throat. "No. That's not how I see myself. And you win. My story is over and you're fully clothed. You don't have to go to bed with me."

Chapter Seven

Cooper couldn't sleep that night. He tried to tell himself that the difference between being inconsiderate and selfish was small and he had accepted himself as inconsiderate, which made him an idiot to care about being called selfish. But it didn't work.

There *wasn't* a small difference between inconsiderate and selfish. There was a pool. A swimming pool. An *Olympic* swimming pool. Inconsiderate people didn't see things, didn't think things through. Selfish people were *deliberately* self-centered. They saw others' needs and ignored them.

Pacing, Cooper tried to remember when he'd seen one of Bonnie's needs and ignored it, but he couldn't recall a time because there wasn't a time. He simply, honest-to-God had never seen what she needed.

He didn't believe that made him a bad person. He thought being inconsiderate made him unfit for relationships. And he accepted that. Hell, he had recognized that as part of the deal back when Seth had kicked him out of the house. He was who he was. Since he couldn't change, he chose to keep his distance from people who couldn't tolerate him as he was.

Except Zoe didn't think that he was inconsiderate. She thought he was selfish.

He fell to the bed and groaned. Damn it! Why did he care?

Because she was a smart woman. She'd seen so much of life he could tell she was a good judge of character. She wasn't just a pretty girl or a sexy woman. She had a real heart. And if she thought being selfish kept him sane and she decided to imitate him, she would lose that heart.

But, he *wasn't* selfish. He was thick, obtuse…or overworked. Burdened with his own problems.

He combed his fingers through his hair. Actually, that *was* the gist of it. When he was with Ty and Seth, his burden had been to do his share of work needed to make Bryant Development great. Ty was a genius planner. Seth was a networker. Cooper was the guy who got things done. While his brothers made deals, Cooper oversaw the resultant projects. Yes, he was tough. But being the voice of the company at the job sites was not an easy task. He took it seriously. It was a responsibility…a burden of sorts. It had hurt that his brothers hadn't seen his value, had only seen him as trouble.

Then after Seth had asked him to leave, his burden had become starting over from scratch and making something of himself. Alone. No money. No contacts. No help. And he'd done that. Until they'd bought his mortgage.

Now his burden had become trying to hold on to the ranch—and not for himself, for his partner. If he failed to get the mortgage money to his brothers' lawyer on time, his partner, Dave, would lose the money he'd invested, too.

There was no way Cooper would let that happen. So, Zoe Montgomery was wrong. He wasn't selfish.

He was who he was.

But if he didn't somehow make her understand the difference between being burdened and being selfish, she was going to imitate all the wrong things and it would be his fault.

That was the part of the situation that made him the most angry. He stayed out of other people's lives not merely because he was inconsiderate, but also because he always screwed things up when he got involved. Now, he would have to fix the impression he'd unwittingly given Zoe.

The only way he could do that would be to talk to her again and if he talked to her again, there was a possibility he'd make a bigger mess of things. Worse, there was also the possibility that he'd like her even more than he already did. He'd fought it and fought it and fought it, but the woman was just plain nice and funny and pretty. But he was trouble. The absolute last thing she needed in her life was a man like him.

* * *

The next morning, Zoe awakened feeling miserable. Now that Cooper Bryant had gotten to know her, even he didn't want to sleep with her. Could a woman get any lower? Sure, he'd tried to pretend he'd lost the bet, but it was abundantly clear to Zoe that he hadn't so much *lost the bet* as he'd *lost interest*. He'd heard her story and metaphorically run for his life.

She slipped out of bed, changed Daphne, then took her to the kitchen for some cereal and a bottle. She made a pot of coffee and toast but Cooper still didn't come downstairs. With a sigh, Zoe put Daphne on the blanket on the floor in the center of the great room, turned on the TV and sunk on to the sofa.

After an hour, Daphne played herself out and fell asleep on the comforter, but there was still no sound from Cooper. Zoe turned and peered up the stairs. She suspected Cooper was avoiding contact with her, but it seemed odd he hadn't come down for coffee. She walked to the French doors to stare outside and suddenly realized that the second storm had stopped. It was even somewhat sunny.

A horrible thought paralyzed her. The snowplow could have come through the night before. If it had, Cooper could have gone.

And why wouldn't he? The details of her life had made him uncomfortable. So uncomfortable, he couldn't even bring himself to sleep with her. If he'd heard the snowplow in the middle of the night he could have taken advantage of the opportunity to skip out.

Something inside Zoe snapped. After four days of being stuck together, he hadn't even had the decency to say goodbye. Was anybody ever going to stick with her to the end of anything?

Wanting to confirm her worst fear so she could get really angry and stop being such a schmuck about people, Zoe bounded up the steps. When she reached the top, she turned into the bedroom she knew Cooper was using and stopped dead in her tracks.

He wasn't gone. He was still asleep.

She took another step into the room. Seeing him tucked under the covers sent a shaft of pure, unadulterated relief through her, but it also confused her. Not once during their stay had he slept in. More than that, even if the snowplow hadn't gone through last night, both she and Cooper expected it to come by today sometime. He should be up and packing, or, at the very least, pacing, dying to leave.

She walked to the bed and peered down at his face. Oh, Lord! His cheeks were red. His brow was dewy with fever-induced sweat. She and her daughter had both exposed him to their virus. She squeezed her eyes shut in misery. She shouldn't be surprised he had caught it, too. But that didn't stop the guilt that spiraled through her. She had been nothing but trouble to this man.

She shook his shoulder. "Cooper?"

He mumbled.

"Cooper, I want you to get up and come downstairs so you can sleep in the bedroom with the bathroom."

He mumbled again.

"That's the spirit," she said, knowing his mumble didn't necessarily mean he was alert, but at least he was awake. She gingerly began to lift the blanket so he could climb out of bed. "Come on. I'll help you walk."

"I'm fine." He took the cover from her hand and put it back where it had been. "I know I have what you and Daphne had. I also know it's smarter to be in the bedroom with the bathroom. But I'm…well, naked under these covers."

She stepped back.

He sort of laughed. "I'm harmless, but I still have my pride. Leave. I'll be down."

Zoe did as he said. Telling herself not to dwell on the fact that she had nearly seen him naked, she ran to the bedroom she was using and quickly gathered Daphne's things. By the time she was done, Cooper was at the bottom of the steps. Though he had put on jeans and a T-shirt, he was also wrapped in the blanket from his bed.

"Just go ahead in and go back to sleep. Daphne and I will be as quiet as we can."

"Great," he rasped, then stumbled into the room.

He closed the door behind him, and Zoe breathed a sigh of relief. But when three hours passed without hearing a sound from him, she decided to make sure he was okay. She sneaked into the room and placed her hand on his forehead. It was hot, but he was sleeping soundly and there wasn't anything she could do for him, so she left.

In the great room she paced, watched TV, then paced some more before she fed Daphne lunch and played with her. When Daphne fell asleep in her drawer, Zoe sneaked into the bedroom again to look in on Cooper. Though he slept soundly and there was no reason to stay in the room, Zoe stood by his bed, mesmerized.

His face was still shiny with fever, and his dark hair was disheveled from a restless sleep, but he was still the most handsome man Zoe had ever seen. She had nearly fainted when he'd kissed her. And, yeah, he was grumpy and self-centred, but he had a kind heart. Whether it was smart or not she liked him.

She took a quick breath. She liked him a lot. That was why she had been so troubled when she'd thought he had left without saying goodbye. Though he tried to pretend he was *The Grinch Who Stole Christmas,* deep down inside he was a good guy. In his story of his life, she had seen a man who had faced adversity and won. She had seen a man who still respected the very brothers who didn't want him around. She had seen a man who was genuine and honest. Even the way he'd stopped the poker game the day before proved he had integrity. Unfortunately, it also quite clearly said he didn't feel about her what she was realizing she felt about him.

Confused by how she could be letting herself fall for another man whose feelings didn't match hers, she sat on the edge of the bed. When her weight shifted the mattress, he opened his eyes and she smiled. "You're up."

"If you want to call it that."

Trying not to succumb to guilt over being the one who had given him the virus, she laid her hand across his forehead. "You feel a little hotter than I remember being."

"I'm fine."

"I'm sure you are, but it still worries me."

He laughed.

"You think it's funny that I worry?" she asked, knowing darned well he thought her a sap and knowing as well as he did that she was going to have to change.

"No, I do not think it's funny that you worry. I was just trying to recall," he said, his voice slow and tired, "the last person who worried about me." He took a breath. "This is the other side of that life of mine that you're trying to learn to copy. This is the empty side." He caught her hand and his weary eyes held hers. "This is what you don't want, Zoe. It's okay for me to be alone. I know how to nurse myself through illnesses that come along. I can entertain myself on lonely nights. I don't need a breakfast companion. But I don't think it would be okay for you."

She looked down at his hand holding hers. Strong callused fingers gripped hers firmly, as if he wanted to be certain she paid attention. But there was also comfort in the gesture, and a strange notion occurred to her. She'd thought he'd stopped the poker game because he was no longer interested in sleeping with her, but what if the conversation had caused him to see enough about her that he was beginning to like her the same way she liked him? He'd appeared angry, but what if that was because he'd recognized he was starting to care about her and he didn't want to?

She stared at their joined hands. Now that he had her attention, he could let her hand go, yet he didn't. It seemed odd that he would allow himself such a quiet gesture of affection, but she realized he might be too sick to fight his feelings. Maybe too sick to understand that something so sweet and simple as holding her hand meant a hundred times more to her than his wonderful, deep kiss had.

"And another thing," he said quietly, then swallowed as if the slight conversation was exhausting him. "Don't get all invested in the idea that you need to be selfish. That's just going to ruin your life."

Her eyes filled with tears. He *did* care. He cared enough to fight his own need to sleep to prevent her from making a mistake. However, she wasn't kidding herself. Cooper was also a loner and loners didn't hang around to help sort through problems. He might like her enough to clear up a misinterpretation, but he wasn't the kind of guy who would work with her to fix what she had done wrong.

All the same, she'd reached her limit. Living her life longing for something she was never going to get was killing her. At the very least, it was killing her spirit.

"I've got to do something, Cooper," she said, staring at their entwined fingers, wishing he were different, wishing he would stay, yet knowing if he were anybody but the stubborn, quiet, determined guy she was coming to know she wouldn't feel the same about him. She liked that he stood his ground, knew his mind, only went after what he wanted. Even though that also meant he stayed away from her.

"I'm sort of breaking. You know how everybody has that point where they can't keep up what they're doing anymore because it's hurting more than helping? That's where I am."

"You've got to find a way to keep going."

She shook her head. "I'm out of ways."

He took a breath and closed his eyes. "When I feel better, we'll brainstorm."

She smiled. "Right."

"I mean it."

His reply came out so slow and sluggish, Zoe knew it would only be a matter of seconds before he drifted off to sleep again. But he still had hold of her hand.

The pool of tears in her eyes expanded to overflowing. Whether he knew it or not, Cooper Bryant had real feelings for her. And she, well, she was falling in love with him.

"Why don't you stay in my life and help me figure out what I'm supposed to be doing?" she asked, half hoping he had fallen asleep because she suspected she already knew the answer. He might have feelings for her, but he didn't want them. He liked his life free of responsibilities. Women in general were a responsibility for men. But a woman with a baby and a past was a burden.

"I'm not the best person to help you figure out anything." He drew a tired breath. "Besides, I don't have time."

"Have you ever tried making time?"

"Did I neglect to tell you about Bonnie?"

Zoe laughed. The fact that he compared her to an old girl-friend, not his brothers, not his partner, not a friend, was very telling and it gave her the courage to be honest. "Things between us would be different. I would be smart enough to know to give you space. I would know how to live with you, Cooper. I wouldn't get in your way."

When he didn't reply, Zoe couldn't tell if he didn't argue because he'd fallen asleep, or if he was actually considering what she had said.

In case he was thinking about it, she pushed on. "You know…we have a built-in opportunity to see if we could have something because the sheriff is selling my parents' house." A new idea came to her and she blurted it out before she could stop herself. "I could move to Texas with you and stay with you until I got on my feet."

But even as she said the words, Zoe knew she wouldn't be staying with him until she got on her feet. She was already halfway in love with him. She would be totally in love with him after a few weeks of living with him. And she knew she'd spend those weeks desperately trying to make him love her.

Unfortunately, she also knew he'd be in his home territory and he could slide back into his routine and easily ignore her. Worse, he could end up wondering what the hell had possessed him to let her move to Texas with him. Assuming he even let her go with him at all.

Her suggestion of moving to Texas with him would only work if she could get him to realize right now, while they were still stuck in Pennsylvania together, that he wanted more from her than something casual.

Recognizing he was asleep by his deep breathing, Zoe rose from the bed. But when she reached the door she stopped. She felt better.

A lot better.

Almost as if she had hope in her life again.

In the great room, she peered into the drawer to make sure Daphne was still napping, then she sat on the sofa and analyzed what had happened in that bedroom. She couldn't feel hope about her feelings for Cooper. He'd probably fallen asleep before she'd made her suggestion about Texas, but if he hadn't, he had ignored it. When he was well again, he could yell at her for even asking. So she knew her unexpected infusion of well-being had not come from him.

She thought about everything they had said in those few minutes of conversation. When that reaped no results, she focused only on what *she* had said and she suddenly realized that buried in their discussion was her admission that the county sheriff would be selling her house.

She gasped softly. Whether she'd intended it or not, in that short discussion, she had let her house go.

She leaned back on the couch and closed her eyes. The truth was the house might come with free rent, but it was an albatross. It cost too much to heat. The roof needed to be patched. The faucets leaked. The furnace was on its last leg. Maybe that was why it didn't hurt to let it go.

Even if Cooper Bryant didn't want her, she was going to be okay. She and Daphne wouldn't end up on the street. They'd end up in an apartment, probably shared with someone she'd find through a newspaper ad. And her new roommate could be good company. Who knew? She might end up with a best friend…or someone who could become as close as a sister.

That thought intensified the hope she felt. But she heard a sound from the bedroom and spun to face the closed door.

The idea of a sisterlike roommate did give her some sense of a happy future, but she'd much, much rather move to Texas. Still, she couldn't be the one to bring it up again. She'd given Cooper plenty of hints that she would be willing to start something with him. But more than that, she couldn't say or do anything that would cause him to put up those walls again. She had maybe one more day before Cooper would leave and she wasn't going to ruin the chance that he might see the obvious for himself.

Cooper awakened at around four o'clock in the morning. Realizing his virus had run its course, he pushed himself out of bed. Though there was a bit of residual stiffness, he no longer felt he could throw up. He no longer felt weak. All of this was very good news.

He pulled on the jeans and T-shirt he had dropped at the side of the bed, then went in search of his boots. He found them, shoved his feet inside, grabbed his jacket and left the house. From the porch he looked out at the moonlight glistening off the packed snow. The air was crisp and clean. The world was a silent winter wonderland, and he let himself absorb the peace before he jogged down the steps and headed for the driveway.

The other good news of the morning was that in spite of his fever-induced delirium, he remembered talking with Zoe about selfishness. He didn't recall exactly what he had said, but he knew he had made his point that selfishness wasn't the way to go. Even though she'd argued a bit about needing to change something in her life, Cooper had no doubt she wouldn't take the selfish route because she was a smart woman. She would be okay. And that meant he had to leave before he did any more damage to her fine, upstanding set of morals.

With the moon lighting his way, Cooper walked out to the road. When he saw it hadn't yet been plowed, he sighed. But he also understood that the state had been busy clearing the main arteries. He was sure this road would fall into the department of transportation's radar some time within the next twenty-four hours and he and Zoe could go their separate ways.

All he had to do was behave himself for about sixteen more hours and he wouldn't have to worry that he'd ruined a perfectly sweet woman.

He trudged back to the cabin and glanced at his wristwatch. It was nearly five o'clock and he knew that Daphne usually woke before six o'clock, so after stripping off his denim jacket, he went into the kitchen and put on a pot of coffee. He watched it brew, then drank a cup, letting the minutes tick away until five-thirty, when he began frying bacon.

Around ten till six, the sounds of Daphne's whimpers and wake-up cries drifted down the steps. At five till six, Zoe padded into the kitchen with Daphne.

"Good morning."

This was where he hit the dilemma. If he wasn't at least polite, Zoe would go back to believing the selfishness theory he had hoped he had wiped clean yesterday. But if he was too nice, she would get all the wrong ideas.... He stopped his thoughts. It might be true that Zoe was coming to like him as much as he feared he liked her, but once they left this house it wouldn't matter if Zoe thought she was head over heels in love with him. They would never see each other again. It was better to err on the side of caution.

He smiled. "Good morning."

"I see you're feeling better."

"A hundred percent better. But you probably know exactly how I feel since you had the same thing."

She smiled. "Yeah."

"Listen, why don't you let me feed Daphne while you go shower? I know what it's like to be her keeper for twenty-four straight hours, so I know you could use a break."

She licked her lips. "Really?"

"Sure." He'd expected a more joyful reaction, not something so analytical, and he concluded he must not have gotten his point across the day before. Knowing he couldn't let her leave this house with the wrong idea, he decided he had more explaining to do. "I remember talking yesterday about selfishness—"

Her eyes widened. "You remember our conversation from yesterday?"

"Yes, and I want to make sure you got my message. I don't want you thinking that by becoming selfish you can make your life better. You can't."

She frowned, then slowly asked, "That's all you remember?"

"Yeah," he said, but he searched her eyes. He experienced the usual slam in the gut that he always got when he looked into their blue depths, but this time he saw something that made him realize their conversation had gone a lot further. And whatever they'd discussed, it was important.

"What else did I say?"

Taking a step back, she licked her lips. "Nothing," she said, but a current of electricity passed between them. More than attraction, it hinted that they'd come to an understanding...or something.

His eyes narrowed. "What else did *you* say?"

She drew a breath.

"Zoe?"

She sighed. "It's not important. Really."

He studied her for a second, feeling a strength of connection to her that had no basis. Finally, he said, "I think it is. I think I must have given you another wrong impression about me and I'd like the chance to fix it."

She sighed again. "All right. What if I tell you this? You didn't give me any wrong impressions."

"I think I did. It isn't just your behavior. I *feel* something—"

"Damn it!" she said, interrupting him. "You just aren't going to let this go, are you?"

"No."

"All right, then, here's the deal. We had a really nice conversation because you were too sick to argue. You even held my hand. So I got brave enough to ask if I could come live with you when the sheriff sells my house."

He frowned as the words began to sink in. Now that she mentioned it, he remembered holding her hand and how right it had felt. He remembered drifting off to sleep picturing her in the house on his ranch. Picturing her with the horses. Picturing her in his bed.

A shaft of white-hot desire shot through him, but he ignored it in favor of getting to the truth. "You asked to live with me…." He closed his eyes and realized what had happened. He'd been too weak to fight his feelings, and she'd seen them.

Unwilling to let her hope for another thing she couldn't have, he shook his head. "Zoe, do not even go there."

Her chin lifted. "Why not? It's my life and—"

"That's exactly the point. This is your life and you're not the kind of girl to live with someone!"

"How do you know that when I don't even know that for sure?"

"*I know,*" he said, getting angry now. She might not have been a virgin when he met her, but Zoe Montgomery was pure. Not the vague kind of pure people associate with sexuality, but pure about life. She wanted life's best. In less than a week, he'd corrupted her.

He headed for the door. "I'm going outside to see if the snowplow came through." He knew it hadn't but she didn't know he knew. "When I get back there'll be no more talk of living together! You're too good for that, Zoe," he said, slamming the door behind him.

Chapter Eight

Midmorning another snowstorm hit. For two solid hours Zoe held Daphne on her lap and stared out the window. She reminded herself that even though Cooper Bryant didn't want her, she could get a roommate. She also told herself that once she got rid of her albatross house, she could get loans and grants and go to school, and eventually land a job that paid well. Things were not *that* bleak. So what if Cooper Bryant didn't want her to live with him? She hardly knew the man.

Daphne made a whimpering sound. As if by rote, Zoe rose from her seat, warmed a bottle, fed her baby and laid her in the baby drawer in the bedroom. Because the sides of the drawer were high enough, she could let Daphne sleep in it without worry that she'd get out, and she acknowledged to herself that Cooper was quite inventive when he wanted to be.

She stopped her thoughts and squeezed her eyes shut. She had to quit thinking about him and giving him credit that he didn't deserve. Yes, he had found somewhere for Daphne to sleep, but he'd done that for his own sanity. Everything he did, he did for himself. He was not nice. He was not thoughtful. If he came up with creative solutions they were to save himself work or ease his conscience. He was *not* the kind of man she wanted to fall in love with, and if it killed her, she was getting over her feelings for him.

Daphne fell asleep. Zoe left the bedroom and walked to the window again. Staring at the big fat flakes as they fell was similar to watching a train wreck. She didn't want to stay another day with Cooper. Yet, for some reason or another, fate had chosen to torture her.

Finally, she decided to indulge herself in her only real activity. Showering. She forced herself away from the window and her gaze collided with Cooper, who lay on the sofa engrossed in an old movie.

She would tell him she was about to take a shower, but she knew he didn't give a damn. He didn't give a damn about anything. That was why he wasn't upset and stressing over the new storm as she was. That was why he could contentedly watch a movie. He didn't invest any emotion in anything—especially not her. No. Not just her. People in general. He didn't expect anything or give too much, and she needed to start doing that, too.

She left the great room, made a quick check on napping Daphne and headed for the shower. She was sure the dull ache in her chest would go away eventually. But for now it wasn't budging.

She sluggishly showered, then stepped out and unenthusiastically toweled her hair until it was dry enough that she could put on her day-old sweater. She shimmied into her already worn jeans and ran a finger full of toothpaste over her teeth, then ambled into the bedroom again.

Unfortunately, when she glanced into the baby drawer, Daphne was nowhere around and all the self-pity in which Zoe had indulged vanished with the violent pump of her heart. Her baby was gone!

She looked around the bedroom, including under the bed, in case Daphne had crawled out of the drawer and had gotten herself stuck there, but she didn't find her little girl. Panicked now, she scrambled out into the hall between the kitchen and great room. Immediately, she saw Daphne's baby seat on the kitchen table, happy baby inside.

"What is she doing out here?"

Cooper shrugged. "I promised to take her this morning, but I went outside. So when I heard her cry, I got her."

Zoe noticed that his answer was simple, to the point, and that he was gathering cans from the cupboard as if he were about to make something for lunch.

She walked to the table. "Come on, Daph—"

Cooper half turned from the counter. "Leave her. We're fine."

Righteous indignation rose up in her. She was *not* accepting any more of his charity. And if he didn't really care about her as a person, then anything he did for her was charity. Or a way to make it palatable to have her around, and Zoe didn't like that, either.

"I don't need your charity."

He shook his head with disgust. "I'm not giving you charity."

"Okay," she said, as pride and anger straightened her spine, "then what would you call it?"

"How about charity for Daphne. She doesn't need a grouchy mother."

Zoe took a sharp breath. He could call her a prude. He could call her stupid. He could call her insane for all she cared. But he could not call her a bad mother. And he knew that. He knew her vulnerable spot and he'd hit it.

Cooper cursed softly. "Sorry. That came out wrong."

Zoe didn't believe it had. Thinking back to everything they'd been through in the past few days, she realized part of the reason Cooper was so good at taking care of himself was that he took things at face value. He didn't read anything into any situation. He dealt only with facts, logic and reason. And the "fact" was he hadn't called her a bad mother. She'd read that into his comment. He'd said she was grouchy. And she *was* grouchy. She couldn't take offense at the truth.

An unexpected sense of calm enveloped her. Using logic and reason really seemed to work.

She took a step back from the table. "Don't worry about it. I *am* grouchy and feeling sorry for myself and all kinds of other stupid things. So maybe I do need a few minutes alone. Though I'm not sure what it'll accomplish." She combed her fingers through her hair. "I wish I had a book...or more space to pace in. I wish I could stop the world long enough to clear up a few of my problems." She smiled uneasily. "But I can't. So maybe a few minutes alone will make me feel better."

"Why don't you put your coat on and go for a walk?"

She laughed and shook her head. Texas boy. Thought it would be fun to walk in the snow. She showed him her tennis shoes. "If I walk in two feet of snow in these, I'll ruin them."

He shrugged. "Sit on the porch. Some days when I feel the weight of my problems, I sit on my porch and look out at how big the world is and realize I'm sort of small and in the grand scheme of things my problems are small and I feel better."

She nodded. Having already made a fool of herself in front of this man, she decided not to argue with his advice or mention that his sentiment was awfully poetic for a man who was so pragmatic. Instead, she walked into her bedroom and put on her insubstantial red leather jacket. Knowing that wouldn't be enough to fend off the cold, she took a blanket from her bed, walked through the hall and front door and sat on the top step of the porch.

And for some reason or another, maybe it was because she was alone in a pristine world, or maybe because she felt as insignificant as Cooper had suggested she would, she suddenly found herself smack-dab up against the truth of why she was so upset. She didn't care about her house. She didn't care about money. She didn't even care about apartments or going to college. She was lonely and tired of being alone. And she thought somebody like Cooper Bryant, who had been deserted by his family and more or less shoved aside by life, would understand that and see her as the answer to his loneliness, too. But he didn't.

Cooper looked out the window and seeing Zoe cry made his chest hurt so much he almost couldn't breathe.

Daphne wailed.

He turned toward the kitchen where he'd left the baby in her travel seat and saw Zoe's energetic daughter slapping her chubby hands against her sausage-like thighs. He pulled her from her seat and instead of grabbing his nose, pulling his hair, or twisting his lips, Daphne cuddled into his neck.

He squeezed his eyes shut. It almost seemed that if one of these two Montgomery girls didn't get to him, the other did. Daphne was sweet and fun. Zoe was sexy and determined. And life was simply kicking the heck out of them. First, Daphne's dad had left. Now, Zoe's parents had let the taxes go unpaid on the only break life had given her.

Daphne snuggled against his shoulder and he sighed heavily. There was no way in hell he was letting his two girls suffer. He couldn't change Zoe's life. He couldn't change that her parents had left her or that her exhusband was an idiot. Yet he wanted to do something. He *had* to do something! He couldn't let life beat her down anymore. He and Zoe might have both lost their parents at eighteen, but he hadn't been left alone. Ty had made sure he had gone to college. Then, even after he left his brothers, fate had been kind to him in finding him a partner. No one had ever done anything for Zoe.

So he had to. But what? Cuddling Daphne as he paced, Cooper racked his brain and suddenly the answer came to him. So simple. So clear. He could pay the taxes on her house. Actually, if he gave her the certified check he'd had prepared to pay off his brothers, he wouldn't be merely paying the taxes on her house. He would essentially be handing her four years of college tuition and support for those years so she could go from poverty to a normal life.

It meant facing his brothers.

No, it meant facing his brothers as a failure. No check. No explanation. Just the simple admission that he couldn't pay the mortgage, so they could foreclose. Seeing him humbled was what they wanted. They didn't want his ranch. His brother had more money and material objects than they knew what to do with. But that was good because that meant he could take care of his partner.

His brothers' lawyer's letter had said that if he couldn't pay the mortgage balance before December 24, he had to tell Ty face-to-face. If he were the only one losing the ranch, he would have ignored that provision, but because he had a partner who stood to lose everything he'd invested, Cooper intended to accommodate it. He would go and see his brother Ty, all right. But it wouldn't be to grovel as he expected was Ty's intent in that provision. No, he would demand a check for the equity he and his partner had earned on the ranch, so Dave wouldn't lose his investment.

Then, Cooper would continue driving truck and saving,

and in a few years he would have another down payment for another ranch.

So he could give Zoe his check. Not because he was a saint. And not because he wasn't selfish. But because for him, starting over wasn't all that hard. He'd played this out once. He knew what to do. Zoe, on the other hand, was trapped and he simply could not stand by and do nothing.

But now that he'd gotten her back up, there was a good possibility she would refuse his "charity" and he had to figure out a way to get her to accept the money. Today's snowfall had granted him the grace of one more day before he and Zoe would be heading home. But it was only one day, so he had to do something quickly. Something he knew she couldn't resist. Unfortunately, the only thing she couldn't resist was him.

He didn't want to give her the wrong idea, but this time tomorrow she'd be in her house on the other side of this godforsaken mountain and he'd be on his way to Texas. Short of seducing her, he had to do whatever it took to get her to accept the check.

When Zoe entered the front foyer, her tears were dry. She blamed her red nose on the cold and happily took Daphne from Cooper's arms, swearing that the hour and a half outside was exactly what she needed.

He sighed with relief. "Great. I fed Daphne a bottle. Why don't you put her down for her nap, catch a nap yourself, and maybe fix yourself up a bit?"

She gave him a confused look.

"I made a special stew for supper and I just thought it would be nice…." He kicked the toe of his boot along the linoleum. "Ah, damn it, Zoe. Look, this storm isn't like the last one. It's passing through. The roads will be cleared late tonight or early tomorrow. We're going to be leaving and there are some things we need to discuss." He paused and caught her gaze. "I think I've figured out a way to solve your problems."

"You have?"

He shrugged. "Yeah, but I don't want to talk about it right now. We both said things we didn't mean this morning and it made me think about you and your life and I have a proposition for you. So you go take a nap and fix yourself up and I'll check on the road conditions and finish dinner. Then while we're eating I can make my proposal."

She drew a long breath. "Let's just talk about it now."

He put his arm around her shoulder and guided her to her bedroom. "No. Daphne needs a nap and I want to check on the road conditions to be sure the road crews really will get to us tonight or tomorrow. And I don't want to rush this. I want it to be special."

He walked away. Zoe stood frozen for a few seconds, then spun to watch his retreating back.

Special?

And hadn't he used the word *proposal?*

Yes, but he'd also used the word *proposition*. It was totally out of the realm of possibility that he would ask her to marry him. But it wasn't so far-fetched to consider that maybe he wasn't going to leave her.... Maybe he'd decided to let her come to Texas with him!

Zoe had never felt her spirits lift so fast. One second her heart was in the black pit of despair, the next it was on the highest mountain singing for joy. From their argument that morning she knew he wouldn't want her to "live with him" in the conventional sense, but because of that argument she also knew he thought of her as someone special. He liked her. And if she went to Texas with him it would only be a matter of time before he loved her.

She put Daphne down for her afternoon nap and then slipped up the steps in search of an attic. Cooper was in freshly laundered clothes. She'd worn the same two sweaters and pants for days. True, she had laundered them, but she was tired of them. She wanted to wear something pretty. And her only shot at something pretty would be finding some discards in the attic that she could somehow mix and match to make herself look and feel beautiful.

But the attic was filled with old hunting jackets, vests and smelly boots. She almost believed she was going to have to be Scarlett O'Hara and make a ball gown out of drapes, when at the back of the attic she saw a trunk. Everything inside looked to be from the forties, and, sadly, everything exceptionally pretty or dressy enough to be worthy of a special dinner was also made from wool. Because everything in the trunk smelled funny, anything she wanted to wear would have to be washed, and that counted out all the wool clothes.

Then suddenly she saw a simple, sleeveless white cotton

dress sprinkled with purple violets. It was sweet and feminine and could be laundered. She grabbed it and ran down the steps to the basement where she tossed the garment into the washer. She waited until the cycle was finished, then brought the dress upstairs. But rather than dry it in the great room, where Cooper could see it, she hung it on a hanger from the curtain rod in her bedroom, right above the furnace vent. Within two hours it was dry. Then she showered, put on makeup and slid into the dress.

When she walked out of her bedroom, all the lights had been dimmed and the television had been tuned to an all-music channel. Soft rock glided through the air. Daphne happily played in the dresser drawer in the center of the great room floor.

At the kitchen table, Cooper glanced up from cutting a chicken and said, "Oh. Well…" He paused as his eyes took a slow inventory. Then he swallowed. "Don't you look nice."

She smiled. "Thanks."

Fighting a serious case of butterflies, she walked into the kitchen. Because she didn't have shoes that complemented the dress, she wasn't wearing any. Barefoot and in the airy sleeveless dress, she probably looked like a woman about to go on a picnic with her lover, rather than a woman stranded in a cabin in the middle of a cluster of snowstorms.

She saw Cooper swallow again. "You *really* look nice."

And Cooper felt *really* funny. If he still had a stomach it had fallen to the floor. He couldn't stop staring at her, but when he noticed it was beginning to make her uncomfortable he reminded himself that he had to get her in an amiable enough mood to take his check.

The gentleman he usually kept buried rose up in him and pulled out her chair.

She smiled. "Thanks."

Zoe made dinner very easy. She kept her voice low, her comments quiet and Cooper relaxed, knowing soft-spoken, quiet Zoe could be persuaded to accept the money. She wasn't the arguer or the spitfire. She was the woman with common sense. The check was as good as in her bank account.

But as quickly as he realized that, sadness enveloped him. He might succeed in putting the money in her hands, but he also knew they weren't going to see each other again. He longed for a kiss. One more kiss. A kiss to remember…

He glanced at her, thinking how pretty she looked, how innocent, and reality intruded. Their attraction was much too potent to risk another kiss.

Still, he wanted something special to make this a night they could both remember. A slow romantic tune floated from the television and, inspired, Cooper rose. "Would you like to dance?"

She smiled shyly and agreed and Cooper's heart did a somersault. He couldn't believe everything was going so smoothly. He'd thought for sure she would immediately demand to know his proposition. Instead, she seemed to want to make this night as memorable as he did.

As he pulled her into his arms and began to glide around

the floor, he realized again how well they fit together. The warmth of her pressed against him felt so wonderful, so natural, he couldn't help admitting that though they might not be perfect partners, they did have "something." He had no idea what it was, but there was clearly a connection between them. Swaying in rhythm with the soft music, they both knew it. And she probably wanted a kiss as much as he did.

Unable to resist, he lowered his head and kissed her. As always, the world spun. But this time it didn't tilt off its axis. This time he understood the sexual attraction had been seasoned with genuine affection and he enjoyed it because it was the last kiss he would get from her, or give her. This was the end for them. Except he had to give her his check.

Compelled by the truth of that, he pulled away. There would never be a more perfect moment. He slid his hands from her waist so he could clasp her fingers and said, "Zoe, I know we haven't known each other very long, but we'd be foolish if we didn't acknowledge that in these past few days we've become very close."

She nodded.

"We've shared a lot of things about our lives that I'm guessing we've never shared with anyone else."

"Yes."

He drew a quiet breath. "So, I want you to have my check."

She blinked. "Your check?"

"Yes." He pulled the folded white envelope out of his back pocket. "This is the certified check I had written to pay off my brothers. It's more than enough to pay the taxes on your house and probably put you through all four years of college. I want you to have it."

She searched his face. "This is what you wanted to talk about tonight?"

"Yes." He opened her hand and placed the envelope in her palm.

She looked at it, then caught his gaze, tears shimmering on her eyelashes. "This is really it? All of it? Everything you wanted to tell me?"

Panic gripped him. He expected her to be overcome with joy or to get angry. He didn't know how to deal with questions or confusion. "Yes."

Holding his gaze, she asked, "So, what was the kiss all about?"

He cleared his throat. "Zoe, you're kind of an irresistible force and we're friends…."

"So, that kiss meant we're friends?"

He studied her for a few seconds, then said, "We're more than friends. And you know that. I wouldn't be giving you my life savings if we weren't."

"But we have no future together."

"We've been through this. I can't commit. If you knew me better—"

"We know each other well enough for you to give me every cent of money you have, but you think we don't know each other?"

He shook his head in disbelief. "You expect to be bosom buddies after six days?"

"No, I expected you to like me enough to want me to go with you."

His eyes widened. "Come with me?"

"Yes. To Texas. I'm losing my house, remember?"

"That's why I'm giving you the check."

"I don't want your check! I want you to love me!"

"*Love you?* In six days?"

"You're giving me every cent of money you have after only knowing me a few days. To me it makes as much sense to think we could fall in love, as it does to give each other our bank accounts."

"You need this money more than I do. I can start over, but you…"

Eyes flashing fire, she said, "I what?"

"You have a baby."

Cooper watched Zoe force herself to be calm. "I know we haven't spent a lot of time together, but you should have known better than this." She stuffed the check into his shirt pocket. "I told you. I don't want your charity."

With that she walked out of the room, and Cooper stood flabbergasted. She'd missed the significance of what he had done. He hadn't merely given her every cent he had. He was willing to give up years of his life for her. But she didn't want what he was offering.

She wanted him to love her. *Love* her. Even if he were the kind of guy to fall head over heels, he wouldn't do it in six days.

This really was the end.

Chapter Nine

The mood in the house the next morning was black. Cooper didn't know whether to be astounded that Zoe could possibly think he could love her in a matter of days, or angry that she'd thrown his generosity back in his face.

When she came into the kitchen and silently gathered Daphne's assorted bottles and half-eaten jars of baby food, her beautiful yellow hair cascading around her, his mind nearly took off in a direction that he knew it wasn't wise to go, so he focused on his anger. She needed that money. Hell, *he* needed that money. But he was giving it to her because her need was greater. That money was her jump start to life.

But she didn't want it because she'd fallen into some starry-eyed vat of stupidity and thought he should love her. Yes, she was beautiful. Yes, he'd love to make love to her. And, yes, under different circumstances—for instance if they lived anywhere near each other—they might be friends. For him, even admitting he wanted to be friends was a stretch. But they didn't live close enough that there was a hope in hell they could maintain a friendship. What would they do? Talk on the phone? Yeah, like he'd spend hours chatting!

But she didn't even want to be friends. She wanted to be lovers. In a real relationship. And she thought they were already on that road. Because the thing left unspoken the night before was that she loved him…or thought she did.

Which astounded him. Even if he did believe in love, even if he believed somebody could love him, there was absolutely no way in hell he would accept that somebody could fall in love with *anybody* in less than a week. Period. So she didn't love him and he sure as hell didn't love her.

She left the room as silently as she had entered and Cooper wilted. He didn't love her. But he did care about her. He cared about Daphne. And he knew enough about life to realize that Zoe had been given a raw deal. He also knew enough about life to suspect that he'd been thrown in her path at the very time that he had a cashier's check because his money was actually supposed to be *her* money. And he knew enough about life to realize that things didn't happen by accident. He'd met her, come to care about her, so he could give her the leg up she needed because he'd already proven that when the chips were down, he could always find a way to save himself.

He frowned. Did that mean he thought she *couldn't* find a way? Was that why she was so angry?

He almost slapped his forehead at his stupidity. He most certainly did not think she couldn't find her own way. He believed she was smart and capable but overburdened. He believed that his money would give her the chance to get the education that would allow her to live the way she was supposed to live. He also believed that if she were by herself, with no baby, no day care, no formula, diapers, or wipes to buy, she would kick life's butt.

But the circumstances were that she had a baby and unusual expenses and she needed a break.

Still, if she assumed he'd offered his herd money because he thought she *couldn't* save herself…well, then he supposed he understood why she was upset. Which simply meant he had to explain that she had taken his offer the wrong way. And once he explained she would see he didn't think her stupid or lazy or incompetent, simply overburdened, she would take his money.

Relief overwhelmed him and he walked into the bedroom where she was stuffing Daphne into her snowsuit.

"Can I talk to you?"

"I think we said everything that needed to be said last night."

"Now, see, there's where you're wrong. Because out there in that kitchen, after only a few seconds of real thought, I realized why you're mad at me. And if we had talked a few minutes longer last night, all this," he said, waving his hands around her room to indicate her quick packing and silent departure, "would be unnecessary."

She turned from the bed, holding grinning Daphne, and pushed past him to the door. "I have to get home."

"And I have to get on the road, too," he agreed, following her. "But this is an easy thing to settle. I figured out that you're mad at me because you think I'm giving you my mortgage money because I think you can't make it on your own. But the truth is," he continued, speaking quickly because she was rapidly striding to the door, "I don't think you're incapable. I think you're overburdened. I think life dealt you a bad hand, and even with your poker skills, it's killing you."

She put Daphne in her baby carrier and set it on the floor in the hall, then turned and ran into Cooper.

She sighed. "Move. I need to get the diaper bag."

"Why don't you let me get the diaper bag?"

"Because I can handle everything myself!"

Her words hit him like a slap across the face, making him see he was right on the money with his assumption that he'd insulted her, so he pushed on. "Yes. You *can* handle everything yourself. That's my point."

She shifted and walked past him to the bedroom. He scrambled after her.

"I'm not giving you my money because I don't think you can handle things. I'm giving you the money because I know you can. With this money you will get a degree—you will have money for both tuition and day care and living expenses for the years it will take. Then you will get a job and become self-sufficient. To me you are a good investment."

"I'm an investment?"

From the tone of her voice, he couldn't tell if she thought that a good or bad thing so he went with the truth. "Yes."

Her eyes narrowed. "So, you want the money back eventually?"

"No! It's not a loan."

"Right, because if it was a loan you would have to give me your address so I could make payments and you don't want me to have your address."

She was right. He didn't like people knowing where he was. He didn't like being accountable or depended upon. He just wanted to give her the damned money.

"Why is it so hard for you to believe that somebody wants to *give* you something?"

"Because no one's ever given me anything! There are always strings attached. There's always a catch."

"This money comes with no catch."

"Except that it gets me out of your hair. This way you leave me without regret. You won't love me. You say you can't, but I say you *won't*. So you give me your money, take the burden of sacrifice on yourself, don't have to worry about me, don't have to think about me…except maybe to have a warm feeling in your heart to know you gave me everything you had." She paused. Her gaze caught his. "But you're not giving me everything you have. I want *you.* You want to take the easy way out. Buy me off. Ease your conscience." She drew a quick breath. "Well, I won't let you. I want you to think about me. I want you to remember me. I want you to know that without you I'm alone and struggling."

The thought of her being alone, broke, hungry, cold, nearly did him in. Until he realized that was exactly what she wanted. She wanted him to feel he somehow was to blame for that. Just as Seth blamed him for the Bryant brothers not getting along. Just like Bonnie blamed him for their relationship fizzling. He cursed. "Take the money."

She grabbed the diaper bag and hoisted it to her shoulder. "No. If you really believe I'm strong, you know I don't need it."

She stormed to the front hall where Daphne sat trying to shove her entire fist into her mouth. Zoe grabbed the carrier handle, adjusted the diaper bag onto her back and headed for the door. But the weight of the diaper bag shifted and she nearly fell.

Cooper sighed. "Let me carry the diaper bag."

With her back to him, she tilted her head back and drew a deep breath. He knew she was debating. He knew she hated to look weak. Because she wasn't weak. But she needed help. He suddenly felt her pain, her burden. How would it feel to be a strong, self-sufficient person, who suddenly needed help? He couldn't imagine it because he'd never needed help. Life had always given him the resources to save himself.

He slowly walked to the door and eased the diaper bag from her shoulders. "No strings attached," he said quietly and opened the door, motioning with his hand for her to go out.

She nodded. He pulled the door closed behind them and followed her, watching her walk, back straight, head held high, to the driveway. His heart constricted. She was so proud. He could feel her pain. He knew she would never let him talk her into taking his money. But now that he was holding her diaper bag, he didn't have to talk her into taking it. He could simply give it to her.

He stopped walking. "Hey, Zoe. I just realized there's no point in me walking this twice. I'm going to run inside and get my duffel and backpack. You keep walking. I'll catch up."

She nodded. He breathed a sigh of relief and ran back to the house. He grabbed his duffel and backpack, which were in the great room where he'd stored them while he'd gone out and shoveled around his truck and her car to assure they weren't plowed in. He unzipped the backpack, pulled out the check and stuffed it into Daphne's diaper bag. Zoe would find it when she dumped the bag to do the laundry.

She'd probably curse him.

She'd probably almost tear up the check at least three times over the course of a long week that she'd spend looking at it.

But he would bet every cent of money in this check that ultimately she'd cash it…because betting every cent of the money was exactly what he was doing. It was a certified check. If she didn't cash it, the money was lost to both of them.

Zoe trudged up the mountain to her car. She remembered making the suggestion to Cooper the day they were stranded that they walk downhill rather than uphill looking for a cabin. At the time, she'd been so engrossed in his thunderstruck reaction to her touching him that she hadn't thought about how walking down to find shelter meant they would have to walk uphill to return to their vehicles.

She took a quick breath. "We're fine, Daphne," she told the baby girl who seemed happy to finally be outside in the fresh air, even if that air was only about thirty degrees. "We survived when your dad left. We'll survive now."

Daphne cooed and Zoe lifted the carrier high enough that she could nuzzle Daphne's face and grin at her daughter. But she knew her smile didn't reach her eyes. She had survived without Brad because Brad was a loser. He was a narcissistic boy. And every time Zoe missed him, if only his companionship, she reminded herself that there was somebody better out there. But she couldn't do that with Cooper because he was her somebody better. Even the way he'd tried to give her his check proved he was unselfish. Kind. Caring. But he didn't see it. Nope, unlike Brad, who only saw his good and never even considered he might do things wrong, Cooper only saw his faults. His mistakes. And he couldn't believe he would ever do anything right, good or kind.

He thought she was the one life had overburdened, but Cooper was the one who would always be trapped. He would always be alone because the person he refused to trust was himself. That knowledge hurt her worse than realizing she might always be alone because she didn't believe anybody would ever compare to him.

She heard the crunch of snow behind her and realized

Cooper was catching up to her. So she put on a brave face. She didn't want his memories to be of her angry with him. After all, he might have decided to live without her, but she most certainly intended to haunt his dreams.

He skidded to a stop beside her. "See, I told you I could catch up."

She smiled. "Yeah. I figured you would."

He adjusted her diaper bag and his backpack on his shoulder and started walking again.

"I don't want us to end on a sour note," she said quietly, hesitantly, because she wasn't sure how this comment would be greeted. But they were only about ten feet from her car. Ten feet of time left together. Ten feet to tell him the things she wanted to say. So it had to come out right.

"I didn't like us leaving mad, either."

She took a quick breath, then smiled at him. "Good, because I never got a chance to say what I wanted to say last night." She took another breath. "I think you're a very, very good person."

He looked away. "Yeah, well, you've got some stars in your eyes."

"And you're too hard on yourself."

Surprisingly, he laughed. "You aren't going to give this up, are you?"

She shook her head. "I have about five more seconds," she said, stopping by her car. She opened the door and slid Daphne's carrier to the driver's seat. Because Cooper had let her car run while he'd shoveled, the inside was warm.

She lifted Daphne from the seat and buckled her into her car seat. She gurgled happily.

"Daphne's glad to be going," Cooper said, nodding inside the car.

"Want to say goodbye?"

He swallowed and looked away again and Zoe's heart broke. He didn't even see that it was more painful for him to avoid love than it was to risk loving.

"Go ahead," she urged, nudging him toward the open door of her car. "Just poke your head in and say goodbye."

He nodded and bent inside her car. "Hey, kid. You be good."

She screeched and slapped his nose with her rattle.

Zoe winced, but he laughed as he pulled out of her car. "She still loves me."

His words shot an arrow in Zoe's heart. She knew he didn't mean them literally, only as an expression, so she smiled and said, "A slap with the rattle is her highest praise."

He nodded, stepped back. "So...you take care of yourself, okay?"

She nodded, and glanced to the right as misery tumbled through her. Damn it. She couldn't believe he could let it end like this. Especially since she couldn't! Before he knew what she intended to do, she took a step forward, grabbed the lapels of his jacket and pulled him to her. Standing on her tiptoes, she kissed him. At first he didn't respond, and then as if he couldn't help himself, he wrapped his arms around her, jerked her closer and deepened the kiss.

But he quickly pulled away and they stared into each other's eyes.

Please, she thought. *Please don't let me go. If nothing else, ask for my address, my phone number...anything!*

But Cooper stepped back. "Be careful going down the hill."

"I'm going up, remember?" she whispered. "I live on the other side of this mountain," she hinted, giving him the chance to say, "Yeah, where on the other side of the mountain?"

But he said nothing. Walking backward, he held her gaze for a few seconds.

Inspiration struck Zoe. "I could give you a ride up the hill to your truck—"

He shook his head. "No. I'm okay. I've been cooped up for so long the walk will feel good."

She nodded.

"Get into the car, Zoe."

Her chest tightened.

He turned away.

Zoe slid onto the driver's seat. The car spun a little as she edged out onto the road, but eventually the wheels caught and she was on her way. Up the hill. Home.

She passed Cooper. He didn't look at her. Didn't wave. Eyes straight head, he continued up the hill. All by himself. Because that's the way he liked it.

A few times she let her gaze stray to the rearview mirror. She memorized his long stride, the straightness of his spine, the sheer determination in his posture and carriage.

She was never going to get over him.

Chapter Ten

Cooper was surprised by the address Bryant Development's attorney had given him for Ty's home. He had expected his successful older brother to have purchased an ostentatious mansion to showcase his wealth and good fortune. Instead, Ty apparently still lived in the old family home where he and his brothers had started their lives.

Familiar with the streets of Porter, which he noted hadn't changed much in eight years, Cooper easily found the house and pulled into the driveway. Overwhelmed with memories, he sat in his four-wheel-drive truck, staring at the front porch, remembering other Christmas Eves.

He could hear his parents' laughter. Remember the gleam in their eyes because there were always Christmas secrets and surprises. Sadness enveloped him. Their parents would be so disappointed in the angry way he and his brothers had parted. They would be even more upset that Cooper, Ty and Seth didn't speak. If it weren't for the mortgage, Cooper wouldn't even be here right now. If it weren't for Zoe, he most certainly wouldn't be civil. But Zoe had changed him. If nothing else, he had to acknowledge that.

He walked up the sidewalk and, rather than take the turn that would lead him to the front porch, out of habit, he ended up at the kitchen door.

A gorgeous redhead answered his knock. "Merry Christmas!" she said.

Cooper cleared his throat. "Merry Christmas," he parroted, if only out of politeness. He felt like an idiot for having waited until he was down to the wire on the deadline, but really hadn't had much choice because of being stranded. His brothers would simply have to accept that explanation, and, if not, Cooper wasn't sure it mattered anyway. They had his mortgage, which meant they had his ranch. There wasn't too much more that could be said about that. "I'm sorry. I think I came at a bad time. Explain to my brothers that I'll come back to talk about the mortgage the day after tomorrow—"

The redhead's mouth fell open. She gasped, "Explain to your *brothers?* Are you Cooper?"

He shuffled his feet. "Yeah. But this looks like a really bad time so I—"

She grabbed his forearm and hauled him into the house. "Oh, no you don't!" She quickly closed the door behind him. "Ty!"

Embarrassed to the tips of his boot toes, Cooper glanced around. The kitchen was much cleaner than he remembered, but otherwise little else had changed. It was as if Ty had decided to preserve the hub of the house exactly as it was.

"I'm Madelyn, Ty's fiancée." She smiled. "I don't know what the holdup with Ty is, but I do know he wants to see you."

Cooper smiled wryly. "Right."

Madelyn put her hand on his forearm again. "No. Really."

Another minute ticked off the clock and Cooper glanced at the door.

"He probably didn't hear me," Madelyn said. "Keep an eye on Sabrina, will you?" she said, pointing at a little girl sitting in a high chair who looked about a year old. "I'll go check things out."

Two weeks ago, that request would have filled him with fear. No, two weeks ago the request that he stay with a baby would have sent him running. Today, after having spent almost a week with Daphne, he said, "No problem."

When Madelyn was gone, the little girl screeched at him, banging her hand on her high chair tray.

Cooper approached the high chair. "What's the matter, kid? Haven't they fed you?"

She bellowed, revealing two bottom teeth and one top.

Cooper laughed. "Damn, you're a cutie—"

"She's Scotty's daughter. Scotty and his wife, Misty, were killed this summer in a boating accident. I got custody."

Cooper spun away from the table to see his brother Ty. Dressed in a forest-green sweater, with the collar of a white shirt exposed, and wearing black trousers, Cooper's dark-haired, dark-eyed brother looked the picture of wealth and sophistication.

Wishing with all his heart that he hadn't come, but knowing he had to stay to get Dave's equity, Cooper quietly said, "Hello, Ty."

"Cooper," Ty said, inclining his head. "Seth's on the way over. I called him when I saw you get out of your truck."

Cooper raised his eyebrows.

"I heard it pull in. Nothing gets by me anymore."

Point for Ty. Apparently his cheating fiancée, Anita, had taught him a lesson or two.

"Let's go back to the den," Ty said as Madelyn entered the kitchen. "Miss Maddy, would you mind making coffee?" He paused and faced Cooper. "Unless you'd like something else."

"Since I'll be driving back to Texas tonight, coffee would be best."

Cooper watched Ty and Madelyn exchange a look. Ty appeared lost. Madelyn's expression egged him on. *Go,* her eyes seemed to say. *Go.*

They arrived in the den. Ty directed Cooper to sit on the brown leather sofa. He took a seat on the wing chair, but the doorbell rang and he rose again. "That will be Seth."

Cooper said nothing. Ty left the room and within seconds, he was back, Seth on his heels. Dressed very similarly to Ty in trousers and a cable-knit sweater, Cooper's pale-haired, green-eyed brother Seth also looked like a man with money. Cooper glanced down at his worn jeans, his battered boots. He hadn't deliberately dressed to celebrate his poverty. He hadn't dressed to make his brothers see the differences in his status. Boots and jeans were who he was now. Ty and Seth might be sweater guys, but Cooper was a boots guy. He raised cattle. He rode fence. He mucked stalls. Luckily, he didn't do any of those in these boots.

And also, luckily, he remembered some of the things Zoe had told him. That deep down inside he was good. Which meant he didn't have to apologize to anyone for who he was.

He rose from the sofa and extended his hand to Seth. To hell with it. If they wanted his ranch, they could have it. But he wasn't begging for Dave's money. He would demand it. He would go down with his dignity.

"Hello, Seth," he said, as Seth took his hand.

"Cooper."

"Let's sit," Ty said, his natural leading abilities taking over. Cooper prepared himself for an argument, but no matter what his brothers decided, he would be as Zoe saw him. He would be strong. He would keep his dignity. His pride.

"Cooper, we're sorry it took the drastic measure of buying your mortgage to get you here."

"Actually," Seth cut in, "it wasn't even our idea. My father-in-law thought of it. He's…well, he's more accustomed to persuading people to do his bidding and he knows a few more tricks than we do."

Cooper looked at his younger brother. "What are you talking about?"

Ty laughed. "Cooper, your idiot brother married a princess. His father-in-law is the king of a small country called Xavier Island. It's off the coast of Spain."

Cooper couldn't help it. He laughed. "Are you kidding?" He glanced from Seth to Ty. "You are kidding, right? This is an icebreaker?"

Seth shook his head. "No. It isn't an icebreaker. I married Lucy knowing she was a princess, but I hadn't thought it was a big deal…until I saw her in action, doing her 'royal duties.'"

"Now, he has to attend royal ceremonies…ride in a carriage…" Ty chuckled, "wave at his subjects."

Seth growled. "Shut up, Ty. I've been to Xavier three times and never once have I waved from a carriage."

"But it's in the cards," Ty said, laughing again.

Cooper glanced from one to the other and suddenly felt eighteen again. The need to tease welled up in his chest so strong and so fierce he couldn't resist it. "Are they going to make him wear purple tights?"

Ty howled with mirth. Seth scowled. "No one wears purple tights. You guys are remembering something from one of mom's old storybooks."

"Right," Ty said.

Cooper grinned. "Right."

Ty took a quick breath. "Okay. We can tease Seth anytime. We need to get down to business."

Cooper's chest tightened. *Dignity,* he reminded himself.

Ty reached behind him to retrieve a manila envelope and handed it to Cooper. "Here's your mortgage. Burn it. Frame it. Shred it. We don't care. It's yours. I'm not a hundred percent sure what happened that caused us to break apart, but I want us back together again."

"And I also want to say I'm sorry," Seth said, jumping in as if worried that he would lose courage. "I was a kid. I shouldn't have said the things I said, and I knew I was wrong two hours after I said them, but by then you were gone."

Cooper stared at the envelope in his hands.

"You also own one third of our company," Ty said. "Seth and I both take salaries for the work we do, but we keep that separate from actual ownership and profit sharing at the end of our fiscal year.

"Profits aren't always high," Ty continued, "because we pour a lot of money back into the company. We've expanded several times so your company shares are worth more than the profits, but you've gotten anywhere from a few hundred thousand dollars to close to a million every year."

Cooper felt his eyes widen. "Close to a *million?*"

"You're rich," Seth said simply. "You shouldn't have a mortgage. When King Alfredo was investigating me he discovered you, and your mortgage. He forgot about it until he found out from Lucy that we wanted to talk to you. Then, he bought the mortgage and gave it to me as a wedding present, suggesting we use it to lure you here so we could tell you about the money you have so you can fix up that ranch of yours."

"Unless you want to move back and work with us," Ty quickly interjected.

Stunned, Cooper looked at him. "Work with you?"

Seth raised his hands. "If you don't want to, that's fine, too."

"But you have a degree in business," Ty reminded him. "And you would fit in perfectly." He paused. "And this company is your heritage as much as it is ours."

"This is it?" Cooper asked, waving his mortgage and looking from brother to brother. "This is why you brought me home?"

Ty and Seth exchanged a glance. "Yes."

"You're not kicking me off my ranch?"

Seth laughed. "No. My God, if King Alfredo dies, Lucy and I are literally responsible for a country until our son Owen is old enough to take over. We don't want any more land, thank you very much!"

"And I have my hands full. So full," Ty said, "that I could use some help."

Cooper stared at him. "Just like that?"

"Just like what?" Ty asked.

"You would take me into your company, give me an upper echelon job, without even knowing me."

"We know you," Ty said. "You're one of us. You're family. We all had things to work out, but that's over now. From today we accept each other as we are and work as a team."

And that was that. Ty told Cooper he had as long as he wanted to make up his mind about working for Bryant Development. A job would always await him. But if he wanted to join the company sooner that would be great since Ty wanted to take an extended honeymoon with Madelyn the following summer. Seth said his wife and his son had come with him when he'd driven over, and they were in the kitchen waiting to meet Cooper. And Ty said that Cooper really hadn't been properly introduced to Madelyn.

The next thing Cooper knew he was in the kitchen. Madelyn's parents had arrived with a baked ham and plates filled with Christmas cookies. He met Prince Owen, Seth's baby son and future king of Xavier Island, and stunning Princess Lucy, and understood why Seth had married her before he'd really thought about the whole purple tights issue. He met Madelyn's two brothers and sister, and so many neighbors arrived that the kitchen rapidly filled with people and the party spilled over into the family room.

For the first time in eight years Cooper was in a house with a Christmas tree. A ham. Cookies. Eggnog. For the first time in eight years he heard carols sung, by family, simply for the joy of it, and he leaned against the doorframe between the family room and kitchen, taking it all in.

He now had everything Zoe wanted.

Chapter Eleven

Cooper stood on the porch of Zoe's small house, not quite sure what he was doing in freezing cold Pennsylvania again. He knocked on the door then blew on his hands before he stuffed them into his pockets.

Zoe opened the door, holding Daphne, who was dressed in red reindeer pajamas. Zoe's glorious blond hair was rumpled. Her jeans were threadbare. Her sweatshirt appeared to have seen more washings than all of Cooper's clothes put together.

She looked wonderful.

"I hope you've come for your check, because I didn't cash it."

"Actually, I didn't." He paused and glanced at the toe of his boot. He knew he was using her and he knew that wasn't right, but he had nowhere else to go. No one else to turn to. "Zoe, I need somebody to talk to."

He raised his head and caught her gaze in time to see her eyes soften with compassion. "What happened?"

"My brothers put a provision in their letter that if I couldn't pay off my mortgage I had to meet face-to-face with them. I thought it was a good idea since I intended to get my partner's equity, but—"

Zoe grabbed his arm and yanked him inside. "Don't stand there on the porch freezing, Arkansas boy. Come in."

He grinned. "I thought you'd never ask."

"Don't mind the mess," she said, kicking Christmas wrapping paper out of the way and Cooper suddenly realized he'd interrupted their celebration.

"I'm sorry," he said, backing away. "I should have thought a little bit about what day it is."

She batted her hand in dismissal. "My celebration is over. My mother called. My dad and his new wife sent a plant." She shook her head. "I didn't even know he was getting married. Hell, I didn't even know he was dating someone. Anyway, Daphne has opened her gifts. For me Christmas is over."

Cooper's heart squeezed with pain. The night before he'd been welcomed with open arms into his family. He'd had an elaborate dinner. He'd eaten homemade cookies, met relatives, been invited to parties. A private plane had brought him to Pennsylvania. "I met a prince."

She turned and smiled. "What?"

"A prince. My younger brother is married to a princess."

Zoe's face lit with happy confusion. "A princess?"

"Her father is the king of an island country."

"Wow!"

"Zoe, that's only the tip of the iceberg. Little Owen may someday be a king, but Ty's already the head of an empire. When I left, the development company was booming but my two brothers have turned it into something that I never envisioned."

"Well, you knew they were rich to be able to buy your mortgage."

"Actually, the king bought that for Seth as a wedding gift."

Zoe grinned, sliding Daphne into a high chair. "What a hoot."

Cooper shook his head. "Ty is marrying a woman who is the public relations director for his company. Her parents and half the neighbors are fixtures in my brother's home."

Zoe sat at the table. She braced her elbows on the place mat in front of her and her chin on her fists and smiled at him. Nobody had ever looked so good to her, or so sad. He had absolutely no idea of what he wanted out of life, because he'd never been allowed to keep anything. His parents had been killed. His brothers had more or less kicked him out of their lives.

"Lots of family."

He nodded. "Lots of family."

"Does that scare you?"

He shrugged. "I was treated as if I had never gone away."

"As if it never happened?"

"No," Cooper quickly said. "Ty and Seth both apologized." He smiled ruefully. "Then they handed me my mortgage, told me to burn it if I want." He shook his head. "I was the one who made the trouble and they apologized to me."

"And…"

"And I wanted to tell them I was at fault, too, but I couldn't. I didn't get time. Before I knew it, we left the den and they introduced me to the rest of the family and suddenly I had a beer in my hand and people were opening gifts and shoving cookies at me." He paused, swallowed. "I never realized how lonely I was."

"Ah."

"Or how empty my life was."

"You filled your time with work. Running a ranch and driving truck." She smiled. "Two jobs. Not much free time."

He shook his head. "No."

"Cooper, you just need a few months to adjust."

He looked at her hopefully. "Really? You think that's it?"

Unfortunately, she did. She had wanted to believe in her heart of hearts that Cooper was here because he finally realized he had fallen in love with her the way she had with him, but there were so many other things going on in his life that she knew he hadn't. When they'd met he was pre-occupied with the fear that if he didn't get his money to Arkansas he would lose the one thing he had worked his whole life for: his ranch. Instead his brothers had handed him his mortgage. Welcomed him with open arms. Given him a family.

Now, he really had no reason to want her in his life. She

was as good as out. Her throat tightened from wanting to cry, but she wouldn't. She refused.

"And they offered me a job."

"Really?"

"I think I could do anything I want at Bryant Development since I own one-third of the company. They've been putting away my share of the profits ever since I left."

And he's rich, too. Great. Now he was really out of her league.

"That's wonderful." She paused, then said, "So why are you here?"

"I'm here because I realized last night that I now have everything you wanted."

"And you feel sorry for me?"

"No! Hell no!" The truth was he had no idea what he felt for her. But whatever it was, it had made his chest ache the night before. When he thought of her, he got hot and cold. He hated that she suffered. He believed she belonged on a pedestal. He knew she could fit in with his family. He believed his family should be hers.

He would give her the moon if he could, and though he knew that financially he could buy her just about anything, personally he had nothing to offer.

"I feel like my family should be your family. They are everything you deserve."

"You came here because you want to give me a family?"

"Don't you understand?" Cooper bounced from his chair at the table. "I have nothing to offer you! You need the real thing. You need a man of character and courage who can stand by you. Someone who will love you forever not just 'while he can.'"

Zoe stared at him. "You don't think it took a man of great character to give me his cashier's check?"

"That was only common sense."

"And you don't think it took great courage to go to Arkansas to meet with your brothers—not for yourself, but so you could demand the ranch equity for your partner?"

"I might agree with that, except I had everything about the situation wrong. They didn't want the ranch."

"You didn't know that. You went there with your head held high, ready to argue for your partner, and ready to start over again because you are strong. You are about the strongest man I know, Cooper Bryant. And why you don't see that I will never know."

He knew she believed everything she was telling him. He had even drawn on her belief in him the night before. But today, sitting in her kitchen, reconciled with his brothers, with more options open to him than at any other point in his life, he realized that none of it had any meaning without her. He suddenly saw that the reason he believed his family should be her family wasn't because she needed them but because he needed...no, wanted...just plain *wanted* her with him.

She brightened his day.

She made him see truth.

She believed in him.

She made him laugh.

She made him angry.

She had done what no one had accomplished in eight long years. She made him *feel*. For Cooper, years of emptiness slid away. Years of self-doubt crumbled. Years of needing to prove himself spiraled into nothing.

And he smiled, then he chuckled, then he out-and-out laughed. "Zoe Montgomery, you are the pushiest female on the face of the earth."

"You need to be pushed."

He caught her hand and pulled her out of her chair and into his arms. "Of course I do."

"Occasionally you need someone to tell you what to do."

"Occasionally." He tightened his hold. "But what I just realized I needed more than anything else was for someone to teach me to feel again."

She pulled back and stared at him.

"When my brothers kicked me out, I turned off my emotions. But you, with your strip poker, your virus, your insistence on washing your clothes and your ever present baby...well, you didn't give me two minutes to turn anything off. I couldn't stop my emotions from pouring out and they all did. I felt more with you and for you in those days stranded on the mountain than I had in eight years and if I hadn't met you before I went to see my brothers I would have stonewalled them. I never would have accepted their apologies let alone their generosity. I owe everything I have today to you."

"Well, you were pretty closed off."

"And rude."

She nodded. "And rude."

"And I think that's why I'm here."

"To tell me you're not going to be rude anymore."

He shook his head. "No."

Her eyes narrowed. "Well, it better not be to give me more money because, damn it, I don't want your money!"

"It will look pretty darned foolish for my wife to refuse my money."

She thought about that a second, then her eyes widened. "What are you saying?"

"I'm saying we should get married."

She gaped at him. "Married?"

"And move to Arkansas."

"Arkansas?"

"Where it's warmer."

She stared at him.

"And where you can meet my brothers and Madelyn and Lucy...and Prince Owen and Captain Bunny—"

"Captain Bunny?"

"Ty's future mother-in-law. It's a long story."

"You and your brother call his future mother-in-law Captain Bunny?"

"Because he's part of her family and her family has become my family." He stopped and his heart swelled. He had something to give Zoe beyond money, beyond even his love. "Say yes and you instantly have a family."

She took a breath. "I want a family, but I also want to make clear that if I choose to marry you it wouldn't be for a family." She took another breath. "It would be because I love you."

And Cooper suddenly realized what he was doing wrong. Why she wasn't jumping for joy and accepting his proposal.

"I love you, too," he said and allowed himself several seconds simply to soak in the fact that he'd actually said that and meant it.

He now had a family to offer Zoe. More than himself. Two brothers. Two sisters-in-law. Two children. A family. A legacy.

But more than that, he was giving her his love.

"So you'll marry me?"

She leaped into his arms. "Yes!"

Epilogue

The following June, Zoe slowly made her way up the aisle of the small country church, holding her bridesmaid bouquet and smiling at the crowd. She and Cooper had beaten Madelyn and Ty to the altar because neither she nor Cooper had wanted a big wedding. Both had been alone so long they were eager to be together and didn't wish to wait the months it would take to plan an elaborate event. Instead, they'd simply surprised Ty, Madelyn, Lucy and Seth with a trip to Las Vegas where Cooper's family had witnessed the wedding of Cooper and Zoe. Madelyn had put the wedding announcement in the paper while the happy couple had honeymooned.

They'd returned in time for Cooper to handle an unexpected problem with the delivery of some materials to a construction site and Cooper had been working with his brothers as a traffic manager ever since. His partner now ran the ranch, which had a full herd and employed ten hands. Zoe had paid the back taxes on the house, but called her parents and told them it was their responsibility to sell it or rent it, and her parents had agreed to call each other about the matter. She and Cooper had bought a huge home in Porter where Daphne had become good friends with Sabrina and Owen.

Making her way to the altar, Zoe smiled at Cooper, then Seth, then Ty, who waited impatiently for Madelyn. All three men looked wonderful in their black tuxes and to see them no one would ever have guessed that the three brothers had been estranged for eight long years. They were happy…. No, they were tight. Like three men who defied anyone who would try to come between them. Exactly the way Zoe believed brothers should be.

From there she cast a quick glance at Daphne, who was in the arms of Mildred Jenkins, Seth's next-door neighbor. Daphne was happily patting Mildred's face, but Mildred hardly noticed because she was too busy peering over the crowd, hoping for a peek at the bride. In the seat in front of Mildred, King Alfredo appeared oblivious to little Owen's singing, as he, too, craned his neck to see the bride. And in the seat in front of the king, Audrey Olsen, Princess Lucy's best friend, held squirming Sabrina and also angled her head to catch sight of Madelyn.

Zoe had discovered she had access to a nanny brigade, friends of Madelyn's mom who didn't merely babysit, they would also make meals and give lessons on anything from cooking to gardening to baby care…as long as you joined their card club and didn't mind getting your butt whopped in pinochle.

At last, Zoe reached her spot at the altar beside Princess Lucy, who looked regal and stunning in the simple green gown Madelyn had chosen for both her bridesmaids.

In her spot at the altar, Zoe turned. The organist changed tunes, and at the back of the church Madelyn and her dad, a short man with a graying crew cut, stood in the doorway. Though Zoe had seen Madelyn a hundred times that morning, she couldn't stop her eyes from misting. Madelyn was the perfect bride with her red hair pulled into a cluster of curls at the top of her head and a veil that made a tulle backdrop for her bare shoulders and sequined gown. Her full skirt swished as she walked. And her smile could have charmed the angels.

Zoe noted that it clearly charmed Ty, who looked spell-bound. Then she caught Seth peeking at Lucy and saw Lucy's answering smile. When she glanced at Cooper, her heart stumbled in her chest.

They were undoubtedly the luckiest six people in the world…the luckiest nine people if you counted the three babies that had brought them together. The luckiest twenty-five people if you counted Madelyn's family into the Bryant clan, and the Bryants definitely counted Madelyn's family as their own. The luckiest five hundred, if you counted the employees of Bryant Development. And fifteen hundred, if you counted the entire small town of Porter.

And Zoe did. Porter was a little place, but it was huge

in the way it had been blessed with love and laughter and friends who were family.

That is…they were family if you believed that love meant more than bloodlines.

And Zoe did.

* * * * *

MEET ME UNDER
THE MISTLETOE

Julianna Morris

JULIANNA MORRIS

has an offbeat sense of humour, which frequently gets her into trouble. She is often accused of being curious about everything – her interests ranging from oceanography and photography to travelling, antiquing, walking on the beach and reading science fiction. Julianna loves cats of all shapes and sizes, and recently she was adopted by a feline companion named Merlin. Like his namesake, Merlin is an alchemist – she says he can transform the house into a disaster area in nothing flat.

Julianna happily reports meeting her Mr Right. Together they are working on a new dream of building a shoreline home in the Great Lakes area.

Chapter One

Shannon O'Rourke pulled into a spot in the post office parking lot and then grabbed her Christmas cards. Normally she would have mailed them at work, but she was reluctantly taking a few vacation days from her job as a public relations director.

In a nearby parking space she saw her new neighbor getting out of his Jeep Cherokee.

She'd only seen Alex McKenzie once, but according to the gossipy head of the condominium association, he was a thirty-four-year-old widowed college professor with a doctorate in engineering.

He was also one of the most ruggedly handsome men she'd ever seen.

"Jeremy, leave Mr. Tibbles in the Jeep for now," he said, unfastening a small boy from a child's booster seat.

The boy climbed down from the Jeep with his father's help, clutching a worn stuffed rabbit to his chest. He was a miniature version of Alex McKenzie, and warmth spread through Shannon's heart at the sight of the serious youngster, his blue eyes older and more worried than they should have been.

"It's okay, son, Mr. Tibbles won't mind staying behind this time," Dr. McKenzie urged.

Jeremy shook his head, holding the rabbit tighter.

His father sighed and passed a hand over the boy's dark brown hair. "All right. Stay here while I get the packages out of the car."

A few moments later he maneuvered his son and a large stack of boxes toward the front door of the post office. Shannon dashed after them.

"Dr. McKenzie…let me help," she called.

Alex turned and saw a flame-haired beauty hurrying toward him. There was something familiar about the woman, though he couldn't place her.

"Excuse me," he said, "do I know you?"

"I'm Shannon O'Rourke, your neighbor."

"Oh, right." Alex remembered the day the previous month when they'd moved into the condo from their apartment. He'd been talking to the movers when a woman had pulled into the next driveway, bundled in a heavy coat, with only her auburn hair visible. She'd waved her hand in a quick hello before rushing inside to escape the rain.

It was warmer today and she was dressed in designer jeans that showed off a pair of long legs, and a cashmere sweater that left no doubt about her slim waist and womanly curves. She exuded confidence and flashed an engaging smile.

One of the packages slipped from his grasp and Shannon caught it. "Let me have some of those," she said, taking several without waiting for agreement. She stepped around him and looked over her shoulder. "Coming?"

One of his eyebrows shot upward. *Shy* and *retiring* obviously weren't in the woman's vocabulary.

Alex took Jeremy's hand.

Everyone said the holidays were especially hard for a spouse who's lost a partner, but the toughest part for Alex was trying to make things right for his four-year-old son. This would be the first Christmas without his wife. Kim's death the past January had left a huge hole in their lives. No matter how good it might be, a day-care center couldn't take the place of a mother like Kim.

The thought of his wife made Alex ache. His friends had called him the most married man they knew, even though he'd spent so much time working out of the country. But they were right. He'd recognized what he had, a sweet, gentle woman who wouldn't tear him apart the way his parents had torn each other apart. You didn't find that kind of love twice.

Shannon nudged the door open with her hip and waited for father and son to go ahead of her.

"That's my job," Alex said, "opening a door for a lady. But I suppose you're one of those modern women who don't believe in that sort of thing."

Shannon opened her mouth, ready to toss out a smart remark, then hesitated. She'd always believed in being herself, and if a man didn't like it, then too bad.

But she wasn't sure what "being herself" was anymore.

She wanted more out of life. She wanted to be in love and married, but lately her love life was practically nonexistent. And now that four of her five brothers were happily wed, the desire to find love such as they had was even stronger. But her life seemed stuck in Neutral, while everyone else's was Full Speed Ahead.

"I don't mind," she said finally. It was true. She didn't object to men being chivalrous; she'd just learned that waiting for a guy to hold a door could get embarrassing.

"All right." Alex rested his shoulder against the door to hold it. "I've got it, then. Go ahead, Miss O'Rourke."

He was close enough for her to smell the faint scent of his aftershave, and Shannon's knees wobbled. That wasn't good. According to her three sisters, Kelly, Miranda and Kathleen, men with children were complicated, especially when it came to their motives toward women.

She glanced down at Jeremy's grave face. "Go 'head," he said, and she melted.

"Thank you," Shannon murmured.

She glanced swiftly at Alex in her peripheral vision, then walked toward the long line of people waiting for service. Her condominium was in a small bedroom community outside of Seattle, but the post office had the usual holiday crowd. It looked as though they'd be waiting for a while, something she was foolishly happy about.

Lord, she had to be crazy.

For Pete's sake, he'd called her *Miss* O'Rourke and said his job was holding the door for a lady. Alex McKenzie was obviously the same breed of old-fashioned guy as the male half of the O'Rourke family. She could spot the type a mile away, and usually ran the opposite direction. She'd dated one in college, only to get her heart broken when he'd dumped her, saying he wanted a homemaker like his mother...something she definitely *wasn't*. Her only talent in the kitchen was turning perfectly good food into inedible, blackened messes.

A tug at the hem of her sweater made her look down. It was Jeremy.

"I can help," he said, pointing at the packages she still carried.

"Oh...all right. May I hold Mr. Tibbles for you? He can sit on top of my purse while we wait."

Jeremy regarded her for a long moment.

Mr. Tibbles was plainly a very important stuffed rabbit not to be entrusted to just anyone. Shannon crouched so she could be eye-to-eye with the boy. Something about him reminded her of how she'd felt after losing her father when she was a child herself, and her heart throbbed with the old grief.

"I promise to take very good care of him." She smiled reassuringly.

After what seemed an eternity, Jeremy nodded and traded Mr. Tibbles for two of the packages. She settled the rabbit so its feet were anchored in her purse, and made sure it stayed in full view of its protective human. Only after the exchange had been completed did she see Alex's stunned expression.

"Is something wrong?" she asked.

"I don't know how you managed that. I haven't been able to separate him from that rabbit since his mother died," Alex said in a low voice. "He only lets go in the bath, and that's because he says Mr. Tibbles is afraid of the water. You must have a gift with children."

Shannon swallowed. What she knew about children could be written on the head of a pin. "Um...I like kids," she said tentatively.

It wasn't a lie.

Kids were great little people and she would love to have one someday. Her three nieces and one nephew were the most precious things in the world.

Alex's gaze was fixed on his son who had wandered over to the Christmas tree in the corner. There was so much pain in his eyes that Shannon's throat tightened. This was a man who'd lost his wife and was trying to raise his child alone. And it was Christmas, a time when absences were felt worse than ever. She remembered what it was like after her father died—nothing had been right, and even now there were moments when emptiness replaced holiday cheer.

"This time of year must be rough," she said softly.

"His mother made things so special for Christmas," Alex murmured, his gaze still focused on his son. "She loved baking and doing crafts with him, and fixing things just right. It's been hard trying to make up for what he's lost."

Shannon shifted her feet, feeling torn.

She couldn't get involved with a man grieving over his wife's death. It was simply asking for a broken heart. Besides, her relationships never lasted. Old-fashioned or not, the men she continually found herself dating inevitably wanted her to be less modern and more a domestic goddess in disguise.

Well, she didn't have an ounce of domesticity in her.

But what about Jeremy? He had responded to her, and that meant something. Didn't it?

"W-why is the rabbit so important to Jeremy?" Shannon asked, despite the internal warnings clanging inside her head. She could tell when a man wasn't interested, and Dr. McKenzie had disinterest written all over his face.

"I'm not sure." Alex gave her a crooked smile. "Maybe you can figure it out."

Shannon knew she should confess her ignorance about children. On the other hand, she did know about hurting. Pain seemed bottled up inside Jeremy and it wasn't right; a child shouldn't have to go through so much.

"I'm sorry things have been so hard. Settling into a new place must make it harder," she murmured instead. "If there's anything I can do, please let me know." She swallowed an offer to babysit while she was on vacation.

"Thank you, Miss O'Rourke. That's kind of you," Alex said formally, in a tone that announced he had no intention of asking for anything.

She cocked her head. "Please call me Shannon. Nobody uses Miss O'Rourke unless they want to annoy me. Even reporters aren't that formal during a press conference."

"Do you talk to reporters very often?"

Shannon shrugged. "It's part of my job. I'm the Public Relations Director for O'Rourke Enterprises."

"Of course," he said. "You're one of the O'Rourkes."

Her nose wrinkled.

Terrific, she was one of the O'Rourkes. Her oldest brother was a talented businessman who'd made truckloads of money. As one of the richest men in the country, Kane had gotten more press than most movie stars, so people tended to recognize the name. Especially in the Seattle area.

"Sorry," Alex murmured, his lazy, comfortable grin sending her pulse skidding. It didn't make sense; he wasn't the type of man she usually dated. "You must get tired of people saying things like that."

"Now and then."

He cleared his throat and motioned to the line that had moved away from them. Shannon strolled forward, making sure that Mr. Tibbles remained within Jeremy's sight now that he'd rejoined them. The boy was so young. She wondered if he remembered his mother, or if it was the sense of abandonment that still haunted him. It was hard for a child to understand that their mommy or daddy hadn't wanted to die. But death wasn't a concept children understood very well.

Nor did some adults, Shannon reflected wryly.

There were times she heard her father's voice in her subconscious and turned around, half expecting to see him standing there.

She let out a breath and looked up at Alex. "I understand you teach engineering. My brother Kane wanted to be an engineer, but he had to quit school."

"Instead he became a billionaire," Alex said dryly. "It must be rough."

Shannon's eyes narrowed. She might complain about her atavistic brothers, but nobody criticized Kane except her. He'd done everything for the family, giving up his own plans for the future. The fact that he'd made a fortune in the process just proved his intelligence and determination.

"Kane is brilliant," she said in a cool tone. "Until he got married he worked fourteen hours a day, so he was hardly living a life of ease and luxury. Money was just his way of taking care of the family after we lost our father. He would have been a wonderful engineer, but he never got the chance."

The corners of Alex's mouth twitched. He'd never have believed the vibrant redhead was capable of looking so frosty. She might be fashion-model beautiful, but when it came to her precious brother, she was pure pit bull.

"I wasn't criticizing," he said.

"Of course you weren't."

She turned her back to him, and he sighed. Women like Shannon O'Rourke were too volatile for a down-to-earth guy like him. And too unpredictable. He liked engineering schematics and formulas, things you could count on. Life was uncertain enough without inviting chaos into the mix.

The line had moved and they finally reached the front, where a postal clerk waited expectantly.

"Our turn," Jeremy said to Shannon.

She nodded. "You're such a big help. Let's put the packages on the counter, so your daddy can mail them." She cast a glance toward Alex. "And I'll mail my Christmas cards."

"Okay."

Jeremy handed up the packages, which Shannon piled on the counter along with the ones she'd carried. Almost as an afterthought, she added her bundle of Christmas cards, which Alex noticed were already stamped. She hadn't needed to wait in line with them.

"Well, Jeremy, I'd better return Mr. Tibbles to you, and then get going."

Shannon took the stuffed rabbit out of her purse and passed it to Jeremy, who didn't seem to hold it quite as fiercely as before. Alex rubbed his chin as he watched Shannon walk away. His son had never accepted someone so quickly. Hell, she'd gotten Mr. Tibbles away from him with just a smile—he hadn't managed that feat and he was Jeremy's father.

"It all goes first-class mail. I'll be back in a minute," he muttered to the postal clerk, shoving his credit card in her direction. Muffled groans of protest came from the waiting customers, but Alex ignored them. "Miss O'Rourke," he said, catching Shannon at the exit. "That is…Shannon."

"Ever the gentleman, Dr. McKenzie," she murmured. "But I can manage this door on my own."

"That wasn't what I meant."

"You mean you don't want to hold the door for me?" Shannon sounded offended and he groaned.

"No, that is, yes, of course I do, but…"

Too late he saw the faint humor lurking in her green eyes.

He'd been had, yet he wanted to laugh as well. There weren't many women who could forgive a supposed insult that quickly. Especially one concerning family. Whatever faults Shannon O'Rourke might have, holding a grudge didn't appear to be one of them.

"So, what did you want?" she asked.

Alex hesitated. He didn't *want* anything, but for Jeremy's sake he should keep things cordial between them. "It's just…I'm sorry I upset you. And I want you to know that I appreciated the way you handled Jeremy. That's all."

"Oh." Confusion filled her eyes.

A woman as beautiful as Shannon O'Rourke probably expected to be asked for a date, but he had no intention of getting involved with anyone, much less someone like Shannon. His friends and colleagues, everyone, kept saying it was just a matter of time, that if you've had one good marriage, you're more likely to have a second good one.

But he didn't buy it.

With Kim he'd gotten lucky, because he sure wasn't good husband material, not with his family background of domestic warfare and divorce. God, he'd hated all the screaming and fighting.

"Sir," called the postal clerk with an edge of irritation in her voice. "There are a lot of people waiting."

"Better go." Shannon flipped her hand and pushed through the double glass doors.

Alex released a harsh breath as he watched the gentle sway of her hips as she headed for her car. Kim had been gone for almost a year. There wasn't any reason to feel guilty for enjoying a woman's legs.

Except he *did* feel guilty.

The rustle of restless feet and throat-clearing dragged his attention back to the post office. He returned to the counter and signed the credit slip, accompanied by applause from the line of postal customers. He walked outside with Jeremy while Shannon was still waiting to pull into the busy street, and his son dragged his feet, watching sadly as her sleek sports car finally merged into traffic.

"Come along, son."

"I like her, Daddy."

"I know. I'm sure you'll see her again. Shannon is our next-door neighbor."

Jeremy let out a very adult sigh. "But you made her mad."

It was undeniably true, even though she'd appeared to forgive what he'd jokingly implied about her brother. Yes, Shannon O'Rourke was temperamental, but she'd also shown that she was loyal.

A far cry from his own family.

After his parents divorced, Alex and his two siblings had been pawns in their incessant power struggles. And now they didn't see one another anymore. They were too far-flung for one thing; his brother was in the Arctic studying global warming and his sister was working in Japan. As for his mother and father, they'd each been married and divorced several times to other people, and they still hated each other with a passion that poisoned everything around them.

"Shannon isn't upset with you," he said finally. "So it's okay."

"But she's mad at you, Daddy." Jeremy was obstinate in his own way, and he obviously felt that Shannon being mad was a problem, regardless of who she was mad at.

Alex rubbed the back of his neck. After his rotten up-bringing, he'd worried he couldn't love a child. But from the minute his newborn son, all red and wrinkled, opened sleepy eyes and blew a bubble at him, he'd turned into a marshmallow where the kid was concerned.

"I know, son, but you still don't need to worry about it." He would have said everything was "all right," but he'd said it too often when Kim was sick, and he'd felt like a hypo-crite each time Jeremy crawled into his arms and believed him.

His son gave him an exasperated look, which would have been comical if his eyes weren't so serious. "Can we get her a Christmas present?"

A Christmas present?

What did you get for a woman who must have every-thing?

"We'll get a poinsettia," Alex promised. Plants were usually safe, especially since it should look like a seasonal gesture. Or as an apology for the verbal faux pas he'd stumbled into over her brother.

Jeremy looked relieved, and as they trudged back to the

Cherokee, he turned his head to gaze in the direction Shannon had driven. For the first time in a year he wasn't clutching Mr. Tibbles to his chest; instead, he was casually swinging the rabbit by one arm.

Alex let out a sigh of his own. He had to be careful. Seeing too much of the woman next door could lead Jeremy into getting ideas about a new mommy.

Yet as he fastened his son into the child's car seat, Alex couldn't help thinking about Shannon. She was undoubtedly headstrong and opinionated, as different from his wife as a woman could be. He'd considered casual dating since Kim's death, but none of the women he'd met were particularly interesting.

And none of them were like Shannon O'Rourke.

Chapter Two

Shannon let herself into the condo and tossed her purse onto the couch before plugging in the lights on the Christmas tree. She had to be out of her mind even to have *considered* offering to babysit.

"Me, babysitting. Hah!"

Yet even as she scolded herself, she remembered Jeremy McKenzie's solemn blue eyes and a familiar ache filled her. She'd been eight when her father died, leaving her confused and hurt. The thought of Jeremy feeling the same way tore at her heart.

"I'm not the motherly type," she muttered. She couldn't change a diaper or even heat a can of soup, though Jeremy was surely old enough not to need diapers any longer. Even that she wasn't certain about, though she was pretty sure most kids were potty-trained by the time they were two or three. How old were her twin nieces when they'd stopped needing diapers? It was embarrassing to realize she didn't know. They were her nieces, and she loved them dearly. Sinking into the chair next to the phone, Shannon dialed her youngest sister.

"Hey, Kathleen. When did Amy and Peggy get potty-trained?" she asked without preamble.

"Shannon?"

"Yes. How old were they?"

"Er...not quite two."

Two. Well, that was good. Undoubtedly kids developed differently, but Jeremy was probably past that stage. Not that it mattered. Alex McKenzie hadn't given any sign of being interested in her, so she wasn't likely to see much of either him or his son.

It was so depressing. Her love life was a disaster area. She wanted an honest relationship with the right man, but what if the "right" man didn't want someone like her?

"What's up, Shannon?"

She shrugged, though her sister couldn't see the gesture. "A little boy moved in next door, that's all. He's really cute, and I started thinking about diapers and stuff. It doesn't mean anything, except I got curious."

"Are you sure that's all?"

"Positive."

Shannon said good-bye and dropped the receiver with disgust. It had to be her biological clock ticking that made her ask stupid questions. She was twenty-eight years old and unmarried—and unlikely ever to be married at the rate she was going, so of course her clock was screaming.

Shaking her head, Shannon walked up to the bedroom to change into a pair of sweats and then began to run on the treadmill in her spare room.

She had a great family, a terrific job, made plenty of money, and was perfectly comfortable, she told herself in time with her steps. It wasn't the end of the world if the love of her life never showed up. Of course, it was hard to keep believing that with the rest of the world obsessed with love, and her own family acting as if Cupid had gone target-happy with his bow and arrows. Even Neil, her brother who had once equated marriage with the plague, had fallen off the deep end. So now Neil had Libby. Her oldest brother, Kane, had Beth and baby daughter, Robin. Patrick had Maddie and their new son, Jarod. Dylan and his wife, Kate, were expecting a baby. Only her youngest brother, Connor, was still unattached. Of course, her sisters weren't married, though Kathleen was divorced. Shannon grimaced at the thought of Kathleen's ex-husband. There were worse things than being single…like having a cheating spouse who'd run off when you were almost nine months pregnant with twins.

A half hour later the doorbell rang and Shannon stopped the machine. She wiped her face with a towel, grabbed a bottle of water from the fridge and took a swig on her way to the door.

"Who is that?" she called on her way downstairs to the door.

She peeped through the curtain and gulped at the sight of Alex and Jeremy McKenzie.

"Isn't this just perfect?" she mumbled. Her face was flushed, her hair damp, and she was wearing an old pair of sweats. Well, it couldn't be helped, so she lifted her chin and squared her shoulders as she opened the door. You could get through the worst situation by acting as if you owned the world.

"Hi."

"Hello." Alex's velvet-rough voice rubbed over her edgy nerves like a silky cat. "Jeremy wanted to be sure you weren't mad at us."

Mad?

Shannon thought for a moment, then recalled the way Alex had seemed to mock Kane, her darling oldest brother. She was willing to give him a second chance, especially with Jeremy looking at her with that anxious expression in his eyes.

"I'm not mad," she said, looking down at Jeremy and smiling. He really was the dearest child, with such a sweet, sad, worried little face. No wonder her scant motherly instincts were clamoring for attention. How could anyone fail to adore him?

"It's for you," Jeremy said, holding out a poinsettia wrapped in green foil and banded by a big gold ribbon and bow. "Can we come in?"

"Of course you may," Shannon said over Alex's attempts to shush his son. She stepped back and raised an eyebrow.

"Thank you," Alex muttered.

"Oooh," exclaimed Jeremy. He'd marched into the center of the living room, and stared transfixed at the Christmas tree, winking and glowing in the corner.

Alex understood his son's fascination. It was a great tree, and at its base a small train ran around and around a miniature Victorian town at the foot of a snowy mountain. The houses were lit, ice-skaters twirled around a silver lake, and even the small street lamps twinkled.

"Sorry about how I look, you caught me exercising," Shannon said. She made no attempt at feminine fussing, and since she was flat-out beautiful with her healthy flush and sexy, mussed hair, it wasn't necessary.

"You look fine," Alex muttered.

In the soft glow from the Christmas tree her hair was a deep rich auburn, and he had a crazy urge to run his fingers through the silken strands, to discover if it was as soft as it looked. It occurred to him that she might not be a natural redhead since there wasn't a freckle in sight on her peach complexion, but he shoved the thought away. Whether she was or wasn't didn't concern him. And he'd certainly never see the proof.

"Well…thanks for the plant," Shannon said. She put it by the fireplace, smiling at Jeremy as he tore his gaze away from the tree. "This is so pretty. Did you pick it out all by yourself?"

"Uh-huh," he said.

"That was nice of you. You got the best poinsettia I've ever seen."

Jeremy's smile was like sunshine, and Alex blinked.

Where was his shy little boy? The grief-stricken, barely talking, rabbit-clutching four-year-old?

"Mr. Tibbles said to get that one."

"You and Mr. Tibbles have good taste." She glanced at Alex. "I don't keep many treats around the house, but are lemon drops on the okay list?"

"They're fine," he agreed, still bemused.

Shannon took a crystal dish from the mantel and removed the lid before offering its contents to Jeremy. Soon his son was sucking on lemon sours and playing with the controls of the train gliding around the extravagant Christmas tree. Steam even came from the top of the engine when a button was pressed on the control panel. Jeremy seemed to enjoy that part especially, along with the train's abrupt stops and starts.

Alex warned Jeremy to be careful, but Shannon seemed unconcerned that the expensive set might be in danger.

"It's all right," she said. "Would you like some soda?"

"We don't want to be any trouble."

"If you were trouble, I'd tell you."

Undoubtedly she would. Shannon O'Rourke was direct, self-assured and definitely wouldn't pussyfoot around. She was also the walking, talking embodiment of everything he'd avoided his entire life—an explosion of emotion and passion wrapped up in flame-colored hair and flashing eyes.

"Tell you what," she said. "If you haven't eaten dinner yet, we can order some pizza. I'm out of milk for Jeremy, but maybe they can bring some with the delivery."

He wanted to say no. He even opened his mouth to say no, only one look at his son's ecstatic face changed his mind. Jeremy loved pizza, but his mother had declared it was unhealthy for children, so they'd rarely eaten any. Come to think of it, he wasn't sure why Kim had disapproved of restaurant and take-out food so much, but she had.

"That sounds good," he agreed. "But it's my treat."

"Whatever. The phone's over there with the phone book, so go ahead and order. I'm going upstairs to change."

"Any preferences?"

"No anchovies, that's all." She glanced at Jeremy. He looked hopeful, and she tried to guess what he might be wishing his daddy would order. "How about one of those dessert pizzas, too? One with lots of sugar and stuff on top." Jeremy's face turned blissful and she winked at him.

Shannon climbed the staircase to her bedroom and willed her heart to stop beating so fast. She'd figured the post office was the last close contact she'd get with Alex McKenzie and his son, but now they were in her living room and her pulse was doing the Macarena.

She took a quick shower, then pulled on a pair of jeans and a sweater. Her footsteps were muffled on the thickly carpeted stairs, so when she descended to the living room, she was able to observe Alex and his son without them being aware of her presence.

With a quiet sigh she sat on a step and watched.

The two of them were lying on their stomachs, side by side, gazing at the tree and the train set her decorator sister, Miranda, had arranged for her a few days after Thanksgiving. This year, Miranda had outdone herself, creating a Victorian holiday wonderland out of the living room.

"Choo, choo!" crowed Jeremy as the train chugged through the tunnel in the snowcapped mountain.

He was darling, yet it was Alex who drew her gaze the longest, his jeans pulled taut over long, strong legs and a tight rear end. He didn't look like any college professor she'd ever studied with, or else she would have paid more attention in class. His rugged good looks had probably turned engineering into a very popular subject—with the female students, at least.

Shannon's eyes drifted half-closed as she imagined what it would be like to be married to someone like Alex.

It was a great fantasy, but reality kept intruding. Alex had said his wife had loved baking and doing crafts and making Christmas special; he'd probably be shocked that she had her home professionally decorated every year and couldn't bake a cookie to save her life. Even Shannon's mother had declared defeat in teaching her eldest daughter how to cook.

The doorbell rang and she jumped up.

"That must be our pizza," she said brightly.

They ate in front of the tree, sitting cross-legged and using the napkins provided by the delivery guy.

"Mommy didn't let us eat pizza," Jeremy said after a while, then looked even more worried than before.

"She didn't?" It seemed odd, but there might have been reasons Shannon knew nothing about, like allergies or another problem.

"Uh-uh." He glanced quickly at his father, then carefully

put his crust down on a napkin. "I get afraid, 'cause I don't r'member her so good anymore."

Alex looked pained, and Shannon bit the inside of her lip. Jeremy had been so young when his mother died, it was inevitable his memories were fading.

She put her forefinger over Jeremy's heart, the way her own mother used to do when her youngest sister had worried about forgetting their father.

"You'll always remember her in here," she said softly. "That's the most important kind of remembering. Your mommy is always right here, so you don't need to be afraid."

The youngster seemed to think about it, then nodded, looking more cheerful. His father handed him a piece of dessert pizza and they ate in silence until Jeremy looked up, his expression brightening.

"Daddy, I bet if Shannon was my new mommy, we could eat pizza whenever we wanted."

Shannon inhaled a crumb and choked. Between coughing, thumps on the back from Alex and her eyes tearing, the moment passed without either of them having to say anything.

Cripes.

How did you handle a remark like that?

"I think it's time for us to go home," Alex said when her windpipe had finally cleared. His face had become closed. "We've imposed long enough on Miss O'Rourke."

"But, Daddy, we—"

"It's time to go, son."

Jeremy's mouth turned down mutinously, but he didn't object again. Shannon insisted they take the last of the pizza, and she sank against the door as she closed it behind them, exhausted.

She didn't know what the expression on Alex's face had meant, but he obviously did not share his son's enthusiasm for getting a new mommy. He didn't know her well enough to object to her personally, so it must be the idea of marrying again that had him feeling grief or guilt or another of the thousand emotions a widower must feel.

Not that it mattered. She just wanted to help Jeremy.

Right?

But as Shannon gathered up the crumpled napkins and put the dirty glasses in the sink, she couldn't shake the melancholy that had overtaken her. It was painfully obvious she was attracted to old-fashioned men, no matter what she'd told herself about wanting a modern guy with modern attitudes. And Alex McKenzie made her nerve endings stand at attention more than any man she'd met in recent memory.

It doesn't matter one way or the other, she told herself. Men usually were drawn to the same kind of woman, and from the little she'd learned about Alex's dead wife, she wasn't the least bit like her.

"I'm going back to work," Shannon told Kane a few days later. Her brother and his wife, Beth, had come to their mother's house for a visit and she'd joined them, more on edge than ever. Not that seeing her brother had helped.

Kane's blissfully happy marriage was another reminder of how alone she felt.

"I don't think so."

"Kane, I want—"

"You've been stressed out, you need to relax," Kane interrupted. He finished diapering his daughter and lifted the baby to his shoulder. Robin looked even tinier against his broad chest, and something inside Shannon ached with renewed force. It was yet another reminder of everything she wanted, and couldn't seem to get.

"I'm fine."

"You can't spend your entire life working," Kane pointed out. His advice would have sounded reasonable except that before he'd gotten married he used to work more hours than she'd ever thought of putting into the company.

Shannon's mother patted her arm. "That's right, darlin'." Her Irish accent lilted, never quite lost despite the years she'd spent away from her native land.

"I'm fine. It's being on a forced vacation that's driving me crazy."

That, and thinking about the McKenzies.

She'd realized that Alex's bedroom was on the other side of the wall from hers, and that knowledge was keeping her awake nights. The walls were too well insulated to hear his bed creak, but she heard other faint sounds and couldn't help wondering about certain things.

Innocent things.

Such as...did he sleep nude at night?

Yeah, that was innocent.

Perfectly innocent.

It had been awhile since she'd thought about a man that way. Her last relationship had turned into such a disaster that she'd become frozen. Now she was thawing, and it was just her luck that a guaranteed heartbreak was the reason.

"You're still on vacation," Kane said calmly. He rubbed the baby's back and smiled at Shannon's frustrated expression.

"You can't be so arbitrary just because I'm your sister."

"I'd do the same for any executive with signs of burnout. You're still getting paid, so what's the big deal?"

"I am not burned-out."

"Then what's wrong?"

Shannon swallowed.

After their father had died, she'd decided she would be the tough one, the one who teased and laughed and smiled when she didn't feel like smiling. If she had trouble at school, she braved things out. If her heart got broken, she turned it into a joke—just so long as nobody found her crying in bed and upsetting her family. Over the years she'd perfected a breezy veneer that made everyone think she was impervious to the usual hurts and disappointments. She was an expert on putting on a good face; now was the time to prove it.

"Nothing is wrong," Shannon said, waving her hand. "It's the holiday season and people slack off. I must have gone overboard trying to keep my staff geared up for any problems that might happen."

Kane nodded, his gaze searching her face. He didn't

seem entirely convinced, though he appeared less con-cerned than before. "All right. But I promised everyone they'd have another few days without the dragon lady, so you'll have to stay away longer."

She wrinkled her nose, making certain none of her frus-tration showed. "Dragon lady? Thanks a bunch. Is it too late for me to cancel a few Christmas bonuses?"

He chuckled. "Way too late."

Shannon kept things light through lunch, working to get her mother, brother and sister-in-law laughing. But it was a relief when she pulled out of her mother's driveway, escaping their watchful gazes. She drove for a long time, up into the hills, finally swinging by Neil's house.

She frowned as she tapped her fingers on the steering wheel and gazed at the modern log structure. She would have sworn that Neil, of all her brothers, would never get married and live outside the city, but he'd fallen for Libby like a ton of bricks. *Two* tons.

Sighing, Shannon headed home, deciding not to call Neil and his wife.

A winter sunset burned pink and gold on the western horizon as she finally pulled into her driveway, but she didn't have time to appreciate it before Jeremy flew across the yard, waving madly with one arm, the other clutching Mr. Tibbles.

An involuntary smile curved her mouth.

"Hey, Jeremy," she said, opening the car door.

"Hey, Shannon."

They had exchanged a few hellos and good-byes over the

past few days, with Alex then hustling his son away with insulting speed. Of course, the speed might have been due to Washington's beastly winter weather, but it was still a little insulting.

"What have you been up to?" she asked as she got out.

"Daddy 'n' me are putting up Christmas lights," Jeremy said solemnly.

She noticed an expandable ladder leaning against the McKenzies' condo. "That's nice."

"But he got hurted and said a bad word."

Alex had followed his son across the yard, and Shannon glanced at him, trying not to laugh at his chagrined expression. She guessed his injury was relatively minor since there wasn't any visible blood and no bones were sticking out.

"He did?"

"Uh-huh. He said—"

"Jeremy," Alex interrupted hastily, "I was wrong to say that in the first place, and it certainly isn't something to repeat in front of a lady."

The youngster quieted and clutched Mr. Tibbles even tighter, mumbling an apology, so Shannon smiled and ruffled his hair.

"That's okay. I'm lucky, I have five brothers to help put up my Christmas lights." Five brothers with the same sort of old-fashioned views about a "lady's" delicate ears and sensibilities—all part of the O'Rourke Code they'd been taught by their father. The "Code" was sacred to the male members of the family, much to the frequent frustration of the *female* members.

"I wish I had a brother," Jeremy said, sounding wistful. Oh dear.

Wasn't wishing he had a brother just one step away from talking about getting a new mommy? Presuming he understood the relationship between the two events.

"I also have three sisters," Shannon said quickly. "Miranda, Kelly and Kathleen. Miranda and Kelly are twins."

"Do they like dodgeball?"

Dodgeball? She searched through her memory and vaguely recalled kids standing in a circle, with others in the middle dodging a large red ball.

"Uh, they haven't played for a while. They're all grown up."

Jeremy sighed. "I wanna play dodgeball, but the big kids say I'm too small."

"That's too bad, but they probably want to be sure you don't get hurt accidentally."

Alex stuck his throbbing thumb in his pocket and watched Shannon O'Rourke charm his son all over again. Jeremy's gaze was fixed on her adoringly, and he was talking like a normal little boy, rather than a traumatized child.

He'd asked around and learned a great deal about the O'Rourkes since meeting Shannon. People in all walks of life counted them as friends. They were highly respected, were active in church and charity work, and gave generously of both their time and their money. Shannon served on the boards of three foundations and was personally credited with saving an inner-city homeless mission.

No wonder, he thought, staring at her stunning beauty and trademark smile—a smile that said she was ready to take on the world single-handedly. The force of her personality alone was probably enough to save a hundred homeless missions, much less one. She was so...electric.

He smothered a half laugh, remembering the way people had described Shannon as cool and sophisticated. They were blind if they couldn't see the wildfire beneath that polished surface.

"Hello, Shannon," he murmured, illogically annoyed that she'd barely noticed him. Once upon a time the opposite sex had found him reasonably attractive.

Yet even as Alex formed the thought, he stomped on it. Shannon O'Rourke might be a beautiful woman, but he'd rather appreciate her beauty from a distance. He didn't have to own Botticelli's *Birth of Venus* to admire the painting.

"Hello." Shannon smiled. "Are you having trouble putting up your Christmas lights?"

"Some." Alex flexed his thumb and a sharp throb went through it. He'd been distracted, thinking about Jeremy and the day-care center's third request for the name and phone number of a backup person to call in case of emergency. He had a babysitter for when the daycare was closed, but except for Shannon, there wasn't a single person in Washington with whom Jeremy would willingly go if his father wasn't available. That was the problem. Shannon was good with Jeremy and had an excellent reputation so there wasn't any reason not to ask...besides wanting to keep that precious distance between them.

Damn.

Around Shannon he felt as if he was being sucked into a whirlpool with no bottom. The sensation reminded him too much of when he was a kid and had no control over his life, or the crazy people masquerading as his parents.

"If you're hungry, I was going to order some Thai food for dinner," she said, breaking into his thoughts. "You're welcome to join me."

He hesitated.

"Consider it a welcome to the neighborhood," she said breezily. "I should have brought you cookies or something, but…" Her voice trailed and she shrugged.

That *but* had some interesting undertones to it. Shannon had a way of saying things that had so many layers of meaning, he could get dizzy trying to figure them out.

"Yeah, you blew your chance of being nominated for the neighborhood welcome party," he said, trying to sound humorous. "Tami Barton made us a casserole. Naomi Hale did Jell-O salad, and Lisa Steeple brought us a cake. And there's also been homemade candy, cookies, several kinds of bread and some sort of cheese log rolled in almonds."

"Let me guess, mostly from the unmarried women in the condo association? I know Naomi, Tami, and Lisa are all unattached."

Alex frowned, realizing there *had* been quite a few single women—divorced or never married—knocking on his door lately. It had been the same in Minnesota. After Kim's death few days had gone by without a knock on the door and a woman standing on the other side. Their culinary offerings had ranged from child-pleasing dishes to gourmet meals. It was one of the reasons he'd come to Seattle, trying to get away from would-be mothers, looking for a ready-made family. Hell. He must have been blind not to see the pattern. Lisa and Naomi had been too friendly, but he'd ignored their flirting the way he'd always ignored feminine overtures that didn't come from his wife.

A pang went through him as he reminded himself that Kim was gone. He'd never put much thought into the marriage vow "till death do us part." Women usually lived longer than men, and he'd figured he'd go first. But he hadn't gone first, and now he had to deal with a reality that didn't include Kim.

His stomach turned as emotions crawled through it, a reminder of those horrible, empty days after the funeral, when he'd cursed himself and God...and his wife for being human enough to get leukemia and die.

"Alex?"

"Yeah," he said tightly. "They were mostly single."

Shannon's gaze flicked over him, seeming almost as tangible as a touch. "I may be single, but I promise not to bake you any cakes or cookies."

"Skip the Jell-O salad and casseroles, too, okay?" Alex muttered. He didn't want anything that reminded him of the food at Kim's wake.

"I promise." Once again something unknown flickered in Shannon's expressive face, but he couldn't begin to guess at the meaning. "And you can skip the offer of Thai food, if you prefer. I may be single, but I'm not on the prowl like Lisa or the others."

"What's 'on the prowl'?" Jeremy asked.

He was examining them both with his serious eyes, and Alex saw that Shannon was as nonplussed as he was over the question. For some reason it reassured him. She was so darned confident about everything, it was nice to know there were some things she wasn't certain how to handle.

"It means that Shannon just wants to be our friend," Alex said.

"That's right," she added quickly. "Just friends."

The emphasis she put on the words drained some of the satisfaction from Alex, which just proved how illogical he could be. The last thing he needed was a neighbor who saw him a potential mate, particularly a neighbor as unsettling as Shannon.

Chapter Three

"Actually, Thai sounds good," Alex found himself saying to his astonishment. "But Jeremy may not like something so different."

"That's all right. I can ask the delivery guy to pick up a hamburger on the way over. Does that sound good to you, Jeremy? We'll have him get french fries, too."

Naturally, Jeremy looked thrilled. He loved fast food, particularly since his mother hadn't allowed him to eat any. Alex had tried to stick to Kim's rules about their son's diet, but convenience foods were called convenient for a reason…they were convenient.

It wasn't that he couldn't cook. His work had taken him to some remote parts of the world where restaurants didn't exist. You learned to cook or you didn't eat. But between work and trying to spend time with Jeremy, it was easier to grab a bag of precut salad mix and a microwave dinner. Now that things were becoming more settled, they would have to start a routine that made them both comfortable.

"That would be fine," Alex said. "Except I doubt you can get the delivery person to run an errand for you."

Shannon's smile turned even more beguiling. "Wanna bet?"

No.

He definitely didn't want to bet.

She could probably charm a perfect stranger into doing something they had no intention of doing. Like him, for example. He'd fully intended to keep his distance, and now they were having dinner together again. He had to be out of his mind.

"You can try the Thai food if you want," Shannon told Jeremy as they went up her walkway. "I just love the peanut chicken. It's sweet and yummy."

"Uh...okay."

They chattered away and Alex nodded in resignation as his son agreed to try a few of the exotic dishes Shannon enthused about. One of the few discordant notes in his marriage had been Kim's lack of culinary adventure, and Jeremy was just as stubborn about trying new things...or had been until now. His son had done nothing but talk about Shannon ever since meeting her, so he'd probably eat live worms if she asked.

"Any preferences?" Shannon asked Alex as she hung her coat in the entry closet. Unlike her orderly living room, the closet was an untidy mess of winter gear and sports equipment. He supposed it was a sort of metaphor, representing the variable sides of her nature. "I like almost everything, so speak up for whatever you want."

Spicy, he wanted to say, but was afraid it would come out sounding seductive. Curiously, her sexual impact was both subtle and overt. The overt part didn't bother him. It was the subtle, vulnerable part of her that had him ready to bark at the moon.

Yet even as the thought formed, Alex shook his head in denial. He doubted there was a vulnerable cell in Shannon O'Rourke's delectable body. She was bright and fiery, like the shining surface of a diamond. Sure, she had a soft spot for his son and seemed to care about people who were less fortunate, but vulnerable?

Not a chance.

"I've learned to like most everything, too, with all the traveling I've done," he said. "But if you hope Jeremy will try something new, I'd get mild." He nearly added *and don't get your hopes up,* then decided Shannon would find out soon enough about his son's preference for unimaginative food.

She picked up the phone. "That's fine. I'll ask them to put some crushed red pepper on the side."

In a short time she'd ordered a number of dishes and sweet-talked the manager into having the delivery driver pick up a burger, fries and a carton of milk.

"I think you ordered too much," Alex said.

"Not if you have a big appetite like my brothers."

Shannon's comfortable references to her family made

Alex uneasily aware that he rarely spoke to his own relatives, even during the holidays.

"You're close to them, aren't you?" he asked curiously.

"Of course I am. Naturally they drive me crazy trying to interfere with my life. And Kane takes his position as head of the family way too seriously, but they aren't bad for big lugs with the mentality of cavemen."

His eyebrows shot upward. "Cavemen?"

"Completely. You should have seen the way they acted when I started dating."

Alex smiled. "That bad, eh?"

"Worse. I swear that Kane or Neil or Patrick followed me on every date for the first six months. Even Dylan and Connor were weird about it. Do you know what it's like to be unable to enjoy your first kiss for fear one of your brothers is going to pounce?"

"Not really." Alex choked, fighting a laugh.

Shannon was trying to sound aggrieved, but he could tell she was touched by her brothers' protectiveness. Yet he sobered quickly, wondering if his own sister had ever had trouble when she started dating, and if she'd ever wished her brothers were there to protect her.

He'd been long gone to college and building his career by the time Gail was old enough to start going out with boys.

"Did you ever have trouble on a date? One you needed help handling?" he murmured.

"Me? Not a chance. I take care of myself."

Something flashed through Shannon's eyes so quickly, it was gone almost before it registered.

She was lying.

Not in a bad way. Just covering up something she didn't like remembering, or didn't want to confess.

It bothered him that Shannon might not be as tough as she appeared—maybe because her brothers were still protecting her, while he'd seen Gail just once in the past three years. Gail was tough, too; you didn't grow up in the McKenzie household without developing a protective shell. But what if his sister wasn't as tough as he thought?

Because it raised a confusing array of emotions that Alex didn't want to feel, he sat next to Jeremy, who was playing once again with Shannon's Christmas train set.

"Choo, choo," Jeremy chanted. Mr. Tibbles had been leaned up against one of the miniature Victorian houses, and he looked decidedly tipsy with one of his long ears flopped over a black button eye.

Sometimes Alex hated that rabbit.

It represented the dark days, the loss his little boy never should have suffered. Only the introduction of Shannon into their lives had lessened his fierce attachment to Mr. Tibbles.

Shannon...

Sighing to himself, Alex glanced across the room. She'd knelt by the fireplace and was lighting a neatly laid stack of logs. The sway of her hips beneath her formfitting jeans made him uncomfortably warm. Her impact on his senses was the most likely explanation for his agreeing to dinner, but knowing that didn't make him happy.

He cleared his throat. "I'm surprised you don't have a gas fire. It's more convenient."

She turned and smiled. "I prefer the light and warmth of a real fire."

"Gas puts off heat and light."

"Not like this." Shannon gazed into the new flames licking across the wood, a dreamy expression on her face. "Every year I visit Ireland with my mother. The cottage she grew up in has a fireplace that fills most of a wall in the kitchen. The light bounces off the polished copper pots and kettles, and it feels so safe and secure, as if nothing will ever change."

"Everything changes." The words came out sharper than Alex had intended, but it was the truth. Things changed, no matter how much he disliked the process.

The corners of Shannon's mouth turned down, and the soft light of memory faded from her eyes. "I know. That's a lesson I received when I wasn't many years older than Jeremy. Anyway, my grandparents still live in the cottage, though Kane wants to build them a modern house with modern conveniences, either in Ireland or here in Washington."

Alex found himself moving closer, drawn partly by the warmth in his lower extremities, and partly by the unguarded emotions he'd seen in her face. "They refused?"

"Yes. Generations of Scanlons have grown up there, and they're not ones to be goin' anywhere that God didn't put them." She said the last in a distinct brogue, and he knew she was repeating something she must have heard often from her faraway grandparents.

"I take it your grandparents didn't approve of your mother going to America."

"It was my father they didn't approve of. That is…" Her voice trailed, and to Alex's surprise, Shannon looked shy, as if she'd revealed something she thought should have stayed private. "They're good people, but my father was wild before he married my mother, and then he took her thousands of miles away."

Wild?

"You take after your father, don't you?" he asked before he could think better of the question. He didn't need to know those kinds of things about Shannon; they weren't even friends, much less lovers.

"Yes, though my third-oldest brother is the most like Dad. Of course, Patrick is settling down now, too. He got married a couple of months after Kane."

"Is marriage the answer for your family? Like a ship's anchor for all that wildness?"

"Maybe." Shannon flipped a curling lock of auburn hair away from her face, and shrugged. "But probably not for me."

Once again there was a confusing emotion in her green eyes, quickly concealed. A man could get whiplash trying to figure her out, and for the hundredth time Alex's head warned him to get out, now, before he got involved. Women like Shannon might be fascinating, but they were also too disturbing.

Despite the warning, he leaned forward. "Why not you?"

"Lots of reasons," she said lightly. "I'm too independent and want things my own way. I enjoy working and keeping my own hours, that sort of stuff."

Once again he had the oddest sensation, as though she'd told him something that wasn't entirely true.

"Seeing how good you are with kids, I'd think you'd want a family of your own."

She lifted an eyebrow. "How do you know I'm good with kids? Maybe it's just a fluke with Jeremy."

Alex laughed. "I don't believe that. Why else would he respond to you?"

"It's…complicated." Shannon's smile trembled and she looked at Jeremy playing with the train set. Her voice lowered. "I think it's because I understand what he's going through. You see, my father died in an accident when I was eight. One minute I was a happy, carefree little girl, and the next…"

Her eyes blinked rapidly, unnaturally bright, and he winced. "Don't, Shannon."

She shook her head. "No, I want you to understand, because if there's anything I can do to help Jeremy, I want to do it. I know how it feels to be young and have your world fall apart, and to hurt so much you want to crawl in a hole and hide," she said, sounding as if the words had been dragged from a deep place in her soul, a place she didn't usually reveal.

Alex felt like a heel for causing her to speak about something so painful. Maybe it wasn't such a terrible thing to ask for her phone number to give the day-care center. Jeremy came first, and Shannon obviously wanted to help.

He raked a hand through his hair, his need to stay uninvolved battling with the seductive desire to be close to a woman as tempting as Shannon. And right in the middle of the battle were his son's needs, more important than anything else.

"Actually, there is something…well, there's a favor you could do for us," he said slowly.

Shannon raised one eyebrow when he fell silent. "Yes?" she prompted.

"The day-care center has been asking for an emergency contact in case they can't reach me. I know it's a lot to ask, but they're right about needing someone local. I understand if you don't want to. It's really all right if you say no."

Alex sent up a prayer she would say no, or seem reluctant, or say something else that would get him off the hook. Then he could honestly stall the day-care center again.

"Of course," Shannon said, reaching for her purse and taking out a business card. She scribbled something on the back and handed it to him. "This has my office number, and I put down my home and cell, along with my executive assistant's phone. She can always reach me. Really, if there's anything you need, just call."

God in heaven…

She was so generous, and Alex gazed into her green eyes for an endless moment, then down at the curves of her mouth. Panic lapped at the edge of his consciousness; he didn't want to be attracted to Shannon or be pulled into her world. He wanted things to be calm and sane, with everything in its proper place. He needed things to be that way.

The doorbell rang before Alex could sort through the

emotional minefield he'd stumbled into, and he let out an unconscious sigh of relief. "That must be dinner."

He pulled out his wallet, but Shannon shook her head.

"It's my treat, remember?"

Letting a woman pay for dinner went against the grain. "But—"

"No 'buts.'" Shannon got to her feet. It had been years since she'd had so much trouble keeping herself from blushing, yet something about Alex was making her say things she never planned on saying.

And those eyes of his…they were too darned intent. She'd bet anything that he wasn't thinking about her the way she kept thinking about him, but that was the story of her love life. Men always had a different agenda, and how was she supposed to figure out a man who'd lost his wife and was worried about his son?

"So, how is everything going with your classes?" she asked after they'd settled at the dining-room table and spooned various portions onto their plates, the food steaming and spicing the air with the pungent fragrances of lemongrass and other herbs.

Alex groaned. "Okay, but I didn't have any idea how tough it was teaching basic engineering principles to under-grads."

"I thought you'd been teaching for a long time."

"No, this is my first year. I used to work on engineering projects all over the world. But now that it's just me and Jeremy, I realized that moving every few months for a job wasn't the right life for him."

"It must have been easier to manage a nomadic life-style with three of you."

He glanced at Jeremy and looked uncomfortable. "It wasn't like that. I enjoy spending time in remote, primitive locations, but Kim didn't feel that way, so she stayed in our house back in Minnesota. I'd fly home as often as possible, but she wanted to have a stable base, especially after Jeremy came. It was for the best."

The best for who?

It wasn't Shannon's business, but it sounded awful. Families belonged together. Her mother had picked up the family and moved with Keenan O'Rourke whenever necessary. They'd lived all over the Seattle region when Shannon was a kid, though mostly in small towns, rather than the city.

"Maybe you should consider working with graduate students," she murmured instead of speaking her mind the way she wanted. Alex's wife had made her decisions; there wasn't any point in criticizing them. "You might enjoy it more."

"They're assigning me a group of graduates after the first of the year. And I guess it isn't that bad," he said thoughtfully. "I miss the work more than the travel, but it's an interesting challenge to mold future engineers."

"How about doing consulting on the side?"

"I've thought about that, but it's taken longer than I expected to get settled."

Shannon made a mental note to talk to Kane. Her brother hired the brightest and best for his company, and she didn't doubt that Alex McKenzie fell into that category. Of course, if she said anything to Kane about Alex, he'd ask questions she didn't want to answer.

Jeremy sat watching them and she noticed a frown growing on his small face. She hadn't said anything more about him eating some of the Thai food, not wanting him to dig his heels in and refuse. She'd simply put the hamburger and fries in front of him, and waited.

"You said I could try some," he announced abruptly.

"That's right. What do you want to try first?"

He pointed to her plate.

"Mmm, yummy choice. That's the peanut chicken I told you about. It's sweet, with ground peanuts and coconut milk." Shannon served some onto his plate, holding back on the fresh spinach that came with the chicken—there was no sense in pushing her luck. "There you go."

Jeremy regarded the food with the expression of a mouse confronting a lion, but he slowly picked up a fork. His smile brightened as he chewed, then quickly finished the sample she'd given him. "Can I have some more?"

On the other side of the table Alex stared in wonder. "*May* I have some more," he automatically corrected.

"Okay. Can Daddy have more, too?" Jeremy asked.

Shannon choked and Alex spotted the smile she was trying to hide. "Yes," she said, "your daddy may have more, too. You both can have anything you want."

Alex doubted that.

What he wanted, and what he should have, were two entirely different things. His attraction to Shannon was inappropriate, ill-timed and utterly impossible. For Jeremy's sake, as well as his own, he had to keep it hidden.

Just then she flicked a small amount of sauce from her lip with her tongue and his body hardened.

Keeping his response to Shannon hidden might not be easy, he thought with resignation.

Much later, after tucking Jeremy into bed, Alex stared into his own dark fireplace and brooded.

He liked sex.

Always had.

After getting married, he'd had opportunities to go to bed with other women, but the idea of being unfaithful to his wife was repugnant. Lack of fidelity, among other things, had cursed his parents' relationship.

What would Kim say if she knew he was having sensual thoughts about Shannon O'Rourke? He shook his head at the question. Kim would probably say something reasonable and measured like…those feelings are normal…don't beat yourself up over it…it's all right. Her Zenlike calm had irritated him sometimes, but he reminded himself it was what he'd wanted. His wife had rarely raised her voice, much less become angry.

He was back to square one, not knowing what to do about Shannon. She might be able to help Jeremy, but what if his son got more ideas about her becoming his new mommy?

And what if he got more ideas about taking her to bed?

Alex couldn't have a no-strings affair with his next-door

neighbor. Besides, for all of Shannon's modern sophistication, he didn't think she was a "no-strings" type of woman.

He rubbed the back of his neck, trying to ease his tight
muscles, but it was useless.

When had life gotten so damned complicated?

Chapter Four

Shannon sipped her cup of tea and glanced around the crowded coffee shop.

The Seattle area was a coffee lover's mecca, and cheerful Christmas shoppers filled the store to capacity. Couples seemed to be in force today, replete with loving looks and affectionate gestures toward one another. For some inexplicable reason the scene made her think about Alex McKenzie. On the other hand, maybe it wasn't inexplicable. *Everything* made her think about Alex.

Sighing, Shannon put her cup on a collection tray and slipped from the store.

Small leaves, scattered by a cold breeze, danced across the sidewalk and into the street. Another sigh escaped as her cell phone rang.

"Hello," she answered.

"Shannon, it's Alex."

She stopped dead in her tracks. "Alex. Hello."

"Are you in the middle of something?" His voice sounded oddly stressed and she frowned.

"I was doing some Christmas shopping, but I'm done now. Is something wrong?"

"No. That is, nothing serious. But I'm involved in something urgent, and Jeremy is at the day-care center. He says he isn't feeling well. I doubt it's anything, and I hate to ask, but I'm really—"

"I'd be happy to pick him up," Shannon said instantly. "He can stay with me until you get home." There was a long silence and she bit her lip. "Alex, are you there?"

"Yes. I appreciate the offer. I shouldn't be too late, I hope no later than mid afternoon." He gave her directions to the day-care center, then rang off.

Shannon stood stock-still for a minute, filled with both shock and alarm. She knew even less about sick children than she did about children in general.

"This isn't about you," she muttered, annoyed with herself. "It's about Jeremy."

It was also about Alex, and the confusing way he seemed to blow hot and cold. She'd hoped they could be friends after their second dinner together, but he'd sounded so uneasy telling her about Jeremy.

She shook her head.

Men were stubborn about asking for help. It seemed to wound their pride to think they couldn't handle everything themselves. Or maybe Alex's problem was something else—something even more incomprehensible than the male ego.

"And men claim women are unpredictable," Shannon muttered as she unlocked her car and jumped behind the wheel. Handling a sick little boy would probably be a piece of cake compared to dealing with a grown-up Alex.

At the day-care center an older woman met Shannon at the door. "Miss O'Rourke? Hello, I'm Helen Davis. Please come inside. I'm afraid Jeremy is upset."

"What happened?"

"We told him you were coming and he seemed pleased. Then one of our aides offered to mend his stuffed rabbit while he waited, and things went down from there."

Shannon's eyebrows shot upward. "She didn't try to take Mr. Tibbles away from Jeremy, did she?"

"Not…exactly."

"Shannon," yelped a small voice, and Jeremy raced forward, practically leaping into her arms. He clutched her neck with surprising strength.

"Hey, kiddo. It's okay."

He looked at her, his blue eyes brimming with tears. "The lady wanted to poke Mr. Tibbles with a needle." He scowled at Mrs. Davis as if she'd sprouted horns and a tail.

"That's too bad. Do you want to come home with me?"

"Uh-huh. Mr. Tibbles wants a nap."

Poor little guy. He couldn't admit he wanted to sleep, so Mr. Tibbles was taking the blame. Shannon stroked the dark hair away from Jeremy's forehead. He felt warm, but kids always felt warm to her.

"Let's go," she said quietly, carrying him out to the car.

When they arrived home, Shannon settled Jeremy in the living room. He quickly curled up on the floor with a pillow and blanket, Mr. Tibbles clutched to his chest. Sucking his thumb, he watched the cheerful village beneath the Christmas tree until he fell asleep.

Alex raced down the freeway, pushing the speed limit, a thousand things on his mind, including the frightened student he'd just left at the University Health Center.

Rita Sawyer, a brilliant sixteen-year-old prodigy, had come to him with a problem.

A *big* problem.

Big enough to make him call Shannon and ask for a favor he would have given almost anything not to ask.

Alex flexed his hands on the steering wheel, angry all over again. If he ever found out which football player had thought it was fun to seduce an underage girl, the slithering little snake would stop laughing in a hurry. Unfortunately, Rita had been too upset and scared to tell him who was responsible.

He pulled into the drive and regarded the side by side condos. Shannon's side glowed with warmth and welcome in the early twilight of the Washington winter day. His house seemed cold and aloof.

"Stop that," Alex ordered beneath his breath.

He wasn't a fanciful person. Buildings weren't endowed with anything more than brick and wood and plaster.

Shannon opened the door before he could knock and she

put her finger to her lips. "Jeremy's asleep," she said softly. "I think he has a slight fever, but it doesn't seem bad."

"You mean he's really sick?"

He practically pushed Shannon to one side. It was only when he saw his son sleeping on a large pillow that his breathing slowed. One of Jeremy's arms was around Mr. Tibbles, and the other was stretched out to touch the controls of the toy train.

"God," Alex muttered, rubbing the back of his neck in an attempt to ease tense muscles. "He's been complaining of tummy aches and stuff every few days, asking to go home. The day-care center thought he was just crying wolf again."

Shannon sat next to Jeremy and stroked the hair from his forehead. It was such a naturally caring gesture that Alex's chest tightened. She seemed able to reach Jeremy when everyone else had failed. He didn't understand why—she was so different from Jeremy's mother.

"He might be getting a cold," she said softly. "But I doubt it's serious." Her auburn hair fell over her shoulders, spilling across a fuzzy white sweater. She looked like an angel, and Alex forced himself to look away, fixing his gaze on Jeremy.

There was nothing angelic about Shannon O'Rourke. Angels did not twist a man's guts into knots.

Seeming unaware of his scrutiny, she smiled and rose. "Would you like some soda, or maybe some wine? You look like you could use a drink."

"Cola, if you have it."

"I'll be back in a moment."

She disappeared into the kitchen and he heard the clinking of ice against glass. Still concerned, he knelt and felt his son's forehead for himself. Warmer than normal, but nothing serious.

Slumping down on the couch, Alex rubbed his face and tried to release the tension gripping him. Everything was all right. In a few days Jeremy probably wouldn't even remember it was Shannon who'd come to the rescue instead of his daddy.

Kids were resilient.

How many times had he heard that?

Doctors, child psychologists, pastors, well-meaning acquaintances—people felt they had to say something when they learned about Kim's death. Everyone had a support group they thought he should join, or a counselor to see…or a single female relative he should call, who was reputed to be a good listener.

He didn't need a good listener; he just needed to take care of his son and make sure nothing ever hurt Jeremy again.

Alex swallowed.

It was hard to escape the feeling that if he'd been home in Minnesota more often, Kim might have been diagnosed earlier. Another few weeks of treatment might have made the difference in her recovery. But he hadn't been there, and all the guilt in the world wouldn't change things now.

"Alex?" Shannon had emerged from the kitchen and was holding out a glass. He didn't know how long she'd waited to catch his attention, but a faint frown creased her forehead.

"Thanks. I appreciate you picking Jeremy up."

She shrugged one shoulder. "I told you I'd be happy to help out."

She astonished him. His parents had shown him that most people needed or wanted *something;* they didn't offer to help someone out of the goodness of their hearts. And a woman like Shannon, whom every wealthy bachelor in Washington must be chasing, certainly couldn't *need* or *want* a widower with a young son who wouldn't let go of his toy rabbit.

Alex cleared his throat. He could go nuts trying to figure out Shannon and her motives; she was far too complicated.

He accepted the glass, took a sip of the cola, then put the drink down on a polished wood coaster. It would be best if he made an excuse, took his son and left as soon as possible.

"So you think Jeremy has been trying to get attention by pretending to be sick?" she asked in a low tone.

"Yeah." Alex grabbed the cola again. "At least I did, but now I don't know what to believe. If he's really ill…it's enough to make me crazy. I can't lose him."

"You aren't going to lose him," Shannon said softly. "Children get colds and tummy aches. It's rarely serious." She'd called her mom an hour earlier and been assured of that fact. "And children make up stories to get attention. It's part of being a kid."

Alex cocked his head. Weary lines bracketed his mouth and she wished she could smooth them away.

"Do you speak from experience?"

"Of course." She smiled. "My youngest sister put on

'dying diva' performances worthy of an Oscar. Fortunately my mother was less gullible than the rest of us."

"What, no award-winning performances from you?"

"Nope. I was the perfect child."

He chuckled, casting a quick glance toward the Christmas tree where Jeremy lay, still soundly asleep. "No way. Didn't we establish that you were pretty wild? You probably gave your mother premature gray hair and an ulcer to boot."

Shannon felt her smile become fixed and she nearly tossed out a smart remark, agreeing to Alex's assessment. But he needed to be reassured that Jeremy would be all right.

"The truth is that after my father…when we lost him, I kept things bottled up." She rubbed the back of her neck, searching for an explanation she'd never voiced aloud. "We all reacted in our own way, and I decided to be the one who didn't cause trouble."

"Shannon, please. You don't have to talk about it."

"I don't mind." She grinned wryly. "Actually, I *do* mind, but that's okay. Dad was killed in an accident working for a lumber company. After it happened, I never let anyone know how I felt, or how much I hurt…about anything. I'd say something clever or tease or make a joke, but I wouldn't cry or make anyone sad. That was my idea of not making trouble."

"That meant you were all alone."

Startled, Shannon gazed quickly at Alex. He sounded appalled, but he also understood. In a house filled with her mother and brothers and sisters, she'd been alone.

She shivered and drew back. She hadn't intended to strip her soul bare, but that was how she felt.

"It wasn't so bad," she said in instinctive denial. "The point is, I got through it, and I didn't turn out to be such a horrible person, did I?"

"Not horrible at all."

"And with some time and a lot of love, I'm sure Jeremy will be all right, too."

Alex swirled the cola in his glass. Shannon hadn't said anything new, but it meant more coming from her. She'd been there, gone through what Jeremy was going through, and she had seen her brothers and sisters go through it as well.

"Then you're saying I shouldn't worry."

She gave him a quick smile. "Of course you're going to worry. You're his daddy. My mom says worry is in a parent's job description."

He liked the way she said *daddy*. Not *father* or *parent*, but *daddy*. Any man could father a child; not all of them were daddies. His own father was the perfect example—a man with so many personal problems, he didn't have energy to think about the kids he'd helped create.

"I'm no expert," Shannon murmured, "but I called my mother and talked to her after picking up Jeremy. I know you've been concerned, and thought she might have some advice. After all, she raised nine children and we all lived to tell about it."

"I don't think I could handle nine. Just having one has me overwhelmed."

"You might surprise yourself. Mom says it doesn't get easier with each child, but you become more shock-resistant."

"She sounds smart. Maybe she can tell me how to help a pregnant sixteen-year-old prodigy," he muttered, his mind unable to erase the memory of the fear in his young student's face, and the knowledge that something had irrevocably changed her life. No matter what Rita decided to do about her baby, it was something she'd live with forever.

"Sixteen?"

"Yes. That's why I asked if you'd pick up Jeremy. A member of the football team seduced her as part of an initiation challenge. She told me after class. She'd been crying...I couldn't leave without doing something."

"I'll kill him." Shannon's eyes flashed furiously.

"Get in line."

"I mean it, Alex. What's his name?"

"I mean it, too, but she wouldn't tell me his name." Alex gazed at Shannon's passionate expression, fascinated. He'd reacted to the situation as an intellectual, coolly, professionally, though he'd been outraged; Shannon's reaction was purely from the heart.

The philosophical concepts of yin and yang, opposites that complemented each other, crept into his mind.

No.

He surged to his feet.

"You've been terrific, but if Jeremy's really coming down with something, then we're exposing you to his germs unnecessarily. I'd better get him home."

Her eyebrows shot upward. "What about your student?"

"She's with the counselors at the school health center. They're going to work with her. I shouldn't have said anything, but I wanted you to know there was a good reason I asked for your help," he said quickly.

It was a lie.

He'd told her because he'd needed to talk about the situation with someone else. It was odd, but the school counselors had frustrated him with their guarded responses. He was a careful man himself—a man who avoided emotion— yet he'd wanted to hear *someone* explode in outrage on Rita's behalf.

He leaned over his son. "It's time to go," he murmured.

Jeremy snuggled deeper into the pillow, so Alex lifted him in his arms.

"No, Daddy," came a sleepy murmur. "Wanna stay with Shannon."

Considering the magical toy train and marvelous Christmas tree, he wasn't surprised by Jeremy's response, yet a piercing ache went through Alex. He'd tried to get Jeremy interested in buying a tree, but his son had just sighed and said it wouldn't be like Shannon's. How a child could fall madly in love with someone in such a short time was beyond comprehension.

Shannon followed them to the door with Jeremy's jacket, and when Alex turned to say goodnight, he caught the faint scent of her perfume.

God, she smelled good.

He stared into her green eyes and felt unwelcome sensations, sensations that reminded him he was still alive, even if his wife was gone.

"Er...thanks again. For everything," he muttered, taking the jacket and tucking it around his son.

Without another word he opened the door and left before he could do something he'd regret.

Chapter Five

"I don't wanna babysitter," Jeremy declared, his small chin setting stubbornly.

Alex sighed. "We need someone for a few days. You can't go to day-care until we're sure you don't have strep throat."

"Not going back there, either. I want Shannon."

Blast.

Alex rubbed at his temples. He'd sat at Jeremy's bedside most of the night, watching him breathe, gauging how sick he was getting. He'd enjoyed few restful nights since losing Kim, but it was his child's health that robbed him of sleep now.

He'd do anything for his son.

Did "anything" include Shannon O'Rourke?

Alex had cashed in her offer of help once already, but

she handled Jeremy so well. By contrast, Jeremy was still convinced the day-care center meant Mr. Tibbles harm by trying to "poke" the rabbit with a needle.

"*Pleeeze,* Daddy. Mr. Tibbles likes Shannon."

The heartfelt plea was more than Alex could withstand. "All right, I'll talk to her," he said.

Feeling as if he was caught in a quagmire that was pulling him down no matter how hard he tried to escape it, Alex stepped outside and knocked on Shannon's door. He'd heard a few sounds from her side of their shared wall earlier that morning, so he figured she was awake.

When the door opened and he saw her, looking bright and beautiful as a new penny, he felt old and tired in comparison. For nearly a year he'd struggled, trying to make sense of his life and figure out how to be a father to a withdrawn, grieving child. Now Shannon had dropped into the picture, and she was like a forbidden Christmas ornament dangling from a branch, just beyond reach.

She represented a sweet escape from the struggle, but escape wasn't possible. He could only endure.

"Is Jeremy all right?" Shannon asked.

"Yeah. He's sniffling and has a sore throat, but it seems to be just a cold like you thought. The thing is, there's a lot of strep throat going around, and the day-care center wants me to wait a couple of days to rule it out before bringing him back. I do have a babysitter I could call, but Jeremy's being difficult and I—"

"If you want to know if I'll take care of him, the answer is yes," she said.

"Are you sure you don't mind? Watching a sick kid is a lousy way to use a vacation day. And there's more chance you'll catch his bug."

"I'm sure. Besides, I never get sick," Shannon said, at the same minute her brain was screaming in pure panic. Taking care of a little boy for a whole day was a much bigger step than watching him for a couple of hours.

"That's great." Alex sounded as if he wasn't actually sure it was great, but he was saying so because he didn't have a choice.

His behavior irritated her. She wished she understood more about single fathers. Then she might know why Alex's face and posture said one thing, while his voice said another. If he really didn't want her to take care of Jeremy, why had he knocked on her door in the first place?

"I'm happy to spend the day with him," she said firmly.

"If he was worse, I'd stay home, only with finals next week it isn't a good time to miss class," he said.

Alex removed a key from his key ring and handed it to her, along with a business card. "Here's a key to my condo so you can spend the day there if you want. Feel free to use whatever you need. My office and cell phone numbers are on the card. I usually turn off the cell in class, but I'll leave it on today."

She glanced at the key and had a sudden burning urge to see the inside of the McKenzie household. Would it be neat? Disorganized? Would it still reflect the influence of Jeremy's mother, who had been the homebody sort who made everything nice? A vision of lace doilies and crocheted toilet-paper-roll covers went through her head—a dizzying image in the face of Alex's rugged masculinity.

"Er...I'll let Jeremy take the lead," she murmured.

Suddenly, Jeremy appeared under Alex's elbow and smiled up tremulously. "Is it okay, Daddy?"

"Yes. Go back inside, son, where it's warm."

"No. Go to Shannon's now."

Quick as a monkey, he scooted past his daddy, and Shannon instinctively crouched to catch him in a hug.

Oh...goodness.

A warm, fuzzy sensation curled in her tummy.

She glanced up at Alex and tingles of electricity gave her a different kind of warmth. Barefoot despite the cold, clad in faded jeans and a University of Washington sweatshirt, he had just the right blend of unconscious confidence and sex appeal to make a woman weak in the knees.

"You—" Her voice cracked and she cleared it.

Alex might be yummier than a chocolate sundae, but she wasn't interested.

Liar, screamed her conscience.

Why else would she keep from confessing that she couldn't boil water and didn't have a clue about kids?

Not for the first time she reminded herself that a relationship between them was doomed. He was a family man who loved primitive countries, and she was a city woman. Her idea of survival skills was knowing how to get rid of the containers that came with take-out food.

Straightening, she plastered a polite smile on her face. "Go ahead and get ready for work. Jeremy is fine here."

"Thanks." Alex's blue eyes darkened and a spasm of emotion crossed his face as he looked down at his son. He still hadn't shaved, but his shadow of a beard and rumpled appearance made him look even sexier. "I shouldn't be too late."

He turned and crossed their side-by-side driveways, then disappeared inside his condo.

Shannon breathed a sigh of relief and directed Jeremy into her house. The less time she spent with his daddy, the better for all of them.

After lunchtime had come and gone, Shannon was exhausted. But it wasn't a bad exhausted. A local store had agreed to deliver groceries—including their "homemade chicken noodle soup," guaranteed to cure colds "just like Mom's did." She'd only boiled a little over in the microwave while reheating it, so nothing disastrous had happened.

Afterward, Jeremy had talked her through making instant cocoa, before delightedly playing with the train again.

The doorbell rang, breaking into her thoughts, and she hurried into the other room, smiling at Jeremy who was curled up on the couch with a blanket.

He blinked sleepily at her. "S'Daddy," he predicted.

Sure enough, Alex McKenzie waited on the step with an anxious expression in his eyes. "Is Jeremy all right?"

"He's fine. I would have called if there was a problem."

Part of Alex's mind registered the annoyed tone in

Shannon's voice, but the other part appreciated the dark green dress she wore. It was made of a soft fabric that clung like a second skin, and he itched to see how it might peel away. Was she wearing underwear? There weren't any obvious lines that—

Damn.

His thoughts were going in directions he'd sworn he wouldn't allow them to go. Shannon was a neighbor— nothing more. It was natural that after a year of being celibate certain feelings would return. And if he felt as if he was being unfaithful to Kim, then that was something he'd have to resolve within himself.

"How did it go?" he asked as Shannon invited him inside.

"Great. We got a few of his toys and books from next door, and we read together, stuff like that. I think he's feeling a little better."

"Uh-uh," Jeremy declared immediately. "Not better. I wanna come back tomorrow."

He let out an unconvincing cough and Alex covered a smile. Mr. Tibbles lay on the floor, over ten feet away from Jeremy, sending a surge of joy through him. After the disaster at the day-care center, he'd worried that Jeremy would be more bonded than ever to the stuffed rabbit, but everything seemed to be all right.

"Maybe Shannon can tell us how to decorate our own Christmas tree," he said, trying to distract his determined son. "How about it, Shannon?"

Alex looked at Shannon in time to see another strange,

altogether unreadable expression on her face. Honestly, how could a man have a prayer of figuring her out?

"I'll give you mine. That'll be easier," she said. "And the train set, of course. That way you can have a tree right away."

He'd expected anything from a polite "Sorry, I'm too busy," to an enthusiastic "Yes," but not such a generous offer.

He shook his head. "We couldn't do that."

"Daddy—"

"No, Jeremy, we can't take Shannon's tree. I know you like coming here because of the train and everything, but we have our own home."

Shannon stayed silent, lips pressed together as Alex collected Jeremy's things and said good-bye. Her eyes narrowed as the front door shut behind them, leaving her in silence.

I know you like coming here because of the train and everything...

Of all the insulting things to say.

Even if it was true, it was still rude. And it wasn't only because of the Christmas tree and train set that Jeremy liked her. He'd liked her at the post office before they'd ever been inside her condo.

Shannon marched to the phone. Her family would think she was acting like a fool, but that was just too bad. She hadn't known what to say when Alex asked for help with a Christmas tree, so she'd panicked and offered to give them her own tree.

Now she had a plan.

"Miranda? It's Shannon. I have another job for you," she said when her sister answered, then settled down to explain what she wanted.

The next day, Shannon waited until after nine in the evening before carrying various boxes out of her house and stacking them near the McKenzies' front step.

She figured Alex was still awake since he seemed to be a night person. Lately she was even more aware of sounds on the other side of their shared wall. Bathwater ran every evening around eight, followed by rustles of noise in one of the smaller bedrooms—presumably Jeremy being put to bed. Later, long after she'd gone to bed herself, she'd hear muffled thuds and bumps and the sound of a shower from the master-bedroom suite that gradually quieted. Usually after midnight.

The lights were still on downstairs, so she tapped on the door and waited, stifling a yawn. Night was not her best time; she liked mornings.

"Shannon?" Alex said, swinging the door open. "Is something wrong?"

"Of course not. I have your tree." She motioned to the boxes her sister had brought to the condo earlier.

"What are you talking about?"

"You wanted my help with a Christmas tree, so here it is."

Alex blinked as Shannon grabbed a carton and pushed past him into the living room. He'd spent the evening listening to Jeremy chatter about Shannon, and couldn't he go to her home tomorrow instead of calling the babysitter again? His son had finally gone to sleep, and now here was Shannon. In the flesh, so to speak, clad in tight black jeans and a black sweater embroidered with green and silver holly leaves across the breast and all that glorious red hair…

He let out a harsh breath.

"Where do you want me?" she asked.

He thought of saying he wanted her in his king-size bed. Much as he didn't want to deal with those kinds of feelings, apparently he didn't have any choice. But he didn't have to act on them. He'd always prided himself on his self-control, determined to be different from his mother and father.

"I asked for advice on decorating a tree. I never thought you'd go out and buy something. How much do I owe you?"

She shrugged, her long hair glinting like fire. "You don't owe me anything. This is a gift."

"I can't accept—"

"It isn't for you, it's a gift for Jeremy," she said coolly. "I'll set it up now, so he can be surprised in the morning when he wakes up."

She seemed edgy, as if filled with suppressed emotion, and he frowned. "Is something wrong?"

"Heavens, what could be wrong?"

Her smile, like her voice, exuded false cheerfulness. Something *was* wrong, but she wouldn't admit it. Moreover, he had the damnedest feeling she was furious.

With him.

What had he done?

Well…he had insulted her brother and generally tried to avoid her whenever he wasn't asking a favor, both of which were probably enough to infuriate most women. But why would she go to all this trouble if she was so mad at him?

They worked in silence, carrying boxes into the house and setting up the artificial tree.

"I prefer real evergreen, but artificial trees are safer," Shannon said as she tugged light strings around the branches. "Especially for children," she added. "They want the lights on all the time, which dries out a cut tree and creates a fire hazard." She sounded as if she was repeating something from a book, or something she'd heard.

It took awhile, but gradually the tree was decorated so it resembled a child's toyland dream. Yet several boxes still remained, and when she unpacked the first two, he saw that they contained a toy train set that was far more elaborate than the one running around the base of Shannon's own tree.

"No," he said quietly. "I either pay for this, or you return it to the store."

"My brother is a generous employer. I can afford it."

"So can I."

"I told you before, it's a gift."

"Why? You hardly know us." Alex caught Shannon's arm and pulled her around to face him. He was stunned to see unshed tears in her deep green eyes. "What's going on?"

"You don't want Jeremy wanting to come see me, so obviously you have to have a better tree and train set. Then he won't want to come over and you can pretend we never met."

Shocked, he stared into her hurt eyes, realizing how it must have sounded to Shannon the night before when he was trying to get Jeremy to leave without fussing. He hadn't meant to suggest his son only wanted to visit her because of her tree and train. And he never would have imagined that Shannon O'Rourke, with her carefree smile and sophistication, would take his tactless words so hard.

But he should have guessed.

She'd told him that as a child she'd locked her hurt away, keeping it hidden from the world. It was obvious that she was still hiding the wounds and hurts from view.

"I didn't mean it, not like that," he said helplessly. "You've been great to Jeremy, and he really responds to you. It's just that we've been through so much and he's so little. He doesn't understand some things. I worry about him getting attached and hoping that something will happen between us."

"And that would be awful, wouldn't it? Getting involved with me?" Shannon asked, the words dripping with injured sarcasm. She busied herself lifting out the train and assembling pieces of track.

Damnation.

It was his own fault for saying something so easily misinterpreted. Still, maybe he *did* want Shannon's Christmas tree to be the reason Jeremy wanted to go to her home so badly. He'd spent so much of his son's childhood in other parts of the world, then Kim had gotten sick, going so quickly, and he'd realized he had wasted three years. Three years when he could have been getting to know his own child. And now Jeremy would rather spend time with Shannon than with his own father.

"I'm not interested in getting married again, that's all," he murmured. "It has nothing to do with you."

"Of course not."

But her hurt look hadn't faded and he groaned silently. He didn't deal well with mixed signals and sensitive feelings. Even with his wife he'd struggled, and Kim had been exceptionally calm and good-natured. They'd rarely argued, and then only about Jeremy.

With Shannon it seemed as if all his nerve endings were exposed. He didn't know why, except she was alive and vibrant, and so obviously off-limits.

"You're beautiful, Shannon, you have to know that," Alex whispered.

"Beautiful." She tested the word as if she'd never heard it before. "What has that got to do with anything?"

"Nothing. Everything. I was just trying to be clear."

Shannon thought Alex was as clear as mud. She didn't even know why she was so stirred up over such an unreasonable man. At her request, Miranda had spent half the day collecting ornaments and specialty items for that darned Christmas tree, and the second half showing Shannon how to properly decorate it.

She had it so bad for Alex, she hadn't even tried to make light of things with her sister. She'd tersely explained the decorations were for her next-door neighbor and his little boy, and to please not ask any questions. By now everyone in the O'Rourke family would know she'd gone around the bend. They would tease and tease, and she'd toss her head and give it right back to them.

Her feelings didn't get hurt.

She was too tough for that. Her heart might have gotten broken when she was younger, but at twenty-eight she'd seen enough of the world to know better.

Right.

And Santa Claus was going to climb down her chimney on Christmas Eve.

"These are stockings for the mantel," she said, getting up quickly.

The mantel didn't have anything on it. For that matter, aside from Jeremy's bedroom, the inside of the condo was generally bleak, with only toys and books adding color to the off-white walls and beige furniture. She arranged the two stockings on their hooks, then stepped back and bumped into Alex.

"Sorry," she muttered, jerking away as every atom in her body reacted to the contact.

Leaning down, she collected a garland of silk holly leaves and berries and arranged it on the mantel, then put two battery-operated candle lights on one end. With her sister's design, Alex McKenzie's living room looked quite festive.

"How's that?" she asked.

When he didn't say anything, she dusted her hands. "Guess I'd better get out of your way. You can finish putting the train together later."

Before she could do something stupid like cry, she headed in a beeline for the door. She had it open a few inches when Alex's hand slapped it shut, his breath coming raggedly as he arched over her. She twisted in the small space between him and the door and looked up.

Blue eyes, dark as a midnight sky, gazed down at her, eyes filled with regret and frustration…and heat.

"You get to me," he said harshly. "You must know that. You're a sexy woman and I haven't been with anyone for over a year. But I can't get involved with my next-door neighbor, not with my son looking on. Particularly when I don't plan to get married again. Do you understand?"

Despite Alex's declaration, she felt the hard bulge at the top of his thighs as he leaned into her. There seemed little difference between the muscled length of his body and the unyielding door, and an answering warmth radiated out from Shannon's breasts.

Her arms found their way around his neck and bubbles seemed to be sliding through her veins instead of blood.

"I understand," she said, though it wasn't true.

Alex's hand cupped her chin, and he pressed a kiss to her mouth, his tongue thrusting boldly inside, claiming her as easily as he breathed.

Shannon's moan was lost in the dark, hot joining. It had never been like this with another man, so out-of-control, so improper, so very good. His thumb rubbed across her nipple, then the world spun and there was a sensation of going down, of weight descending on her. She squirmed, inviting it.

He shoved her sweater and bra out of the way and his hands closed over her breasts with a hungry demand. She arched into the caress. Suddenly, Alex froze...and a second later she knew the reason. From the second floor came the faint sound of coughing.

Alex stared at her as she breathed in deep gasps, trying to clear her head. His eyes darkened, his gaze lingering on the sensitive peaks of her breasts. Her nipples tightened as if they'd been stroked and a low moan rose from her throat. She couldn't remember the last time she had felt anything close to the way he was making her feel.

"Daddy?" Jeremy called in the silence, still sounding hoarse from his cold. "Can I have a drink of water?"

"Stay where you are," Alex ordered hastily. "I'll be right up."

Finally coming to her senses, Shannon bolted upright and yanked her clothing into place. Her first thought was escape, but Alex put a hand on her arm as she scrambled to her feet.

"You stay, too," he said. "We have to talk."

Chapter Six

What a mess.

Shannon sat on the floor, blindly assembling the toy train she'd brought, and tried to understand why she'd let Alex kiss her like that.

Because you *wanted* to kiss him, that's why, you idiot, her conscience taunted, and she rolled her eyes. Kissing Alex was a lost cause. He'd made it clear he wasn't getting married again, and she was tired of being single and pretending to like it.

The O'Rourkes were marrying kind of people.

Even Neil had accepted the truth, and sooner or later her youngest brother and three sisters would find their soul mates, as well. The brides would toss their bouquets and they'd go on their honeymoons and start their families. She was happy for them, but it was hard feeling left behind.

She wanted to believe she had a soul mate, too, but she'd stubbed her romantic toes too many times to have much hope of finding someone to love her as she was, domestic limitations and all.

Face grim, Alex walked down the staircase and sat on the bottom step. He didn't say anything and Shannon tried to calm her queasiness. Was he angry, blaming her for that brief moment when the needs of his body had outweighed the caution in his mind?

Taking a deep breath, she squared her shoulders. "Aren't you glad we got that out of our systems?" Her voice cracked a couple of times, but it was the best quip she could devise in her current state of mind.

"Did we?"

Her eyes narrowed.

If Alex said something chauvinistic or crude, she was going to kick him. "At least you could pretend."

He sighed. "I'm not good at pretending, Shannon. I spent my childhood in a marital war zone, followed by divorced-parent hell, never knowing when the screaming was going to start. I got lucky with Kim, but I don't expect to get lucky a second time. That's just one of the reasons I'm not getting married again."

"I don't remember asking you to marry me."

"I can't have an affair, either. It's nothing against you, but I have to think about Jeremy."

Shannon glared. The male half of the human race was so arrogant, she didn't know why women bothered with them. "That's fine, because I *also* didn't ask you for an affair. Have you forgotten I was leaving when you stopped me? Besides, it was just a kiss."

"I'm not so sure." Alex let out a low curse. "This isn't going to work. I can't let Jeremy start hoping for something that isn't going to happen."

"What isn't going to work? We're agreed we aren't getting married, and we aren't having an affair. So I wouldn't worry about Jeremy getting his hopes up about anything."

"You heard him that first night." He gave her a moody look. *"If Shannon was my new mommy, we could eat pizza whenever we wanted."*

Shannon sighed. Even *she* knew children said things they didn't understand. "That was just wishful thinking. It surprised me, but he would have said the same thing to a ninety-five-year-old grandmother who suggested pizza for dinner."

A faint smile pulled at Alex's mouth. "Ninety-five?"

"Yes. You don't actually think Jeremy knows why people get married, do you? He's too young for that."

"I should hope he doesn't," Alex said fervently. He had a sudden vision of trying to explain the birds and bees to Jeremy in a few years. It was enough to turn him gray. With his luck, his precocious little boy would start noticing girls by the time he was five.

Shannon chuckled and he looked at her. "What's so funny?"

"You look as if you're contemplating a snake-infested swamp."

"Worse, I was imagining having to explain sex to my son. It's pure luck that I'm not explaining it right now. The modified version, of course."

"Of course." She laughed harder, and after a moment he grinned, as well. There was nothing coy or shy about Shannon and it was surprisingly refreshing.

"Hey, someday you'll be in my shoes and it won't seem so funny."

"Maybe, but it's further away in my future."

"Don't you want kids?"

Her smile faltered. "One day. Maybe." She began working on the train again and he sat next to her, fitting pieces together, as well. The town took shape, along with a small forest of trees and a mountain with a tunnel.

He sighed. "You were supposed to take this back. And here I am, helping put it together."

"Call it a permanent loan. I don't need two toy trains."

He opened his mouth, then closed it again, instead snapping together the last piece of track. Jeremy would love the tree and train, but he doubted his son would talk less about Shannon just because they now had their own Christmas wonderland.

There was something about Shannon that was hard to forget. The more Alex saw of her, the less he saw the breezy sophisticate from their first meeting. He wasn't sure if that was good or bad, because the woman beneath the surface was intelligent, charming...and ever so appealing.

It was baffling, but he just plain *liked* Shannon. She was far too emotional, something he'd always avoided in both male and female friends. And he would have expected her to act like a spoiled princess given her family's wealth, but she was down-to-earth and generous to a fault. It made him uncomfortable in ways he hadn't expected, raising questions about the way he'd lived, the way he'd denied the deeper workings of his own soul.

The train's power cords were hidden from view and Shannon flipped a switch on the control board. The lights of the Victorian town twinkled merrily beneath the tree.

"How's that?" she asked.

"It's great. You have a gift for this sort of thing."

She had a gift for handling public relations problems, not decorating or cooking. But she could write a check and wield a credit card with the best homemaker on the planet.

"My sister is responsible," she admitted. "Miranda is a professional decorator, and she had most of this stuff in stock already. Anything you want, she can take care of."

"Can she take care of my big mouth?" Alex rubbed the back of his neck. "Please believe me, I never meant to hurt your feelings yesterday. The truth is, I was jealous. Jeremy is the most important thing in the world to me, yet you've been able to reach him, when I can't."

The pain in Alex's face turned Shannon's stomach into mush. "You mustn't worry, he adores you," she whispered.

His mouth lifted in a brief smile. "I appreciate that, but I still can't reach him. Why, Shannon? Why can't I get through to my own son?"

She thought about her day with Jeremy, and the quick,

almost guilty look he'd given his father when he had said
he couldn't remember his mother's face.

"Maybe he's trying to protect you," she said gently.

"Protect *me?* What are you talking about?"

Shannon let out a breath and wondered if she was
mistaken. Her instincts told her she was right, but her instincts might be wrong. Still...

"The thing is...I don't see any pictures or keepsakes of
your wife around, and you seem reluctant to talk about her
in front of Jeremy. Maybe he's decided it hurts you too
much, and he's trying not to upset you." She lifted her shoulders in a shrug. "Problem is, those feelings don't go away."

"He's a child. I'm supposed to take care of him."

"Yes, but when someone dies, people say odd things.
Things like 'smile.' 'Don't be so sad.' 'Be strong for your
family. For your mommy. For your daddy.'"

"Damn." Alex rubbed his face, his mind working furiously.

Could that be it?

Jeremy thinking he had to grieve in silence...the way
Shannon had grieved? He gazed at her and wondered what
other secrets were hidden behind her green eyes and bright
smiles.

"Somebody said that to you, didn't they?" he murmured.

She shrugged noncommittally. "Isn't it strange that
people tell you not to be sad when you've lost someone?
Why shouldn't you be sad when that happens?"

A long sigh came from Alex's diaphragm.

Shannon scared the hell out of him, but he was also

starting to understand how seductive powerful emotions could be. Time after time, his parents had torn each other to pieces. They should have called it quits after their first knock-down-drag-out fight, but neither one of them had been able to leave, not for fourteen years.

And he'd bet that a man, once hooked, wouldn't be able to leave Shannon any longer than it took to turn off the lights and pull her close.

"What are you thinking?" she whispered, and Alex fought the appeal of her sweet concern.

He inhaled sharply…a mistake.

His senses were filled with the subtle perfume of her skin, a scent that teased and tempted. He'd prided himself on his control, determined to be different from his parents, but now that control was vanishing.

Alex closed his eyes and tried to summon Kim's image, but all that came was a twinge of guilt and the warmth of a cherished memory.

No. He clenched his fists in denial. He didn't relish the role of grieving widower, but Kim had deserved better than a husband who spent most of his nights in a foreign clime. At the very least she deserved a man who grieved for her properly.

"Shannon…we changed the subject, but nothing has actually changed," he forced himself to say. "Seeing you isn't good for me. Truly, it's my problem. You're terrific, but I don't want to be involved with anyone. Jeremy has to come first."

Shannon looked down, her heart aching for a thousand

different reasons. She'd been drawn to Alex from the beginning, and it hurt to have him push her away. But some
things were more important than her feelings.

"I agree that Jeremy comes first," she said quietly. "But
you said yourself that I've been able to reach him. Are you
willing to throw that away? We can make it clear that we're
just friends. And we can make sure it stays that way when
we're alone," she added.

Alex was silent for so long she wondered if he'd heard,
or was thinking some dark thoughts of his own. Then his
eyebrows lifted. "Friends? After what just happened?"

"Men and women can be friends without sex and
romance coming into it," she said, exasperated. She had
good male friends. And while she'd never tried to be friends
with a man she found as attractive as Alex, it had to be
possible. Her brother, Dylan, had been buddies with Kate
Doug-las since they were kids before he'd finally woken up
and married her.

Swell.

Shannon shook her head in disgust.

Dylan and Kate were *not* a good example. But she was
still certain it could be done.

"We'll just have to work at it," she said.

"All right," Alex agreed slowly, though he didn't seem
a hundred-percent convinced.

"Good. I'm still off work, so if you need someone to sit
with Jeremy, I'm available."

"That would be great."

She stuck her hand out and they shook, a silly formality

that should have made her laugh. But it was hard to laugh around the lump in her throat, or the tears trying to find their way to the surface once again.

"How's that, Jeremy?"

Jeremy solemnly regarded the cup of flour Shannon held up. "It's s'posed to be at the line."

"Oh. Right." She scooped some flour from the measuring cup and shook it a little. "Is that better?"

"Okay."

She dumped the flour into the bowl with the other dry ingredients and gave the mixture a dubious look. The cookbook she'd bought claimed this was a foolproof recipe for gingerbread cookies, but she had her doubts. Nobody had Shannon-O'Rourke-proofed a recipe yet.

At least her agreement to be "just friends" with Alex meant she didn't have to worry about him discovering she was the domestic equivalent of a shipwreck. On the other hand, she still hadn't rushed to tell him the truth, either, particularly when he'd asked if she'd make cookies with Jeremy.

The words had stuck in her throat.

Instead of saying, "Sorry, but I couldn't bake a cookie to save my life," she'd agreed to his request. Worst of all, she and Jeremy were making those cookies in the McKenzie kitchen, rather than her house, so anything she broke, spindled or mutilated would belong to Alex. Fortunately, he was upstairs, looking for something, instead of sitting in the kitchen watching her make a fool of herself. But sooner or later he'd come down and see her mess up the place.

At least Jeremy looked content. He had smudges of flour on his cheeks and a smile on his mouth; it was worth a little humiliation if it made him happy. And he was so smart. He could already read words like *flour* and *sugar* and *ginger,* and he understood measurements.

He was *also* smart enough to understand the difference between really being sick, and pretending because he didn't like the changes in his life.

"Jeremy, have you ever heard the story about the boy who cried wolf?" she asked casually.

He shook his head. "Uh-uh."

"It's about a little boy who was given the job of watching the sheep for his village. A village is a small town," she explained. "It was an important job, making sure a wolf didn't come and scare the animals."

"What was the boy's name?"

Shannon blinked and thought furiously. She didn't know the story that well, just the highlights and the message behind it. "I think...I think his name was...Bob." She cringed the moment the name came from her mouth, but she was new to this storytelling thing.

"Bob?"

"Y-yes. Bobby. Bobby liked watching the sheep, but sometimes it was boring, and he wanted to get the villagers' attention. So he'd cry 'Wolf!' and everyone would drop what they were doing and come to help chase it away. But when they got there, he'd laugh because they were out of breath and worried, and *he* knew it was just a joke."

Jeremy darted a look at her. "That wasn't nice."

"You're right, it wasn't nice. Unfortunately, he kept doing it and the villagers stopped believing him. Then one day a wolf *did* come."

"What did he do?"

She swallowed, suddenly unsure of herself. A sheep-eating wolf was a grim tale for a four year old; it might have been better if she'd asked Alex before starting the story.

"Uh...Bobby called, but no one came from the village."

This time Jeremy didn't even look at her; he just nodded.

"Do you understand why it was so important for Bobby to tell the truth?" she asked, brushing some of the flour from his cheek. "It's like when you say you're sick, except you really just want to see your daddy. After a while nobody knows if anything is really wrong."

Jeremy's small lower lip pouted out, then a huge sigh rose from him. "But I don't like day-care." He planted his elbows on the table and looked angry. "Why did Mommy have to go away?"

Her chest tightened. He'd gone right to the tough question, the question she'd asked so many times about her own father.

"I don't know...but I know that she didn't want to leave you." Shannon pushed the bowl of flour and other ingredients to one side and sat next to him. Some things were more important than cookies. "Tell me about your mommy."

Standing outside the kitchen, Alex fought a thousand different emotions as he listened to Shannon. Pain at the emptiness Kim's death had left, love for the woman who'd been his wife...anger at life's injustices.

And hope, hearing Shannon encourage Jeremy to talk.

Soon his son was pouring out stories about Mommy taking him to the pond to sail paper boats, about cookies and bedtime stories, and the songs she used to sing. Things Alex had thought Jeremy was too young to remember, but which had actually been carefully guarded in his heart.

Alex looked down at the picture he'd unearthed from storage in the attic, one of the rare photos taken of him, Kim and Jeremy as a family. And beneath it was another of Kim with her swollen tummy, proud and happy, just days before giving birth to a healthy baby boy.

He had to wonder if he'd hidden the pictures away to protect himself, when he'd believed he was doing the right thing for Jeremy. How long could you deny feelings you simply didn't want to accept?

"I bet it was funny when your mother dressed up like that," Shannon said in the other room.

Alex's eyes widened as Jeremy giggled. "Mommy drew whiskers on her face and wiggled her nose. Just like a kitty."

Halloween.

Kim had been terribly sick by then, but she'd made them laugh when she'd donned cat's ears and painted her cheeks. She'd been determined to make it through the holidays, to spend that special time with her "men." How could he have forgotten those moments when she'd pushed the dread away and let them be a family?

Fighting the tightness in his throat, Alex stepped into the kitchen and looked at Jeremy, smiling and happy, the shadows chased from his eyes as he talked about the things that he'd loved about his mommy.

Gratitude filled Alex as he turned his gaze to Shannon. He felt the inevitable throb of desire as well, but he didn't mind it as much as usual. He'd never believed in divine intervention, yet Shannon's fortuitous entry into their lives was enough to make him wonder about the possibility.

"Jeremy, I thought you'd like to have some pictures of your mother," he said, determined to continue the good his beautiful neighbor had started. "You're in this one." He sat at the table and showed his son the one of a very pregnant Kim.

"That's not me, that's just Mommy," Jeremy denied, but he gazed at the photo with growing delight.

"Nope." Alex pointed to the bulge in Kim's tummy. "That's you, a few days before you were born. And you're the reason she's smiling. You made your mommy so very happy."

He glanced at Shannon over his son's head and wished he could tell her how he felt, but gratitude was mixed with other feelings, less easy to understand.

She challenged him.

Somehow he knew it was because of Shannon that he'd listened to his distraught student, instead of avoiding the tears in her reddened eyes, the way he always avoided emotional scenes. It wasn't that he didn't care about people, but it was easier to give money than get involved.

Shannon had gotten involved with his son because she knew what it was like to lose a parent and was willing to open that old hurt to help a child she barely knew.

"How about pizza for dinner?" he asked, his gaze still fixed on Shannon. "We'll go over to that new Italian place that everyone says is so good."

"Yummy," Jeremy exclaimed.

"Shannon?" Alex prompted when she didn't say anything.

She nudged the bowl on the table. "What about the cookies?"

"Finish them tomorrow. Unless you're tired of us and want some time off."

"If I get tired of you, you'll know it," she said, giving him one of her exasperated looks.

"Let's go then." It seemed only natural to put out his hand and she took it with a questioning smile. When she stood, he was surprised to see the top of her head only came to his shoulder. He kept thinking of Shannon as tall, but it was an illusion of her leggy beauty and vibrant nature.

They were friends, Alex reminded himself. Her height— or lack of it—wasn't something he should be thinking about.

"You put on your coats. I'll start the Jeep and get the heat going," he said quickly.

"All right."

Outside, he saw that clouds had rolled across the Puget Sound area. A misting rain drizzled through the twilight, so fine it was like fog shrouding the landscape. The windows clouded up the moment he got inside the Jeep, and it took several minutes before warm air began coming through the vents.

"I don't know about this. Maybe you'd prefer staying in," he said when he'd returned inside his condo. "It's a miserable night."

Shannon smiled. "I don't mind, if you don't. This is Christmas weather."

His eyebrows shot upward. "Snow is Christmas weather. This is just cold and wet."

"Give it a chance. We don't get many white Christmases in this part of the country, but there's the smell of wood smoke and fresh-washed evergreen in the air, and all those strings of lights sparkle through the rain like tiny jewels."

Alex shook his head, yet when they walked outside to the waiting Jeep, he realized that the scent of wood smoke and evergreens did fill the air, and the early twilight was indeed brightened by the Christmas lights strung on trees and bushes and houses. He'd deliberately chosen a place that was different than their old home in Minnesota, but while they probably wouldn't have snow for Christmas, they'd have stands of pine and cedar keeping the forest green.

And they'd have Shannon.

The errant thought shook him. Desire was one thing, but he didn't want to need anyone...the kind of needing that tied your heart in knots and made good-byes so terrible.

"You're quiet all of a sudden," Shannon commented as he pulled out of the driveway. "Is something wrong?"

Alex summoned a smile. Shannon was a nice woman, and she was doing a lot for his son, but that didn't mean he needed her. He had to get a grip.

"Nothing's wrong. I just hadn't realized we wouldn't have a white Christmas."

"Well, we *might* get some early snow, but we usually don't before January. Even then it's iffy, and doesn't stay long on the ground unless an arctic storm comes down from Canada."

Using the discipline he'd honed over the years, Alex forced his brain into less disturbing directions.

Snow was a perfect distraction.

He mentally noted where he'd stored the snow shovel, and calculated how long it would take to shovel the walks and their two driveways. He'd shovel snow for any neighbor, so it wasn't significant that he planned to deal with Shannon's snow.

They were friends, weren't they?

Chapter Seven

Alex doggedly read the term papers piled on his desk and tried to ignore the cheerful sounds rising from the first floor of the condominium.

Jeremy hadn't forgotten about the half-finished cookies, and at 5:00 a.m. his son had been standing by his bed, asking if they could call Shannon to come and help finish making the "ginger people."

"You mean gingerbread men," he'd said groggily.

"Shannon says they're ginger people."

"Did she say gingerbread people?" Alex was never at his best in the morning, and getting into a semantics discussion with a four year old before the crack of dawn hadn't been the brightest idea in the world.

"Shannon says ginger people."

Of course. Whatever Shannon said was the gospel truth

as far as Jeremy was concerned. It didn't matter, anyway. In the end they were just cookies.

"Okay," he'd muttered.

"Goody." His son had picked up the phone receiver and pushed it into Alex's hand. "Call now, Daddy."

Oh, God.

Why couldn't children sleep when other people were sleeping?

"Son, I didn't mean it was okay to call. I meant okay, they're ginger people."

"But, *Daddy*—"

"You don't want to wake Shannon up, do you? She's on vacation. Besides, you don't call friends this early in the morning."

Jeremy had reluctantly agreed, then he'd crawled into bed with him and talked for three straight hours, with liberal references to their neighbor and the things she'd done and said when they were together.

So much for his *daddy* sleeping late. Alex had finally given up and called Shannon at a more reasonable hour about the cookies. She'd come over looking fresh and wide-awake, while he felt like Grumpy and Sleepy from the Seven Dwarves rolled into one.

Conceding defeat, Alex abandoned the term papers and walked downstairs. His son and his neighbor were lying on their backs by the Christmas tree, holding kaleidoscopes in front of their eyes as cheerful Christmas carols played in the background. He smiled at the scene.

Shannon's auburn hair tumbled about her head and her

knees swayed in time with the music. Her feet were bare, toenails painted pink. Snug jeans that showcased her legs were topped by a T-shirt with the words, Dear Santa, Just bring the five gold rings, printed on it. She looked like an unruly teenager, though he knew she must be in her late twenties.

Next to her was Jeremy, singing "Jingle Bells" off-key. Mr. Tibbles wasn't anywhere in sight.

"Hey, I thought you were baking cookies," Alex said, his grin broadening.

"The dough has to chill before we roll it out," Shannon explained without looking up. She spun the dial on the end of the kaleidoscope and whistled a few notes in tune to the stereo. "I thought you were grading term papers."

"I'm taking a break."

"You ready for the final exams?"

"Yes. And I've been trying to work out a time for a makeup session, if the student has a good excuse."

Shannon sat up. "Really? I never heard of a professor willing to have a makeup session."

"Yeah? You couldn't charm them into it?" His comment felt dangerously like flirting, but it was hard to believe Shannon O'Rourke failing at anything she might go after.

"I never needed a makeup test. I was the perfect student."

"How perfect? No-skinny-dipping-in-Lake-Washington-during-Christmas-break perfect? Or grade-and-attendance perfect? There are different levels of perfect, you know. Some students are more perfect than others."

She laughed. "Nobody in their right mind skinny-dips

in Lake Washington in December. Of course, one of my brothers did it, but he was crazy."

"What's 'kinny-dipping?" Jeremy asked.

Alex stifled a groan. He had a big mouth, and he obviously didn't know how to guard what he said around his own son. Jeremy was smart and precocious and he understood things far too well for comfort.

"Skinny-dipping is going swimming without your bathing suit," Shannon explained. "It sounds like more fun than it really is, especially when it's cold."

"Okay." Jeremy rolled over onto his stomach and started the toy train chugging around the tracks.

Alex sighed. Why was it so easy when Shannon explained something like that, and so difficult when he tried? Their gazes met and another grin curved his mouth at the merry humor in her eyes. In another life he would have thought it was funny as well, watching a parent squirm over the innocent things a child asked...and the loaded answers that followed.

He wanted to promise retribution, because it was guaranteed that Shannon O'Rourke's children would be a wild handful. But he bit his tongue, remembering her reaction the last time he'd said something about her having kids—a faltering smile and a flicker of unhappiness. He didn't want to spoil the moment.

"I need some coffee," he said, a yawn splitting his mouth. "How about you?"

"Sure."

In the kitchen Shannon sat and watched as Alex filled

the coffeemaker with water. His hair was rumpled and his eyes sleepy. She didn't doubt that if it wasn't for Jeremy and term papers to grade, he'd still have his face stuffed in a pillow; he definitely wasn't a morning person.

Lord, she'd been up since before six, writing memos, responding to e-mails from the office…and sending a message to Kane that she wouldn't be at work for another week or two. He'd wonder about it, particularly since she'd just begged him to end her forced vacation, but it didn't matter. She was having too much fun.

Fun?

Shannon smothered a chuckle. Playing with Jeremy and trying to figure out how to bake cookies weren't her usual ideas of fun. Her family would die of shock if they discovered how she'd been spending her days. Her reputation as a disaster in the kitchen had reached epic proportions, a reputation that had spread to the office after she'd twice set fire to the break-room microwave.

"You have that devilish twinkle in your eyes. Promise you aren't laughing at me," Alex said, plunking two steaming mugs of coffee on the table. He dropped into a chair with a groan.

"Why would I laugh?"

"I open my mouth in front of my son and dumb things come out. Like mentioning skinny-dipping." Beard stubble rasped beneath his fingers as he rubbed his jaw and yawned again.

"Didn't you get any sleep last night?"

"Not enough. Jeremy decided that 5:00 a.m. was the

perfect time to start making gingerbread men. Only he insists they're called ginger people, because that's what you call them."

Shannon dangled the cookie cutters she'd bought in front of Alex. "There are two sexes. I don't want to be exclusive. Besides, I have a politically correct cookbook that calls them ginger people."

He lifted one eyelid and glared at her. "Next time, I'm teaching him how to dial the phone so he can wake *you* up in the middle of the night."

"Five isn't the middle of the night."

"I knew it. You're one of *those* people, aren't you?"

"If you mean a morning person, the answer is yes."

"I mean one of those people who wakes up early and thinks it's the best time of the day." He made a disgusted sound and gulped his coffee, yelping a second later, "That's hot!"

Shannon couldn't help herself, she dissolved into laughter. "You just made it, what would you think it is?"

Alex leaned back in his chair, regarding her. "Aren't you going to mother me? Where's the usual feminine sympathy like running to get an ice cube for my burned tongue?"

"Do you want to be mothered?"

"No."

"Then I'm not going to do that."

An odd gleam entered his eyes. "I think I'm going to like being friends with you, Shannon."

That was a switch. Alex had only agreed to a friendship for Jeremy's sake. Shannon swallowed a stab of regret and told herself to be grateful he'd agreed to anything. He was proof that her luck in the romance department hadn't changed.

She sipped her coffee and thought about the men she'd dated over the years. Some had hoped to get close to her wealthy brother through her. Others had been allergic to marriage or, on the flip side, had secretly wanted a perfect homemaker for a wife. Few of those had been as callous as her college love, who'd decided he couldn't handle her lack of homemaking skills and made sure their mutual friends knew exactly why they'd broken up.

She'd forced herself to joke about the split, but she'd died inside each time she laughed about the end of her first love.

"Are you asleep, too?"

Startled, Shannon lifted her head. Alex had leaned forward and seemed wider awake now that he'd burned his tongue and gotten more caffeine into his system.

"No, not asleep. But your coffee could put hair on my chest."

"Too strong for you?"

Her pulse jumped, but it had nothing to do with coffee, just the tug of her heart. If she wasn't careful, she could risk having it broken again, and she wasn't certain how many times a broken heart could heal.

"It's a little strong."

"I assumed morning people lived on coffee."

"Not me, but I can't speak for all morning people."

Shannon traced a circle on the table and tried to regain the peace she'd felt lying next to Jeremy, rediscovering the beauty of light and color captured in a kaleidoscope. How long had it been since she'd felt at peace? Children seemed to have a marvelous gift of simplicity, a way of cutting through the chaos of the world.

"Do you have something against being mothered?" she asked idly. She'd been thinking about inviting Alex and Jeremy to her family's Christmas celebration, and Pegeen O'Rourke mothered anyone who would let her.

"I'm an adult, I don't need mothering."

"Don't tell my mom that. I think she secretly wishes we'd never grown up, though she probably doesn't mind as much now that she has grandchildren to spoil."

"She sounds nice."

"Thanks. She is." Shannon didn't ask about Alex's mother, remembering how he'd described his childhood— *a marital war zone followed by divorced-parent hell.* Given his experience, he must have loved his wife beyond belief to have risked getting married.

Sorrow crowded Shannon's throat—sorrow for what Alex had lost, and what she might never have.

"I think that cookie dough must be cold enough," she said huskily. "And you have term papers to grade."

"Cracking the proverbial whip, huh?"

"Sure, that's what friends do."

Alex smiled and rose. "About the mothering," he said, "don't get the wrong idea. I've just had my fill of women rushing in and trying to take Kim's place."

"They probably mean well."

"Maybe. But I like your style better."

He sauntered out and Shannon shook her head. He liked

her style. What did that mean? Maybe it didn't mean anything. Men thought they were direct and to the point, but they were beyond confusing.

"Jeremy?" she called. "How about making those ginger people now?"

Alex studied the term paper in front of him. He was trying to figure out a reason not to flunk the author, when the smell of something burning crept into his consciousness.

At almost the same moment the smoke alarm screeched and he jumped to his feet.

"Shannon?"

He raced downstairs, grabbing a fire extinguisher on the way. Smoke filled the kitchen, with the thickest billows rising from the stove and sink.

"It's…" Shannon coughed. "Everything is under control. Yeow!" She dumped a blackened cookie sheet into the sink and began flapping a dish towel.

As a precaution, Alex sprayed the smoking mess with the fire extinguisher, then grabbed Shannon and Jeremy and shoved them out the back door.

"Stay there," he ordered.

Inside, he opened windows, started the exhaust fans blowing and turned off the oven. When he was certain nothing was actually on fire, he put a cap over the smoke alarm to silence it. The sound of Christmas music replaced the shrill screech.

"It's all right now," he said, stepping into the backyard again.

Shannon had her arms wrapped around Jeremy, keeping him warm. She was shaking from the cold and he swore beneath his breath, realizing he'd overreacted when he'd shoved them outside. But when it was his family involved, he couldn't take any chances.

"Come back in, the smoke is nearly gone." Alex put out his hand and she released Jeremy.

"Go inside where it's warm," she said, her voice shaking.

Jeremy skipped through the door, but Shannon remained on the garden bench.

"Shannon?"

"I think I'll go home," she whispered.

He frowned. "Why?"

"It's better if I do." She blinked and a tear dripped down her cheek.

Damn. He wasn't good at this sort of thing, especially when he couldn't see any reason for her to be so upset. So some cookies got burned, it wasn't a disaster. On the other hand, he had a strange feeling that if he let Shannon leave, she wouldn't come back. And that *would* be a disaster, for reasons Alex didn't want to think about.

"Better how?"

"Just better." She swallowed hard and two more tears spilled over. "I'm sorry about the cookies. I should have told you that I can't cook, but I thought if I paid attention it would be all right."

She jumped up and rushed across the empty flower bed separating their small yards.

Oh, man. This was exactly the type of situation Alex

hated dealing with the most. And if any other woman had cried over a burned tray of cookies he would have been exasperated, but it obviously meant something significant to Shannon.

"Shannon, don't go."

"It's really...*better*."

Shannon pulled at her sliding-glass door, but the dumb thing was locked. So much for a speedy exit. She spun around, not wanting to see Alex's face and the disappointment that must be there, but not having a choice.

"Hey, it's all right." He put his arms around her, warmth radiating from his body.

It was nice.

Strength and heat and comfort. She'd ached after their brief kiss, ached for a deeper touch, and the kind of tender holding that only came in her dreams. She'd wondered if Alex could be the man in those dreams, but it was useless to think that way. He'd pushed her away from the moment they met; the barriers around his heart were higher than the castle walls in any fairy tale.

"It's not okay." She sniffed, the scent of burned gingerbread mixed with his masculine scent. "You have no idea. Maybe it doesn't matter to you because you don't want me, but it matters."

"God, Shannon, it isn't you I don't want."

She knew that tone. Or she thought she did. He was trying to be gentle and not hurt her feelings.

"It's all right. Don't worry about it. I'm not your problem," she said tiredly. In an hour she'd manage to get some perspective, but right now she felt as if she'd crashed into a brick wall. She hated failing at anything.

Alex leaned into her. "You aren't a problem at all," he breathed in her ear.

She knew that tone, too.

The husky murmur.

The suggestion of awareness.

A swollen heat burned against her abdomen and she swallowed. "Alex, this isn't—"

His mouth smothered her protest. She resisted for a split second, knowing he'd regret touching her the minute he came to his senses. But when his strong hands closed over her breasts, her own senses scattered.

His touch wasn't the least bit hesitant, and the bold, kneading strength of his fingers sent streamers of longing through more than her body. She felt him to her soul.

Knowing that Alex didn't feel so strongly about her cooled her response. Then his knee pressed between her legs and she lost touch with reality.

Her life had been spinning nowhere, but with Alex holding her, she had an anchor. Yet it was curious that an anchor would make her head whirl and her blood bubble like champagne.

Their tongues met, velvet on velvet, framed by the hard lines of his mouth.

The only other time she could remember a kiss being so good was when he'd held her before, that night she'd brought the tree and toy train.

Mmm…

Beneath Alex's sweatshirt his muscles were hard and she explored the contours of a man who'd worked not only with his mind, but his body. She didn't feel cold, though her thin shirt and jeans were hardly protection against the bitter chill that had descended over Puget Sound.

Pleasure shimmered in wave after wave as Alex began kissing his way down the curve of her neck. Then suddenly, a loud, raucous sound pierced the air.

"What?"

Alex jerked away, looking horrified, and Shannon dropped her hands to her side.

Think fast, she ordered her frozen brain, but it wasn't cooperating.

"Merrooow."

Thank God.

She edged around Alex's stiff figure and looked for the source of distress. A kitten, all ears and eyes, stuck its head from under a bush and cried again.

"You poor thing," Shannon said, kneeling and holding out her hand. "Come here."

The kitten had obviously been fending for itself for a long time, because it hesitated, looking suspicious.

"It's all right, little one, I won't hurt you."

Alex stared at the ragged feline and wondered how it could resist that coaxing voice.

Damnation. How could he have kissed Shannon again?

He couldn't even blame her. She'd done everything but climb the wall trying to get away from him.

The cat put a hesitant foot on the flagstone patio, ready

to bolt backward if the gentle voice turned out to have a mean hand attached to it.

"Come here, baby. No one is going to hurt you."

"Meooooow."

"Yes, I know. It's all right now." She cuddled the feline against her breasts and the air hissed from Alex's chest. He ached, but the physical pain was less intense than the torment in his mind.

Shannon O'Rourke had a filthy kitten tucked lovingly to her body, and he couldn't remember the last time he'd seen something so beautiful. Panic screamed through him, a warning of everything he didn't want to feel again.

"Shannon, we have to talk about what happened."

She glanced at him...and rolled her eyes. "For goodness sake, Alex, don't go melodramatic. I was upset and you gave me a friendly kiss. I'm surprised you didn't laugh your head off."

"About what?"

"What do you think? Remember the smoke alarm going off? Black smoke filling the air? I must have looked ridiculous."

The cookies.

Right.

His brain wasn't working correctly, but it was a relief to know Shannon hadn't taken him seriously. In fact, she'd been so upset, she probably hadn't noticed the more than friendly way he'd groped her body.

"I'm not being melodramatic, I was just wondering what you plan to do with that cat."

"Take it into your house, of course."

His eyes narrowed. "If you're thinking about giving it to Jeremy, the answer is no."

"I'm planning to adopt him myself. But I don't have a drop of milk in my house, so you're going to have to cough up the white stuff."

She strolled past him as if the last fifteen minutes had never occurred, and Alex shook his head. He'd missed something significant, but since he didn't have a clue what that significant something might be, he focused on a real problem.

"Wait, Shannon. Jeremy is going to see that cat and want it."

"You fuss too much. I'll explain everything to him," she said over her shoulder.

"Men don't 'fuss.'"

"Yeah, right."

She disappeared inside his house and he remained where he stood, amazed at the way the tables had been turned on him again. For a man who prided himself on being in control, he was losing it faster than a barrel sailing over Niagara Falls.

"Cats usually only clean themselves after they've eaten," Shannon told Jeremy as he sat in her arms, watching the tired kitten lick his oversize feet. "That's why he's so dirty. He hasn't eaten regularly for a while."

"Is he gonna be okay?"

"I think so. I'll take him to see my brother tomorrow.

Connor is a cat doctor, and he'll make sure nothing is wrong."

"He looks scared."

"I know. He's been alone and trying to take care of himself for a while. I'm sure he wants to be loved, but it will take time for him to feel safe again."

Jeremy released a sigh and snuggled closer. "What's his name?"

She kissed his cheek; names seemed to be important to him. "Cats reveal their names when they're comfortable with you. He'll tell me when he's ready."

"*Shannon,* that's too fanciful," Alex warned.

She lifted her chin and gave him a narrow look.

Children needed a little fancy in their lives, and Jeremy had already seen too much reality. Besides, as far as she was concerned, Alex was skating on very thin ice. His relief at the way she'd dismissed their kiss had been practically insulting—particularly when she was certain that the kiss had shaken him as much as it had shaken her.

"You don't know much about cats," she retorted, "if you think that's fanciful."

"Oh?" He didn't say anything more, just crossed his arms over his chest and reminded her with his silence that he'd gone out in the rain and purchased the supplies she needed for a feline housemate.

Well, maybe the ice beneath his feet wasn't as thin as she'd thought.

The need to be fair did battle with her feminine pique, and fairness won. Alex *had* to be careful. He had Jeremy to think about, and she was never going to be nominated mother of the year.

The faint scent of smoke lingered in the house, and she wrinkled her nose. "I'm sorry about the cookies," she said to Jeremy. "I'm not very good at cooking."

He twisted and put his arms around her neck. "That's okay, Shannon. I don't care."

She blinked, still fighting those annoying tears. "I know a great bakery. They'd probably let us come and watch them bake a gingerbread house. We'll ask your daddy if it's all right."

"Can we go, Daddy?" Jeremy asked eagerly. "You can come, too."

It sounded like a careless afterthought and Shannon smothered a laugh. Yet she sobered quickly, remembering the pain Alex had expressed about Jeremy wanting to spend time with her rather than him. He worried about his son, like any good father. But while Jeremy was looking for a way out of the sadness, his daddy seemed determined to look backward, instead of reaching for the future.

Like the kitten, Alex probably wanted to be loved…he just didn't trust that it wouldn't end up hurting him.

She looked again at Alex's handsome features and the shadows that lingered in his eyes. He needed laughter. He needed to learn how to play and enjoy life.

He needed to stop being stuck in the past.

And so did she.

Chapter Eight

"**D**own you go, son," Alex said as Shannon opened the door of the bakery on Saturday. He lifted Jeremy from his shoulders and then held his hand as they stepped into the crisp outside air.

The scents of spice and vanilla and chocolate clung to their clothing and Shannon smiled.

It wasn't the New Year yet, but she'd made a resolution to look to the future, instead of being afraid of what it might *not* hold. Of course, that didn't mean she shouldn't be careful about Alex. He'd made it abundantly clear that he didn't want a permanent relationship with any woman, so falling for him wouldn't be smart.

In the meantime, it was almost like having a family of her own, the three of them walking down the holly- and pine-decorated street. She carried a box filled with perfect gingerbread people; they would add some to the Christmas tree when they got home, and others would be eaten with milk.

Naturally Alex hadn't let her pay for them. His stubborn pride was sweetly annoying, but she could forgive him. He hadn't teased her once about the burned cookies, or complained about the odor of smoke in his house.

"Ho, ho, ho," cried a sidewalk Santa, ringing his bell. "Merry Christmas."

Shannon reached into her purse and withdrew several bills and a handful of change to throw into his kettle.

"Why'd you do that, Shannon?" Jeremy asked

"Santa is trying to help people," she explained.

"Daddy doesn't believe in Santa."

She gave Alex a stern look. The man needed a kick in his scrumptious rear end.

He cleared his throat. "Actually, I said that Santa is more like a state of mind than someone real."

"Pop psychology rears its head again."

They stopped and Jeremy pressed his nose against a store window where mechanical figures simulated Santa's workshop. Santa wore striped stockings and glasses and peered intently at a half-finished fire engine.

"A little fantasy can't hurt," she said softly. "What's wrong with letting him believe?"

Alex pulled her farther from Jeremy's ears. "I can't do that, not after telling him everything would be all right when his mother got sick. It wasn't all right, and I knew it wouldn't be, but I still said it."

Shannon's heart skipped a beat. "Mom said it would be all right the day we buried my father."

"Then you know what I'm talking about. I've seen the way you miss your dad. What's all right about that?"

"You never stop missing the people you love," Shannon said, understanding better than ever before what her mother had tried to tell her. Life was a bittersweet tapestry, with sorrow and joy mixing into the pattern until they were nearly inseparable. "But Mom wasn't saying we'd forget Dad. She meant that we would go on and that there still would be good days. And there have been, even though he's gone…and the good is better because of who he was and what he left behind."

"Jeez, Shannon. How can you open yourself up like that?" Alex sounded almost angry. "You barely know us."

"I'm doing it because I don't want Jeremy to *be* like me, keeping it all inside. And I don't think his mother would want it, either."

Alex closed his eyes, shutting out the sight of Shannon's generous face, the gentle light in her eyes as she gazed at his son. Her breezy sophistication hid a tender side she had trouble revealing. But not when it came to Jeremy.

His chest ached, only he didn't know if it came from old sorrows, or the space Shannon was forcing him to make in his heart.

When they'd first met, her volatile nature had reminded him of his mother and father, but the comparison was fading. He found himself looking forward to each day, to their conversations and even to not knowing what to expect.

There was a depth to Shannon that fascinated him…almost as much as it scared him.

Were there other choices? Other possibilities than the ones he'd chosen? Or would he just fall into the same angry hell that had destroyed his parents? He didn't believe he could ever break a marriage vow, but would he find himself stuck in the same screaming rounds of arguments and the bitter chill between those arguments?

Alex instinctively stepped backward, only to jump at the sudden blare of a car alarm.

"What the…?" He stared at the Jaguar parked at the curb. "I barely touched the damn thing."

Shannon shook her head. "I hate those things. They're so sensitive. I think just breathing sets them off."

"What happened, Daddy?" Jeremy's eyes were round and he clasped his fingers over his ears. "Make it stop."

Before Alex could answer, a man ran from a nearby jewelry shop and yelled. "What are you doing to my Jag?"

"Breathing," Alex shouted back.

Shannon burst out laughing, and he watched, loving the way she didn't care that they were attracting attention. It should have bothered him; he'd hated it when he was a kid and his parents fought in public places with everyone looking at them. But this was different.

The man bent over, anxiously checking the paint of his Jaguar, and Shannon impudently thumbed her nose at him.

Laughing now himself, Alex swung Jeremy into one arm, and put the other around Shannon.

"Is that any way for the O'Rourke Public Relations

Director to act?" He thought for a moment. "For that matter, is it any way for an O'Rourke to act?"

"I'm on vacation."

She might be on vacation, but within minutes she had the Jag's owner eating from her hand, even getting him to admit he'd been in the wrong for yelling.

In downtown Seattle, the commotion would have hardly been noticed, but in their small community, it was an event. Christmas shoppers filled with seasonal goodwill paused and chatted. A policeman stopped and asked if he was needed. Assured he wasn't, he stayed nevertheless and ate the gingerbread cookie Shannon offered him.

Something that could have turned ugly became a social event, and it was all because of Shannon. She had a gift for bringing out the best in people—a sincere concern for others, a loving spirit that accepted human foibles and graces alike.

"We need more of these," she said when everyone had gone about their business. The box of cookies dangled from one finger, empty.

"Let's go back. They're yummy," Jeremy said, munching the cookie she'd given him first.

Alex thought about the excuses he ought to make, the things he had to do, the term papers and projects still to grade.

"I think we need more, too," he agreed. "And let's get some cocoa. I'm cold."

As they retraced their steps to the bakery, it occurred to him that he was getting too involved, but it was easy to push the worry to the back of his mind.

Because for the first time in longer than Alex could remember, he was happy.

Shannon hummed to herself as she read the new cookbook by the author of the not-so-foolproof ginger people recipe.

She'd always hated cookbooks—they seemed to be a reminder of something she couldn't do. But even if she couldn't cook to save her life, it was surprisingly interesting to see what was involved.

From the corner of her eye she saw the kitten, miraculously improved in appearance, sidle into the living room. He was at that awkward growing stage—all ears and brown tiger-stripe legs.

She knew if she was patient, he would eventually work his way up the couch and into her arms. It was the same every night. He'd watch from the doorway, resistant to coaxing, but by morning he purred beneath the comforter, curled against her tummy.

Would Alex be like that someday?

Cautious, guarding his heart, before finding himself in a woman's arms and loving her completely?

Shannon closed the cookbook and clung to her newfound peace. The restlessness that had worried her family and taken its toll on her staff was nearly gone, but that didn't mean she'd stopped wanting more from her life.

Her feelings for Alex had nothing to do with his proximity or the wonderful child he'd fathered, and they weren't because of her physical attraction to him, though heaven knew that was intense. Just kissing him was more exciting than anything she'd experienced with another man. But more than that, he was smart, hardworking and adored his son. He had a good sense of humor and a core of strength and integrity that was all too rare.

It would be so easy to love Alex, to give him the part of herself that no one had ever seen. She hadn't loved that boy in college; she realized that now. Not really. Not the way a woman loves a man. Her pride had been hurt, and she'd lost her girlish dreams, but there were other dreams.

A soft, warm body wriggled along her thigh, and she glanced down to see the kitten's anxious eyes.

So needy.

So ready to bolt.

So afraid to accept that his life had changed. To believe that food and kindness weren't a deception. That he could trust again.

Oh, Alex, she breathed silently. If there was ever someone who needed to be loved by a woman, it was him. But that woman wouldn't be her. He hadn't seemed to care about her culinary disaster, but he would eventually choose someone more like his first wife, if only for Jeremy's sake. That was what they both deserved, a real homemaker, and all the stolen kisses in the world wouldn't change that.

"I wish I could stay with you all day, little one," she whispered to the kitten. "But I can't."

He blinked and stretched out one paw, touching her arm.

A small overture that tugged at her heart.

At almost the same moment, sounds outside the front

door made the feline's ears stand at attention. He darted into the kitchen when the bell rang.

It was the McKenzies. During their cookie outing the day before, they'd talked about having lunch together, though a time hadn't been discussed.

"Shannon?" Jeremy called. "Hurry."

"Coming." Shannon opened the door. "I take it you're hungry."

"More like cold." Alex shivered and stuck his hands in his pockets. "How can it feel colder here than in Minnesota?"

"It's the damp. You'll get used to it."

"If we stay."

The casual words made Shannon colder than the worst arctic storm. Swallowing, she stepped back to let them inside. "I didn't realize you were thinking about leaving."

He shrugged. "Just keeping my options open."

"Kitty, kitty," Jeremy called, looking hopefully around the room.

"He's still shy," Shannon said, trying to compose her expression. "You have to be patient." Excellent advice for herself, as well, except that men weren't cats, and they generally couldn't be won over with food and a warm place to sleep.

Alex wouldn't have had anything to do with her if it hadn't been for Jeremy. She needed to remind herself of that at frequent intervals.

"We called earlier, to see if you'd prefer having brunch, but you weren't here," he murmured, standing close to the embers of the small fire she'd built.

"I went to church."

"Oh."

His flat tone confirmed what Shannon had already guessed. She would have invited them to attend the service with her, but she figured Alex had turned his back on the church, along with so many other things.

"Um, I'll get my purse," she said quickly.

"There's no rush." He crouched by the hearth. "This feels good."

His jeans were stretched over his muscled legs and she held her breath, remembering how they'd felt, pressed against her.

Friends, she reminded herself.

Just friends.

She decided hurrying was a good idea, and she grabbed what she needed in record time. "I'm ready," she said, in case he hadn't noticed.

Standing, Alex closed the glass doors across the hearth— to prevent any sparks from the dying embers popping into the room while they were gone. His gaze went to the coat she wore, and she knew he'd expected to help her with it. The perfect gentleman. Just like her brothers, but it didn't make her knees weak to have *them* ease a coat up her arms.

"So…where do you want to eat?" he asked.

"Anywhere is fine."

Fine.

Inadvertently, Alex thought about the milk and cookies they'd eaten the evening before, made even better by laughter and talk. They'd discussed art and literature, history, travel and world affairs. Shannon was naturally curious and had asked perceptive questions about engineering and his work in less-developed countries, showing a healthy grasp of math and sciences.

His mind had shied away from thoughts that would only make him feel guilty, but the guilt was inevitable. Kim had been the dearest of women, and he'd loved her, but her interests had revolved around children and their home. Her priorities had made him comfortable; they hadn't always challenged his mind.

Shannon wasn't comfortable, he told himself firmly.

He still wanted comfortable. Things were comfortable the way they were, with just him and Jeremy.

Yeah? jeered Alex's conscience. So why are you spending so much time with Shannon?

The answer was something he didn't want to know.

"We're going, Jeremy. Where is Mr. Tibbles?" he asked.

Jeremy looked thoughtful, then he pointed to the rabbit, sitting by the Christmas tree. "Shannon says Mr. Tibbles might wanna stay home sometimes. He could stay here with kitty, and then he wouldn't be alone."

"That's a...a good idea." Startled, Alex looked from the rabbit to his son, and last to Shannon. She was watching Jeremy, nodding agreement, and he'd never felt so grateful in his life.

The hell with guilt, at least for today.

She'd performed a miracle and if they didn't have Jeremy as an audience, he'd give her another kiss. A friendly one, of course.

In fact...

"Shannon, may I see you in the other room for a moment?"

"Sure."

They walked into the kitchen, and Alex saw what he should have seen before: a room obviously not used for any serious cooking. He felt badly that he had asked her to do something she wasn't able to handle, though it had been endearing to see her so upset when she did everything *else* so well.

"Alex, is something—"

He smothered her question with his lips.

It was just a little, *friendly* kiss and he released her as fast as he'd grabbed her.

Shannon's green eyes were wide and startled. "Alex?"

"Thank you for Mr. Tibbles," he said, still exulting in the progress Jeremy had made.

"I...I didn't do anything."

"You did. I was right that first day—you have a gift with children. You're great with him."

He'd pleased her, he could tell by the way her cheeks bloomed pink. When was the last time Shannon had blushed? He'd bet it had been awhile.

"I'm going to warm up the Jeep," he said. "Be back in a few minutes."

Shannon touched her fingers to her mouth after Alex had disappeared. That kiss had been an impulse he'd probably regret, but she couldn't be sorry herself. His unstinting approval of her time with Jeremy filled an empty place in her soul.

Vacations weren't so bad, she thought.

Not if you could spend them doing something special.

A few days later, Shannon was even more convinced that vacations were a splendid invention. Instead of running her staff ragged with her favorite community projects for the past two and a half weeks, she was having fun. Going back to work would be a drag, but she'd survive. Besides, Kane was exceptionally generous with time off.

Shannon grinned.

If her brother had his druthers, the family would be living a life of perfect ease and luxury. He'd always wanted to give them far more than they wanted to take.

Still, as much fun as it was taking care of Jeremy, she *would* have to go back to work, and he'd have to go to day-care again. It might have been better if she and Alex had insisted he return once his cold was better, but they hadn't.

They?

Hmmm. *They* felt like a team, but Shannon wasn't good at deceiving herself. Alex was Jeremy's father; she was just the neighbor.

Torrents of rain splattered the window and Shannon frowned, uneasiness replacing her contentment. The rain had begun Sunday night and hadn't stopped since. The ground was already saturated with water and flooding was predicted in the lowland areas and along the White River.

It was silly, yet the feeling that something was wrong grew over the next hour. She checked on Jeremy several times, but nothing was amiss.

Was it Alex?

She wished he was safely home, but he was in the middle of giving his last exam, with the afternoon session yet to come. Anyway, he was driving the Jeep, and it was designed for rugged driving. She recalled some of the stories he'd told her about building dams and roads in parts of the world where rain and mud were a daily part of life. The simple stories had revealed a man who worked hard and well; Alex could handle anything Mother Nature threw at him.

But she still felt uneasy. She often got those sensations at work, the prickling at the back of her neck when something wasn't quite right. The public relations staff claimed it made them nervous the way her instincts worked, but they'd learned to pay attention.

Shannon finally dialed her deputy, waiting impatiently while the phone rang several times.

"O'Rourke Enterprises." Chris's normally measured tone sounded slightly frantic.

"Chris, it's Shannon."

"Where have you been?" he demanded. "I've been calling and calling."

She winced, realizing she'd left her cell phone at her condo. "I'm at a friend's house. What's wrong?"

"The factory near Bolton is flooding and we have two employees missing. Please come, Shannon. I don't want to be the one to tell their wives."

She closed her eyes and said a silent prayer for the missing men. "I'll be there as soon as possible. Do you know if any of the roads between here and Seattle are closed?"

"No. I checked with the roads department in case you were already on the way and had got stuck."

"All right. I'm babysitting a friend's little boy, so I'll have to bring him with me. Have someone meet us in the garage and make sure they understand Jeremy isn't to be left alone for a minute. Tell them if he gets scared about anything, they'll answer to me."

She issued several additional orders then put the phone down, thinking carefully. She'd dealt with numerous crises since becoming her brother's public relations director, but she'd never had a child to worry about at the same time. No matter what else happened, Jeremy mustn't get frightened.

"Jeremy?" she said, going into the den where he was watching a Christmas video.

He gave her an angelic smile.

"I hope you don't mind, but I have something to do at my office. We need to drive into Seattle." Luckily, Alex had insisted they put a spare booster seat in her Mercedes in case it was needed.

"Can we have pizza?" he asked hopefully.

Pizza seemed to be the magic cure-all, and despite her concern for the missing employees, Shannon smiled. "Sure, we can have pizza. Go get your coat."

Jeremy sang "Jingle Bells" all the way, and by the time she pulled into her reserved parking spot by the executive elevator, she was certain that "Jingle Bells" had been written by a sadist.

Three members of her staff were waiting, including her deputy, and he rushed over with a relieved smile on his face. "It's all right," he whispered the minute the driver's door opened. "The men have been found. Only minor injuries."

Most of Shannon's tension vanished.

That was all that mattered. Damage to property could be repaired—it wasn't the first time it had happened, and it wouldn't be the last. Damage to lives couldn't always be fixed.

"Great. Everyone, this is Jeremy," she said, lifting him in her arms. "He's a special friend of mine, and he loves pizza. So we need to order a whole bunch."

Chapter Nine

Alex turned into the underground parking garage of O'Rourke Enterprises and stopped at the security gate.

A uniformed guard stepped from the kiosk. "Can I help you, sir?"

"My name is Alex McKenzie. My son is—"

"Yes, Dr. McKenzie, we've been expecting you," the man said quickly. "Ms. O'Rourke said you wouldn't want to be delayed. Follow the white arrows to the center of this level. A parking space is available by the elevator."

"Thank you." Alex pulled forward, eyebrows raised. Shannon appeared to have thought of everything.

He'd been thrown by her phone message saying she'd brought Jeremy into the office. He trusted her, but he knew how hard it was for his son to adjust to new people.

The elevator doors opened as Alex got out of the Jeep, and a woman in a business suit hurried over.

"Hello, Dr. McKenzie. I'm Claire Hollings, Ms. O'Rourke's executive assistant. Welcome to O'Rourke Enterprises. Jeremy is doing fine," she said before Alex could ask.

He smiled faintly. Shannon had her staff well-trained. He was impressed. "Thank you."

"Come with me, sir."

When the elevator doors closed, Alex rolled his shoulders to release his lingering tension. Shannon's brief message had only said there had been an incident at one of the O'Rourke companies, and that she'd needed to take Jeremy to the office with her.

"If you don't mind my asking, what happened?" he asked.

Claire Hollings inserted an override key into the control panel and pushed the button to one of the top floors. "Flooding at our textile factory in Bolton. Our emergency response team is on the scene."

"I hope no one is hurt."

Claire flashed a bright smile, which melted her brisk demeanor. "Minor injuries, that's all. Two men were missing, but they've been found and they're fine except for one broken arm and some cuts and bruises."

The elevator rapidly ascended and opened to a spacious office suite.

"This way," Claire said, gesturing with her hand.

They threaded their way through a beehive of activity.

He overheard references to Shannon, what she'd told them to do, wondering what would she think, relief that she'd come. Their destination was a glass-walled office in the very back and Alex saw his son sitting behind the desk, looking intently at a laptop computer. The woman with him said something and he looked up, waved madly, then focused on the computer again.

It was disconcerting.

Until recently, Alex had been the focus of his son's life, the linchpin in a world that had lost its balance. But things were changing now that Shannon's outgoing nature was rubbing off on Jeremy.

"Ms. O'Rourke is in the middle of a press conference," Claire explained, pointing to a bank of televisions.

Shannon was speaking on the muted sets, her name and title emblazoned at the bottom of the screen, where microphones featuring various television station logos could be seen.

"Would you like to listen?" asked her assistant.

Intrigued, Alex nodded, and Claire increased the volume.

"…just grateful the injuries weren't more severe."

"What about the employees' jobs, Shannon?" called a reporter from offscreen. "How long before the mill is up and running again? Christmas is a tough time to go without a paycheck."

"No jobs will be lost, and there won't be any loss of wages," she answered. "But it will be several weeks before production begins again."

"We've heard a number of homes were damaged, as

well. Do some of them belong to your workers?" asked someone else.

"That's correct. We have emergency response teams assessing the needs of each family, and assistance will be offered as needed. But let me emphasize that our services are available to everyone. Bolton is a fine community and we want to help wherever it's needed."

"Are any relief agencies on the scene?"

"Yes, shelters are being set up…" She continued, explaining the locations and aid available. Alex leaned against a desk and watched, fascinated by the play of emotions on her face. Efficient, reassuring…compassion for the injured and distressed. Anyone watching would soon be convinced the world would right itself.

The way she'd been making Alex believe. The kernels of hope Shannon had managed to plant were taking root.

"She's good, isn't she?"

Alex tore his attention from the television. A man stood nearby, and though his hair and eyes were dark, there wasn't any question this was one of Shannon's brothers.

"She's great."

"Kane O'Rourke," the man said, putting out his hand.

"Alex McKenzie."

"So I'm told. Shannon says you're an engineer. If you're interested, I may have a consulting job for you on that factory."

Alex frowned. "You don't know whether I'm qualified."

"Don't worry, I'll check your credentials," Kane said dryly. "But I know my sister, and she thinks you're the man for the job."

"They called, Mr. O'Rourke. Your helicopter is ready," interrupted Claire Hollings.

"Thank you, Claire."

Kane turned back to Alex.

"Glad to meet you, McKenzie. I'm flying over to see my injured employees, but I'll be in touch."

Alex shook his head as Shannon's brother strode away. Consulting for O'Rourke Enterprises would look good on his résumé, but he wasn't sure how he felt about his life becoming even more entangled with those of the O'Rourkes.

He went into Shannon's office and ruffled his son's hair. "I appreciate you staying with him," he told the woman sitting with Jeremy.

"It was a pleasure. Your son has a strong aptitude for computers," she added. "I hope to see you again, Jeremy."

"Bye, Bobbi. We don't haf to leave yet, do we, Daddy?"

"Yes, we do."

But he'd barely gotten Jeremy's coat fastened before Shannon appeared, surrounded by people clamoring for her attention. She gave him an apologetic smile. "I'm so sorry about bringing Jeremy into Seattle," she said when the tumult had settled. "But things were frantic here."

"Don't worry about it," Alex assured. "It probably was good for him."

It was true, yet the truth bothered him, because it led to questions without answers. *Would* Jeremy have had an easier adjustment the past year if his mother had encouraged him to be more independent? Kim had spent every waking moment with their son and had wanted him to be educated at home. Was that why Jeremy was desperately unhappy in day-care? Would he hate school even more?

A weary sigh escaped his throat, and Alex felt the inevitable stab of guilt. Kim wasn't here to defend her decisions—decisions she'd had to make alone because *he'd* been off building roads and bridges in remote corners of the world.

"I'll get Jeremy out of here, so you can work," he said. "And I'm the one who should apologize. You've done more than anyone has a right to expect. It must have been inconvenient with everything you had to do."

Emotions he couldn't read shifted in Shannon's eyes. "It wasn't inconvenient. He ate pizza and played on the computer."

"Well, thanks, anyway."

Jeremy gave her a hug, dragging his feet and making it plain he wanted to stay. Alex knew how he felt, and he turned around at the door.

"How long will you have to stay in the city?"

"I don't know. A few more hours. But I shouldn't have to come in tomorrow, so I can still sit with Jeremy."

She would be tired when she got home. Alex had dealt with emergencies when he was working in the field, and knew what it was like once the pressure and adrenaline wore off.

"I..." He cleared his throat. Stepping along the edge of a precipice was never easy, and that was what it was like around Shannon. But surely he could be a good enough friend to do something for *her* this time. "If you want to talk later, I'll be up."

Surprise flickered across her face. "All right."

He hustled Jeremy away, aware that curious glances were being sent in their direction. The O'Rourke employees were wondering who he was, and what he meant to Shannon. It wouldn't have been so bad if he could tell them, but he couldn't.

It was another one of those damned questions without an answer.

Stomach churning from her encounter with Alex, Shannon sank in her chair. He hadn't seemed upset about her bringing Jeremy into the city, yet who could tell?

"Nice kid," Claire said, sticking her head inside the office. "And nice man. I haven't seen a body like that since I went to Montana last summer."

She gave her assistant a dismissive look. "He's a widower, Claire. We're just friends."

"What? Widowers don't need sex?"

Needing sex wasn't the problem. Shannon had seen and felt the intensity of Alex's response to her, a response he didn't welcome. He insisted it had nothing to do with her, but it still hurt.

Shannon pasted a practiced smile on her lips and waved her hand. "Go back to work," she ordered. "I have things to do, even if you don't."

"Hah. I always have work. My boss is a slave driver."

"Slave driver? I thought I was the dragon lady."

"Knew we'd get a rise out of you over that one."

"And I knew you were the one to come up with it. So scat."

Claire grinned and returned to her desk, while Shannon pulled up damage reports on her computer. Things were settling down. Kane would visit the various emergency shelters and decide if more needed to be done, but his response teams were well-trained. She was lucky to work for a company with near-limitless resources, and a CEO willing to use them.

Shannon sighed. It had almost been a relief to handle something familiar. Spending time with Jeremy was easy; figuring Alex out wasn't.

Alex.

She spun her chair around and gazed out at the city. Rain continued to pour and she knew there'd be more flooding, more problems. It was inevitable. Mother Nature was stronger than the best-laid plans.

Like her plan to help Jeremy.

Dear heaven. Her eyes closed. Where was her common sense? She was running headlong toward another heart-break, seduced by a sweet little boy and a man who made her feel more than she'd believed possible.

But she couldn't help herself.

Five hours later, Shannon was grateful she'd promised Kane not to drive herself home. The company driver detoured to avoid one flooded street after another, but peace reigned inside the limousine. The trappings of wealth weren't important to her, but they could be convenient.

She was drowsing when the door opened and the chauffeur extended his hand. "Miss O'Rourke, we're here."

"Thanks, Ted." She slid from the limo and looked to see if the lights were on in Alex's condo. The downstairs windows were still lit; Jeremy would be in bed, but his daddy seemed to be awake.

"I'll just walk you to the door," Ted insisted when she tried to take the umbrella he held over her head. "And check the house for any problems."

"You need to get home, Ted."

"I have my orders, ma'am."

"I'll take care of Miss O'Rourke," said Alex as he walked down the driveway.

"Sheesh. Doesn't anybody think I can take care of myself?" Shannon demanded.

The two men looked at her blankly. They didn't get it, but neither did any of her brothers. Ted's orders might have come from Kane, but the driver was the father of three grown daughters and would have walked her to the door without being told. He was the old-fashioned type, just like Alex.

She sighed. Her independence wasn't being challenged. They were just big, dumb brutes who couldn't help themselves.

"Never mind. Thank you, Ted, for driving me home. I'll be all right with Alex. He's a friend."

Ted examined Alex the way a cop would examine a suspect in a police lineup. "Very well. I've arranged for your car to be delivered in the morning."

Shannon chuckled as the limo rolled smoothly away.

"I'm glad you think it's funny," Alex muttered, pulling her into his house. "Half of the state is flooded. How do you handle this much rain?"

"We tread water." Shannon dropped onto the couch. "I suppose Jeremy is in bed already."

"An hour ago. Have you had anything to eat?"

She thought about it. "Cold pizza around six. We were going to order food, but most of the restaurants aren't delivering because of the weather."

Alex let out a disgusted sound. "I'll get you something."

"No, I'm fine."

She might as well have been talking to a rock. He tossed the umbrella into a corner and headed for the kitchen.

Shannon hauled herself to her feet and followed. "Do you ever listen?"

"It's one of my failings. Deal with it."

He was so endearingly rumpled and belligerent that she laughed again.

Alex gazed at Shannon, her face less weary now that she was laughing, and realized he must have done something right. Who could have guessed that being grumpy and out-of-sorts would do anything but start an argument? In his family it would have triggered World War Three.

She was amazing, and while he wanted to tell her that, the words stuck in his throat.

"Do you like omelets?" he asked instead.

"Yes. You cook omelets?"

"Sure, they're…" Alex stopped. He'd almost said they

were easy, but cooking was a touchy subject for Shannon.
"I manage."

He pulled eggs from the refrigerator, then nearly dropped
them when she yawned and stretched, her body arching like
a sensuous cat.

Friends, he reminded himself.

With a sleepy smile she drifted into the utility room and
he heard the dryer being opened and closed. Sounds of
daily tasks that were never quite done.

"Come out of there, you're supposed to be relaxing," he
called.

"In a min—oh, *damn.*"

Alex had never heard Shannon curse and he hurried to
see what had happened. The smell of bleach hit him instantly, and he saw that she'd somehow upended the bottle
in a basket. A basket full of his jeans.

It struck him as inordinately funny, but he didn't think
she'd agree. He dumped the contents of the basket into the
washing machine and hoped for the best, though he had a
feeling the jeans were beyond rescue. He hoped Shannon's
pride wasn't in the same condition.

He cast a cautious glance in her direction.

She'd backed against the wall, her face stormy with
frustration.

There was only one thing Alex could think of doing. He
put an arm around her waist and used his free hand to cup
her chin so she'd have to look at him. "If you think I give
a hoot about what happens to those jeans when you can
make my son smile, then you're crazy."

"I'm a real riot."

"Treasure is more like it," he retorted. "I can pay people to clean and cook. What you do for Jeremy is priceless."

"You sound like a credit-card commercial," Shannon grumbled, but he could see a smile overtaking her scowl.

"Not a chance." Alex dropped a kiss on her nose. "Did you know that in some cultures the smell of bleach is an aphrodisiac?"

"You're making that up."

He wasn't so sure. In the right circumstances bleach probably could excite a man. *Like now.* Like when a beautiful, sensual woman crowded everything else from his mind.

This time his kiss landed on her mouth and lingered for an endless moment.

Definitely an aphrodisiac.

"Um…mmphf…Alex?" Shannon said. "What about our agreement?"

"It's just a friendly kiss."

"Oh. Okay."

He gave her another, deeper and friendlier than ever, his tongue thrusting into the warm recesses of her mouth. She had textures a man could spend forever exploring, from the top of her fiery head to the bottom of those determined feet.

Like her hips.

They were slim and curved in the right place. Blood gathered, hot and heavy at the top of his thighs, and he pressed his forehead to Shannon's in a desperate attempt to regain control.

Yeah, friendly.

So friendly that in another minute he would have invited her to share his king-size bed for the night.

Their breaths intermingled and he swallowed. A month ago, he would have believed the need in him was because he missed Kim so much. But Shannon wasn't a substitute for anyone; she'd created a whole new kind of needing.

"I better get that omelet going," he said hoarsely.

Or you'll be eating it for breakfast.

The unspoken words hung in the air, and he knew Shannon had heard them in the silence. But he couldn't be the man she deserved. He was too damaged, grieving his first love, unwilling to take a chance that his life wouldn't turn into the turmoil he remembered from his parents' marriage.

Yet he knew if he had met Shannon in a different space and time, he would have held on to her like a child grabbing the shiniest star in the sky.

"I'll go now," he whispered and she nodded.

Eggs had never been beaten with more vigor than the ones Alex broke into the bowl, or cheese more fiercely grated and peppers chopped. His preference would have been to lift weights or go running to release the energy twisting his nerves, but neither was an option.

"My salsa is the atomic-heat variety," he said, plunking the plate in front of Shannon. "But you're welcome to it."

"I like spicy, remember?"

Alex pulled the jar from the fridge and put it next to her plate. He liked the way she wasn't cautious, the way she spooned the salsa generously over her eggs and ate, sighing with pleasure at the simple fare.

He liked being around her, even enjoyed her unpredictability, and that was new for him, as well.

"I must have been hungry, after all," Shannon said when she'd taken the last bite of omelet.

"Cold pizza isn't very satisfying."

"I know, but I'm not allowed to use the microwave in the employee break room."

Alex managed to keep a straight face, but it was a struggle. He could well imagine what had led to her being banned from using the microwave. And Shannon, being Shannon, wouldn't ask someone else to do it for her. "That's too bad. How about going into the living room and putting your feet up?" Changing the subject seemed prudent.

"I should go home. The cat will think he's been abandoned."

"Relax for a while. I'll go get No-Name so you can reassure him."

"No-Name?" she repeated.

"That's right. I'm assuming he hasn't 'revealed' his name to you yet. I have to call him something, so No-Name fits."

"You're a riot," Shannon said, but she let herself be convinced. She wanted to stay. Her condo might be beautifully furnished and decorated, but she felt more comfortable in Alex's home than in her own.

She was half asleep when Alex returned, dropping the kitten on her tummy. The feline let out a cry that sounded more annoyed than mournful, and cocked his head to one side.

Alex grinned. "He didn't like you being gone."

"He's been getting friendlier. It's hard learning to trust again," she murmured idly, extending a finger to the cat.

The kitten was already gaining weight, the bony ridges on his back no longer so prominent. In a few months he'd be a magnificent long-haired tabby, filled with the arrogance of his species. She didn't know why she hadn't gotten a cat years ago. They were amazing creatures, filled with secrets and purring wiles.

Alex sat at the end of the couch, pulled her feet into his lap and began massaging them.

Mmm. She'd never had a foot rub before, and it made her tense muscles turn to warm honey. How had he known exactly what she needed, when she didn't know herself?

"Alex?" she murmured.

"Yes?"

"Um…never mind." She wanted to ask why he had kissed her, but didn't want to spoil the moment. If she asked, he might stop rubbing her feet, and that would be a shame.

Yet the thought lingered, adding to the slide of heat in her veins.

Alex hadn't wanted her to be upset or hurt, and instead of getting annoyed that she'd spilled bleach on his clothing, he'd kissed her. Men had romanced her with flowers and jewelry and expensive restaurants over the years, but none of them had come close to Alex McKenzie and his simple omelet.

The Christmas-tree lights winked and twinkled, Alex's

thumbs moved in slow, easy circles, and the kitten purred on her tummy.

She smiled and closed her eyes.

For the first time in forever, she was right where she wanted to be.

Chapter Ten

The phone on Alex's bedside table rang. He opened bleary eyes and looked at the clock.

Six?

What maniac would call at six in the morning?

"Yeah," he mumbled into the receiver.

"Where in hell is my sister, McKenzie? She isn't answering her phone."

Alex rubbed his face and yawned. The voice sounded like Kane O'Rourke's, and his tone was a far cry from their cordial encounter of the previous day. So much for a consulting job with O'Rourke Enterprises.

"She's here."

A harsh breath came over the line, followed by a woman's muffled voice, saying that Shannon was an adult, entitled to her own life. And would Kane please not interfere.

Good advice.

Alex yawned again. "Shannon fell asleep on the couch. She'd had a rough day and I didn't feel like kicking her out."

"I...see."

"Is this just a social call or is it something important?"

A brief silence was followed by a laugh. "Not important. I just wanted to talk to my sister." The woman whispered again in the background. "And my wife says to apologize for waking you up."

"Would you apologize if I'd said Shannon was in bed with me?"

"Probably not."

At least they understood each other.

"Okay. Wait while I see if she's awake." Leaving the phone on the table, Alex wandered downstairs. Shannon lay on the couch and he tried not to see how she made the room seem alive, though her eyes were closed.

He drifted back upstairs. "Sorry, O'Rourke. Out like a light," he told Kane. "I'll let her know you called."

He crawled back into bed, but sleep proved elusive. While Kane O'Rourke had been out of line, his love and concern for his sister was undeniable. Alex wasn't even sure he had Gail's current phone number, and the last time he'd seen her was at Kim's wake. They hadn't really talked, but not talking was a McKenzie trademark.

Mentally calculating the time difference between Washington and Japan, Alex reached for his address book. But when the ringing began, second thoughts had him ready to disconnect.

The Japanese greeting on the other end of the line momentarily threw him, then he said, "Gail?"

"Yes, this is Gail McKenzie."

Cripes, she didn't even recognize his voice. "It's Alex."

Silence, likely from shock. "Alex? Hi."

He swore to himself. This was even harder than he'd imagined. "How have you been, Gail?"

"Busy. You know how it is."

Did he ever.

"Yeah, I'm busy, too."

They exchanged painful small talk for five minutes before Gail excused herself. Alex was never more grateful to end a call, and he swiped beads of sweat from his forehead. Why had he bothered?

Shannon, he thought. He'd bothered because of Shannon. Beneath her polished veneer was a woman with old-fashioned family values, who prodded his conscience without even trying.

Like a ghost creeping through the house, Jeremy walked past Alex's bedroom door, dragging his blanket behind him. He spent a lot of time in front of the Christmas tree, probably dreaming of Shannon becoming his new mommy. Alex groaned, knowing his son would find the object of his dreams on the couch. Still, it wouldn't help to rush down and explain things Jeremy wouldn't believe anyway.

A delighted "Shannon" drifted up the stairs, his son's voice filled with the breathless excitement most children reserved for Disneyland and Santa Claus.

"A man ought to be able to sleep in his own house," Alex

grumbled. But when the house was quiet again, he found sleep was the last thing on his mind. It was too full of visions of Shannon, the frustration in her eyes turning to laughter. Of her breathless anticipation before a kiss. Of Shannon holding his son, reading or just talking to him.

Why should *that* be so haunting? he wondered.

Over the past months he'd seen too many women trying to mother his son, their gushy concern spilling over to him. He moved across the country to get away from it.

"Damnation." Alex kicked the blankets away. He preferred sleeping in the nude, but with Shannon spending the night on the couch, he'd opted for pajamas. *That* was why he couldn't sleep. Those damned pj's.

Yeah, right.

A grim smile twisted Alex's lips as he got dressed. He was lousy at lying to himself.

Shannon read a story to Jeremy, her senses tuned to Alex's movements on the second floor. She hadn't slept so well in months, though it *had* been a surprise to wake up on her neighbor's couch with Jeremy standing over her. She must have fallen asleep after Alex's wonderful foot massage.

A smile curved her mouth.

Alex would probably never know how much his touch had stimulated other parts of her body. But it was his gentleness that had truly melted her.

Footfalls on the staircase had Shannon looking up. "Good morning."

"Morning." Alex yawned. "Your brother called. He's prepared to beat me senseless for letting you spend the night."

"He is not."

"Yes, he is. He tried calling you at home, then decided you might be here. I don't know why. Maybe he interrogated the chauffeur or something."

Shannon wanted to crawl under the couch. "Honestly, I told him we were just friends."

"Uh-huh."

"He means well."

"His wife told him you were an adult and not to interfere. She also told him to apologize." Alex grinned. "Do you want to go out for breakfast? I have a meeting with some folks at the university, but not until ten."

"I'd like that." She breathed a sigh of relief. At least he thought Kane's reaction was funny. "Do I have time to shower and change? It won't take long."

"Go ahead. I need to get Jeremy dressed, anyway."

Shannon carried the kitten home and got ready in record time. The phone rang before she could leave, and she picked it up, knowing it would be her oldest brother.

"Hey, sis."

She scowled. "Don't hey me. How could you call Alex like that? It's none of your business whether or not I'm sleeping with him. Besides, I told you we were just friends."

"I overreacted."

"As usual." She looked at her watch. "But we'll discuss it later. Do you have a reason for calling? I'm on vacation."

Kane chuckled, kindly refraining from reminding her that he'd forced her to take that vacation. "Nothing that can't keep. Talk to you later, sis."

Shannon said good-bye and hurried outside. It was still raining, and Alex got out of the Jeep to help her into the front seat. He looked wider awake than she'd ever seen him look in the morning, and his smile was brighter than sunshine.

"Thank you," he whispered.

"For getting ready so fast?"

"Better than that." He went around to the driver's seat and got in. "Jeremy, why don't you tell Shannon what you've just told me."

She twisted in her seat to look at the four year old. "Yes?"

"I'm not playing wolf an'more, 'cause Daddy has to work." He sighed a very adult sigh. "An' I guess I haf to go to day-care. After Christmas," he added hastily.

Pleasure went through Shannon. She'd wondered if she was doing the right thing, talking to Jeremy about his pretending to be sick and needing to accept day-care. She'd also planned to tell Alex about those talks, but there had never seemed to be a right time.

"You're a good boy. I'm so proud of you."

Jeremy glowed.

And Alex…the warmth in his eyes was the best reward she'd ever received. But it didn't mean anything had changed between them. He'd told her often enough he wasn't interested in a permanent relationship.

They drove to a local café. As they walked inside, Alex put his hand on the small of her back, sending shivers in all directions. "That okay?" he asked, pointing to a booth by the window.

"It's fine." He could have suggested a bench in the middle of a rain puddle and it would have been fine. She had it bad, and there wasn't a single reason to hope things were going to change. Yet a bubble of hope kept rising, demanding attention.

"I've been thinking," Shannon said once the waitress had taken their orders. "If Kane didn't annoy you too much, would you and Jeremy like to spend Christmas day with my family?"

A dark expression flickered in Alex's eyes, his barriers popping up one by one. "I don't know…"

"Oooh. Can we, Daddy?" Jeremy begged.

Alex hesitated, torn.

His first impulse was to refuse, but it *was* a chance for his son to see a real family celebration. On the other hand, Jeremy already had too many dreams about Shannon. It was Alex's fault. There was something he hadn't anticipated in his agreement to be just friends…Shannon was too irresistible.

To both of them.

"I'm sorry," she said worriedly. "I should have asked when we were alone. I understand if you have other plans."

He couldn't handle her apologizing. Not when she'd done so much for both of them.

"Actually, we don't have plans. We accept."

"Does that mean yes, Daddy?"

He nodded and Jeremy wriggled with excited anticipation.

"Goody!"

"What should we bring?" Alex asked, already regretting the decision. He didn't know how to act with big families. His own was a mess, and Kim's only relatives had been distant cousins. Was there a particular protocol that was expected?

"Just bring yourselves. I have twin nieces who are close to Jeremy's age. They'll love playing with him."

The nieces sounded good; Jeremy needed to learn how to play with children his age. The day-care center had said he stayed too much to himself. Of course, Kane O'Rourke would be more convinced than ever that his little sister was involved with someone he didn't know anything about, but Alex took a perverse pleasure in the knowledge. If he ever *did* take Shannon to bed, he didn't plan on answering to anyone about it.

What about Kim?

It wasn't a new thought, and he knew it was something he'd have to deal with sooner or later. Strangely, he wanted to talk with Shannon about feeling guilty. Would she understand?

"We still should bring something," he said gruffly.

Shannon nodded. "You can bring me. I always have a mountain of stuff to take, and your Jeep would be perfect to pile it into."

"Then it's at your service."

"Good. We'll go Christmas morning and spend the day, if that's okay with you. Someone could drive me home if you decide we're too much for you."

"Mmm," he said noncommittally.

Their meal came and they talked about the weather and other safe subjects, and Shannon couldn't help being discouraged again. Alex had places inside she couldn't reach.

"You didn't eat much," Alex said when she pushed her plate away.

"I'm still full of omelet."

His eyes asked silently if something was wrong and she bit her lip. She doubted he was aware of the way he posted barriers and stay-out messages.

"It's after eight-thirty," she said, gesturing to the clock on the café wall. "You don't want to be late."

He agreed and took care of the bill.

It was funny, Shannon thought as they walked out to the Jeep. The more they seemed like a family, the more it hurt to know they were just playing a game.

Later in the morning, Shannon summoned her courage and opened Alex's washing machine. At home she managed basic care of underclothes and such, but the cleaning service took care of the big stuff. She knew what bleach could do to clothing, though, and she held her breath as she pulled Alex's jeans from the machine.

"Drat," she muttered, looking at the faded blotches. The two well-worn pairs didn't look so bad; they'd already lost a lot of color. But the newer ones were a mess.

The intimacy of doing a man's laundry had never struck her before, but now she was acutely aware of how those jeans wrapped around Alex's hips and muscled thighs.

Maybe that was why some women liked doing laundry; it made them feel closer to their men.

She hastily shoved the jeans into the dryer and set it to low, the way the labels suggested.

"I am losing my mind," she said, glaring at the machine that thumped and thudded as the heavy jeans tumbled around inside. "Positively bonkers. Laundry is just work, not a mission in life. And I'm terrible at it."

Besides, it was too disturbing spending time in the utility room. All she could think about was Alex's kisses, the mix of tenderness and laughter. He'd been so kind about her fumble with the bleach bottle, though it must have been annoying.

She went into the kitchen and picked up the phone. She didn't have to be good at domestic skills if she knew who to call. The service who cleaned her condo could do an emergency job on Alex's house, instead of her taking the chance of ruining something else.

He'd probably be relieved.

As Alex parked in the drive late in the afternoon, he saw a car pulling out of Shannon's. Despite the rain he was able to make out two women inside, and they were waving at him.

"Can I help you?" he asked when the driver stopped and rolled down her window.

"No, we're from the cleaning service," the woman explained. "You must be Dr. McKenzie. Sorry about your jeans," she added with a grin.

Alex realized they must have talked to Shannon. She would have hated admitting what had happened. "It was an accident."

"Obviously. Gotta go."

He frowned as he opened his front door and the scent of lemon and baking surrounded him. They were fragrances from the past, a time when he'd arrived to a house freshly cleaned and a cobbler cooling on the stove. After being raised as an unwanted foster child, Kim had been determined to do things right. Maybe that was why she'd kept Jeremy close at home and insisted he eat a certain way.

"What is going on, Shannon?" he asked the minute he saw her on the couch wrapping gifts.

"Nothing. Jeremy is taking a nap and I had the cleaning service come," she said, looking up from the package she was taping. "They baked an apple cake, too. I figured you wouldn't want me to destroy anything else."

She'd assumed her polished veneer, the one that hid everything, and he sighed.

"I told you that stuff doesn't matter."

Her eyelashes swept down and she carefully measured a length of silver Christmas ribbon. "It matters to most men."

Maybe. Once upon a time he'd even been that kind of man. Hell, he'd *enjoyed* the way Kim catered to his every whim. Unfortunately, it had also let him off the hook to be a real father and husband. He ought to have insisted Jeremy be allowed to play with other children and have occasional treats like pizza, but he'd chosen the easy route.

It was sobering to realize that in his efforts not to repeat the mistakes of his parents, screaming and yelling and never agreeing, he'd made a different mistake. Parenting ought to be something a mother and father did *together,* balancing each other's strengths and weaknesses.

Shannon tied the ribbon around the package and he sighed again. Someone had hurt her in the past; probably someone a lot like him.

"Who told you men were like that?"

"I didn't have to be told."

"We both know there's more to it," he said, sitting and taking the spool of ribbon from her fingers. "Talk to me."

"Hey, if we're trading failed romance stories, you have to go first." She made it sound like a joke, and breath hissed through his teeth. *Damned stubborn woman.*

"There isn't much to tell, except for the way I left my wife and child eight months out of the year to pursue work I could have done at home. Does that qualify?"

"Alex. That isn't…that's not what I meant."

"I know." His tone gentled and he traced the line of her jaw. "But I don't know how to make you believe me."

She wrinkled her nose. "For heaven's sake, it's no big deal. It's just that your wife was a gifted homemaker, and I obviously come up short compared to her. Even successful career women have episodes of insecurity, you know."

"You could never come up short," Alex said, appalled. "You made my son come alive again."

You made me *come alive again.*

He now understood at a gut level why his parents had

gotten married despite their gross incompatibility—they'd felt more alive together than apart. To be really alive, you had to feel deeply, and Alex had done his best to wall himself away from emotion. Shannon tried to hide her deepest emotions, but they were an integral part of her heart and soul.

What would it be like being the man she felt safe enough to turn to when she was vulnerable and upset, instead of trying to be strong for everyone else?

Alex swallowed.

He wasn't that man.

Was he?

"Listen to me. I don't give a hoot about the cooking or cleaning," he insisted. "It was never about housekeeping when I said I wasn't...well..."

"Getting married again?" she finished for him.

"Yes. The truth is, I wasn't a great husband," he admitted. It was a relief to say it out loud, maybe because he knew Shannon wouldn't judge him.

Shannon shook her head. "I saw Kim's pictures. I know you made her happy. Isn't that the real measure of a husband?"

He hoped that was true.

Alex had never been a cuddler, but he had a sudden need to do just that. He gave Shannon a sideways glance, wondering how she'd feel about it.

"Do you have to leave right away?" he asked.

"No. Do you need to go out again?"

He shook his head. "Just checking." Getting up, he

turned off the lights except those on the Christmas tree, then he sat on the floor and pulled Shannon down with him.

"Alex?"

His "just being friendly" routine from the night before stuck in his throat, so he settled her against his chest and inhaled the fragrance that clung to her hair and skin. He was still concerned about Jeremy and spending Christmas with Shannon's family, but he needed a moment of peace. The curious part was seeking peace with a woman who'd turned his routine and self-control on its ear.

"Aren't you worried about Jeremy finding us like this?" Shannon asked after a while.

"I worry about everything. It's one of my defining characteristics."

He sensed, more than heard, her laugh.

"Then why are we still sitting here?"

"I don't know, but it feels good. Tell me more about No-Name," he whispered, wanting to prolong the stolen interlude.

"His *name* is Magellan, for the explorer, because he has a tendency to find unusual routes through things. But there isn't much to tell. He's skittish and distrustful and hates loud noises, and he's so anxious to be loved that it breaks my heart."

Alex wondered if Magellan knew his good fortune.

"Then he isn't sleeping with you?"

"Not when I first go to bed, but by morning he's snuggled under the blankets. It just takes him awhile to get there."

Sheesh.

He'd definitely chosen the wrong topic if he'd hoped to keep his mind from going haywire again. Visions of Shannon in bed were a sure guarantee of heat and guilt and other emotions he didn't want to confront. Yet the guilt seemed further away now. Maybe he'd just needed to hear someone say that he'd made his wife happy. Kim's love hadn't been the selfish kind; she wouldn't want him to be alone.

And Kim *had* been happy. She'd made the most of their time together, and found things that contented her when they weren't.

"How did the meeting go today?" Shannon murmured.

The ordinary "how was your day" question made Alex smile. "Great. It was about me being assigned grad students next term. They sound like a good bunch. And Rita—the pregnant student I told you about—came by and said she's decided to keep her baby. She still won't say who the father is, but at least her folks have calmed down and want to help."

"I should think they would," Shannon said indignantly. "That poor kid. Kane has a corporate program to keep young mothers in school, but it's easier when the parents are supportive. I'll give you the number for her to call."

"Thanks."

Rain continued to patter outside, and the swish-slosh of cars driving the wet streets came more often now that commuters were arriving home from the city. Everything was dark except for the lights twinkling on the Christmas tree, and Alex wished it was possible to freeze time.

Sitting there in the holiday warmth that Shannon had created, there wasn't any past or future, or any bad mistakes to repair or decisions to make. He could be like Magellan, exploring his way toward love and trust, nothing more to worry about than an unkind hand and sharply spoken words.

If only it were that easy.

Chapter Eleven

"Prooomise," pleaded Jeremy.

Shannon hesitated. Jeremy had asked her to be there when he woke up on Christmas morning, but that meant she would have to spend the night. It was one thing to sleep at the McKenzies' accidentally; it was another to do it deliberately.

"Yes. Promise?" Alex repeated his son's request. "You can sleep in Jeremy's room, and he can sleep with me."

What about Jeremy getting the wrong idea? She asked the question silently, and Alex shrugged. She would be returning to work after the New Year, so maybe he figured they would gradually see less and less of each other, that way letting Jeremy down lightly.

It was depressing, but she summoned a smile. "All right. Except I'll stay on the couch."

Alex frowned. The proposed sleeping arrangement probably didn't suit his notions of gallantry.

"Oh, pleeeze sleep in my room," Jeremy begged before his father could say something.

"Uh-uh, I want to be down here and see Santa coming down the chimney." She ignored the choking sound that came from Alex. "I never could catch him when I was little, but this might be the year I get lucky."

"Santa?" The youngster's face was scrunched up, doubtful but wanting to join in the fantasy at the same time.

"That's right. We'll put cookies and milk by the fireplace for him to eat, and leave the Christmas lights on all night."

"So he can find us?"

"Santa doesn't need lights to find us. He already knows you're a good boy."

"Daddy, I wanna sleep with Shannon and see Santa," Jeremy declared firmly.

Shannon clasped her hand over her mouth to keep from laughing as Alex sighed, long and hard. She now knew where Jeremy got his heartfelt sighs—from his daddy.

"Okay, you can sleep downstairs," Alex said, conceding defeat. "But Santa is hard to catch, so don't get your hopes up."

He received a spontaneous hug that nearly knocked him backward. "Goody. My daddy is the bestest daddy," Jeremy declared proudly.

That was one of the reasons parents made bad decisions, Alex decided wryly, so they could hear their kids saying they were great. Despite Shannon's chiding, he'd intended to stand firm on the subject of Santa Claus. The jolly old guy was merely a Christmas icon; his son needed to understand that it was the spirit of giving that was important.

Then Alex thought of the gifts for his family that he'd shipped the day he'd met Shannon and realized the spirit of giving had little to do with his efforts. It was duty—the tired habit of sending gifts to people he hardly knew any longer.

What *had* he gotten for Gail?

He remembered. A gold chain. Something light for mailing to Japan. Probably similar to what he'd gotten the year before, and the year before that. Now he wished he had chosen something with more care.

"You *are* the bestest," Shannon said, smiling faintly. She rose and asked Jeremy to come with her into the den, so she could show him the computer games she'd brought.

How quickly she'd become a part of their daily lives. Now that it was the Christmas break and he didn't have to fight Jeremy over day-care, he ought to have begun the painful process of limiting their time together. But he hadn't been able to do it. The way his son's face lit up whenever he was around Shannon was too hard to resist.

After Christmas, Alex resolved.

He would break things off after the holidays. Shannon had restored the security his son had lost, and it must not be taken away too quickly.

What about *your* security?

Alex scowled at his nagging conscience. His next-door neighbor had become far too important to him, as well. She was so beautiful, it took his breath away, but that wasn't the problem. It was the way she made him believe in possibilities that truly disturbed him.

He'd believed Kim was the perfect woman for him, with her calm and gentle nature. Shannon was nothing like that, yet she was loving and generous and filled with the joy of living. Could she be his second chance?

"You push that button, and see what happens?"

Jeremy was all smiles as he played on Shannon's laptop. She'd ordered several games after he'd shown so much interest in computers at her office.

"You're spoiling him," Alex murmured when she walked into the kitchen. He gazed at her over the edge of his coffee cup, still blinking groggily, though he'd been awake for a couple of hours.

"They're educational games. I did my research. You can't spoil children with educational toys."

"Uh-huh."

She thought of the call she'd taken for Alex the previous day while he was out shopping, and smiled with secret delight. It had been Alex's sister, trying to reach him on his home phone. They'd introduced themselves and talked for a few minutes. Apparently Alex had called Gail a few days before, which started her thinking about coming to Seattle for Christmas. Hearing that, Shannon had instantly invited her to the O'Rourke holiday celebration. But because Gail still wasn't sure she'd been able to get a last-minute ticket for the nine-hour flight from Japan to Seattle, she'd asked

Shannon not to tell Alex in case her travel plans fell through.

Shannon hoped Gail would be able to come. Families should be together for Christmas.

"I suppose you're grinning like a Cheshire cat because of that Santa Claus stuff," Alex grumbled.

"He's only four years old, not twenty-four. When did you stop believing?"

"I never believed."

Sadness filled Shannon at his flat tone. She'd been raised by parents utterly devoted to each other and their children, who'd taught them about Irish mysticism and endless love, gifts she'd never fully appreciated before meeting Alex.

She'd fallen in love with him, the way her mother had fallen for a wild Irish lad. But it was by no means certain that Alex felt the same. He was so closed, so determined not to be disappointed again by love and life.

She'd thought her inability to be domestic was the biggest obstacle to love and marriage, but not with Alex. Those things faded into insignificance next to the big issues.

"Come on," she said suddenly. "Let's go someplace."

"Huh?"

"Jeremy?" she called. "We're going out." Shannon smiled at Alex. "It's December twenty-third and it has finally stopped raining. Let's celebrate."

She didn't want him to object; she wanted him to forget to frown and have fun. Grabbing his hands, she pulled.

"I'm twice your size," he said, beginning to smile.

With a neat twist of his wrists he tumbled her into his lap and laughed.

"The wrong idea," she reminded, but wanting very much to be kissed.

"Right." Alex's gaze lingered on her lips. "Little pitchers have big ears—and eyes."

Shannon pursed her mouth. "There's always the utility room," she suggested.

Apparently it was a suggestion he liked, because he swept her into the small dark room, slammed the door shut and cupped the back of her head. "I thought you'd hate being in here."

"I'm a woman. I change my mind easily."

That was all she got out, because Alex was kissing her so hungrily it was all she could do not to fall down. She felt him from her head to her toes and everywhere else between.

"J-just a friendly kiss," she managed to say when his hands travelled up her rib cage.

"You don't think this is friendly?" Alex's thumbs rotated over her nipples and she moaned.

"Daddy?" came a plaintive voice on the other side of the door. "Where are you an' Shannon?"

Alex uttered a single curse and Shannon grinned. "You bet it's friendly," she whispered. "But being *that* friendly is the way little pitchers get started in the first place."

Didn't he know it, Alex thought ruefully as Shannon eased free and opened the door.

"My goodness, Jeremy, you're all ready to go," he heard her exclaim. "You are growing up so fast. Let's go get my coat, too. I...um, think your daddy needs a couple of minutes to himself."

Alex took deep breaths and wished he was wearing loose sweatpants instead of jeans. When he could walk without cutting off his circulation, he followed Jeremy and Shannon into the living room. She looked at him with a merry expression.

"Feeling better?"

The little witch.

She knew exactly how aroused he'd been.

"Yes, I'm better. Where are we going?"

"I don't know. Malls. Toy stores. Chocolate shops."

"Yum," Jeremy crowed. "I like chocolate."

"So do I. Bet we can get your daddy to buy us a big chocolate Santa."

Alex was resigned as he followed Shannon and Jeremy to the Jeep. A man could only fight the tide so long before getting pulled under, and Shannon was like the tide. An inexorable force sweeping through his life.

An ancient memory came to him of his father at the beach, solemnly explaining it was best not to fight a wave. If you got knocked over, go with it and then find your footing. A rare family vacation, beset by the usual arguments and recriminations, but in the middle was the remembrance of something good.

"Did you see him, Shannon?" Jeremy asked on Christmas morning as he danced around the living room in uncontained excitement. "Did you see Santa?"

Shannon shook her head. "Nope, I fell asleep like always."

"Me, too. But he came, didn't he?"

She looked at the packages around the tree. She'd put some of them there after Jeremy had drifted into slumber, but more had appeared. Alex must have sneaked down after they were *both* asleep.

"Yes, he came," Shannon said, a silly grin on her face. The last two days had been glorious, a wonderland of time spent with the man she loved to distraction, and a little boy who was as dear to her as if she'd given birth to him. She wouldn't let herself think about what would happen once the holidays were over. Not now, not until she had to.

"I gotta get Daddy." Jeremy went racing across the room, only to find his father on the staircase. "Santa came! *He came!* See, Daddy? An' he ate the cookies and drank all the milk."

"I see."

Alex sat on the steps, dressed in jeans and a sweatshirt—he was everything she'd ever wanted for Christmas.

The scent of coffee came from the kitchen, the machine's timer set by Alex the night before, but it was the empty plate of cookies that Shannon looked at. She'd forgotten to make it appear as if Santa had enjoyed his midnight treat. Alex had handled that little detail, and her heart swelled. Christmas was truly a miraculous time of year.

"Can we open presents now, Daddy?" Jeremy begged.

"Uh…okay." He still didn't look fully awake.

"Let your daddy have some coffee first." She went to the

kitchen and poured a large cup. Alex accepted it with a smile and tugged her down next to him. She did wonder if he was thinking about Kim and wishing she was there, but Shannon couldn't resent the other woman's memory. Kim had loved her family, and was surely watching over them the way Shannon knew her father was watching over her, comforting her in dark times, and rejoicing in the good ones.

"Do you want cookies with that?" she asked softly, to keep Jeremy from hearing.

"Cookies?"

Her gaze flicked to the empty plate by the fireplace and back again. "Yes. Thanks for remembering. I was so sleepy, I wasn't thinking."

"I didn't eat anything. It must have been Santa."

"You…" Shannon laughed and leaned into the arm Alex put around her.

After a while he shook himself. "I think it's time to open presents," he said, and Jeremy clapped his hands.

Soon the living room was a sea of paper and ribbon, something that Magellan—who'd also been a McKenzie houseguest—enjoyed immensely, along with the cat toys Santa had left him. Shannon held her breath when Alex opened her gift, an old ship's sextant. He'd confessed a fascination with early sailing ships, but she couldn't be sure it was something he'd like.

"Shannon…it's extraordinary." He lifted the instrument from its velvet-lined case and checked the settings, peering through the eyepiece. "But you shouldn't have."

"I wanted to. And you should talk," she said, her fingers stroking the antique copper teakettle Alex had gotten to put by her fireplace. It was perfect. A little bit of Ireland, like her grandparents' home.

"This is from me, Shannon." Jeremy gave her a package and crawled into her lap. She had given him a telescope and books and other toys, but it was the picture of his mother that she'd sealed in a plastic key chain that he wouldn't put down.

"Thank you, Jeremy. It's darling—just like Magellan." It was a silver pin of a skittish cat, dancing on his toes.

He kissed her and sat looking at the picture of his mother. They had talked the night before, Shannon guessing that one of his wishes to Santa was that his mommy come home from heaven. Another was that he get a new mommy—Shannon.

The conflicting desires weren't troubling to a child Jeremy's age. She'd simply told him that Santa couldn't bring those kinds of gifts, but to remember that his mother wasn't any farther than his heart, and that grown-ups had to work things out for themselves.

"I'd better get ready to go," Shannon said after they'd bagged the paper and ribbons.

"We'll get ready, too," Alex promised.

He looked tense, she realized as she crossed to her condo carrying Magellan; she'd probably blown everything, asking him to have Christmas with the rest of the O'Rourkes. She should have remembered he didn't have the best experiences with families. Yet surely it would be better once his sister arrived.

If she arrived, Shannon reminded herself. Gail McKenzie had sounded uncertain about her plans, saying only that she hoped to arrive on Christmas day from Japan and would prefer to rent a car rather than have anyone meet her. But it would be a great surprise gift if she did get there.

Alex bathed Jeremy and tried not to think about the way Shannon had looked when he'd gone downstairs to put Santa's packages beneath the tree. Angelic, her fiery nature muted by sleep. If Jeremy hadn't been dozing by the tree, he might have kissed her again.

"My son, the duenna," he muttered. A four-year-old chaperone.

"What's a dwayna?" Jeremy asked.

"It's just a word. You'll find out when you learn Spanish."

By the time they were both dressed and on their way next door, Shannon was already hauling boxes from her house and stacking them by the Jeep. "Why didn't you wait?" Alex asked, hurrying to help her.

"I didn't want to take longer than necessary."

He scowled, wanting to remind her that men had muscles to do the heavy work, yet knowing she'd just say something sassy and laugh at him. But he was particularly annoyed when he discovered one of the boxes was filled with bottles of sparkling grape juice, and another with sparkling cider. They really *were* heavy.

"Don't be mad," Shannon said winsomely, handing him a bag of gaily wrapped packages.

"I'm not mad…yes, I am. *Was* mad," he amended when

she smiled. Though she'd said to dress casually, she wore a soft, expensive-looking sweater and a velvet skirt that hugged her faithfully. The cat pin Jeremy had given her adorned her shoulder. Once they were in the Jeep, she hummed a Christmas tune as they headed for her mother's house.

It all seemed so *right*. Still, panic skirted the edges of Alex's consciousness. He didn't want to examine what he felt for Shannon. It was much easier dismissing his feelings as simple physical need and gratitude for what she'd done for Jeremy than acknowledging that something deeper and more complex had been growing since the day they'd met.

Shannon gave easy-to-follow directions and it wasn't long before they pulled into a tree-lined driveway. Alex didn't know what he'd expected to see, but the big old rambling house wasn't close. A porch wrapped around the house, and people spilled from the doors as they parked. It was the homiest place he could have imagined.

"Merry Christmas. You're late," cried a collection of voices, followed by hugs and exclamations of, "We missed you last night."

"What about last night?" he whispered in Shannon's ear when they stepped inside the front door. "Were you supposed to be here?"

She bit her lip. "The family usually has dinner and attends a candlelight service on Christmas Eve. I didn't have to go. We would have been welcome, but I figured… well…you know. And I didn't want to disappoint Jeremy."

Alex knew why Shannon hadn't said anything; she'd known he wouldn't want to attend the service.

"Goodness, is this Jeremy?" asked an older woman, who approached them with a warm smile.

Jeremy nodded, still clinging to Alex's hand, but he looked intrigued by the color and laughter and happy chatter that filled the comfortable house. It was a new experience for both of them—like walking into a Norman Rockwell painting.

"My name is Pegeen," said the woman, introducing herself. "I'm Shannon's mother, and you must be Alex." Her Irish brogue had been softened but not erased by her years in America.

"I like Shannon," Jeremy declared before his father could say anything.

"So do I, darlin'. Do you want to meet my other grandchildren? The two oldest are close to your age. You'll enjoy playin' with them."

Jeremy readily released his grip on Alex's hand and followed Pegeen.

"I should have known," Alex murmured, shaking his head. It had been days since Jeremy had wanted Mr. Tibbles with him, and though Alex had put the rabbit in the Jeep as a precaution, it seemed apparent the stuffed animal wouldn't be needed.

"You should have known what?" Shannon asked.

"That your mother is a Pied Piper, just like you."

She grinned and drew him into the living room, introducing family as she went. The names became a blur of brothers and sisters, in-laws and children. And Kane O'Rourke, who held a small baby on his shoulder, was no longer the brisk executive or accusing brother, but a doting father. Meeting him that way, Alex would never have guessed he owned a multi-billion dollar corporation.

"Who's going to help bring everything in?" Shannon said, and though they complained, her five brothers donned coats and trooped out to the Jeep Cherokee.

"You always bring too much," Kane said when they were piling gifts near the Christmas tree, then carrying her contributions to the meal into the kitchen.

"But I didn't do it all. Alex, what is this about?" she asked, looking into several of the boxes.

"I had to contribute something and you wouldn't tell me what to bring."

An arm reached over Shannon's shoulder and took a can of cashews from the box she was examining. "Great, I'm starved."

"You're always hungry, Connor."

"Dinner isn't for hours."

With Alex distracted by her brothers Shannon took his coat and hung it with hers in the hall closet on the way to the kitchen. She wanted a word with her mother.

"Mom," she said, entering the kitchen.

"Yes, darlin'?"

"You do remember what I told you about Alex being just a friend, don't you? There's nothing going on between us." It wasn't quite a lie, but Shannon crossed her fingers nonetheless.

"He seems a fine young man."

"Yes, but what did you mean by asking Jeremy to meet your 'other' grandchildren? Like he's one of them?"

"A slip of the tongue, love."

Her mother never had slips of the tongue.

"Do *not* get carried away," Shannon warned. "Alex doesn't want to get married again. He has been very clear on the subject, so nothing is going to happen between us."

"Now, darlin', you can't blame me for bein' a bit hopeful. You've never brought a young man to dinner, much less Christmas dinner. I haven't seen you so happy in a long while."

"He's a widower, Mom. It hasn't even been a year," Shannon said desperately. All she needed was to have her mother try some misplaced matchmaking. "*Please* don't say anything."

Pegeen touched her face. "I'll only say that I love you, dear. Now go on, and don't worry. It's Christmas."

Shannon hurried back to the living room and Alex made room for her on the couch. He was debating a point in football, and she rolled her eyes at how quickly the men had found a topic of common interest. There were times she felt like the odd person out in her own family. The women would congregate in the kitchen, talking about cooking and babies and other domestic interests, her brothers would talk sports or some other manly pursuit, and she didn't fit with either.

"How is that new kitten of yours doing?" asked Connor after several minutes. "Except for being skin and bones, he seemed to be healthy when I checked him."

"He's doing fine." She looked at Alex. "Connor has to endure the entire family bringing their animals to him for treatment."

"Like having a doctor in the family?"

"Something like that."

Alex nodded and wondered why he'd worried about coming to dinner at the O'Rourkes'. They were normal people, down-to-earth and thoroughly likable; no one would know they had access to inconceivable wealth. And Jeremy was having a ball, laughing and running around with two little girls who were as alike as two peas in a pod. His son was too young to think about the implications of having dinner with a woman's family, anyway.

Other O'Rourkes arrived, aunts and uncles and cousins whose names Alex didn't have a prayer of remembering. Children were hugged and given treats. Food was everywhere, snacks to hold everyone until the main event. Which, judging by the rich scents rolling from the kitchen, would be a feast of grand proportions.

Shannon divided most of her time between him and Jeremy, and Alex found himself missing her whenever she disappeared to chase after his son. It wasn't as if he'd barely seen her that day, or any other day in the past few weeks, and he didn't want to think about the implications.

"Try this," Shannon said, appearing after a particularly long absence.

He bit into the pecan and butter pastry. "It's great, but I'm not going to be able to eat dinner if you keep feeding me."

"Just be grateful she's not trying to cook dinner," joked Connor. "Or you'd need your stomach pumped."

Everyone laughed, and someone else added, "Or we'd be out on the street, waiting for the fire department to arrive."

"Hey, I only set fire to stoves, not houses," Shannon said lightly, but Alex saw her lips tighten. She left a couple of minutes later and he frowned, surprised her family didn't know she was bothered by their teasing.

He gave Connor a cold look. "If you had half the brains of your sister, you wouldn't say stupid things," he said, not caring if he sounded rude, or what they would think about him defending Shannon when it had obviously been a family joke.

He followed Shannon, grabbing both their coats when he saw her stepping out onto the front porch.

"Hey," he said, closing the door to shut out the prying ears of her family. "You're going to freeze out here."

"I'm tougher than I look."

Alex wrapped her in a coat. "Tough, right. You're shivering and turning blue. Why didn't you tell Connor and the others to stuff it?"

"Why should I? Everyone had a good laugh."

He caught her chin and made her look at him, frustrated by the way she guarded her deepest feelings. "*You* didn't enjoy it. You act like you don't care, but I know that isn't true, so don't pretend with me. Please, Shannon."

The remote expression in her eyes slowly vanished. "I'm used to the kidding. It's just that with you and Jeremy here…" She shrugged and rubbed her arms. "I mean, I explained we were just friends, so they don't have any reason to think it would embarrass me in front of you. But with families there's always this…I don't know…*thought* when someone new comes. An anticipation, wondering whether that person could be the 'one,' no matter what has been said."

Alex waited, trying to understand.

"New relationships are fragile and you have a son to think about. So having Connor joke around like that without thinking…it just…"

"Hurt?" Alex finished for her.

"Yes. He didn't know if we might really be involved, and if you'd get second thoughts about a woman who can't cook."

"Only an idiot would think that was important when it comes to you," Alex said adamantly.

Shannon tried to smile. "Don't get the wrong idea," she said. "My family is great, but all families have their moments."

"So, how long are you going to be mad at Connor?"

"Who said I was mad? My brothers can't help having the sensitivity of bricks. They've been handicapped from birth with the problem."

Alex laughed and hugged her close.

"You are the most amazing woman," he whispered in her hair. "I wish you could see yourself through my eyes, then you'd know what a miracle you are. If things were different…"

He stopped speaking, and pain lanced through Shannon. It meant so much to have Alex wanting to comfort her. She'd longed to find someone who would accept who she was. Yet now that she'd found the perfect man, he just wanted to be friends. But even that wouldn't last; they couldn't continue the dance between friendship and desire for much longer. It would tear them apart.

A light breeze ruffled the pine swag on the porch railings, and she thought ironically of the Christmas mistletoe her mother always hung above the front door.

She looked up.

Sure enough, it was there, tied in a bright red bow.

Alex looked, too, and shadows haunted his eyes. "Oh, Shannon, I wish—"

"No, don't talk about it. Let's pretend for one more day. It's Christmas."

"Yes, it is." Alex bent his head and his kiss, filled with passion and regret, brought tears to her tears, even as it sent streamers of fire through her blood.

When they were both gasping for breath, Alex released her. After a long minute regaining his composure, he looked over her head and lifted an eyebrow.

"It seems we have an audience. A very unhappy audience."

Shannon spun and saw three of her brothers. They were glaring through the window at Alex as if he was a randy teenager groping their underage sister.

"Okay," she admitted grudgingly, "they have the sensitivity of bricks, but they're *protective* bricks."

Alex promptly burst out laughing.

Chapter Twelve

Shannon marched into the house, grabbed her eldest brother's arm, and dragged him into Pegeen's unoccupied sewing room. She slammed the door with a satisfying thud.

"What do you think you're doing?" she demanded.

"Nothing."

"Nothing my foot. How could you watch us through the window like that? It was none of your business."

"It most certainly *is* our business," he retorted. "You told Mom he didn't want to get married."

"I said he didn't want to get married *again*. He's a widower, with every right to make his own decisions. Besides, this isn't the eighteenth century. I can do what I want to do."

"I'm aware of that, but I don't want you getting hurt," Kane said quietly. *"Again."*

Shannon swallowed, shaken. She would have sworn the family knew little, if anything, about the times she'd had her heart broken.

"Alex is trying to survive," she whispered. "He's had too much happen, lost too much to risk it all again. Yes, I wish he'd change his mind, but he isn't responsible if I get hurt. I went into this knowing there wasn't a future."

"Ah, Shannon." Regret tinged Kane's voice. "Are you sure?"

"I've been able to fool myself a few times, but yes, I'm sure. So please let it alone. I want to spend Christmas with Alex and Jeremy, and for once not think about tomorrow."

She could tell he was reluctant, but he finally nodded. "All right. I'll tell Neil and Patrick to back off."

"Oh, no."

Shannon suddenly remembered she'd left Alex alone and sped out the door, Kane following close behind. She had visions of Alex and her other brothers rolling around on the living room floor, punching one another while the Christmas tree went flying in ten directions. Her brothers had primitive-level responses when it came to protecting the family. They became cavemen. Barely standing upright.

"How about playing some football later?" Neil said as she rushed into the room. He was standing with his arms crossed, practically nose-to-nose with Alex, who had assumed an equally aggressive stance.

"Yeah, football," agreed Patrick, a glint in his eyes that suggested he wouldn't mind tackling his sister's guest. In a purely friendly, I'm-gonna-kill-you way, of course.

"No football," Shannon said hastily.

"That's right." Kane stepped between the two men. "No contact sports. Shannon wouldn't like it."

"Is that right, Shannon?" Alex asked with a wink. He looked ready to laugh again, and she loved him even more for understanding that her brothers were a bunch of lovable lunatics. Considering what he'd told her about his parents' endless fighting, she would have expected him to grab Jeremy and march out at the first sign of dissent.

She turned to her four sisters-in-law. They were watching their husbands with a mixture of love and exasperation.

"Can't you control them?" she demanded.

Patrick's wife, Maddie, shifted the baby in her arms. "Nope. I'm afraid we're stuck with the bozos," she said cheerfully. "Let's have some hot cider."

The other women agreed and dragged their spouses into the dining room.

Alex tugged a length of Shannon's hair, seeing that she was still outraged. "Isn't this the point where you're supposed to tell me that they mean well, then assure me they're harmless?"

"They do and they are, and that's no excuse."

"But it's understandable." He knew why the O'Rourke brothers were hostile. They were a close-knit Irish family, with unshakable family values, and they saw him as a threat to their sister's happiness. It was a fascinating glimpse into a world he'd never seen before.

Shannon sighed finally and focused on him. "At least you're not running for the hills."

"I'm looking forward to dinner too much to run. Besides, I don't think I could drag Jeremy away from your nieces."

"He does seem to be having fun."

"Just like his daddy. Let's go have some of that cider."

Alex tucked Shannon's arm into his, and headed for the dining room. He *was* having fun. Food and laughter were a seductive combination—not as seductive as Shannon, but few things could compete with Shannon.

She had said they would eat around two in the afternoon. Alex wondered why it was planned for so late, then learned why when the family gathered around the Christmas tree, crowding into every possible corner as they opened packages.

Somehow, he wasn't surprised to find Jeremy and himself the recipient of several thoughtful gifts. There were a number that Shannon looked at, then put back under the tree, whispering instructions to her eldest brother who was playing Santa by reading labels and passing out packages. She seemed to be anticipating something, and when she heard a car turning into the driveway, she jumped to her feet.

"I hope this is another Christmas present," she said, touching Alex's shoulder before hurrying out to the foyer. When she returned, another woman stood behind her.

Alex froze.

"Everyone, this is Alex's sister, Gail," Shannon announced, drawing Gail forward. "She's here from Japan. Gail, this is everyone. Don't worry about anyone's name, just say 'hey you.'"

Gail.

Remembering their agonizing phone call of just a few days before, Alex felt his stomach clench. Gail looked tired and unsure of herself, but she smiled gamely at the huge, welcoming family. "I hope I'm not intruding."

"Nonsense," Pegeen said. "Come in, child, you look worn to a frazzle."

Alex belatedly rose and gave his sister an awkward kiss. "Jeremy," he said. "Do you remember your Aunt Gail?"

Jeremy didn't, but he'd been hugged so much that day, he was more than willing to get another. Soon he and Gail were sitting together, with Shannon pulling out the packages she'd set aside and giving them to the newcomer.

"Thank you...that's so thoughtful." Gail sounded overwhelmed, and Alex clenched his teeth. Shannon had obviously known his sister was coming, but why hadn't she told him?

After a while Gail seemed to relax, even joining with the O'Rourkes as they sang Christmas carols. Shannon shot him curious glances as she eased his sister into her family circle, the way she had done with him and Jeremy.

What could he say?

You should have told me that my sister, whom I barely know, is coming to Christmas dinner?

Yeah, that would really add to the spirit of the day.

Shannon knew something was wrong. Alex had hardly said two words during dinner, then shortly after his sister left for her hotel, turning down his offer to stay at the condo, he'd suggested they go home.

"Jeremy is already asleep," she murmured as he drove steadily through the darkness. Fog had crept over the Puget Sound area, but Christmas lights still glimmered in the murk.

"Yes."

"I think he had a good time."

"You know he did."

She expelled a breath. It was hard having a conversation with someone who was so tight-lipped. Had he taken a belated offense to her brothers' behavior? Or was it something else? She tried to think of anything else that might have disturbed him, but the worst offense of the day had been Patrick and Neil threatening his well-being in a game of tackle football.

At the condo Alex carried Jeremy upstairs and Shannon sank onto a chair in the living room, waiting for him to come down again. The holiday meal that had tasted so delicious only two hours before, now sat like lead in her stomach.

What had gone wrong?

When Alex returned, he didn't say a word, and she followed him into the kitchen. "I can't take the suspense any longer. What's wrong?"

"Nothing."

"I don't believe that."

"All right, I don't want to discuss it."

"Alex! Look at me. *What is wrong?*"

He threw his keys onto the counter, then turned to her, a fierce glare in his eyes. "Why didn't you tell me Gail was coming to Seattle? How did you even know she was coming?"

The question made Shannon's eyes widen. "She called you, one day while I was watching Jeremy. She wasn't sure she'd be able to get here, and because her plans weren't settled, she decided it was better to make her trip a surprise."

"You should have told me."

"It was what Gail wanted. For Pete's sake, Alex, she's your sister. I thought you'd be thrilled to see her."

"You don't know the score with my family," he retorted. "And you have no right to interfere. You should have discussed it with me before issuing invitations and keeping secrets. *You're not my wife.*"

"I know I'm not your wife," she said tightly. "And you've certainly made it clear that I'm never going to be. So why don't you take a flying leap and see where it takes you?"

Shannon spun, too angry to see straight. It didn't seem possible that Alex could be so awful. Even if he didn't know she was in love with him, he had to know she had strong feelings for both him and Jeremy.

"Where are you going?" he demanded.

"Home."

"I'll walk you over."

"Don't bother." She grabbed her purse and fished her keys from the outside pocket.

If it hadn't been for Jeremy, she would have slammed the door, but she remembered in time that he was asleep. He deserved a night of sugarplum dreams before he learned that his daddy was a confounded *jackass*.

Despite her refusal, Alex came outside and watched her walk the thirty feet to her own door safely. But it wasn't any comfort; it was just aggravating.

She had never *once* asked him to change his mind.

She'd tried to be a friend the way he wanted, and what had that gotten her?

Accusations and anger.

He was impossible.

But as she sank into a chair after letting herself into her condo, she remembered the tormented look in Alex's eyes. Tears streamed down her cheeks. Without even knowing what he was doing, he must have been looking for a way to break things off, a way to feel he was right about banishing her from his and Jeremy's life.

"Oh, Alex," she moaned.

She *could* be a good wife and mother, and still be herself. She finally understood there was more to making a home than being able to cook and clean. But their problems were about Alex's personal demons, not domestic responsibilities.

Alex had never had a family that was a haven, caring and supportive—even when they tried to interfere. Despite that, he had taken a chance by loving Kim, and he'd lost her. Shannon had wondered how many times a shattered heart could heal, and she was afraid Alex was beyond that limit. He was hurting, and there wasn't anything she could do about it.

"Meoowr?" Magellan cried and jumped onto her lap, looking at her anxiously.

"I'm afraid it's over, baby," she whispered.

He lapped a tear that had fallen onto her hand, then rested his chin on the spot.

Shannon looked around her home and realized there *was* something she could do to help Alex, but not with useless crying or reminding him of what they might have had together.

A strength she hadn't known she possessed filled her. She would call a Realtor first thing in the morning and list the condo for sale.

"Are you sure you can't stay longer?" Alex asked his sister as they waited for her plane to board.

"I wish I could, but I didn't plan this trip enough ahead of time." A light blush spread across Gail's cheeks. She had admitted to impulsively deciding to visit Seattle after his telephone call, only to be riddled with second thoughts of how he'd feel about seeing her.

"I'm glad you came," Alex said. He meant it, though he still winced when he thought of how he'd overreacted to Shannon's "surprise" two days before. Even at the time he'd known his response was hugely out of proportion. She hadn't interfered; her loving spirit simply couldn't imagine a sister being anything but a welcome visitor—especially not on Christmas day.

The O'Rourkes celebrated Christmas with all the excitement of small children, but they hadn't forgotten its meaning. Alex, who'd smugly told Shannon that he wanted his son to understand the spirit of giving, had lost its meaning completely.

The boarding call came and Alex hugged Gail close, only to find heat pricking his eyes. "You'll call," he said gruffly. "When you get in?"

"Of course."

"And if there's anything you need...*anything,* you let me know. We'll be on the next plane."

It didn't help his own composure when she gave him a watery smile. "Yes."

"Bye, Auntie Gail." Jeremy gave her a noisy kiss. "You promise to come see me again?"

"I promise."

Alex knew Gail would keep her promise. They had only begun talking, sorting out the tangle of their childhood, but it was a beginning that was long overdue. He and Jeremy would visit her in Japan, and Gail would come to Seattle. And in the meantime, they would force themselves past the awkwardness of talking on the phone, and find a way to be brother and sister, rather than strangers.

Thanks to Shannon.

The thought was uppermost on his mind during the drive home. Shannon had reshaped his life, and all he'd done was wound her, like all the other men who hadn't valued the remarkable woman inside that sophisticated package.

He wasn't ready to end things between them, no matter how often he'd thought it would be for the best. But what could he do to fix what had happened? Fixing relationships wasn't his forte; he was better at screwing them up.

When Alex turned into their shared driveway, he braked to an abrupt halt.

A For Sale sign stood on Shannon's lawn.

He cursed.

"You said a bad word, Daddy," Jeremy said placidly. "Can we go see Shannon? I miss her a whole bunch."

They were going to see Shannon, all right. He was going to find out why she was leaving without even telling him. Jeez, one little fight and she was bailing out.

"Stay here, Jeremy. I'll see if she's home." Alex left the heat running in the Jeep, then stormed up to Shannon's door. He pounded on it furiously. "Shannon, what in hell is going on?"

It opened abruptly and he scowled when she didn't say anything right away.

"Explain that." He pointed to the Realtor's sign.

"Where is Jeremy?" she asked instead. He wanted to shake her.

"Jeremy is in the Jeep, keeping warm." Alex looked at her hungrily, aching at the dark smudges beneath her eyes. "I don't understand. I was a jerk the other night, but that's hardly a reason to do something so drastic. Can't you just blame it on faulty male chromosomes?"

"It isn't that simple. I really can't—"

"I just want an explanation," he shouted, not caring who heard him, or what they'd think. That was what Shannon had done; she had finally made him as nuts as the insane people he'd grown up wanting to escape. "Please explain," he said more quietly. "*Please,* Shannon."

"I...I know that it's hurting you, me being here."

"It isn't that bad," he said, his throat tight from everything he wanted to say, but couldn't.

"Yes, it is. We're tearing each other apart. We can't keep living next to each other, and since I don't have a child to think about, it's only right that I'm the one to leave."

Alex stared. The stark unhappiness in Shannon's eyes wasn't about wounded feelings. She loved him, with more intensity and goodness than he could ever deserve.

Memories flitted through his head: raging battles between his parents, the big and small cruelties they'd handed out on a daily basis. They'd loved each other, too, before it turned to hatred. But he finally knew why they could hurt each other so badly...it was because they'd cared more about their own concerns and well-being than about each other.

But Shannon cared about him.

She cared so much, she was willing to put him and his son's welfare ahead of her own. She would never intentionally use his heart against him. All he had to do was find the courage to risk losing everything again.

And to gain everything.

Because he already loved her. She'd become more important to him than breathing, though he had done his best to deny the truth and push her away because of fear and guilt.

"I love you," he breathed, suddenly free in a way he'd never been. The decision was really very simple—life might be uncertain, but without Shannon, it wasn't worth living. "I know I was a fool, but don't leave us. Jeremy and I can't make it without you."

"You can't...it's too soon."

Alex put her hand over his heart, pressing her fingers to its beating rhythm.

"You're wrong, Shannon. You were just in time. All my life I've been afraid of emotions because of my parents' mistakes. I married a woman I loved, but I let my childhood keep us from the closeness we should have had."

Shannon watched him doubtfully.

"I don't want to make that same mistake twice," he said urgently. "You showed me that hiding from what I feel isn't really being alive, and I want to be alive. But can you trust me enough to share all the things you've kept hidden since your father died?"

Shannon trembled. She'd expected Alex to be relieved she was leaving: expected that he would allow a polite good-bye to Jeremy and be glad he didn't have to deal with her any longer. Yet now he was offering her the world.

"I…are you sure?"

"More sure than I've ever been. Please marry me, Shannon. Love me forever. Trust me enough to be strong for you when things are bad."

Shannon searched Alex's face and saw unqualified adoration. Love and trust and a thousand other promises were vowed in his level gaze.

"I've never spoken about my father with anyone, not the way I talked to you about him," she said softly. "Or of most of the things I've told you about, and it wouldn't have happened if I didn't trust you already." Alex's heart pounded furiously beneath her fingers. "But as much as I trust you, I love you even more," she finished.

He pulled her close and she laughed.

"Jeremy can see us. What if he gets ideas?"

"My son had the right idea all along. But come on, let's tell him."

She laughed again as she was rushed across the lawn to the Jeep Cherokee.

"Good news, Jeremy," Alex said exultantly. "We have a late Christmas present for you."

"What is it?" Jeremy asked, wriggling impatiently as his father released him from the car seat.

"Shannon is going to be your new mommy."

Jeremy became very still. "For honest real, Daddy?"

"For honest real, son."

Jeremy lunged into Shannon's arms. "I was afraid, but on Christmas, my first mommy told me it would be okay," he said, his voice muffled against her shoulder. "She sang me a song and said Daddy just needed to let go. I didn't know what that meant, but she said Daddy knew."

Shannon blinked away tears, though she didn't know how Alex would react to his son's declaration. She'd always accepted there was a larger world beyond human perception, but Alex had never been taught that love didn't know any boundaries.

"Then it's unanimous," Alex said, smiling as if he'd never stop. "Trust me," he whispered.

She nodded and he gathered them both into his arms. Their lips met in a kiss that drove away the last shadows and doubts, everything but the miracle of two people finding each other.

Epilogue

"Did you convince her?" Alex demanded as his wife put down the phone.

"I talked to her, that's all," Shannon said. "You know Gail has to make up her own mind, and it won't help if you pressure her one way or the other."

"But her firm is opening a division in the Seattle area," Alex fumed. He'd become much closer to his sister in the past year and wanted them to spend more time together. "And if she lived here, then she wouldn't have to miss Christmas with us because of some idiotic project."

Shannon laughed and rubbed the small of her back. She loved being pregnant, but the baby's size was beginning to interfere with daily activities...like getting dressed and climbing the two staircases of their 1890 farmhouse.

She sighed with pleasure as she looked around the living room. It was the last sort of house she'd wanted to live in again, but she'd changed her mind the moment they'd seen it and Alex had gotten a kid-in-a-candy-shop look on his face. The old place was great to decorate for Christmas…something she'd actually managed to do on her own.

Of course, she might have gone overboard. With the lighted pine garland on the staircases and fireplace mantels, dozens of poinsettias, and Christmas trees in every window, it was a holiday wonderland. Kane had insisted she take maternity leave early, so she had used the time to decorate to her heart's content.

She had also come up with the idea of having several cookie-baking parties at the house, so Jeremy's cookie cravings had been handled by his new aunts and his grandmother—no fire extinguishers needed.

"Are you all right?" Alex fussed as he pushed pillows behind her back. "You need to rest more."

"I'm fine. If I didn't know better, I would think you'd never gone through this before. But I do know better, because the proof is attending kindergarten this year."

"It's the first time I've gone through it with *you*," he retorted. "And you're so damned uncooperative about following the doctor's orders, you're making me crazy."

Shannon grinned. "She said to put my feet up several times a day, not to become an invalid."

"She also said not to get too tired."

"You're the one getting tired, running around and waiting on me. It's your Christmas break. You have to quit—" Her scolding was smothered by Alex's kiss, which started out teasing, and ended with them both out of breath.

"Have I told you today how much I love you?" he whispered.

"Yes, but I never get tired of hearing it," she murmured.

The past year had seen them through a family wedding, fierce disagreements, home-selling and buying, and the kind of passionate loving that made her current condition all the sweeter. Things hadn't been easy, they'd both needed to make adjustments and compromises, but Shannon hadn't expected easy. Anybody could have easy; she wanted something worth working to have and to keep.

"Jingle Bells, Jingle Bells," sang Jeremy as he trotted into the room. He was a year bigger, and even dearer to Shannon's heart, if that was possible. A few months before, he had given Mr. Tibbles to her for permanent safekeeping, and she'd carefully packed the tired rabbit away with the baby clothes that Kim McKenzie had saved. "Mommy, when are we gonna go singing?"

Alex raised an eyebrow at his wife and tried to look stern. "Singing? In your condition?"

"It's Christmas Eve." She smiled innocently. "I thought everyone could go caroling before we attend the candle-lighting service. Jeremy has never gone caroling before, so it's an educational experience. Besides, he'll have fun."

By "everyone" Alex knew she meant the entire O'Rourke clan. Little by little, Shannon had given him her family, pulling Gail into their circle of love, as well. She'd been making noises about his brother lately, and Alex knew as soon as Sam emerged from his research assignment in the Arctic, he'd be overwhelmed by his sister-in-law.

Alex grinned.

Sam didn't stand a chance against a determined redhead. None of the McKenzies did. To Alex's never-ending amazement, he actually enjoyed the inevitable battle of wills between him and his wife, knowing that love hovered as an ever-present peacemaker.

"Am I gonna have a new brother or sister for Christmas?" Jeremy asked, eyeing Shannon's nonexistent lap. He had to be content with sitting next to her on the couch.

"Santa is working on that," Shannon said, squirming in an attempt to get comfortable.

Alex felt a familiar anxiety. The baby was already overdue. He wanted to suggest that they stay home where it was warm and dry and quiet, but knew his wife would laugh and say that he worried too much. It was hard to believe how much she'd changed his life, opening his mind and heart, refusing to back down on anything she thought was right and important.

As the afternoon and evening progressed, he tried to push the worry to the back of his mind. And, amid the peace of the candlelighting service to celebrate the birth of another small baby, he breathed a prayer of thankfulness and hope for the future.

When Shannon opened her eyes on Christmas morning, she decided she must be in heaven. Magellan—now a magnificent adult-size cat—purred contentedly at the foot of the bed. Small flickers of flame still danced in the bedroom hearth. And her husband held her close, his warmth stretching from the back of her head to her heels, while his hand rested carefully on her rounded tummy.

Alex still didn't like waking up, but that was okay. Shannon knew how to make him smile, even if it *was* morning.

She grimaced at the persistent ache in her back. Correction: she could make him smile when she *wasn't* nine months pregnant and ready to pop at any moment. Seducing her sleeping husband wasn't a problem when she could do more than just *think* about it.

"Mommy, Daddy, Santa came again," Jeremy shouted, bursting through the door. "An' he ate all the cookies and drank the milk. He even lef' me a card. See? I can read the words. It says Thank you."

Jeremy dropped the card on the bed and went tearing down the stairs again.

Shannon smiled.

"Nice touch," Alex murmured behind her.

One of her eyebrows lifted. "Don't look at me. I didn't leave a card—you're the one who ate the cookies and milk."

"I thought you ate them."

Shannon squirmed awkwardly to face him. "Not a bite."

They looked at each other, then they shook their heads. Some mysteries were better left unanswered, though Shannon privately thought Alex was pulling her leg. He loved teasing her about "Santa," declaring she probably still believed in the jolly old fat guy.

Maybe.

She'd never received a greater gift than her family, both the one she'd been born into, and the one given to her only a year before. If Santa truly represented the spirit of love and generosity, then she believed in him wholeheartedly.

After their own celebration around the living-room Christmas tree, they drove to her mother's house, with Jeremy singing his new favorite song, "Silent Night."

"It's an improvement on Jingle Bells, but he's still off-key," Alex murmured after they arrived and Jeremy went tearing across the yard to leap into his Uncle Kane's arms.

Shannon patted Alex's hand. "That's okay, honey, he gets his singing ability from you."

A mock glare was followed by a kiss as he lifted her from the high seat of the Jeep. "Are you sure you shouldn't be home in bed?" he asked.

"Positive." Shannon kissed his nose, but she was grateful for his strong arm as they climbed the porch steps. She hadn't told him about the contractions she'd felt before leaving their house. They were barely noticeable, and she wanted them to enjoy Christmas before making a mad dash to the hospital. Of course, O'Rourke babies had a habit of appearing at the most inopportune moments, and she figured this one wouldn't be any different.

"Surprise," Pegeen said as she pulled Gail out from behind the Christmas tree. "Look who flew into Seattle this morning."

"You said you couldn't come," Alex exclaimed as he embraced his sister.

"I didn't want to disappoint you if I had to cancel." Gail hugged her nephew as he launched himself at her. She smiled at Shannon and gave her a kiss over Jeremy's head. "Pegeen helped to arrange it."

"Now, none of that. I said you're to call me Mom, like all my other children," Pegeen scolded.

Alex saw the pleased blush on Gail's cheeks and felt regret for everything his own parents had missed over the years. But as Shannon snuggled next to him on the couch, he decided that Christmas wasn't a time for regret; it was a time for counting blessings.

Like the Christmas before, there was food and laughter, eggnog and hot cider to drink. Jeremy played with his cousins, and babies were passed from one welcoming arm to another.

Before dinner, Shannon went into the kitchen and sat in a chair, watching the bustle. She no longer felt left out because she didn't cook or do things like the other women in the family; she was truly Jeremy's mother and a passionately loved wife, and those were the only things that counted.

But Pegeen's sharp gaze wasn't to be discounted, and after a few minutes she leaned over her pregnant daughter. "How far apart, darlin'?"

Shannon laughed and shook her head. "I should have known you'd guess. The contractions are over thirty minutes apart, and my water hasn't broken yet, so there's plenty of time."

"Hmmm. 'Tis a good thing your cousin, Liam, is here."

Liam O'Rourke was a doctor, but Shannon had every intention of having her baby at the hospital, or her husband would never let her hear the end of it.

"I'll be fine," she said. "You had nine babies. You should find this stuff old hat. Positively boring."

"Never. And to think we'll have a Christmas babe…" Pegeen gave a happy sigh. "'Tis even better than I'd hoped."

"Bet you never thought I'd be next," Shannon said, smiling as she patted her drum-tight tummy.

"You're wrong." Pegeen kissed her daughter's forehead. "I knew when I met Alex and saw the way he looked at you. A fine man denyin' his own heart, but lovin' you with all of it, just the same."

Much later, as Shannon sat with Alex's fingers intertwined with her own, she knew they couldn't wait any longer. She'd managed to slip out of the room whenever a contraction was coming so he wouldn't guess, but something told her it was time.

"Um…Alex?" she murmured.

"Yes, darling?"

"I think it's time to get the Jeep warmed up."

"Are you…" He took one look at her face and leapt to his feet. *Oh, my God, the baby's coming!*

She laughed through the pain gripping her abdomen. "Well, it's not coming this minute, but let's not wait too long."

Liam was at her side in an instant, asking questions and taking her pulse. When Alex raced back into the room, her cousin calmly assured him they had plenty of time.

While everyone talked, assuring them Jeremy would be taken care of, Shannon donned her coat. She wanted to walk out under her own steam, but her husband would hear none of it. He carried her outside and in the glittering illumination of Christmas lights she saw excitement and worry on his handsome face.

"We'll be fine," she said as he put her in the passenger's seat. "Babies have been getting born since the beginning of time." But Shannon knew he would worry just the same.

They were met at the hospital by an efficient contingent of medical personnel, including her own obstetrician. Liam had come, as well, and the two doctors consulted as she was prepped.

An hour passed, then another, with Alex holding her hand and counting the way they'd practiced in childbirthing class. Her water broke late, and then everything happened in a rush. Twenty minutes later, she delivered a healthy, six-pound-nine-ounce daughter.

The nurse went out to the waiting room, where Gail McKenzie and the O'Rourkes had crowded together in anticipation. A happy roar burst out at the announcement, discernable even from the delivery room. Jeremy's excited cries rose above the rest; he'd gotten a sister for Christmas and it seemed to be exactly what he'd wished.

Later in her room, Shannon drowsily watched as Alex sat by the bed and gazed at their little girl, awe and adoration in his face. They had counted fingers and toes together, marveling at her dark red hair and angelic face, but this was her daddy's time; a time for silent promises and hopes for the future.

Tears pricked her eyes and Shannon knew that tonight, of all the nights in her life, she missed her own father the most. Yet even as the thought formed, she heard echoes of Keenan O'Rourke's voice in her mind and heart, and knew that he was watching and rejoicing.

Alex tore his gaze from the sleeping baby. "What is it?" he asked, knowing instantly that the darkness in his wife's eyes didn't come from discomfort or exhaustion.

"I was just thinking about my father...wishing he could be here."

"He *is* here, Shannon. Nothing could keep him away."

"I know." She smiled and held out her hand. "I've been thinking...we've talked about so many names, but maybe we should consider using Kimberly."

Alex swallowed, trying to control the lump in his throat. Shannon accepted the life he'd once shared with Kim; she even celebrated that life because of her love for Jeremy. Few women could have been so generous.

"I think you're wonderful," he said when he could talk. He looked down at the precious bundle he held, the tiny infant who already possessed his heart and soul as completely as her mother did. "But I can't think of a better name than Holly Noel for a little girl born on Christmas."

"Oh...all right."

Shannon's radiant smile filled Alex and he leaned forward.

"I love you, Shannon McKenzie," he whispered against her lips, and heard it returned with sweet promise.

Sometimes the greatest miracles of all were the ones you never knew you needed.

* * * * *

This book is dedicated to my good friend,
Darlene Hanson,
and her mother,
Pearl Hanson

STRANDED WITH SANTA

Janet Tronstad

JANET TRONSTAD

grew up on a small farm in central Montana. One of her favourite things to do was to visit her grandfather's bookshelves, where he had a large collection of Zane Grey novels. She's always loved a good story.

Today, Janet lives in Pasadena, California, where she works in the research department of a medical organisation. In addition to writing novels, she researches and writes non-fiction magazine articles.

Chapter One

Zach Lucas stood on a weathered old porch in the small town of Deep Gulch, Montana, and scowled as the gray sky darkened even further. "It's going to snow."

Dr. Norris, the only vet in Deep Gulch, Montana, shrugged as he cheerfully slipped another handful of candy canes into the mail bag Zach had slung over his shoulder. "Don't worry about the snow. The postal truck always makes it through. You'll do fine."

The doctor had made a bargain with Zach. It was Saturday, December 23, and Zach was to deliver the mail along the rural route outside of Deep Gulch so that the doctor, who had promised he would do his sister's mail route in her absence, could tend to Zach's sick horse instead.

It was a perfect bargain except for one small thing. Zach hated it.

If he wasn't so worried about his horse, Zach would never have agreed. It wasn't that he had anything against delivering the mail. That was no problem. What was a problem was delivering it the way the doctor's sister wanted it done. She wanted it to look like Santa himself was out there delivering the letters this close to Christmas.

Zach pushed his Stetson hat lower on his head. He didn't know anyone in this crazy one-stop town, but he still hoped no one saw him as he stood on the doctor's porch. He was Zach "Lightning" Lucas and he had a reputation to uphold—a reputation that didn't include a fuzzy red fat-suit and a plastic black belt. It was bad enough that the four-wheel-drive postal truck had a fake set of reindeer horns tied to the grill and a ball of mistletoe swinging from the antenna. He didn't need Christmas fuzz all over him, too.

Zach grimaced as red and green flashes met his eyes. The lightbulbs hanging from the reindeer horns were on a timer. When he first saw them, he'd hoped they were merely ornamental. No such luck.

Zach didn't know how much holiday nonsense he could take. After all, he was Zach "Lightning" Lucas. He had more gold-plated champion belt buckles than most men had ties. He had fans who knew his name—lots of fans since he'd endorsed that Ranger breakfast cereal. People recognized him in grocery stores and in laundromats. He was famous, for Pete's sake. He was entitled to some dignity.

Unfortunately, the doctor did not care about Zach's dignity. And it was all because of Christmas. Not that Zach should be surprised. Christmas had been giving him trouble for years. It always depressed him with all that family stuff. Not that Zach had anything against families—it's just that that family stuff wasn't for a man like him.

That's why, this year, he had made a plan.

Zach and Thunder were only passing through Montana, heading over to Interstate 15 for the long stretch down to Las Vegas. Once there, Thunder would board at a ranch some miles outside of Vegas while Zach hit the Strip. The neon lights and showgirls—well, if her return message was to be believed, one showgirl in particular—would make him forget the holidays were even here.

He and Thunder had been making good time, too, Zach thought mournfully, until Thunder got a fever.

"You've got the map." The older man patted his pockets as though the slip of paper showing all the county roads might still be there instead of taped to the dashboard of the postal truck.

"Yes, sir."

The winter air had a bite to it, but Zach was in no hurry to leave the doctor's porch and get into that decked-out postal truck. He might as well ride around in a clown's cart and be done with it.

"Well then, let me get that apple pie my sister baked for the Collins family." Dr. Norris ducked inside his house, his muffled voice continuing, "That'll be the last stop on your list. And the box in back is for them, too. Their car is broken. Radiator. So Delores said she'd pick some things up for them." The doctor appeared again with a foil-wrapped pie. "Two of the cutest kids you'll ever meet."

Zach nodded. He'd already met every kid on the planet—both the cute and the ugly. The ones he missed at the rodeos he met because they ate Ranger breakfast cereal. Not that he was complaining. He liked kids better than he liked most adults.

The doctor smiled and looked at Zach slyly. "'Course, one look at their mother and you'll see why they're so cute."

Zach grunted. Now that was the part of meeting kids he didn't like—their mothers. Even the women who were married always seemed to have a scheme to get him married off to someone. You'd think there was something wrong with a man choosing to live in hotel rooms and wash his socks in bathroom sinks.

The doctor shook his head. "The poor woman. Such a pity—"

The doctor looked at Zach as though he expected some curiosity.

Zach had none.

The doctor ploughed ahead, anyway. "Jenny Collins is a widow. Not that she's old, mind you. No, sir. Moved up here a couple of months ago—surprised us all. She'd been married to Jeb Collins's nephew." The doctor nodded at Zach as though Zach had known this Jeb, whoever he was. "Jeb had left the place to his nephew, but we all thought the nephew would have sense enough to sell it before he started dying of that cancer of his. But he didn't. Don't know what he was thinking. Surely he didn't expect his widow to move up here with the two kids. What do you think a city woman's gonna do with a place like that anyway?"

Zach shrugged. He didn't like to get involved in the problems of strangers.

The doctor had no such hesitation. "Delores says the woman's been getting magazines on farm management!" He shook his head. "She's a game one, I'll give her that. But it's no place for her and the kids—even old man Collins used to move into town here for the winter months. The house doesn't even have a decent road leading up to it. Ruts a mile deep, and it drifts closed every time there's a blizzard."

The doc took a breath before he continued. "Delores always drives the mail right up to the house for them. But with the next hard snow they won't get mail for a week. The county snowplow doesn't go that far out. Most farmers out that way have plows on their tractors or something. But all the woman's got is that car of hers—and with the two little ones—Delores worries about their car not working."

Delores, Zach had already learned, worried about everything and everybody.

The doctor stopped suddenly and squinted at Zach. "What Jenny Collins needs is a husband."

Zach looked at the doctor in amazement and then pushed his hat farther down on his head. "Don't look at me. I'm just trying to get my horse fixed up. Besides, from the sounds of it, she needs a tractor worse than she needs a husband."

The doctor shrugged. "I doubt you'd stand a chance, anyway. I hear Max Daniel is planning to ask her out—he's a rancher north of here. 'Course Tom Fox might beat him to the punch. A good-looking woman like Jenny can have her pick of the bachelors around here."

Zach grunted. Ever since he started making money at rodeoing, he'd had women who wanted him to settle down. Made him nervous as a rope-tied calf every time a woman talked about it. Anyone with any sense could see that the life he'd led didn't prepare him for marriage.

Not that he didn't like women. He did. He just had sense enough to know his limitations. He didn't even have a year-round mailing address; he'd be a fool to think he would be any good at marriage.

"Yeah, well, it was only a thought," the doctor said as he pointed to the back of the truck. "Now, you remember what I said about the camera back there. Delores promised Jenny pictures of her little boy with Santa, and I'll never hear the end of it if you don't remember to take one."

"Pictures." Zach grimaced. "I'm not much good at pictures."

"What? You can't tell me that. Even I've seen your picture in the paper. You looked okay to me."

"Well, the news photos—and the ads—they're all right. But they're not, well, personal."

Zach didn't know how to explain his reluctance to have a picture of him in some family album along with pictures of babies and grandmas. He'd feel a fraud. A family photo album was one place he didn't belong.

"There's nothing to a Santa picture," the doctor said, pushing ahead anyway. "It's one of those cameras that prints out a picture while you wait. Jenny will even take the picture for you. And Delores said to leave it, in case Jenny wants to take other Christmas shots."

Zach nodded in defeat. What was Delores going for... mail carrier of the year?

"And don't forget about old Mrs. Goussley. She has a sweet tooth. Delores always gives her a few extra candy canes." The doctor winked "Say they're for her cats. She'll give them back if you say they're for her."

"Cats," Zach repeated bleakly. Forget mail carrier of the year, Delores must be going for sainthood.

"Mrs. Goussley likes her visit from Santa. She gets a kick out of the suit." The doc eyed Zach. "I know my sister got carried away this year with putting those flashing lights around Santa's belt, but you can keep them pressed off if you want. Plus the suit's warm—all that padding. Still it might not be enough. Gets cold out there. Could drop to zero before you get back."

"I've got a sheepskin coat if it does." Zach had put his duffel bag and the coat in the postal truck. The sheepskin was imitation, but of good enough quality to be worth a pretty penny. It wasn't something he'd leave behind. Not that he didn't trust the doctor, but he'd worked enough rodeos to know never to leave his duffel with strangers.

"Oh, well then," the doctor muttered as he walked toward the truck. "I'll just put this pie inside and let you get going. Remember, now, the brakes turn a little to the left if you happen to be going downhill."

Zach nodded. He was definitely going downhill. Playing Santa to an old lady and her cats. Zach "Lightning" Lucas. He shook his head and pulled his Stetson down farther.

He sure hoped no one saw him.

Jenny Collins looked out the kitchen window again. Gray stormclouds almost covered the square butte west of her place. It was starting to snow, and the mail hadn't come yet. Delores had told her the doctor might be late with the mail, but he'd see the package got to them. It wasn't much, but it had the few presents she'd been able to get for the children, and she was anxious for them to arrive. Tomorrow was Christmas Eve day and, since it would be Sunday, there'd be no mail delivery then.

She had kept thinking she would get the car running, so Jenny had not sent her list in with Delores until a few days ago. The box should contain a water pistol for Andy, a paint kit for Lisa, and much-needed mittens and scarves for them both. Four-year-old Andy really wanted a cowboy outfit with a hat, and eight-year-old Lisa really wanted a princess tiara, but they were both too expensive and nowhere to be found in Deep Gulch anyway.

Maybe next year, Jenny consoled herself. She'd surely think of a way to make some money soon. She had to. She'd just spent everything except a few hundred dollars filling the propane tank so the furnace would keep going for the next few months. If nothing else, she wanted to be generous with heat when it came to their place.

Their place. She repeated the phrase to herself in satisfaction. This Christmas it would be enough that they had a home that was all their own, even if the roof leaked on the south side of the living room and the linoleum in the kitchen had more cracks than color left. Still, the place had three bedrooms and no mortgage. She was glad her husband had forgotten he had the deed to this place. It was the one thing she had left when the estate was settled.

She'd go looking for a job after Christmas. She'd have to go to Deep Gulch each day, anyway, once she enrolled Lisa in the school there.

Jenny had talked to the second-grade teacher, and they'd agreed Lisa could start in January. Surely by then Jenny would have the car running.

In the meantime, they were happy enough. Maybe more than happy. Jenny had always dreamed of living in a small town like Deep Gulch. Her dreams even included a mail carrier like Delores.

Jenny and her family had rented a house for eight years on that wretched street in El Monte, just east of Los Angeles, and the mail delivery people there changed routes so often she doubted any of them knew her face let alone her name. Here, Delores greeted Jenny like a friend and spoiled the kids with dinosaur candy and news of her own grandchildren.

Yes, Deep Gulch was home. Jenny just needed to find a way to make her piece of home support them.

"Mom, I see her coming!" Andy's voice carried from the back bedroom. He was obviously looking out the window himself.

"Get down off those boxes, Andrew Joel." If he could see

out the window, it meant he was standing on the boxes again. Jenny didn't intend to leave everything in boxes for long. She just hadn't been able to buy dressers or book shelves or cabinets—none of the furniture that stored things.

Jenny had left all their furniture in California. She'd had to. Their savings wouldn't stretch to paying off the funeral expenses and hiring a moving van, as well. Besides, she'd hoped there might be furniture in the house already.

That hope died when she took one look at the outside of the house and realized the inside probably wasn't much better. The property wasn't what she had expected. She doubted anything but thistle had grown on the place for the past ten years. The acreage was fenced, but half of the fence was down. The only trees were short scrub ones, and she'd already heard from someone at the store in Deep Gulch that the creek at the bottom of the coulee had been dry for the past five years.

Still, Jenny knew this was their home. Even though it had already turned cold before they moved, the children liked to be outside. They had a freedom they had never known around Los Angeles.

If the children were happy, Jenny could live without furniture for a few months. She'd told the kids they'd pretend they were camping. So far, they hadn't complained.

"But she's coming!" Andrew said as he ran out of the bedroom door and down the small hallway. "She's coming to get my letter."

"Oh, dear. I forgot," Jenny remembered that Delores had

promised Andy she'd take his letter special delivery to the North Pole so that Santa could read it before he began his trip tomorrow. Jenny had helped him write the letter so she had known for days what it said. She just hadn't realized he wanted the letter mailed until recently. "I'm afraid it won't be Delores getting the mail today. Her brother is taking the route for her."

"The guy who showed me that runny pig?"

"Runt. The pig was a runt. And, yes, that's the man."

"Can he find the North Pole?"

"I'm sure he can," Jenny said. Dr. Norris was a nice man. She was sure he'd play along with Andy's fantasy. Andy was at the age when he was starting to doubt Santa Claus, but he wasn't ready to give up hope yet.

Or maybe, Jenny thought, she was the one not willing for him to give up his fantasy. His young life had been so difficult. He'd never really had a father. At least not one who showed any interest in him.

Stephen had made it plain to Jenny even before they married that he wasn't a family man. Jenny had thought he would change—surely a man would care about his own children. But Stephen never had. Stephen had lived his life apart from the family as much as possible ever since her oldest, Lisa, was born.

No, it wouldn't hurt Andy to believe in Santa for another year.

Zach twisted the wheel to keep the postal truck on the road. The doctor hadn't exaggerated when he'd complained about the ruts to the Collins place. No wonder the woman's car was down for the count. There probably wasn't a nut or bolt in the vehicle that hadn't been shaken to within an inch of its life.

The road matched the house at its end. A bright patch of white paint around the door made the rest of the house look even more faded. He suspected this Collins woman didn't know that paint needed to be applied in warmer, dryer weather. Of course, he supposed it did get the message across that someone was living there. Without that paint and the yellow curtains in the kitchen window, the place would look deserted.

The land itself looked like no one had ever cared for it. Flat and gray, the land stretched out in all directions with nothing but half-melted lumps of old snow drifts and a few scrub trees on it. The gray patches were gathering a coating of white as the snowflakes started to fall. In the distance Zach saw a few buttes rising up from the ground, but they were so far away he didn't pay them any attention.

A woman opened the door as Zach pulled the postal truck to a stop. She was hugging an unbuttoned man's flannel shirt around her shoulders and was wearing a T-shirt and jeans. A young girl stood on one side of her and an even younger boy on the other.

Zach unlatched the side door and stepped out of the postal truck. The north wind was already turning bitter, so he walked along the south side of the truck until he reached the vehicle's back door. Cold, hard flakes of snow hit against his face.

Zach had given up and put the Santa beard and hat on before he even got to Mrs. Goussley's. It was the cookies that had done it. Every place he stopped someone shoved a plate of homemade cookies into his hands. He explained that he wasn't Delores—shoot, he wasn't even the doctor—he wasn't entitled to any cookies. But no one listened. It was Christmas, they said, and he looked like a nice young man.

He hadn't been called a nice young man since he'd started riding rodeo.

He was getting soft, he thought glumly as he yanked the furry red cap farther down on his head and snapped the fake white beard into place. The cardboard box marked "Collins" and the pie were all the mail left to deliver.

Zach lifted the two things up. It would only take a minute to get the box up to the porch. Once there, he'd see about a quick Santa picture with the kids and head back to town. Maybe Thunder would be able to travel by then. If Zach was lucky, he'd be in the arms of that showgirl by Christmas after all.

Even from a distance Zach could see the woman was younger than he'd thought she would be. He'd guess her age at twenty-five or twenty-six. He shared the doctor's surprise that she'd taken on a farm in the middle of Montana. He would expect someone like her to move into one of the cities like Billings or maybe Missoula. Someplace that had a video store and a beauty shop.

Not that it was any of his worry. She could live on the moon for all he cared.

"Package," Zach said when he got close enough to the porch to thrust the package at the woman.

Short blond curls blew around her face, and up close he confirmed his opinion of her. Even in the cold, she would draw some attention in a crowd. The wind had turned her nose pink to match her cheeks.

Zach had a momentary wish he'd taken the Santa suit off before he'd made his last delivery. Lots of women had a weakness for cowboys. He'd never heard of a woman yet who thought a fat, polyester Santa was sexy.

Not that he was interested in what this woman or any woman in this part of Montana thought about him. What he'd told the doctor had been true—he was just delivering the mail and then passing through.

If Zach had been paying attention to what he was doing instead of admiring the woman in front of him, he would have seen her eyes sooner. Startled blue eyes looked straight at him.

"It's the mail," Zach clarified. No one else had greeted him with anything remotely like panic. Maybe she thought he was some kind of kook. "The suit's for the old ladies. Well, that and the pictures. Delores wanted you to have one with your kids."

"Where's the doctor?"

"Back in town looking after my horse."

"You've got a horse." The young boy looked around his mother's thigh and up at Zach. His eyes shone with wonder. "A real horse."

The two children stood on either side of the woman. The

boy's jeans were neatly patched at the knees, and he obviously took his fair share of tumbles; the girl's clothes were well washed but showed no sign of stains or tears. Not even little ones. The boy's eyes had already welcomed Zach, but the girl's were more careful.

"Thunder's as real as a horse can be, even when he's sick," Zach said. "In his day, he was the best bucking bronc around."

"Santa has reindeer—not horses," the young girl pointedly corrected Zach as she crossed her arms. Zach pegged her age at seven. Maybe eight. "You need to get the story straight."

"It's no story," Zach protested. "I'm not—"

The woman's eyes widened in even more alarm and Zach stopped. He looked back down at the young boy.

"—in a hurry," Zach fumbled. Were there still kids left that believed in Santa Claus? Apparently so. "I'm not in a hurry at all."

The woman smiled in relief.

Now, *that* woman should smile more often, Zach thought. She was pretty without it, but when she smiled she made him think of one of those soap ads where they try to picture springtime. It might be twenty degrees below zero on this porch right now, but when he looked at her he could almost see the green meadow she should be walking through.

But, Zach reminded himself, he wasn't here to think of meadows. He was here to deliver the mail, snap a picture and give away the last of those blasted candy canes.

"I have something for you in my pocket." Zach had moved the last of the candy canes from the bag to his pocket several stops back. "Just let me set this box down inside the house and I'll get it out for you."

Zach didn't notice that the alarm on the woman's face turned to dismay.

"I can take the package," Jenny offered. She wasn't ready for company.

"No problem. I've got it," Zach said as he stepped up to the door the boy was opening.

"But I can—" Jenny started to repeat even as she watched the man walk into her kitchen. Great, she thought. Just what she needed—some man in a Santa suit seeing her house. Every man she had ever known expected a woman to keep a neat house. Stacks of boxes and fold-up furniture would hardly qualify as neat.

She hoped the beard would hide his disapproval. Although, she told herself with a tilt of her chin, it wasn't any of his business what kind of a housekeeper she was.

Chapter Two

"I haven't had a chance to get to town much yet," Jenny said defensively as she stepped through the kitchen doorway behind the man. She hadn't minded when Delores Norris had come inside and sat on one of the folding chairs. But a strange man was different. "I've been meaning to find some used furniture or something."

The man set the box and a foil-wrapped pie down on the kitchen counter and started patting his pockets.

The kitchen counter was covered with tiles so old the white had turned yellow, but Jenny had scrubbed the grout clean. The floor, too, was spotlessly clean even though the linoleum was cracked. No one could say the place was dirty, she reminded herself, even if they could say it lacked almost everything else to recommend it.

"I've asked about garage sales—then I'll be able to buy

a few things," Jenny continued before realizing the man was not only not listening, but he hadn't even taken a good look around. He probably didn't realize that all that stood in the kitchen was a broom in one corner and the folding card table and chairs that sat square in the middle.

"I must have another candy cane here someplace." The Santa man turned and held up one candy cane. The plastic around the red-and-white cane was wrinkled and looked as if it had been slept on. "I'm sure I couldn't have given them all out already."

The man continued patting his pockets a little frantically. "I gave one for each of the cats—that was five—and a few extra when she said one of the cats was going to have kittens—and then she gave me that plate of cookies, and I had to give her some for that—but I should still have—"

Zach made another pass at checking the pocket on his right. The suit only had the two large pockets, and they had both been full of candy canes. He shouldn't have given so many to Mrs. Goussley and her cats. Not when two children were waiting at the end of the route. "Maybe one dropped out in the truck. I'll go see."

Zach smiled at the kids to show they could trust him. The boy smiled back, so excited he was almost spinning. The girl eyed Zach suspiciously. No smile there. She clearly had her doubts about him and the promised candy cane. Well, he didn't blame her. At least she wasn't whining about it.

Zach walked toward the door.

"I'll go with you," Jenny said, as she turned to the two children. "You two stay here."

"But, Mom, I gotta—"

"Stay here," the woman interrupted the young boy. "We'll be right back. I want to talk to Santa."

"But, Mom," the boy persisted. "I gotta—"

"Later. I need to talk to Santa *alone*." The young woman used her best mother voice. Gentle but firm.

Zach forgot all about the candy canes. Maybe Santa did have a little sex appeal if an attractive young woman was willing to take a walk in freezing temperatures just to talk to him privately. But he knew that a woman like her was trouble. He'd feel hog-tied after the second date. He'd have to tell her he was just passing through.

Zach took another look at the woman's face and hesitated. Maybe he was being too cautious about dating. Just because a second date was out of the question, that didn't mean a first date was impossible. Even a woman like that wouldn't have expectations on a first date, would she? A first date was a test with no commitment whatsoever. And that's all it would be. One date. He could put off starting down to Vegas until morning and still make it. Maybe he should ask her out for dinner tonight. He didn't see any restaurants in Deep Gulch, but people must go out somewhere.

"Where do people go around here for fun?" Zach asked as he opened the door for the woman.

It was only four o'clock in the afternoon, but the cold pinched at Zach's nose and he was grateful for the warmth of that beard on his face. The temperature had dipped a few degrees just in the time they had been inside. A full-fledged storm was coming.

"Fun?" The woman looked at him blankly. She crossed her arms against the cold and walked out the door, headed toward the postal truck.

Zach closed the door and hurried to follow. He could see the goose bumps on her neck in the strip between her collar and her hair. Pinpricks of snow still swirled around in the wind. "You need to wear something heavier than that flannel shirt when you're outside."

The woman walked faster. Her teeth chattered so he could hardly make out her words. "It'll do."

Zach opened the passenger door to the postal truck. The handle was icy to his touch. "Here. Sit inside."

Zach closed the passenger door and quickly walked around to the driver's side.

"You've heard of the North Pole?" the woman asked when Zach was inside and seated.

"That some kind of night club?" Zach was feeling more hopeful. Now they were talking fun. She didn't look like the kind of a woman to go to some pole-dancing night club, but you never could tell. Maybe he wouldn't even need to go to Vegas to find some Christmas cheer. Pole dancing was as good as the showgirl stuff anyday.

"Huh?" the woman looked bewildered.

"The doc could watch the kids," Zach thought out loud. He felt a little bad about the kids, but the old doctor would treat them fine. He probably even had more of those candy canes. The kids could do without their mother for one night. Shoot, some kids would be glad to spend a night apart from their mother.

"The North Pole," the woman repeated as if she had doubts about his mental abilities. "You know—that place where Santa Claus makes his toys."

"Oh." So much for pole dancing.

Zach reached up and turned on the heat. The engine was still warm and gave off a soft wave of hot air. "I didn't know you meant *that* North Pole. Sure, I know it."

"Well, Andy is going to give you a letter to deliver to Santa Claus at the North Pole. Just go along with it, okay?"

"Sure," Zach shrugged. "I'll tell him I ride my horse, Thunder, right up there every night."

Jenny frowned. "Don't overdo it. He's four, but he's not gullible."

Zach refrained from pointing out that the boy still believed in Santa Claus. "Anything you say."

Zach smiled.

Jenny frowned.

Zach got a glimpse of himself in the rearview mirror and frowned, too. No wonder the woman was still cool to him. He looked like a lunatic. His beard was crooked and, instead of hair, it looked as if it were made of yarn that some cat had chewed. Zach pulled the beard down past his chin and let it settle around his neck. He pushed the Santa hat far enough back on his head so that she could see his hair. That should make her relax.

It didn't.

Jenny's frown turned to an expression of alarm. "You look just like that…that cowboy on the cereal box."

Zach relaxed. He was home free. She'd seen the Ranger boxes. "He's me—I mean, I'm him."

"But you can't be."

Jenny tried not to stare at the man's face. His cheekbones were high; his eyebrows black and fierce looking when he wasn't smiling. It was the middle of winter and his tan was only partially faded. The golden flecks in his brown eyes saved his face from being too severe. Nothing saved it from being the handsomest face she had ever seen.

Jenny had dreamed of that face ever since Andy had convinced her to buy the first box of that cereal a year ago. She must have bought three dozen boxes this last year alone. And that wasn't the worst of it. She'd been talking to the box.

Jenny was a private person and she didn't admit her unhappiness to anyone. But, one morning at a solitary breakfast, she'd poured out her troubles to the face on the back of the box and she'd been talking to it ever since. Only the face on the box knew of her disappointment with her marriage. To the rest of the world, her marriage was fine and her husband was the good-natured man he appeared to be to others. But the box knew the truth.

She'd told that box things she wouldn't have admitted to a priest, and now it sat before her. She felt betrayed. Pictures on cereal boxes were not supposed to spring to life in front of your eyes.

"—you just can't be him."

"Well, everybody's got to be somebody."

Jenny panicked. Not only was the face here, it was—unless she missed her guess—also teasing her. Maybe even flirting with her. It was awful—like the Pope asking you out on a date. "You'll have to go."

Okay, Zach thought to himself. Definitely not a pole dancer. Which was fine. He had his good time waiting in Vegas. "Just give me a minute to find another one of those candy canes and I'll be happy to head out. I need to get back before the storm hits anyway."

Jenny looked up. "I thought you said you'd take a picture with Andy."

"I did, but I thought you were, well, in a hurry for me to leave."

"No, I'm just, well, I don't want to take more of your time. But a picture only takes a second."

Jenny forced herself to look the man in the face. It wasn't his fault she'd started talking to his picture.

"Okay. Fine. Whatever you want."

Jenny forced herself to smile. "It's just that you're the only Santa around."

Zach grunted. "No problem."

"And I appreciate you bringing out everything for Delores. And the candy canes, too. That was very nice of you."

"Delores bought the canes. I'm just passing them out for her."

"Still…"

Zach noted that the woman's face had relaxed. The goose bumps had left. The air inside the truck wasn't white with trails of exhaled air. "Not a problem. I'll even tell that boy of yours I'll take his letter to Santa."

"I'm sorry I can't—I mean, I don't date anyway—not that you were asking me out." Jenny stopped in embarrassment.

"Oh, but I was asking you out. At least I was heading in that general direction."

Jenny couldn't help but notice he sounded a little too cheerful for someone who had just been turned down.

"Well, I appreciate that. I'm just sorry I can't accept."

"It's okay," Zach felt around the side of his seat and found not one but two candy canes. Hallelujah! He'd soon be out of here. "I suppose you tried the cereal and didn't like it—or you thought the manufacturer shouldn't say it is the cereal real cowboys eat when everybody knows cowboys don't eat anything but beans and trail dust."

"No, actually, I like the cereal. And I think cowboys would like it if they had a chance to try it. It's great—real nutty."

Zach nodded and didn't make the obvious comparison. "So you like the cereal. You just object to the box."

Jenny nodded sheepishly. "I guess it is kind of odd."

"No problem." Zach smiled to show it was okay. He'd been bucked by broncs. He'd learned how to take his lumps in life. If the woman was that set against him, he'd let it be. Better times were waiting for him. "I'll just take this other candy cane into the house and pick up the letter from—what's the kid's name again?"

"Andy."

"So I'll pick up the letter from Andy, do our bit with the camera and be on my way back to the doctor's."

"Thank you for understanding."

Zach shrugged as he opened the driver's door on the postal truck. "Don't mention it."

To show there were no hard feelings, Zach walked around and opened the passenger door, as well. "Some folks think the picture on the box is just some dress-up modeling job. But it isn't. The cereal company asked to put my picture on the box because I won the All-Pro Championship in bronc riding last fall."

"Oh, I didn't think they used your picture because of your looks." Jenny gracefully stepped out of the truck and almost immediately folded her arms in front of her for warmth.

Zach admitted complete defeat. Most women found him attractive. He wasn't fool enough to go after one who didn't. Especially not when he was out in the middle of nowhere and the sky was turning a serious gray.

"Storm's coming," Zach offered as they walked toward the house. He suddenly understood why Delores worried so much over this little family. He felt some of that same worry tugging at him. There wasn't another house around for miles. "You got enough supplies stored up and everything? A winter storm in southern Montana can be a fierce thing."

"I know that."

Zach wondered how she could know that. He didn't ask, but she must have caught the drift of his disbelieving thoughts.

"I may not have lived through one of the storms here,

but even in Los Angeles they have guidebooks that talk about Montana."

Zach groaned inside. She'd learned about Montana storms from a guidebook.

The few snowflakes that were falling had a dry sting to them. Zach knew that meant the coming storm would be cold enough to freeze a person. Some folks thought the large wet flakes signaled the worst storms, but they didn't. The wet flakes generally meant more snow, but the dry ones foretold a swift and merciless drop in temperature. And with the wind that could be dangerous.

"The electrical will probably go out. Are you set for that?"

Jenny turned to look at him squarely and lifted her chin. She was standing on her porch and she could still feel the pinch of the cold in her nose. She could see the sky was going deep gray and she could hear the grumbling in the air. "We have a propane furnace. And I have some oil lamps if the lights go out."

Zach grunted.

The door on the house popped open when they stepped near it. Andy, the little boy, had been waiting for them to come back and must have heard their steps on the porch.

"Hi, there, Andy." Zach stepped inside behind Jenny. At least the little boy liked him.

Zach revised that opinion. The boy was looking at him like he'd sprouted a second head.

"Santa Claus?"

Zach grabbed for his chin. He'd forgotten the beard.

Jenny met his eyes in alarm. She took a quick breath. "Santa shaved."

Zach slipped the beard back over his chin. But it was too late. The kid was bewildered.

Then the confusion on Andy's face slowly cleared as though he finally understood a big secret. Zach felt a momentary pang, but then decided it was just as well the kid learned the truth about Santa Claus.

Zach looked over at Jenny. She was signaling him desperately to do something.

Zach figured there wasn't much to be done.

"He'd find out someday anyway—now that he's a big boy." Zach threw the boy a bone. He knelt down until his eyes were level with the boy's. "Isn't that right? You're a big boy and big boys can handle the truth about Santa Claus, can't you?"

Andy nodded happily.

Zach threw Jenny a self-righteous look. He might not be a parent, but he did know some things about little boys. "You're a real smart big boy to figure out Santa's secret."

Zach noticed the girl who stood beside her mother. She rolled her eyes as if Zach was hopeless.

Andy nodded eagerly and leaned forward to whisper. "I know the secret. Santa's a cowboy—he's you—Lightnin' Lucas."

"Well, now, that's not exactly true." Zach stalled. Maybe he didn't understand a little boy's mind as much as he thought he did. "I am Lightning Lucas—that's true—but I'm just wearing a Santa suit. I'm a pretend Santa."

"I have cowboy pajamas," Andy nodded happily as he danced from one foot to the other. "That's pretend. Want to see?"

"Sure, I guess." Zach looked up at Jenny to get direction.

Jenny gave a reluctant nod. The pajamas had been Andy's present last Christmas and they were still his most prized possession. "Why don't you bring them out here and let Mr. Lucas see them when you give him your letter? I think he'll still take it for you."

Jenny lifted a questioning eyebrow at Zach.

Zach bristled. He was a man of his word. "Of course I'll still take the letter. I'll see the letter gets to the North Pole tonight. Before Santa leaves on his trip tomorrow. I'll take it personally."

"Can you fly?" Andy looked at him in awe. "Like the reindeer?"

Zach swallowed and shifted his weight onto his knee. "No, but I know the way to the North Pole and I can drive fast in my truck. Zoom. Zoom. Of course," he said, fumbling, "nobody should drive fast."

Zach hoped the kid forgot this conversation before he turned sixteen and got his driving permit.

"Will you take me with you?"

Zach looked over at the little boy looking at him with such shining trust. Like a shy deer, the boy had edged closer and closer to Zach as he knelt beside him until now the boy was practically leaning against Zach's shoulder. Zach had to swallow again. "Not this time."

"Why not? I'll be good."

Jenny looked down at the man and her boy and felt sad. Andy yearned for a father even more than he yearned to be a cowboy. Maybe after Christmas she should accept a date from that rancher up north who kept asking her out. Even if Jenny didn't find him very exciting, he was stable.

Jenny had learned the hard way that exciting men weren't the best family men. She had a second chance to provide a father for her children, and this time she was going to choose carefully. Her children had never known the warmth of a real father. If she married again, it would be for them.

"Of course you'll be good," Zach said. "But you see, well, you have to stay and help your mother. There's a storm coming and she'll need a big boy like you to help her."

"Lisa's bigger. She can help."

Jenny looked at the helpless expression on Zach's face and almost laughed. Not many men were a match for a determined four-year-old.

"Of course she can." Zach searched the room for the girl and didn't see her. He wondered where she had gone. "It's just that—" Zach had an inspiration "—Santa's too busy to see people before he takes his trip. He only talks to the elves."

The boy looked up in sudden worry. "But my letter."

"Oh, I'm sure he has time for letters." Zach started to sweat. He decided he was better off facing a bucking bronc like Black Demon than a child like the one in front of him. He understood a thousand pounds of angry horse better than he did this little boy.

"I'm sure Santa reads all his mail," Jenny explained. Andy had labored for a full afternoon on his Santa letter, patiently copying the letters Jenny had printed for him.

Jenny hoped that Mr. Lightning understood how precious the letter was he'd offered to deliver. Andy hadn't thought of anything for days since he wrote that letter.

"Lisa can come, too." The little boy leaned closer to Zach and confided, "She told me there's no Santa at the North Pole." The boy's voice dropped to a whisper. "She has to do dishes for a month all by herself if I show her that Santa lives there. It's a bet."

Jenny saw her son's blond head leaning close to the man's dark one. The man's arm had gone around her son's shoulders and they were whispering about something she couldn't make out. She knew children liked their secrets, but she wasn't sure she wanted this cowboy to share them.

"Mr. Lucas needs to leave soon, Andy," Jenny reminded her son as she picked up the camera from the counter. Lisa had insisted she was too old for a Santa picture, so Jenny only had to worry about Andy. "Why don't you go get your letter for him, and I'll take your picture while you give it to him."

"It's here," Andy said as he moved away from Zach enough to pull a crumpled letter out of his pocket. He handed it up to Zach. "I've been saving it."

The camera flash went off as Jenny snapped a picture.

"I'll deliver it express mail." Zach blinked as he took the letter in his hand. The woman hadn't even given him time to force a smile. "You can trust the U.S. Postal Service."

Zach saluted the boy even though, as far as he knew, the postal service had never had a salute of any kind. But it seemed to reassure the boy.

Zach stood up and looked at the woman. "If you want, you can try a second picture."

Jenny looked at him.

"I wasn't smiling." Zach almost swore. It wasn't his idea to have his picture in some family album, but if his picture was going to be there it seemed only right that he be smiling.

Jenny shrugged. "The beard covers most of your face anyway."

Zach nodded. If the woman didn't care if Santa was smiling, he shouldn't care. It did make him wonder what Christmas was coming to, however. If anyone should be smiling at Christmas, it was Santa and his helpers. "It's your picture."

"Did you get my letter in the picture?" the boy asked.

The woman nodded.

"I drew the stamp myself." The boy looked up at Zach. "Mom said it was all right."

Zach bent down and shook the boy's hand for further assurance. "It's just the right kind of stamp."

The kitchen had a window by the sink and one on the opposite wall. The sky was gray out of both windows, and Zach heard the rattle of the wind as it gathered force.

He watched as Jenny pulled the stub of a picture out of the camera.

"Here." Jenny held the camera out to him.

Zach shook his head. "The doc said you were to keep it over the holidays in case you want to take more pictures."

"Well, that's kind of you."

"Not me. It's Delores." Zach shuffled his feet. He wasn't used to getting so much credit for things he didn't even do.

"I better get out of here before the storm hits." Zach pulled his Santa hat back on his head. No one had flipped any light switches, and the light coming into the windows was thin. Fortunately, he could hear the hum of the furnace and a floor vent blew a steady stream of warm air into the room. At least the family had heat.

Zach looked over at the woman who held a still-developing picture in her hand. "You're sure you'll be all right now in this storm? If you need to call anyone on the telephone to come sit this storm out with you, I'd do it now. The lines might go down anytime now."

"Thanks. I'll do that." Jenny said. She smiled confidently as if she had someone to call.

Zach nodded. He figured that cereal box wasn't the only reason the woman wouldn't go out with him. She must have a boyfriend. Well, he shouldn't be surprised. The doctor had as much as told him she did. Some rancher—what was his name? Max something.

"Well, I'll leave, then," Zach said as he walked toward the door. "I'll close the door quick behind me so you keep your heat in."

Jenny watched the man walk to the door. Suddenly she didn't want him to leave. There was a blizzard coming and she didn't know what to expect. Even a cereal-box cowboy was better than no one when it came to facing a storm. But she couldn't ask him to stay. He was a stranger, for goodness sake. Just because she was used to telling her troubles to his face didn't mean he had any obligation to her.

"You've got holiday plans?" she squeaked out as he put his hand on the doorknob.

He turned around and looked at her. "Vegas."

"Oh. I see. Well, have fun."

Jenny could kick herself. Of course, the man had plans. It was Christmas, after all. Everyone had plans.

"Thanks." Zach hesitated. "I could change them if—"

"Of course you can't change them." Jenny stiffened her resolve. "I was just asking because I…I mean we…we have plans of our own and I was hoping you had plans, too."

"I see. Thanks." Zach turned the knob this time. No sense staying where someone had plans that didn't include him.

Zach leaned into the wind as he walked to the postal truck. The sky was getting darker in the east. A spray of snowflakes hit his face, even with the beard pulled up. He noticed that he hadn't closed the back door to the postal truck completely. He walked over and snapped it shut. He didn't want a chill at his back while he raced this storm back to Deep Gulch.

Zach started the engine on the postal truck and released the brake. Time to get back. It was probably too late to beat the storm to the pass. Unless he missed his guess, he'd be sleeping in the horse trailer tonight while Thunder boarded at the doctor's barn. In a few hours no one would be doing much driving. Zach just hoped he made it back to the doctor's before the roads were snowed shut.

He could feel the hard boards of that trailer on his back already.

It was going to be some merry Christmas.

Chapter Three

Andy wanted a peanut butter sandwich.

"Just let me be sure the oil lamp is filled and I'll make you one," Jenny said as she watched the taillights of the postal truck pull away. The red lights were the only bright thing in the dark gray of the afternoon. A layer of snow had already fallen and she could see the tire tracks of the truck.

Jenny had made a mental list over a week ago of the things she needed to do to prepare for a winter storm. Making sure the lamp was full was the first one. The other was to be sure the curtains were drawn on all the windows so that there was a little extra insulation. Delores had insisted Jenny buy a case of beans and another of assorted soup when she moved here. The older woman had also urged her to always keep the propane tank that fed the furnace at least half-full.

"Heat and food is all you really need," the older woman had said. "If your pipes freeze you'll more than likely still have snow around that you can melt for water. Not that it's as pure as you might think. I'd get some water filters if I were you and run the melted water through them. Outside of that, keep healthy and you'll do fine."

Jenny didn't feel as if she was doing fine. She hadn't been able to get any filters for water. But the small stove in the kitchen fed off the propane tank out back so she could use that to boil snow water if necessary.

Just keep focused, she reminded herself. Like Delores had said, she'd do just fine.

Ten minutes passed before she realized Delores was wrong. Jenny wasn't fine. She'd made one big mistake. The number one rule of surviving a blizzard with your children was to actually have your children inside the house with you. Andy was here, but Lisa was gone.

Jenny had searched every room in the house twice before Andy confessed that Lisa had sneaked out the door in the laundry room and hid in the back of the postal truck. Jenny was accustomed to watching Andy. He was the one who got into trouble and scrapes. She never had to worry about Lisa.

"We got a bet going," Andy explained without a trace of worry. "Lisa's gonna go see all about Santa and let me know."

Jenny's heart stopped. "You mean she went off alone!"

"The Lightning man's with her," Andy said calmly. "He'll take care of her until they get to Santa's workshop."

"But Mr. Lucas is going to Las Vegas!"

"Not until he takes my letter to the North Pole. He promised."

Jenny was speechless. Her daughter had run off with some cowboy on his way to Vegas, and she was only eight years old.

"He'll bring her right back," Jenny promised herself aloud. The man had to bring her back. "When he sees her in the truck, he'll bring her right back."

But what if he didn't see her? Lisa was obviously hidden or she'd be back already unless he was—Jenny stopped herself. No, she wouldn't even think that. She was sure he wasn't that kind of a person.

Jenny looked out the window. The tracks left by the postal truck had been filled in with new snow.

He's not going to see Lisa in time to bring her back, Jenny thought to herself in despair. Oh, she supposed he would leave her with Dr. Norris—when Jenny thought about it she had no worries that the man would actually want to take Lisa to Las Vegas with him—but still, Lisa would miss Christmas. Lisa had never been away from home at Christmas before.

Jenny looked around. She wished now that she had swallowed her pride and asked someone to bring them a Christmas tree from town. She had told herself it would be okay for this Christmas to be plain. Her children would understand and share her gratefulness that they had a new home. They'd hang their stockings and read the Christmas story and that would be enough.

But she was wrong. Lisa wouldn't have come up with a ridiculous bet like this for Andy if they had both been busy decorating a tree or putting gumdrops on cookies. Her children needed Christmas and she had failed to give it to them.

Zach swore under his breath. The snow blew thicker every minute. And enough of it covered the road so that he couldn't make out the ruts. He was lucky to keep this tin can of a postal truck on the gravel road.

But the snow wasn't his big problem. His big problem sat on the passenger seat next to him.

"I knew you couldn't go to the North Pole," the girl said smugly as she bit into another oatmeal cookie. "There is no North Pole."

Zach gritted his teeth. "Didn't your mom teach you not to go off with strangers?"

He'd been halfway back to Deep Gulch when he'd heard the muffled sneeze from the back of the postal truck and had been so startled he'd almost driven off the road. In fact, he did pull to the side of the road so he could twist around and take a good look back there. The girl had been hiding under his sheepskin coat.

"We're not in Los Angeles anymore." The girl took another bite of cookie. "There aren't any strangers here. Only farmers."

Zach had given her the plate of cookies he had gotten from Mrs. Goussley. So far she'd managed to polish off half of them.

"There are things to be careful about in Montana, too."

"I know." The girl brushed the crumbs off her jacket sleeve. "There's snakes in the coulee. And bees in the summer."

"And strangers. Weird people are everywhere. You can never be too careful with strangers."

The girl shrugged. "You got any milk?"

"Of course not, this is a postal truck not a lunch truck."

Zach strained to see through the snowstorm outside his windshield. He'd guess there was four inches of snow so far on the ground—maybe more. He hoped that was the final turn to the Collinses' place up ahead.

"Your mother's going to be worried. She won't know where you are."

"Andy will tell her. He can't keep a secret."

Zach hoped the girl's mother didn't jump to any wild ideas like that maybe he had asked the girl to come with him. He had given her the candy cane, but no mother would think that would be enough to entice a child to climb into his truck. Of course, he had said he was going to see Santa. A court of law might see that as enticement enough for any child.

Zach started to sweat. He'd best get this little one home soon. "Ah, good, that is the turn."

The snow was blowing so much he could only make out the outline of the house and the yellow glow of the windows.

Jenny thought she heard the sounds of a car and ran to the window. An hour had passed since Mr. Lucas had left, and the day had turned to evening. Jenny opened the door to see better. Stinging snow hit her face, but she only leaned out farther to try and see more clearly. If it weren't for those red and green lights on the postal truck, Jenny wouldn't have been sure it was Mr. Lucas coming back up her long driveway.

The truck stopped a few feet from the porch, and the lights went out. The driver's door opened and Jenny breathed easier. It was him.

"Lisa!" The wind blew the call away from Jenny and she wasn't sure her daughter would hear it, but the man did and he gave her a reassuring wave as he walked around to the passenger side of the truck.

Her daughter started to walk to the porch, but the wind made her stumble. The man picked her up and took her up the steps in long strides. Snow clung to her daughter's hair as the cowboy brought her across the porch and into the door that Jenny held open.

The temperature had dropped even more than Zach had figured when he was inside the truck. He knew that was why the girl clung to his neck. All that Santa suit polyester was warm and fuzzy. Still, he liked having her nestled there. It made him feel, well, a little fatherly, he thought defensively. Nothing wrong with that.

"Lisa! Are you all right, honey?" The woman opened her arms, and Zach reluctantly gave the girl to her.

"She's fine," Zach said curtly.

"I don't feel so good," the girl moaned.

"What'd you do to her?" Jenny shifted Lisa in her arms and glared at Zach.

"Me?" Zach looked around. Even the boy was looking at him suspiciously. "I swear. All I did was give her the candy and some cookies."

"You did find Santa's!" Andy gave a triumphant war whoop and jumped down off the chair where he was sitting. "No more dishes."

"The cookies came from Mrs. Goussley. Honest, you can call her up on the phone and ask her."

"That won't be necessary." Jenny set Lisa down on the floor and knelt at her eye level. "How many cookies did you eat?"

Lisa gave Zach a look of appeal.

"They were oatmeal cookies," Zach offered in her defense. He hadn't even counted how many were on that plate. "Oatmeal is good for you. Builds bones or something."

Jenny reached over and smoothed down her daughter's hair. It had been a long time since Lisa had been disobedient. Or done anything like eat too many cookies. It was good to see her daughter be a child again. "I guess a few extra cookies won't hurt anything."

A gust of wind rattled the house, and the overhead light flickered.

"I hope you have that lamp handy." Zach looked out the kitchen window. The sky was completely dark now, but he could see flakes of snow being whipped past the glass by the wind. "I should call the doctor, too, before everything goes down."

"The phone's over there." Jenny pointed to the wall opposite the sink.

"Did you get a chance to make your call earlier?" Zach stepped over to the phone. Whoever she had been planning to call earlier hadn't been much help to her. If she had called Zach with a storm like this on the way, he'd have been on her doorstep by now.

"I, ah, I thought I'd wait."

Zach pulled a slip of paper out of his pocket. The doctor had written his phone number on the same page he'd written the other instructions. Zach dialed.

"This is Zach Lucas." The phone only rang once before it was answered; the doctor must have been waiting for a call. "I'm at Jenny's—"

"Thank God someone's there! My sister's already called. There's a real blizzard coming through and she's worried—"

Another gust of wind hit the house and the phone went dead. Then the overhead light in the kitchen flickered again before it went out. Jenny's heart stopped. Her house was completely dark. There was no moon outside to provide a soft hint of light. There was nothing. Just the howl of the wind and the rattle of the windows. Followed by a whimper and the shuffle of little feet.

"Stay still, Andy, I'll come to you." Jenny said as she slid one foot out across the kitchen floor. Andy didn't like the dark. She had to get to him. He had nightmares.

"That's okay. I've got him," Zach said as he felt the boy's arms grab his thigh and hug tightly. Zach bent down to lift Andy up in his arms. "We're just fine, aren't we, partner? It's just a little darkness."

The boy burrowed into Zach's fuzzy suit. There was something about a Santa suit, Zach thought to himself. Even a crazy Santa suit like the one Delores had put together. It made the kids feel at home with him. He realized with surprise that he kind of liked it.

"I don't like the dark," Andy whispered softly.

"It's okay," Zach muttered as he shifted his arm so one of his hands would be free to feel the grooves along the belt of the Santa suit. If he remembered the doctor's words correctly, there was a switch here someplace that would turn on the flashing lights surrounding the belt. Zach had only seen the lights flash for a minute or two when the doctor first asked him to put on the suit.

Jenny kept taking small steps in the general direction of her son. What had made Andy slide over and grab on to the cowboy? She had been as close to Andy as the cowboy had been. "Mama's coming."

Zach's hand found the switch on the belt at the same time as he smelled the perfume. He stopped to take another breath. It was a simple perfume—peach, if he wasn't mistaken. But it made him want to keep the darkness around him for just a minute or two longer.

Jenny reached out to where she thought Andy was and touched the cowboy's arm instead. The softness of the Santa suit could not hide the solid steel of the man's muscle. Jenny knew she should move her hand when she discovered it was the cowboy she was touching and not her son, but she didn't. It was dark all around her and he was an anchor.

"Jenny?"

Jenny snatched her hand away from his arm. She was glad it was dark enough to hide the fierce blush she was sure was on her face. "I'm just worried about Andy."

"Of course," Zach shifted the boy's weight in his arms. "He's right here."

Jenny was close enough to sense the cowboy turning his body slightly so that her son was in the arm closest to her. Jenny reached out her hand again. This time she felt Andy's soft hair. She also felt the edge of Zach's shoulder.

It was ten degrees below zero outside and only about fifty degrees above zero inside the house, but Zach felt like he didn't need to see another fire again as long as he lived. Jenny's touch had been tentative, but it scorched him.

"Can you hold him while I get the lamp?" Jenny asked.

"You got oil in the lamp already?"

"It's right next to it." Jenny felt disoriented. The sink had to be in that direction. "Under the sink."

Zach groaned. "You better light me up, then, so you don't break your neck walking over there."

"What?"

"It's the belt," Zach interrupted. "It's got built-in Christmas lights. I had the switch a minute ago, but I had to let go when I moved Andy."

"But how do I?"

"Just feel along the belt until you come to a clicker kind of a thing. It attaches to the batteries."

"Your belt?"

Zach's mouth went dry at the breathless way she said

it—as if he was asking her to do something a whole lot more intimate than turn on some lights. "It's about where Andy's feet are."

Jenny moved her hands away from Andy's hair and let them slide down Andy's back until the man shifted her son in his arms and suddenly her hands were sliding down the man's torso. Even the softness of the Santa suit couldn't hide the lean muscles of his chest and then his stomach underneath.

"I can't find it." Jenny stopped. It suddenly occurred to her she didn't want to go too low. But she left her hand on his stomach. The whole world was dark around her and she wanted an anchor. Besides, she could hear his breathing.

Zach felt his breath catch. He shifted slightly to balance Andy in his left arm. He put his right hand over the one that Jenny had on his stomach. It wasn't until he touched her that he felt her pulse. Her heart was fluttering like a bird's.

"Scared?" Zach whispered.

"Me?" Jenny braced herself. It was only a man's stomach for goodness sake. "No, I'm fine."

"Good. I'd begun to worry I scared you with what I said about storms earlier. There's nothing to worry about. We'll be fine."

Jenny had completely forgotten about the storm. "Of course."

Zach reluctantly guided Jenny's hand to his belt buckle. He realized he could have just flipped the switch on his belt himself, but it was much more satisfying to feel Jenny's hand under his.

"I found it." Jenny felt the ridge of a button on the side of the smooth plastic of the belt. She slid the button to the right. "That's it!"

A dozen tiny lights flickered. The kitchen was no longer dark. Instead, long shadows filled the corners and a soft glow surrounded Santa.

"Mama." Lisa ran to Jenny and stood beside her.

Zach felt as if time had stopped. There was just enough light in the kitchen to see Jenny's eyes. Zach didn't even realize he was staring at her eyes until she blinked.

"I better go get the lamp." Jenny didn't move. She meant to move, but she didn't. In the light coming from Zach's belt, the man looked more like his cereal picture than he had since he'd pulled down his beard. It was his eyes, Jenny thought to herself. He was looking at her as if she'd just given him a championship trophy.

"I didn't know those lights would work so well." Zach tried to rein his mind back to the present. He would start counting to ten if he had to—he couldn't stand there staring at the woman. She'd think he was a lunatic.

"Oh." So that was it, Jenny thought. That's what pleased him so much. Men and their mechanical toys. "Yeah, they're something. Great lights."

Zach felt Andy squirm in his arms.

"I'm hungry," Andy said as he wiggled his way down Zach until he reached the floor.

"Let me get the lamp set up first." Jenny patted Andy on the head as she turned toward the counter. "Then I'll see what we can fix for dinner."

Jenny mentally catalogued the cans in her cupboard. She wished Delores had warned her to keep more than soup on hand for blizzards. She didn't have anything suitable for company. "I'm afraid it won't be fancy."

"I don't need fancy," Zach said.

One hour later they sat down to the table and there wasn't one hot thing on it. Even soup was impossible. "I never thought the pipes would be a problem."

The outside pipe on the propane stove had shaken loose in the wind. Zach had capped it off, but needed better light to fix it completely.

"This is just fine." Zach grinned. They were having cereal for dinner. His cereal. "I didn't know you ate this stuff."

"It's my favorite." Andy pushed his chair closer to Zach before he climbed up on it.

"I thought we should use some of the milk up since the refrigerator is off." Jenny set a plate of bread on the table and sat down. "I had a coupon for the cereal."

"So you're just trying the cereal out?"

"I wouldn't say that exactly." Jenny casually turned the cereal box so the man's face wasn't staring at her. "We eat lots of kinds of cereal."

"It's my favorite," Andy repeated as he picked up his spoon and waved it around. "Cowboys eat it."

"It's only your favorite because Mom bought a ton of it." Lisa unfolded the napkin by her plate.

"Mr. Lucas doesn't want to hear about what we eat." Especially not how much of his cereal we eat, Jenny thought frantically. "We should talk about—" She tried to remember what single people talked about. "We should talk about— That's it…" Jenny turned to face the man. "How was your day today?"

Zach watched Andy take a spoonful of the cereal dry. He could hear him crunching away. "My horse got sick, but I ended up having a good time delivering the mail. Met some nice people. How was your day?"

"Oh, your horse. Did the doctor get a chance to say how he was before the phone line went dead?"

"I'm sure he's fine. It was just a low-grade fever." Zach noticed Jenny hadn't answered his question. Now what would a mother with small children do during the day? "I'll bet your day was spent getting ready for Christmas."

Jenny gasped and dropped her spoon on the table.

"What'd I say?" Even in the dark of the kitchen, Zach could tell he'd asked the wrong question.

"Nothing. It's just—" Jenny looked at her two children sitting one on each side of the stranger who should be a stranger but who wasn't because his eyes were looking straight at her just like he did from the cereal box. She couldn't keep it in any longer. She was used to making her confessions to that face. "I'm a terrible mother."

Zach saw the tear in her eye before she bent her head down, and he said the only thing he could. "That can't be true."

Jenny looked up at him. "I don't have a proper Christmas for my children, and that's why Lisa ran away with you."

"Lisa didn't run away with me. She didn't even run away, really. She had a bet she wanted to win."

"Yeah, Mama. I wouldn't run away. I just wanted to show Andy that there's no Santa at the North Pole."

"See what I mean?" Jenny wailed.

Zach half nodded. He didn't see at all, but he could tell the woman needed sympathy. "It's a shame they make all this fuss about a day—all it is is December twenty-fifth. Just the day after December twenty-fourth. No need to go on so."

Zach heard three gasps all at the same time. One good thing—he was pretty sure Jenny's tears had stopped.

"But Christmas is the birthday of Jesus," Lisa announced primly.

"All children need a Christmas," Jenny said at the same time.

"Don't you believe in Christmas?" Andy cut right to the important question. His eyes were wide in shock.

Zach squirmed and did the only manly thing he could. He lied. "Sure I believe in Christmas."

Jenny looked at him skeptically.

"Christmas just doesn't believe in me," Zach added softly.

"Well, surely you're going to celebrate Christmas," Jenny said. It was really none of her business, but everyone needed to celebrate something. And then she remembered that he was. "Of course, that's why you're going to Las Vegas."

Zach snorted. "I'm not going there to celebrate Christmas. I'm going there to forget there *is* such a miserable day."

"But I thought you had plans. That you were meeting a friend, or…" Jenny squinted at him. Surely nobody went to Las Vegas to be alone for the holidays. Come to think of it, it wasn't that easy to just go alone to Las Vegas at Christmas, especially without planning. "You won't get a hotel room, you know. Not over the holidays. All the hotels will be booked."

"Patti already has a room for me."

"I see." Jenny's voice tightened.

Jenny didn't know why she cared that the person he was driving hundreds of miles to see was a woman. And not just any woman. A woman with a name. She should be glad he was driving off to meet some woman. It would keep her focused. The last thing she or her family needed was a man like him around. They needed someone stable. Someone who would be a good husband and a father. "Well then, you don't have to worry about reservations."

Zach nodded.

Jenny knew she should let it go, but she didn't. "Maybe you'll see a show while you're there. I hear they have some wonderful Christmas shows."

"You're thinking of the family shows. The kind of show Patti and the girls do isn't what you'd call family fare."

"This Patti—she's a singer?"

Zach shook his head. "Naw, she's just one of the show-girls."

"With the feathers in her hair?" Jenny knew what those showgirls wore and didn't wear. "She must be very pretty."

"I suppose so."

Jenny stiffened. "Of course she's pretty. They all are."

Zach told himself Patti would have to be pretty. He'd only spent several hours with her last year. He knew she was a blonde. But outside of that… "I don't remember her eyes."

"Well, maybe you should try looking at her eyes instead of her—" Jenny broke off. Her children were at the table. Besides, it was none of her business who or what the cowboy admired. "Would you like some more cereal?"

"You know that showgirl stuff is mostly aerobics." Zach took the cereal box that Jenny offered.

"Aerobics?"

"Like cheerleading," Zach said firmly as he poured more cereal into his bowl. "Yeah, it's like cheerleading. Only with feathers and a bikini full of sequins."

"Mama was a cheerleader," Lisa offered proudly as she paused with her spoon halfway to her mouth. "Weren't you, Mama?"

"A long time ago."

"Really?"

"A very long time ago."

"We still have her pom-poms," Lisa said as she set down her spoon. "She didn't have any feathers or a bikini. She was a great cheerleader, though."

"I'm sure she was." Zach had a vision of Jenny bouncing around doing cheers. He wasn't sure it was at all the sort of vision he should have while he sat at the table with her children eating cereal. "She must have been wonderful—even without the feathers."

Jenny could feel the blush on her cheeks. She needed to

change the subject. "The snow should be gone by tomorrow. It's too early to have a blizzard that sticks. You should still be able to make it out of here and catch your show."

Zach looked at her as if she was crazy. "What makes you think that?"

"The guidebook says—"

Zach snorted. "You have that guidebook here? Let me see it. I can practically guarantee you that this blizzard will last forty-eight hours."

"But that's impossible." Jenny looked stunned. "Montana doesn't have long blizzards before Christmas."

"Tell that to the sky," Zach said.

Jenny would tell it to the sky if she thought there was any hope the sky would listen. "So you'll be here for Christmas."

"Looks like it."

"I'm afraid it won't be nearly as exciting as Las Vegas," Jenny said. Surely he would be able to leave tomorrow. The postal truck was a four-wheel-drive. It could go places her car couldn't go even when it was running. The house suddenly felt much too small, and the Christmas she'd planned much too humble to share with this man. "We don't even have a tree."

Zach felt the collar of his shirt get smaller and he swallowed. "I'm not worried about a tree. They aren't anything but a fire hazard anyway."

"You don't like Christmas trees?" Lisa asked him in a voice that suggested he hated babies.

"Well, I…I don't have anything against them, I guess."

Zach tried to make amends. "Especially if they don't have lights on them."

"No lights!" Lisa scoffed at him. "If there's no lights, it's not even a Christmas tree. Everyone knows that."

Jenny knew she should have tried harder to get a tree. Christmas was important to children. Well, it wasn't too late. "I'm going to go out tomorrow and get us a Christmas tree."

"Really?" Lisa turned to her mother breathlessly. "You are?"

"Of course," Jenny said. "This is Montana. There's lots of trees around. It might not be a pine tree like the ones we used to have in Los Angeles, but I can find something to decorate."

"It'll be ten below zero tomorrow." Zach thought he should mention the fact. "You'll freeze to death."

"Tomorrow will be a fine day." Jenny lifted her chin. "Montana blizzards this time of year never last."

Zach groaned. Even if the sun did shine tomorrow, he couldn't leave this family in this kind of weather. They'd never make it through Christmas without help the way they were carrying on. Jenny would freeze out there trying to chop down some fool sage bush. "And don't try baking any Christmas cookies until that propane line is fixed."

"Cookies," Andy sighed blissfully as he looked at Zach. "Are you going to make us some Christmas cookies?"

"Me?" Zach didn't like the trusting look in the boy's eyes. "I don't cook."

"I'll help you," Andy said, his trust not wavering. "I know how to stir. We can make cookies, can't we, Mom?"

Jenny looked at her son. She'd never seen him this anxious to spend time with a man before. It must be because Zach was a cowboy. How could she explain to her son that this man was not the kind of man to put on an apron and bake cookies with a little boy. "Mr. Lucas might be busy."

Fortunately, Andy didn't ask what the man would be busy doing. "Busy" was the excuse his father had always used when Andy asked to do anything with him.

Zach watched the joy flow out of Andy's eyes, and he found he didn't like it. "I guess I could learn to make cookies. How hard can it be?"

"Really?" Andy's eyes shone again.

"What?" Jenny's eyes stared at Zach like he'd offered to fly to the moon. "Are you sure?"

Zach nodded. He wasn't going soft, he told himself. He was snowed in with this family. Stranded, really. He was just making the best of a bad situation. Anyone would do the same. It was that time of year, after all.

He sure hoped he wasn't going soft.

Chapter Four

Jenny had no choice but to follow the cereal cowboy and her son deeper into the house. They'd all cleared their bowls off the card table, and there was nothing to keep them in the kitchen.

"We've only been here a little over a month." Jenny carried a flashlight even though Zach and his lit belt showed everyone the way.

The living room was almost empty. She had a cork bulletin board hanging on one wall that was covered with snapshots of the kids, but it was the only thing hanging on the walls.

A few boxes stood along the other wall. The flaps of the boxes were pulled up and showed a jumble of children's books. They didn't have television so the children each picked a favorite story each night and they sat together while Jenny read to them. Lisa loved fairy tales. Andy liked animal books.

"We're camping," Andy confided in a loud whisper as he led Zach through the living room. "That's why we don't need no furniture."

Jenny winced. The one piece of furniture that had been there to welcome them was a rust-colored sofa that sagged and had a grease spot on the right cushion. Jenny had covered it with a light-blue afghan she had knit when she was pregnant with Andy. It was a baby's afghan, but she'd made it large and it almost covered the sofa. "I plan to get some used furniture just as soon as I can get to Billings."

"Yeah, I hear your car isn't working," Zach said as he followed Andy's lead and sat down on the sofa. "Doc Norris said it was the radiator."

No sooner had Zach settled on the sofa than Andy burrowed into the cushion next to Zach's elbow and whispered, "The doctor—he's got pigs."

"Is that right?" Zach looked down at the boy. The living room was full of crazy red and green shadows from the Christmas lights on the Santa belt, but no matter what shade of light surrounded the boy's face it just seemed to keep shining. Zach had a pang of wistfulness knowing he'd never been that trusting. Certainly not at four years old. Maybe not even at four months. Not with the kind of parents he'd had. He'd had to learn to take care of himself early. By the time he was Andy's age, he was taking care of his alcoholic parents as well as himself.

"I've got pigs, too," Andy said as he jumped off the sofa and headed toward the books. "They huffed and puffed."

Zach felt as if he'd fallen down a rabbit hole.

"It was the wolf that huffed and puffed," Jenny clarified. She had to admit that the cowboy was taking her sparse furnishings better than she would have expected. He didn't look around with anything like pity in his brown eyes.

Andy found the book he was looking for and waved it at Zach. "Read me the story."

"Mr. Lightning might not have time." Jenny wished Andy wasn't so intent on relating to the cowboy. She supposed Andy would be that way with any man these days. But a drifter like Zach would have no patience with a little boy, and she couldn't bear to see Andy hurt. "He's resting."

Andy put his book down easily and looked at Zach with round eyes. "Is he sick?"

Zach heard Jenny's quick intake of breath at the same time as he saw the worry flare in Lisa's eyes as she stood next to her mother. Then he remembered what the doctor had said about Jenny's husband dying of cancer. "Don't worry. I'm not the kind of guy who gets sick. I'm healthy as a horse."

"Your horse is sick," Lisa reminded him as she walked over to the books and stood next to Andy.

"That's just Thunder's disposition," Zach said. He couldn't help but notice how the girl came close to him, but not too close. "He just likes to complain about his aches and pains. He's not a sunshine guy like me."

Zach saw the quick smile that crossed Lisa's face before she rolled her eyes.

"Let me see that book," Zach held his hand out for the book Andy had picked up again. He patted the sofa on the side opposite where Andy sat. "No reason we can't all read it together. I've always wondered about wolves. Thought I might get one for a pet one of these days."

"Wolves aren't pets," Lisa informed him. She sat down next to Zach, but her back was straight and she perched cautiously on the edge of the sofa. "They're dangerous animals."

Zach had no idea how it happened, but the wolf led to some ballerina Lisa was anxious for him to read about.

"She has a tiara," Lisa told him solemnly as she pointed to the shiny circle on the girl's head in the book. By this time, Lisa had snuggled close to his other elbow.

"She looks like a real princess," Zach agreed. Zach decided he liked being enclosed by the kids. Now if only Jenny would join them on the sofa.

Jenny sat on a folding chair and looked at the cowboy and her children. She could not remember a scene like this one in her whole life. Even if her late husband, Stephen, unbent enough to relate to one of the kids, he never included them both at the same time. He certainly never read to them.

It was past bedtime for Andy, but Jenny let the time pass. If it wasn't that she thought she might destroy the moment by capturing it, she would take a picture of the three of them. Her children would remember this cowboy reading to them for a long time.

"I asked Santa for a tiara," Lisa sighed as Zach finished reading the last page of the book. "But it's too expensive."

"Santa doesn't need money," Andy said cheerfully as he wiggled even closer to Zach. "He's got elves. They'll make you up one of those things."

"Elves can't make tiaras," Lisa said as she straightened her back and took the book out of Zach's hands. "They don't have any jewels. You need jewels for a tiara."

"Oh." Andy thought about this. "But they have cowboy stuff. Cowboy stuff doesn't take jewels. You could ask for some of that, like me."

Lisa stood up to take the book back to the box. "I hope you didn't write that in your letter. If I can't have a tiara, I at least want something that's pretty. I don't want anything cowboy."

Jenny knew what was coming and tried to head the question off before it was formed. "Time for bed, Andy." Jenny stood up and added another distraction. "You can wear your cowboy pajamas." Jenny kept her voice cheerful and calm, but she could see the frown forming on Andy's face.

"When are you going to take my letter to Santa, Mr. Lightning?" Andy asked in a soft voice. "Lisa said you had to bring her back. You never got to the North Pole."

Zach reached out automatically and patted the pocket that held the letter. Oh, oh. He'd forgotten it was still there. He looked to Jenny for help.

"Mr. Lightning did his best," Jenny said softly as she walked over to her son. "But there's a blizzard outside. The roads are all full of snow. He had to turn back before he got to the North Pole."

Andy looked up at Zach in alarm. "But you're still going

to take my letter, aren't you? It's almost time for Santa to come. He has to get my letter or he won't know what to bring me."

Zach knew he was a sucker. There was no longer any doubt. "I'm just waiting for everyone to go to bed. Then I'll crank up the old truck and make a quick trip."

Andy looked up at Zach in relief. "It won't take long. You can go fast. Zoom, zoom. You said so."

"That I did."

Lisa rolled her eyes and Jenny opened her mouth to protest, but neither of them said anything.

"The quicker you get to bed, the sooner I can get going to the North Pole," Zach said.

Jenny had never seen her son so anxious to get to bed. Andy ran into his room and changed into his pajamas in the thin streaks of light that shone into his room from the living room. Even Lisa seemed content to go to her bedroom.

Jenny had managed to get a single mattress for each of the bedrooms, but she hadn't prepared for company. "I'm sorry, all I have to offer you is the sofa."

Zach smiled. "The sofa's fine."

"It's really not too bad," Jenny apologized as she went over to a box and pulled out several wool blankets. "And I have some blankets, of course, that you can use. I don't have a spare pillow, but we can roll a blanket up and—"

"It's fine," Zach repeated.

Jenny had been worrying. The Santa letter had become more complicated than she'd ever imagined. "Andy can be persistent."

"That's a good thing."

Jenny kept her voice low as she put the rolled-up blanket at one end of the sofa. "We'll just tell him in the morning that you went to Santa's while he was asleep."

"You think he'll believe that?" Zach whispered in amazement. "If I know him, he's going to lie awake in there until he hears me leave." Zach shook his head in pride. "He might only be four, but he's awfully sharp."

"But what else can we do?"

Zach no longer bothered to lower his voice. "In just a few minutes, I'm going to go out to my truck and start driving it away."

"Oh." Jenny knew she shouldn't have expected him to stay. "I see."

Jenny swallowed before it occurred to her that even if the man wasn't the kind who stayed around, he didn't look like the kind who was crazy enough to head back to the main road in this weather.

"There's a blizzard out there," she whispered just in case he had forgotten. "You won't get halfway to Deep Gulch without getting stuck."

"Ah." Zach smiled and winked at her. "But I don't need to get to Deep Gulch. I only need to get to the North Pole."

They both heard the sigh of deep contentment that came from Andy's room before they heard the boy's voice. "It won't take long."

"No, it won't, partner," Zach agreed as he stood up. "It won't take long at all."

"Mom can go with you," Andy offered from the bedroom. "Just in case you have trouble on the way back. She knows the way back here real good."

Now that's an idea, Zach thought to himself, before he realized how unlikely that would be with the kids in bed. "Your mom probably needs to stay with you."

Zach glanced sideways at Jenny just in case she was the kind of mother who was willing to leave her kids alone on a dark night so she could go for a freezing-cold drive with a bachelor.

Zach had known women who would have left their kids in strip joints if it meant they could spend time with a cowboy. Not that he was passing judgment on those women. He knew plenty of men who were just as irresponsible. Who was he fooling? He *was* one of those men who were just as irresponsible.

"It sure would keep me warmer if I had some company," Zach said softly as he followed Jenny out into the kitchen. If Jenny was the kind of mother willing to leave her kids, she'd be the kind of woman to give him a friendly kiss or two out there under the night sky. He had a sudden, powerful urge to know if her wide blue eyes changed colors and danced with stars when she was kissed. "I wonder how cold it is out there, anyway."

"Give me a minute and I'll let you know. I've gotten pretty accurate at guessing temperature." Jenny turned back to look at Zach.

Zach stepped closer. He wondered if Jenny could tell how much the kitchen had heated up since she'd turned to face him. He knew his temperature had risen by ten degrees.

Her face was dusted with pink. And it was more than the red in the lights at his belt. The kitchen was still in shadows but her face looked petal soft. He could almost taste those kisses. He figured her for a sweet kisser. He couldn't wait to find out just how sweet.

It took a second or two for Zach to get past his thoughts of kissing and realize Jenny was willing to leave the kids and go off with him for a long ride into the night. It took another second for his disappointment to settle. He'd have wagered his saddle that she was a better parent than that. Not that his disappointment would stop him from showing the lady a good time, he told himself. "It doesn't matter how cold it is out there, I'll keep you warm."

Now that Zach realized Jenny wasn't a saint, he figured the same old lines would work with her that he'd used in the rodeo for years. He was back in the game.

Jenny rolled her eyes, but didn't even respond to him. She just turned and walked toward the far kitchen wall. "I hope you don't mind if I drive the postal truck. The kids will be fine with you here."

"What?" Zach couldn't believe it. He was still stuck in his fantasy of her hot lips in the cold night. What had she said? He followed her through the kitchen. "You're going without me? Without me? Out there—into that blizzard?"

Was the woman crazy?

"Do you know how cold it is out there?" he asked, just to be sure. "It isn't anyplace for a woman alone—not on a night like tonight. This windchill is nothing to mess around with—especially for a woman alone."

Zach knew he had said the wrong thing even as he saw Jenny bristle. She turned to face him.

"Actually—" Jenny's voice was chilly enough to match the outdoors "—a woman alone is just fine—inside or outside. Especially if she's read her guidebooks. The fact is women are better suited for the cold than men."

Zach lifted his eyebrow.

Jenny put her chin up in the air slightly. "It's true. It's because of body fat. Women have more body fat."

"But only in—" Zach stopped. He wasn't sure Jenny would like him to tell her where her body fat was stored. Especially since it was in places that were causing him some discomfort now that the idea of kissing her had taken hold of him with a vengeance. Maybe he was the one who was crazy here.

Jenny turned and reached up to the coat hooks that were next to the door. "Well, we both can't go." Jenny lifted off a drab blanket that was hanging on the hook. She'd grown accustomed to being both mother and father to her children years ago. "I wouldn't expect a stranger to do this for my children. It's my responsibility. Besides, I should have gotten the letter to Santa some other way before you came. It's not your problem."

The kitchen windows all looked out at the black night. Zach took a breath.

"It might not be my problem, but it is my truck." Zach put his hands on his hips. Let her argue with that. "I'll drive the thing."

"You hate that truck. You said so earlier." Jenny wrapped

the blanket around her shoulders like a shawl. "Besides, we both know it's not your truck. It belongs to the post office."

"That truck is entrusted to my care," Zach said stubbornly. He'd moved his hands away from his hips. The extra Santa padding under that suit he still wore made him feel ridiculous. "The doctor didn't say anything about me lending it out to folks to go driving around in it like it's some kind of do-it-yourself taxicab."

"I'm a good driver," Jenny held out her hand for the keys. "You can wait in the kitchen until I get back so the kids think you're gone, too. Just keep an eye on that furnace."

"Well, if they think I'm gone, maybe I should be."

"Somebody needs to be here in case something goes wrong." Jenny flashed Zach a smile. "Don't worry—the kids won't be a problem. They don't come out of their beds once they get settled. That's one good thing about it being cold. They don't want to leave their bed once they get the sheets warm."

Zach's frown turned to a scowl. Speaking of sheets, something was wrong with that blanket Jenny was holding like a shawl. "Is that what you use for a coat?"

Jenny lifted her chin as she wrapped the blanket more closely around her shoulders. "We used to live in Los Angeles. It wasn't cold enough there to need heavy coats."

"Well, this isn't Los Angeles." Zach looked at the other two hooks. They both held new snow coats, one in pink for Lisa and one in red for Andy. "You should have bought a coat for yourself when you bought the ones for the kids."

Jenny shrugged. "The kids needed the coats more than I did. I can get by until spring."

Zach didn't say anything. Boy, was he wrong to think she was an irresponsible parent. She was halfway to sainthood. Which made him proud in a funny sort of a way. Until he figured it out. If she was that kind of woman, his odds of getting a free kiss in this house were about the same as they would be at a PTA meeting filled with Republican grandmothers.

He'd learned long ago that kissing good women was complicated. They tended to take their kissing seriously. A kiss or two and they started thinking about china patterns and meeting your family. Zach didn't even know where his parents were anymore. Even if he did know, he sure wasn't going to take any woman to meet them.

Jenny lifted the blanket up to wrap it around her head as well as her shoulders.

"Andy asked me to deliver his letter." Zach pulled up the collar on his Santa suit. His hopes of a kiss might be gone, but he still would do this his way. "I'm responsible for the U.S. mail. I'm the one who's going."

Jenny looked at the man. The kitchen was in shadows, but she had no problem seeing the face before her. Faint red lines marked his cheek where the Santa beard had rubbed. A strong chin was brushed lightly with late-day whiskers. Brown eyes met hers with determination. She'd seen that same steady look in his eyes in rodeo pictures of him on those cereal boxes. He made one fierce-looking Santa.

"But it's cold out there."

"Then make me something hot to drink when I get back." Zach reached for the knob on the door. He wasn't going to argue on this one. He wouldn't be able to think straight if he let her take off in a night blizzard while he stayed in the kitchen. What kind of man would he be if he did that?

"I don't know what to say," Jenny tried again. The blanket around her shoulders was stiff, but she held it firm. "You shouldn't have to do this. You don't even like Christmas."

"Yes, I do." Zach gritted his teeth. What was it about this family? "I just don't see the need to go overboard and fuss about everything."

"You mean fuss about things like delivering a child's Santa letter?" Jenny asked softly.

"Well, no. The letter, now that's important. U.S. Postal Service business. I'm just doing my job."

Jenny smiled. "You're losing money. There's not even an official stamp on the envelope."

"It's official enough for me." He paused and added, "Besides, I gave my word. He's counting on me."

Jenny was speechless, and Zach took that as sign enough to open the door and leave.

The cold outside air lingered briefly inside while Jenny stood at the door's window and watched the red and green lights bump their way down her driveway. So that's what this man did when he gave his word. He actually carried through with his promise.

All Jenny saw of the postal truck was lights. She could, of course, hear the truck. She suspected Zach revved the motor a little extra just so it was very obvious that he was driving away.

Jenny was amazed. This cowboy was actually honoring his word. Her late husband had only considered promises made to adults to be binding. And then only if the adults were other men. Jenny was beginning to wonder if she hadn't misjudged the cereal-box cowboy. Not that it would make much difference. A man with that much sexual magnetism was not the kind of man she wanted in her life the second time around.

If and when she married again, she would marry for the sake of her children. And she wouldn't take any chances. She'd marry a solid citizen. Maybe a banker. Or a schoolteacher. A teacher would be nice. But a cowboy? Not a chance.

Jenny pulled the blanket closer around her shoulders as though she could press the heat into her skin. She wished the cowboy had let her make the drive. She felt beholden enough to him already and didn't relish adding a favor like this to the list. She had her pride. She just had no way to repay him.

Unless—Jenny still had a few dollars in the bank. She could write him a check. Yes, a check, she thought to herself in satisfaction. A check should even the score nicely.

Outside in the cold, Zach stopped the postal truck. He'd driven a quarter of a mile away from the house when he stopped and turned out the lights, just in case Andy had watched him leave the house. He'd leave the lights off for a few minutes so that it would look like the truck was far, far away on its way to the North Pole. He knew Jenny had said that the kids both stayed tucked into bed once they were down, but he also knew that Christmas changed the rules for kids everywhere.

Without the heater on, the temperature inside the postal truck dipped quickly. If Jenny was sitting next to him, Zach knew he'd ask her what the temperature was just to challenge her skill. He smiled. She was some amazing lady. He wondered if she really could tell temperatures like that.

The black night, even with the cold outside, was peaceful. Zach clicked on the lights on his belt so he could read his watch. He'd had the lights off for five minutes. He wondered how long a kid would figure it would take to go to the North Pole.

Speaking of the North Pole, Zach pulled out the letter Andy had written. He wasn't curious about what the requests were. The kids had already told him what they wanted. But he was beginning to worry.

The box he'd brought out to this family hadn't been heavy enough to satisfy any child's Santa wish. Besides, he knew what was in it. The camera, a frozen ham that Jenny had already put in the unheated laundry room, the pie from Delores Norris, and two small brown bags from the one store in Deep Gulch.

Those brown bags looked awfully puny.

Zach sat in silence. He knew firsthand how it felt to be disappointed at Christmas. He'd never believed in Santa Claus, but when he was ten years old someone had sent his parents a Christmas card with a family picture on the front of it. Everyone in the picture was standing beside a Christmas tree and looking happy. That was Zach's first glimpse of what the day was like for other families, and that Christmas Zach had decided Christmas should be that way for his family.

Zach had begged a scrawny leftover tree from a nearby lot on Christmas Eve and set it up in the living room. He'd thought a tree would make the difference. He'd believed the tree would turn his family into a Christmas family like the one on that card. But his parents had only used the tree as an excuse to drink more than usual, quarreling over who should propose the next toast to it.

No one in his family smiled that Christmas and Zach threw the tree away the next day. That was the last time he had had any hopes at Christmas. But he'd never spent Christmas with children like Andy and Lisa. They were good kids. They deserved a good Christmas.

Zach did not know exactly when in the darkness the idea came to him, but it somehow did. He, Zach "Lightning" Lucas, knew what the children wanted. They knew that he wasn't the real Santa but they had still both trusted him with their Christmas wishes.

Maybe it was time Zach lived up to the red suit he wore. In this snow-covered corner of Montana he was Santa. He would see that their hoped-for presents were delivered.

At first Zach thought about driving into Deep Gulch tomorrow, but then he realized he had the same limitations that had faced Jenny. The one store in Deep Gulch, a multipurpose little store with everything from bread to automotive oil, would not have either Lisa's tiara or Andy's cowboy outfit.

Of course, the cowboy outfit—Zach looked into the back of the postal truck. His duffel bag was still there along with his sheepskin coat. He hadn't packed much for his trip to Vegas, but he did have the latest championship buckle in there that he had just won last month.

He knew how to work with leather and he had a broken bridle in his duffel that he'd been meaning to fix. He might be able to fashion a belt for the boy. And he could put a thick lining in his Stetson hat to fit the kid. He didn't have a toy gun, but he could make a small rope with some of that postal twine in the truck.

Lisa's tiara would be more difficult. Especially because, as she'd reminded Andy, a tiara needed to have jewels.

Zach grinned to himself. Now that he thought of it, he did have jewels. Zach reached into the back and pulled the duffel toward him. He unzipped the bag and felt around in the contents until his hand found what he was seeking. He'd brought a Christmas present for Patti.

He twirled the lacy leg garter on his finger and grinned.

The showgirl would never miss the fancy garter he'd bought her. But Lisa would love the rhinestones that circled it. There were pink rhinestones and clear rhinestones and small pieces of ruby. And, if Jenny had a metal clothes hanger that he could bend, he'd be in business.

By the time Zach turned the engine back on in the postal truck, he'd decided that this Christmas might be tolerable after all. Imagine Zach "Lightning" Lucas filling in for Santa Claus.

Zach ho-ho-ho'ed to himself just to see if he had the knack.

He didn't.

But that didn't matter. Zach would pretend to have the Christmas spirit even if it killed him. He'd do it for the sake of the kids.

He only hoped Jenny would cooperate.

Chapter Five

Jenny looked out the window again. It had been totally black outside the last time she'd peeked, but now she could see the lights of the postal truck coming closer to the house.

Jenny was beginning to have second thoughts. She'd looked at her bank book, and the crude budget she'd worked up to see them through the winter, before deciding to write the check for seven dollars. It wasn't much, but it was all she dared give away until she knew how much it would cost to fix the radiator on her car.

The truck engine came to a stop near the house, and Jenny smoothed back her hair. She'd put some water into her fondue pan and lit the candle underneath. She didn't know how long it would take the water to heat, but she intended to have a hot drink for Zach when he came inside. That and the check would make her feel less indebted to him.

Zach sat in the postal truck. While he was driving back up the path that led to Jenny's house he'd noticed the ball of mistletoe Delores Norris had hung on the antenna of the truck. It would freeze solid if he left it outside over night. He might as well haul it in with his gear.

Zach opened the door and stepped outside into the snow.

The night was kinder to Jenny's house than the light of day had been. In the dark, the flickering light through the kitchen window gave the house a warm look, as if some-one was waiting up for the last one of the family to come home.

Maybe, Zach thought wryly, that's why he preferred busy hotels. With all the neon flash of a hotel at night, everyone knew there was nothing personal about the fact that someone was waiting up inside. It was strictly business. Zach liked it that way.

If no one was waiting up, there would never be anyone to be disappointed when they discovered that Zach knew absolutely nothing about the things other people took for granted. The Christmas tree failure had only been one les-son he'd learned as a child. It was that same year he'd dis-covered other families ate their meals together at a table. He'd asked his mother if they could do the same. One meal together had cured them all of the idea.

No, Zach knew he wasn't meant for family life. Not that he usually thought about such things, Zach told himself with a shake of his head. He'd made peace with his limita-tions many years ago. He wouldn't wish the life he'd had growing up on anyone, but that was what he knew. Zach figured he was destined to follow in his parents' footsteps, and it wasn't a path he wanted anyone else to have to walk with him.

Besides, he was fine with being single. The rodeo life was a good life, even if the thrill of it had grown decidedly thin in the past few years. Maybe next year he'd see about having some kind of a home base. He didn't mind washing his own socks, but he sure did miss a steady drawer to put them in.

Still, rodeo riding was what he knew and what he was good at. No one expected anything from him in the rodeo world that he did not know exactly how to give them. That should be enough for any man, he told himself as he reached Jenny's door.

Zach stamped his feet lightly outside the door, shaking the snow off them. He wore his heavy coat over the Santa suit and carried the mistletoe in one hand and his duffel bag in the other.

"What the…?" Zach muttered to himself as the mistletoe pricked him. The spikes on the holiday weed were big enough that the whole thing should be declared a lethal weapon. Zach half hung the mistletoe on his coat pocket and reached for the doorknob before he hesitated.

Polite manners were never his strong suit. But he figured even if the light in the window was for him, he was still company in this house and would be expected to knock rather than just come inside as though he belonged here. No matter how tempted he was to do just that, it wasn't right. He didn't belong. So he knocked.

The window on the door was frosted over, but the light from inside shone through the iced pattern.

"Come in," Jenny called softly from inside the kitchen.

Jenny had decided payment of a debt required some special touches. She brought down two cups and saucers from her good china set. She'd even put a lace cloth on the folding table. That should be enough, Jenny thought to herself when she heard Zach on the porch. The tea and the check should bring them about even.

When he opened the door, however, Jenny decided she should have forgotten the tea and left the check until the morning. She should have done whatever was necessary to be as far away from this man as was possible in her old house. The cold had turned the man into someone who looked as if he belonged on one of those calendars for single women. He was Mr. December.

Jenny shivered all the way down her spine. She told herself it was because of the cold wind that blew into the kitchen in the quick second before Zach turned to close the door.

But it wasn't.

Just look at him, she thought in dismay. Zach was the kind of man she had moved a thousand miles to avoid. Montana men were supposed to be farmers. Steady, reliable men with faces one learned to love. She wasn't supposed to meet a man like Zach, whose face would make a nun shiver. But there he stood against the black of the night like some mountain man covered with snow.

The kitchen was dark except for the half dozen candles Jenny had lit, some on the counter and some on the table in the middle of the kitchen. The candlelight made the snow scattered over Zach's dark hair glisten like confetti. The cold had turned his skin to marble. His brown eyes simmered beneath strong brows, and snow had settled on his eyebrows. More snow had fallen on the shoulders of his heavy leather coat as it hung from his frame.

In that long coat, all hints of a friendly Santa were covered.

"Thanks for waiting up," Zach said as he stood on the rug by the kitchen door and set his duffel on the floor nearby. "It was nice of you."

Jenny was speechless. Then she decided the best way to deal with the situation was to meet it rationally.

"It was only for a few minutes." Jenny took a deep breath and walked closer to him as he tried to get his arm out of his coat. If she could only get that coat off him, she'd be fine. She could cope with a man dressed as Santa. "Here, let me help you with that."

Zach stopped in surprise. He couldn't remember the last time anyone had offered to help him with anything. He'd always had to fend for himself. "I can get it."

"Not with that Santa suit on under your coat. Believe me, I know. Andy has a playsuit out of that fuzzy material and it's almost impossible for one person to get the coat pulled off the sleeves."

"Oh."

Zach was pretty sure Jenny was wrong, but he hoped she didn't discover the fact. She had moved close enough so he could inhale the pure soap smell of her.

Jenny gripped the edge of Zach's coat sleeve and tugged.

"Something's caught." Jenny pulled on the sleeve again before looking up at Zach.

Jenny looked back down at the sleeve. Looking up was a mistake. She needed to keep focused on the Santa material. Polyester. That wasn't sexy. Think of Andy's playsuit. "It'll come off in a minute."

Zach wasn't paying any attention to her words. He wondered if she knew what the candlelight did to her blond hair. She'd combed the short curls back and had them clipped with some combs. But little wisps of hair escaped here and there making it look as if she wore a halo.

Zach caught his breath. His skin was still cold from outside, but Jenny slipped her hand inside the sleeve of his coat and his skin warmed up in a hurry.

"Andy's coat never did this." Jenny bit her lip as she frowned up at Zach.

"Huh?" Zach stopped breathing as her hands slid farther under the Santa suit and up his forearm. Her hands were soft as an angel's beneath the weight of both the Santa suit and his sheepskin coat.

"Ouch!" Jenny said.

"Ouch!" Zach said.

The ball of mistletoe dropped to the floor and rolled.

"Sorry. I forgot I'd hung that halfway in my pocket."

"It's mistletoe."

Zach noticed Jenny didn't sound any too happy about the fact.

"It was on the truck antenna. Delores put it there," Zach said.

Jenny nodded curtly. Delores was a matchmaker. She'd put mistletoe on a hearse just in case the corpse met anyone on the way to his own funeral.

"I couldn't just leave the stuff outside. It'd freeze." Zach bent down and gingerly picked the mistletoe up by the string that had tied it to the antenna. "Besides it is a Christmas decoration. Thought you might be able to use it."

"I guess we could put it in the laundry room," Jenny offered after a moment. After all, Delores did mean well. "With the ham."

"What's a ham need with a wad of mistletoe like ours?"

"Ours?" Jenny looked up at him quizzically. The shadows in the kitchen left her eyes in darkness. Zach wished he could see them more clearly. Her eyes gave away her emotions, and he felt that he was flying blind when he couldn't see them.

"Well, you know—you and the kids," Zach stammered, before he added himself to the list. Man, that woman made him nervous. "You don't need to worry about it being mistletoe. I mean with the kissing and all. It's not like I'm planning to kiss you."

Jenny blinked. She wasn't planning to kiss him, either. Of course not. "Good…that's good."

It was good they understood each other. Very good. She would have had to speak to him if he intended to kiss her and assure him that they had no prospects. That would have been awkward, and she was glad there was no need to do it. But still…

"Not that I don't want to kiss you." Zach threw that in

for good measure. Jenny still wasn't smiling. "Any man would want to kiss you. I mean you're very, ah, pleasant. Very pleasant."

Jenny frowned slightly. *Pleasant* sounded like someone's grandmother. No wonder he was stuttering and stammering all over himself. Apparently she wouldn't have had to speak to him at all. "You don't want to kiss me."

"Huh?"

"Not that it's a problem," Jenny chattered. When she was upset, she always talked too much. "Which is for the best. Of course. In fact, you shouldn't even think about it. I mean, there's no need—I mean, well, you're just snowed in for Christmas. Stranded, really. We're not even each other's type—I mean, it's not like we're—that is—you just brought the mail and I'm grateful for that."

Sometimes a man has to gamble with his life, Zach thought. Sometimes he even has to gamble with his heart.

Zach bent down and kissed Jenny.

Or at least he thought he did. Maybe she was the one who tilted her head back and arched up to meet his lips. He would never know. All he knew was that he was kissing Jenny.

Zach had never expected the rush of pure sweetness to be followed by a hint of fire. That was his only excuse for lingering over the kiss.

Jenny stood rooted to the floor. She knew it was a mistake to kiss this cowboy, knew it when she'd told herself to step back and then found herself unable to do it. What was wrong with her, anyway? She usually had more sense.

Something was wrong with her. It was— "Christmas," Jenny whispered the word to herself as if it was a lifeline. Of course. It must be because of the holiday that she was letting this man kiss her senseless. That was it. The holiday.

People did strange things at holidays. They ate fruitcake. Rang old metal bells. They even forgot their very sensible vows and kissed good-looking cowboys who were just passing through.

"Hmm." Zach smoothed back Jenny's hair. "What about Christmas?"

"It's making me crazy." Jenny tried to collect herself. What was that purring in the back of her mind? "Well, not just me—both of us—Christmas and mistletoe. You know, it's crazy."

Zach didn't like this line of thought. "Christmas doesn't make people go crazy."

Kisses like the one we'd just shared might make people go crazy, Zach conceded to himself, but a date on the calendar never would. He'd missed out on a lot of things about Christmas, but crazy wasn't one of them.

"Of course it does." Jenny stepped farther back and kept chatting. Even her teeth were nervous around this man. She was lucky she wasn't blabbing. "There's the Santa fantasy. Every kid gets carried away with Santa. Even when we're adults we expect magic at Christmas."

"You think us kissing is about Christmas?"

Zach's voice was quiet, but Jenny didn't stop. She couldn't stop.

"Well, you know the goodwill, peace toward men—that kind of thing."

"I see." Zach turned slightly and, even with one hand holding the mistletoe string, pulled his arm away from his coat sleeve. A slight buzz of static filled the silence.

So that's why Jenny kissed him—goodwill? A man certainly couldn't go very far with that. A woman kissed her uncle for goodwill, or a child. She probably got extra points for cozying up to a sick orphan.

"It didn't mean anything. The kiss, I mean," Jenny stammered. The man was scowling about something. She supposed it was the kiss. He was experiencing after-kiss remorse. She'd seen it before. "We were just—"

"I know—" Zach hung his coat on one of the hooks and tried to stop scowling "—crazy at Christmas."

"Yeah."

Zach could vouch for the fact that at least one of them was crazy. The bottom had sure fallen out of his stability. And people wondered why he wasn't overly fond of the holiday.

Jenny shook herself. "It was only a kiss." And a tidal wave is only a little water, she mocked herself. She felt as if she'd jumped into the deep end before she'd learned to swim. She'd never meant to be this vulnerable again. And him, he was only passing through on his way to— "You were just lonesome for your friend."

"Huh?"

"The showgirl."

"Oh, Cathy."

"I thought you said her name was Patti."

Zach didn't like the way Jenny was looking at him—as though he was such a roving cowboy that he didn't even remember names. "It is Patti. I just call her Cathy sometimes."

Now she'd think he was certifiable, for sure. Zach assured himself the only reason he couldn't remember names was because Jenny was making him nervous. Usually he did fine.

Jenny continued chatting. "Speaking of your trip…" She willed herself to stop, but it did no good. She didn't even like to think about his trip to Las Vegas. She surely didn't want to talk about it. "You'll be needing some money."

"What?" Did she think he was paying for it? "Patti's a showgirl, but she's not—I mean, she doesn't charge."

Zach wondered if she thought he was so unattractive he needed to pay for it. She'd already made it clear she didn't particularly like his looks. But to say that—well, it was pretty discouraging when he'd just kissed her.

"I meant for gas. You'll need to buy gas to get there." Jenny willed her mind to focus. There she'd gone and insulted his girlfriend. And him, she supposed. "All I mean to say is that I have a check for you."

"Gas money?" Zach repeated in disbelief. He wondered if the woman knew how much money he had in his bank account. When he compared it with what was probably in hers, he was speechless. He could buy her miserable little farm a dozen times over and still have change. "I don't need gas money."

"Well, you'll need something someday—and you've done so much for us tonight." Jenny made the mistake of looking up directly into Zach's eyes. She'd heard of eyes that smoldered, but she'd never actually seen any that did until now. He was angry. The gold in his eyes sparked until it melted the brown. She completely forgot what she was going to say.

"You don't owe me anything."

"Still." Jenny gathered herself together. She needed to be strong for her children. She walked over to the counter and picked up the check. "I don't want to be beholden."

Zach saw the cornered pride in Jenny's eyes. So that was it. His face softened. "You're not beholden. You've offered me shelter in a storm. That's worth more than some ride in the dark."

"But it's just an old sofa."

"I've slept on worse. Many nights."

Jenny held out the check. "I'd still feel better if you took this."

Zach didn't want to take her check. Of course, it probably didn't make any difference since he'd never cash it. "I guess."

Zach reached out to take the check with one hand. The other hand held tight to the mistletoe string.

The kitchen was quiet except for the tick of the battery-operated clock on the wall. The candles carved out pockets of golden light by the counters and the table in the middle of the room.

Zach heard a shuffle in the corner and a yawn. Come to

think of it, he'd heard the shuffle for some time now. He wondered how long the little feet had been standing there.

"Mama, it's too late to give Santa a letter." Andy's voice came from the doorway to the kitchen. "Mr. Lightning already took the letters to Santa Claus, didn't you?"

Andy padded over to Zach and wrapped his arms around one of Zach's thighs. "You're cold."

Zach was surprised the cold didn't stop Andy from hugging his leg. "It was cold out there—going to the North Pole."

Zach let his hand rest on the boy's head.

"You should be in bed," Jenny gently scolded. Jenny didn't like the fact that her son had gone to the cowboy instead of her for the third time tonight.

"But Santa won't get your letter," Andy said worriedly as he looked up at his mother. He didn't leave his post by Zach's leg as he pointed to the check Zach held in his hand.

"That wasn't a letter. It was a check." Jenny hoped her son's fascination with the cowboy didn't turn to tears when the man left.

"Santa doesn't need a check."

"No, the check was for Mr. Lucas." Jenny hoped the formal title would remind Zach that just because her son wrapped himself around his leg at every opportunity he got it did not mean they were anything but strangers.

"It should have been a list," Andy protested. "What you want from Santa."

"Santa doesn't come to mommies," Jenny said.

Andy's eyes grew wide. "Because they've been bad?"

Jenny smiled. "No, it's just that Santa is special for little kids."

"But won't you get any presents?" Andy was frowning
as he clutched Zach's leg even harder. "You've gotta have
a present."

"Of course she'll have a present." Zach frantically
thought about what else might be in his duffel bag that
could be made into a present for Jenny. No wonder Santa
was fat. The stress of thinking of all those Christmas gifts
would drive anyone to eating too many cookies. "I just
don't know what yet."

"We could give her the Christmas ball," Andy announced
as he pointed to the mistletoe that hung from Zach's other
hand. "I've seen those. They're for kisses. Mommy likes
kisses."

"She does?" Zach watched the pink sweep across
Jenny's face. "Now isn't that nice."

Andy nodded happily. "I kiss her every night and she
sleeps with my kiss under her pillow."

"She does?"

Andy nodded as he pretended to scoop a kiss out of the
air. "I blow one to her so she can catch it."

"Isn't that nice." Zach wasn't at all in favor of that kind
of kissing. Not when it came to Jenny. Of course, the pillow part sounded nice.

Andy squeezed Zach's leg tighter. "Is Mommy going to
keep your kiss under her pillow tonight?"

Zach heard Jenny's gasp.

"Mommy, ah…" Zach jumped in to explain before Jenny

could deny everything. He knelt down so he was facing Andy directly. "Your mommy only has room under her pillow for kisses from her little boy. You give her special kisses."

Andy nodded happily. "I blow them to her."

Zach nodded. "That makes them easier for her to catch."

Andy leaned closer to Zach and whispered into his right ear. "I could teach you how to make special kisses. Then you could blow some to Mommy, too."

Jenny didn't like seeing the two heads together. Plus she couldn't hear what her son was saying. She didn't want to spoil Andy's illusions about the cowboy, but she didn't like him sharing his innocent thoughts with the man. "What's the secret?"

"Nothing." Zach knew Jenny wouldn't like what her son was saying.

Her son has no such hesitation. "I was just telling Mr. Lightning how to give you kisses that you keep under your pillow."

Jenny blushed.

"You should be back in bed," Jenny reminded her son. "It's cold out here."

"Tomorrow night Santa comes," Andy said blissfully as he continued to hug Zach's leg. "We're going to make cookies for Santa tomorrow, aren't we?"

Zach wondered when he'd become such a sucker for little boys. Maybe it was when they offered to teach him how to kiss their mothers. "Sure enough."

"I can stir," Andy offered proudly.

"You'll do a fine job," Jenny said firmly. "But first, you need to go to bed and sleep."

Andy yawned as he let go of Zach's leg and walked back out of the kitchen. "Good night, Mr. Lightning."

"Good night."

Zach watched Andy go. Now there was a sweet little boy, full of hope and enthusiasm. "His father must have been something."

"What?" Jenny looked up at Zach in alarm. Now where had that come from? She never talked about her husband. She'd not even told Delores about Stephen. At first, she'd never told anyone about Stephen because she kept intending to talk to him first. But then he was sick. And now she felt it was disloyal to voice her disappointment about someone who was dead. "What about Stephen?"

"To have raised a boy like Andy, he must have been a good father is all."

Zach was surprised at the surge of envy he felt. It must have felt good to be a man like Stephen and have something steady and loving to give to a wife and kids.

Jenny bit her lip. "Stephen wasn't well."

"I heard…the cancer." Zach could have kicked himself. Jenny's face had gone closed and pale. What kind of a brute was he, bringing back painful memories. "I'm sorry. You must miss him."

Jenny nodded. That was the sore truth of it. Even though he had kept to himself, she missed him. She had loved Stephen. For years. He had been her chosen one. She'd been hopeful. She'd prayed. She'd bargained for his attention.

She'd lived expecting the day would come when Stephen would look around himself and realize the value of his family. That day had never come. She always felt there had been some trigger in Stephen that she hadn't been able to find. Something she should have known that eluded her.

Zach called himself ten kinds of a fool. "I should be telling you about my trip to the frozen north instead of stirring up sad memories—especially at Christmas."

"And I should be offering you a cup of tea." Jenny gestured to the table. "And thanking you for making this Christmas a better one for my children."

Zach tried not to notice that she didn't include herself. "The Santa stuff was all Delores's idea."

"Do you like your tea plain or with lemon?" Jenny walked back to the fondue pot. "I'm afraid it will only be a tea bag in a cup. I couldn't get enough water to heat to make a pot."

"A cup will be more than fine."

Jenny poured him a cup of tea in silence and took it to the table. "I'm sure you'll enjoy some peace and quiet while you drink this."

Zach could have told her that he'd lived his life with peace and quiet. It wasn't what it was cracked up to be. But he didn't. She was rattled. He hoped she'd sit down at the table with him and have a cup of tea, as well.

"The tea smells good," Zach offered. "If you don't have enough water for two cups, I could get by with a half cup."

There. He'd asked her to share.

Jenny shook her head. "It's cold out there. You'll need your whole cup. Besides, I think I'm going to head to bed."

Zach watched Jenny walk out of the kitchen. "Good night."

Zach told himself he shouldn't mind. He was, after all, used to sitting at a table by himself and eating. It shouldn't even bother him after all those years. He'd sat alone in coffee shops. In hotel rooms. In bars. He should be used to it.

Zach looked around at the shadows in the empty kitchen. Yeah, he should be used to it by now.

Suddenly he had no appetite for the tea.

Chapter Six

Jenny woke with her pillow twisted around her shoulders. She'd had a dream of hot coals hiding under her pillow, and it took a couple of deep breaths to assure herself that everything was all right. She could feel her cheeks were aflame even though the air around them was cool.

She was lying on the mattress in her bedroom of the old house in Montana. The faint light of daybreak streaked into the room through the gap between her drapes. The day looked subdued. It was probably cloudy outside. Most likely the electricity was still off. At least the wind had died down.

Jenny heard the quiet giggling before she even had a chance to turn over again. She couldn't mistake the sound of Andy's laughter, and it didn't take too many guesses to place the deeper tones. Zach.

Jenny wondered what she was going to do with her son. How did you tell a four-year-old that it wasn't wise to become attached to a man who was going to be gone in a couple of days?

Maybe you didn't, Jenny said to herself as she stood up and slipped on her robe. Maybe all she could do was distract Andy as much as possible so that he was busy with other things and stopped spending time with the cowboy.

Jenny looked at her face in the mirror on the back of her bedroom door and grimaced. Her blond hair was naturally curly, and this morning it was flyaway. Usually her hair was only like this when it was going to rain. She wasn't sure if her hair would react the same way to snow.

Fortunately, no one would notice her hair once they got a good look at her puffy eyes. She looked like someone who had been doing battle all night with her dreams. Too bad she was out of eyedrops.

She was a mess. But she wasn't in a beauty contest today. All that mattered today was getting Christmas ready for her children. She, like her son, would do well to forget the cowboy was even here.

"Whoever gets the pan out of the cupboard gets the first pancake," Jenny announced firmly as she stepped into the living room.

Three pairs of eyes turned to her. She hadn't realized Lisa had joined the other two. Her two children were in their pajamas. The cowboy had at least put a shirt on with his well-worn jeans. The three of them were huddled around something on the living room floor.

"Mama!" Lisa squeaked.

"Don't look," Andy added in panic.

The cowboy simply pulled a blanket off the sofa where he had slept and spread it over something on the floor. "It's okay now."

Jenny eyed the blanket-covered lump on the floor. "What's that?"

"Well, now," the cowboy drawled. "That depends."

My goodness, Jenny thought as she looked at him closer. Didn't the man ever have a bad day? He looked just as pleased with himself as the children did. And his excitement made his brown eyes—well, it wouldn't do to look him in the eye for too long. "Depends on what?"

"Whether or not I tell you depends on whether you can keep a secret."

"She can't keep the secret. It's—" Lisa protested before she bit off her words and looked at Zach with reproach. "You're teasing."

Zach grinned back at Lisa. "Sure am."

Lisa smiled back before she rolled her eyes.

Jenny felt the need to sit down. Lisa never took to strangers. Granted, she'd run off to the North Pole with the man, but that was only to win a bet. Now Lisa was talking to him as if he was her best friend. Jenny wasn't sure she liked it. "You've got a secret?"

"Don't you know you're not supposed to ask questions at Christmas?" Zach finally said as he stood up.

Jenny was momentarily distracted. She thought rodeo cowboys were supposed to have aches and pains in every joint. Zach moved with a smoothness that made her mouth grow dry. If he ached anywhere it was unnoticeable. His whole body was a symphony. Even his hair behaved. And that little dimple she sometimes glimpsed on his chin— Jenny stopped herself.

"Huh?" Jenny looked away from the cowboy and back at her children. They were sitting on the floor and both smiling at her.

"Oh, it's a Christmas something? For me?" Jenny finally understood. Now she was completely dumbfounded. Jenny couldn't remember the last time she had gotten a real present. She'd always bought herself some soap or bath gel and put "From Stephen" on the package at Christmas. When the children asked, she'd told them all she wanted was a kiss and a smile.

"It's a surprise," Andy said in satisfaction as he stood up and walked over to her. "From us."

"You'll like it," Lisa added confidently as she stood up. "But you can't see it. Not until you open it up on Christmas morning. We're going to put it under the Christmas tree."

"I wouldn't dream of peeking," Jenny said. She hadn't seen her children so excited for months. And Zach—the man stood square in the middle of their excitement, looking just as pleased as they were.

Well, almost as pleased. The dimple was hidden, and she could see a small frown starting on his forehead.

"Where'd you say that frying pan is?" Zach asked as he sat down on the sofa.

"Me first," Andy squealed as he ran out of the living room with Lisa following close behind him.

"I hope you don't mind us doing this," Zach said quietly to Jenny. "Andy woke up first, and we didn't want to wake you. It was early. So we had this idea of making a present. I didn't think to ask you. Maybe, as I think about it now, I should have gone in and woken you."

No, Zach said to himself, that wouldn't have been a good idea at all. The sight of Jenny all warm and curled up in her bed would not have been—well, it would not have been a good idea at all.

"Ah, no." Jenny felt her cheeks blush. She'd already had hot coals under her pillow this morning. "You don't need to ask permission. But Andy can be a handful."

"He's just excited. Christmas, you know."

Jenny knew Christmas wasn't what was exciting Andy. It was having a grown man sit on the floor and pay attention to him.

"He's a good boy," Zach offered. He didn't want Jenny to think he minded spending time with Andy.

Zach had always liked children, but most of his encounters with kids were short and came about because the kid wanted his autograph or wanted to pet Thunder or something like that. He'd never had a chance to spend this much time with individual children like Andy and Lisa. He hadn't known what he was missing.

"I just don't want you to feel you need to spend all of your time fussing with the children. I know you don't like all the stuff that goes with holidays."

"I don't mind the children." What did she think he was? A monster? "It's only the holiday that I said that about— just the day on the calendar. Never the children. Children are supposed to like holidays."

"Oh." Jenny tried again. "Still, if you have other things to do—reading or something."

"The only books here are the children's books."

Jenny shrugged. "I thought maybe you brought something to read."

"I guess I could go check out the mailbag and see if I forgot to deliver any letters to Mrs. Goussley," Zach teased. What did she think? That he hauled around a library in his duffel bag?

Jenny gave up. Stephen had always found some excuse to avoid spending time with the children. She figured she had given Zach enough excuses he could pick one up anytime he wanted. She'd given him all the help she could.

"Unless—" Zach finally figured out what was giving the woman heartburn "—unless you'd rather I not spend time with the kids."

"What?"

"I know some women think that a rodeo man might not know how to act around kids," Zach said, ignoring the fact that even he knew he didn't know how to act around kids. "But I've been watching my language. And I don't tell them anything that they shouldn't know about."

Zach almost mentioned that he hadn't even explained what a showgirl was when they asked again this morning. He'd let them keep thinking a showgirl was nothing more than a cheerleader with feathers in her hair. Zach stopped himself from speaking of the showgirl, however. Jenny didn't seem to approve of showgirls.

Instead Zach decided he'd list his good points.

"I might not be as well mannered as their father... and educated," Zach continued. She could stop him at any time, but she didn't seem inclined to do so. "And I'm sure they still miss him something fierce. But, one thing I can guarantee, and that is you can trust your kids with me."

Jenny was speechless. Zach wanted to spend time with her children.

"They're not perfect children." Jenny felt she should let him know. "Lisa bites her nails."

Zach nodded. "I noticed. But I thought maybe she'd grow out of it. It's not something to worry about, is it?"

"I asked Delores about it. She said maybe it's just the move."

Zach nodded. "I'm sure moving around is hard on kids."

Moving around is hard on everyone, Jenny thought, but didn't say it. Maybe she should have stayed in Los Angeles. At least in Los Angeles she would never have gotten stranded miles away from the nearest neighbor with a man who cared about whether or not Lisa bit her nails.

"Mommy!" The call came from the kitchen.

"Oh, the pancakes," Jenny said. "I better get going."

"Take your time," Zach said as he turned toward where he'd laid his coat. "I need to get those pipes put back together before you can cook anything, anyway."

"Oh, I forgot."

"Now that it's light, it'll only take a few minutes." Zach walked out of the living room and into the kitchen.

Jenny stood up. "In that case, I'll dress first."

"Wear something warm," Zach called back from the kitchen. "We need to get that tree in before it starts to snow again. I told Lisa I think I know where we'll find one."

Jenny nodded. How was she supposed to protect her children's hearts from this man when he promised them a Christmas tree in the middle of a Montana blizzard?

Jenny wore panty hose under her jeans and two flannel shirts over a T-shirt. She figured that should keep her warm enough outside. She figured wrong.

The pancakes had fried up nice and brown and she'd even been able to warm the maple syrup. Everyone had eaten their fill. They had barely pushed their chairs back from the table before Lisa asked if it was time to go to get the tree.

"I don't see why not," Zach said. He didn't like the looks of the heavy gray clouds outside.

"There's the dishes," Jenny reminded everyone.

Lisa and Andy groaned.

"It's going to snow later," Zach said. "Maybe we should go right away."

Lisa and Andy looked at Zach and beamed.

"Well, maybe just this once we can do the dishes after we get back," Jenny conceded.

"You can put them to soak," Andy offered. Soaking the dishes was Andy's favorite way to cope with them. Lisa, on the other hand, carefully scrubbed each dish with a sponge.

"I'll at least clear the table while everyone gets dressed," Jenny said to her children. "And remember double socks today."

"Don't you have anything warmer than those shirts?" Zach asked when the children had left the kitchen.

It wasn't until this morning that Zach figured out that the men's flannel shirts Jenny was wearing had to be left from her husband's wardrobe. No wonder the woman wouldn't let them go. If they were real flannel, they'd probably keep her comfortable in the cold. But they were the thin, city flannel that was set for style instead of weather.

"What's wrong with these shirts?"

"Nothing. They're just not warm enough."

Jenny lifted her chin. "They'll have to do."

"You could borrow a sweatshirt from me," Zach offered and then held his breath. "I've got a new one—not even worn—picked it up at a rodeo in Fargo a couple of weeks ago."

"What makes you think it's warmer than my shirts?"

"Those are California shirts. Made for the beach. The sweatshirt was made for North Dakota wear."

"I wouldn't want to impose."

"And I wouldn't want you to catch your death of cold." Zach thought he had the upper hand, but he decided to cinch it. "Who will take care of your kids if you come down with pneumonia?"

"I won't get sick," Jenny assured him. She couldn't afford to get sick.

"Then you'll wear the sweatshirt," Zach ordered. "And the sheepskin coat."

"Oh, I can't possibly—I can't wear your coat," Jenny sputtered. She needed to draw the line somewhere. She was used to taking care of herself. It wouldn't be good to let down her guard and become used to someone doing things for her. She'd have to cope on her own again when he was gone. Besides, she'd always been a fair person. "You will get just as cold as me. It's your coat. You'll need it."

"I can't wear it, anyway, while I chop down the tree." Zach only hoped they found a tree to chop down. He'd look foolish chopping down a thistle bush. "You might as well wear it. If not, it'll just stay sitting on the seat behind me."

Jenny looked at the coat. Maybe she could let her guard down a little. It was Christmas, after all. And the coat was lined with a heavy knotted wool. "That's not real sheepskin, is it?"

Zach grinned. "Imitation."

Jenny walked over and touched the coat. The rough, knobby lining was warm.

"Try it on."

Zach held the sleeves to the coat as Jenny slipped her arms into it.

"Feels like fur," Jenny said. The coat made her feel warm for the first time in days. She almost felt like purring.

"Now you're ready to go." Zach looked at Jenny with satisfaction. She finally looked like a Montana woman.

Lisa was the first one to spot a tree. After Zach had scraped the ice off of the front and side windows, the four of them had squeezed into the postal truck and driven down the road that ran along the fence of the Collins property.

Just like Zach remembered from the previous day, the only trees around were at the bottom of the coulee about a half mile past the fence, just as the road turned up the hill to go to the house.

Zach had to give Lisa credit. She had leaned over her mother's shoulder so she could look out the side window. Since Lisa had already insisted Jenny roll down the window on their side, that meant Lisa's nose was cold enough to be red.

"I see one. I see one. I see one. Stop right here." Lisa bounced on her feet as she stood on the floor of the postal truck and half leaned out the passenger-side window.

"We need to pick one that doesn't have any pinecones," Jenny announced as she pulled out a narrow, green book from a bag she carried. She started to flip through the pages. "And, it's also good to find one that's at least—" she turned a page "—eight, maybe even nine feet tall."

Lisa seemed familiar with her mother's green book. The girl didn't even look at the book, she just nodded dutifully. "We will, Mama."

"What's that?" Zach eyed the book that Jenny read. He had assumed the bag held cookies or crackers in case the kids got hungry.

"It's my Montana Guide Book. It's got a chapter on caring for local trees." Jenny lifted her chin. Jenny had ordered the book when she first discovered that Stephen had not sold his uncle's property. The guidebook had given her the courage to move north. "I don't know very much about Montana. But the people who wrote this book do. They say there's no excuse for just stripping the land of its trees. A good farmer doesn't do that."

"We're only talking one tree," Zach reminded her as he turned the ignition off on the postal truck. He'd already pulled the truck to the side of the road in an area between two snowdrifts. "That's hardly stripping your land."

Jenny tightened her grip on the green book. "The trees with pinecones are needed to make seeds for new tall trees."

"Well, there is that." Zach nodded.

He didn't have the heart to tell her that it would take more than a few pinecones to make nine-foot pine trees grow on her land. The trees at the bottom of the coulee were hunched over from the wind. He doubted any of them would ever grow more than four feet tall. And those were the lucky ones. Any tree seed unfortunate enough to fall on the top sides of the coulee would never live to grow even to four feet. The wind would see to that.

"I want a tree with an angel hook," Lisa announced as she sat back down on the floor at the back of the postal truck and pulled on her mittens.

"That's just something they put on trees at the lot where we got them in L.A., dear," Jenny said as she sat her book down on the tray that ran along the front of the postal cab. "These trees won't have them."

"Will they have one of those kissie-toe things?" Andy asked as he crawled up front and held out a mittenless hand to his mother.

"You mean mistletoe?" Jenny asked hesitantly. She had hoped Andy had forgotten about the kiss he'd seen last night. She put her hand in the pocket of Andy's coat and pulled out his missing mitten. "No, the tree won't have that."

"Then how is Mr. Lightning going to learn how to kiss?" Andy forgot about his mitten and just stood in the space between Jenny and Zach.

Zach felt a little hand clamp on to his arm and looked over to the boy. Andy's eyes were earnest with worry as they looked back at him. Zach would have joked with the boy, but he looked over the little one's head and saw Jenny. Joking might not be the best idea, Zach decided.

"Mr. Lightning doesn't need to learn how to kiss," Jenny finally said firmly as she reached around the truck's gearshift to capture Andy's bare hand. Jenny pulled the mitten on Andy's hand. "Now, be sure you have your coats buttoned up tight before you go outside."

Zach held back his grin until his muscles ached. He could watch Jenny's face blush a hundred times and not grow tired of the wonder of it.

"I'm zipped," Andy said happily as he wiggled back into the back of the postal truck.

"Me, too," Lisa said as she unhooked the back door of the postal truck.

"And wait at the edge of the coulee. We'll all walk down together," Jenny called out as the two children scrambled out of the back of the truck. "I need to talk to Mr. Lucas for a minute first."

Jenny wished she didn't blush. "I'm sorry. Sometimes kids say the craziest things."

"I suppose it's because of Christmas." Zach agreed solemnly. It occurred to him he hadn't been able to get a clear picture of Jenny's eyes last night when they had kissed. The candlelight didn't give off enough light. "I hear everyone's crazy at Christmas."

"Yes, yes, that must be it." Jenny was relieved he seemed to understand. "They just get excited, and... well, they don't mean anything by it."

"I must say, though, it is a little troubling." Zach turned so that he was looking squarely at Jenny.

"What is?" Jenny turned to face Zach.

Zach reached up to touch Jenny's cheek. It was cool and smooth as silk. "How can I let your son think I don't know how to kiss his mother?"

"He's talking about air kisses," Jenny whispered. She felt the man's thumb as he rubbed it down her cheek. Her cheek was cold, and his thumb felt like a hot brand, marking her cheek as his own. "The kind you blow across the room."

"Seems an awfully risky way to send a kiss," Zach said softly as he moved closer. "And not nearly as satisfying."

Jenny swallowed. Or at least she tried to—she was having a hard time even breathing. "We need to go get the tree."

Zach must have kissed over a thousand women. Never once in all those times had he wanted a signal as desperately as he wanted one from Jenny. He didn't want to kiss her unless he knew she wanted him to kiss her.

"Is that what you want?" There, he thought to himself,

he'd just put the question out there. He didn't want to have any doubts. "The kids are warm. They can wait a minute."

"No, I don't want to…yes, I mean…the kids—" Jenny stumbled. She needed to remember the kids. She was going to find a steady, stable man to be a father to her kids. She couldn't afford to be sweet-talked by a cowboy who was just passing through. "The kids want a tree."

Zach swallowed. Never let it be said he took rejection badly. He was a grown man. He knew the odds. He put his hand on the door handle of the truck and pushed. "Well then, let's go get us a tree."

The tree was deformed. But Lisa had chosen it, and Zach had dutifully cut it, and they had all dragged it up out of the coulee.

"It's got a place for stars," Lisa said as she patted one of the branches.

They had set the tree up in the middle of the living room. Jenny had produced a plastic bucket, and they had poured rocks around the tree trunk to make it stay upright. Even with the extra height of the bucket, however, the tree didn't top four feet. It also had a tendency to tilt to the left.

"It's beautiful," Jenny declared loyally.

"It's crooked," Lisa confessed, a worried frown on her face.

"Some of the most beautiful things are crooked." Zach anchored the tree deeper into the bucket of rocks. "Remember that leaning tower in Italy."

"Yeah." Lisa smiled. "We'll just have an Italian tree."

Jenny had taken Delores's camera with them and she'd taken a picture of Lisa, Andy and Zach as they all measured that tree down at the bottom of the coulee. And then she'd taken a couple more of them dragging the tree up out of the coulee. "And I'm sure we'll think of something for decorations."

"We don't have decorations?" Lisa stopped studying the tree and turned to her mother. It was clear all worry about the tilting of the tree was forgotten. "We have to have decorations."

"We can make decorations," Jenny said firmly. She should have shown her children how to make decorations in the years past. It's just that Stephen never liked the mess that projects like that made and so it was easier to just buy things at the thrift stores.

"But how can we make stars?" Lisa said worriedly. "Stars need to sparkle."

Zach sat down on the sofa to get a better look at the tree. He didn't know whether he was coming or going. He'd looked ahead down the road on the way back from getting the tree just to see if he could make it into Deep Gulch. He could tell it would be foolish to leave this house, especially because the clouds had started to grow gray and heavy again.

Of course, no matter how foolish it would be to leave, staying would be worse.

Life had really pulled a fast one on him. Here he was, snowed in with a family that was everything like the family on that Christmas card he'd seen when he was ten.

Everyone cared about each other. They didn't need a tree to be happy together, but they had a tree anyway.

They made a perfect Christmas card picture. Sure, the father might be missing from the picture, but the man used to be in the picture. For years and years, this Stephen guy had been the husband and father in this family.

The man was dead and buried. And Zach still envied him like he'd never envied anyone in his life. That man had had it all.

"I bet he never rode a horse, though," Zach said aloud to himself.

"Huh?" Jenny looked over at Zach. For the first time today, he looked a little frayed around the edges. Zach was sitting on the sofa with his shoulders hunched forward and his hands clutching an empty cup that had held coffee.

"Horse." Andy caught the one word that interested him. He had been sitting on the floor at Zach's feet. Now he jumped up and stood at Zach's knee. "Are we going to ride a horse? Huh? Are we?"

"We don't have a horse," Jenny answered her son.

"And lights," Lisa moaned. She was still looking at the tree. "We don't have any lights."

"I can take the lights off those reindeer horns on the postal truck," Zach offered as he stood up. He might not be part of this family, but he still wanted this Christmas to be perfect, Italian Christmas tree and all. "They are on some kind of batteries."

Lisa brightened. "That's right."

"And we can make stars out of aluminum foil." Jenny

started toward the kitchen. "And I have some red yarn for bows."

"Mr. Lightning has a horse," Andy said softly as he watched Zach walk toward the kitchen door.

"That horse is sick," Lisa said in disgust. "You can't ride a sick horse."

Zach stopped himself from promising the boy a ride. It would be a promise he couldn't keep. Once Thunder was well, they needed to keep driving down to Vegas. He and Thunder were both roving souls. Besides, he doubted Jenny would ever invite him back for a visit. "I'll bring in the reindeer horns. Maybe we can rig you up a horse to ride from them."

"See," Andy said to his sister. "I am going to get to ride."

Lisa just shook her head. "First you have to help make stars."

Zach stepped into the kitchen. Jenny had opened a drawer on the counter and was pulling out slender tubes. "I know I had tinfoil here somewhere."

"I have some foil in the truck."

Jenny looked up, relieved. "You do?"

"Wrapped around half a dozen plates of cookies."

"I could replace the foil with waxed paper," Jenny offered. "That way your cookies won't dry out."

"I thought I'd bring them in anyway. The kids will like them."

"Oh, we couldn't take your cookies."

"They're not my cookies. They were meant for Delores. She'd want the kids to have them."

Why was it, Zach asked himself, that it was so difficult to give that woman anything? Even a porcupine had fewer prickles.

"Well, thank you." Jenny pushed the empty tube of foil back into the drawer. Why was it that the man insisted on being so nice? Couldn't he see that she was determined not to let him get under her skin? "I'll pay you for them, of course."

Zach just looked at her as he grabbed his coat off the hook. What was it with this woman? "I don't need your money."

Jenny was going to point out that everyone needed money, but the man was out of the door before she could. Still, she had made her point. She wanted to keep things on a businesslike level between them. Money helped do that. She didn't like accepting things from him. It made her feel as if they were friends.

No, she admitted to herself, it didn't make her feel as if they were friends. Friends stayed around. They didn't leave and take your heart with them. No, the last thing Zach offered was friendship. At the moment he was a stranger, just passing through, and she would do well to remember it.

Chapter Seven

Zach had a towel wrapped around his fingers and a hot sheet of metal in his hand. It wasn't the best time to be watching Jenny as she watched the sky. He wondered if she knew her blond curls shone with golden highlights as she stood in the thin light that came through the window above the kitchen sink. And the long curve of her neck as she looked up—well, as Zach already knew, it wasn't the best of times for him to be holding a hot sheet of metal.

He'd already burned himself once today when Jenny bent over to pick up a spoon that fell on the floor. Of course, it had almost been worth it when Jenny insisted on rubbing some kind of an ointment on his thumb. She'd been shy about touching him, and Zach had found it more arousing than any flirtation he'd ever encountered.

"Expecting geese?" Zach carefully set the cookie sheet

on the pot holders Jenny had laid out on the counter. The kitchen was warm and the sounds of the children in the living room made him feel a contentment he'd never known. For one brief day he was inside the Christmas picture.

Andy had gone into the living room to fold tinfoil stars with Lisa. Jenny had been doing dishes, until she stopped to look up at the sky.

Jenny turned toward him. "It's below zero out there. There's no geese."

Zach nodded. "I know, but the way you've been watching that sky I figured you must be watching for something."

"I was looking at the clouds." Jenny had resisted the temptation to bring her green Montana Guide Book out from her bedroom. Before starting the dishes, she'd carefully read the different cloud descriptions. If she could just match the clouds outside with the right picture in her guidebook, she should be able to tell if it would snow more today. Unless there was more snow, Zach might leave. She didn't want that to happen—for Andy's sake, she told herself. Gray and heavy clouds meant snow. The clouds outside were gray, but she wasn't sure if they were heavy enough.

"Ah." Zach started lifting the cookies off the pan and onto a platter.

"What makes air heavy?"

Jenny hardly recognized the cowboy. He had flour on his face and a sprinkling of cinnamon on his shirt. He'd tied an old dish towel around his waist. If the cereal people could only see him now, they'd take a whole new set of pictures for the backs of their boxes.

"Moisture, I guess." Zach carefully nudged the angel cookies to the left of the platter so there would be room for a few sugar-cookie trees. He'd never thought he would ever be baking Christmas cookies. "Don't tell me you're worried, too. I thought Andy was the only one."

"Andy's worried?" Jenny didn't like that her son was worried about whether or not it would snow. Of course, Zach had probably mentioned the roads to Andy. "Have you said something to make him worry you'd leave?"

"Me, no. He's not worried about me. He's worried about Santa Claus. Andy's afraid that if it rains instead of snows Santa won't be able to land his sled on the roof because it'll be too slippery." Zach kept his tone light. "It seems he remembers when you tried to fix the roof."

"Oh."

"Something about the roof being slippery because it was raining." Zach took a deep breath so his panic wouldn't show. He knew it was none of his business what this woman had decided to do last month. But what if she had fallen off the roof instead of just sliding down the roof a bit? He wouldn't have even been there to get her to the doctor. "I guess that guidebook of yours didn't tell you that you shouldn't be climbing around on a roof in the rain. Especially not a pitched roof like this one. It's dangerous."

"Well, I didn't know the roof leaked until it started to rain."

"That's what buckets are for." Zach put the empty cookie sheet back on top of the stove. He had one more pan in the oven. "You wait until the roof is dry to work on it. Besides, you shouldn't be fixing your roof, anyway." Zach bent his head down to open the oven and mumbled the rest. "I'll see it gets done for you."

Jenny didn't think she had heard him right. "But you can't do it, either. Snow's no better than rain. Well, it has to be worse—snow is wet and ice both at the same time. Besides…" Jenny didn't finish. They both knew he would be gone before the snow melted.

Zach swallowed. The hot air from inside the oven felt good on his face. He reached in for the pan of snowman cookies. He might as well say this while he was facing the oven. He didn't expect Jenny would like it. But he had given it some thought. "I've decided—when I go back to the doc's—I'm going to give him money to hire someone to put a new roof on this house."

Jenny gasped. She forgot all about the dishrag in her hand. "But, you can't. Why, that's way too much…you can't possibly."

Zach pulled the pan of cookies out of the oven and straightened up. "Consider it a Christmas present."

Jenny dropped the dishrag back into the dish water. "That's not a Christmas present—a Christmas present is socks or a pin—something small. A roof is way bigger than a Christmas present." The warm air from the oven floated across the kitchen toward her. "Besides, you don't even like Christmas."

"Maybe not, but I like solid roofs."

"But you can't pay to have a new roof put on my house. Why, what would the doctor and Delores think?"

"They'd think you were getting a new roof."

No, Jenny thought to herself, they'd think she was getting a new husband. Which was ridiculous, of course. Anyone could see the cowboy wasn't the kind of guy to marry anyone. He would never settle down. He'd just—no, Jenny realized with a start, the doctor and Delores wouldn't think of marriage at all.

She'd been out of the dating game for so long, she didn't recognize the obvious. They wouldn't think the cowboy was doing any favors, they'd think she'd been the one to be generous to the cowboy. Anyone would think that. Even Zach. "I could never accept a gift that expensive. It'd be hundreds of dollars."

Try thousands, Zach thought. But he wouldn't sleep well nights thinking Jenny might be crawling around up on that roof. And paying someone to do it was the only way. Unless… "If you won't let me pay someone, I'll come back and put a new roof up myself."

Jenny looked at him as if he'd offered to burn her house down instead of seeing that it stayed dry. "I have the children to think of, you know. Not to mention the fact that I have to live in this community." Jenny paused. "I'm afraid you wouldn't get anything in exchange for the roof."

"I wouldn't—" Zach had been scooping the cookies off of the sheet and turned too fast. The back of his hand hit the hot sheet. He barely felt the burn. He'd figured out what Jenny was saying and he didn't like it. Not that he wouldn't have tried to find an angle with any other woman he found attractive. "*I* can think of the children, too, you know. And I wasn't expecting anything in return for the roof."

Jenny had noticed his wince when his hand hit the sheet. She reached in her pocket for the tube of ointment. "Then why were you offering it?" She held out her hand. "Here, let me see your hand."

Zach held out his closed fist. The ointment felt cool until Jenny rubbed it around on the back of his hand. Then his whole body heated up. "Can't someone do something nice for you just because—" Zach scrambled for a reason "—just because it's Christmas."

"You're doing it because of Christmas? You?" Jenny obviously wasn't convinced.

Sometimes, Zach decided, a man needed to stay with the cards he'd been dealt, even if they were losing cards. "I have a lot of Christmas presents to make up for. From the past."

"I didn't know you in the past." Jenny held Zach's burned hand while she reached over to the counter and picked up the roll of gauze she'd used on Zach's thumb earlier. She started to unroll the gauze. "You don't owe me any presents."

Zach closed his eyes. Why did she have to make it so hard? "Maybe I've decided it would be too difficult to track down everyone I've known over the years and give them a belated present."

Jenny wrapped gauze around Zach's hand. "So this roof—it's like penance for all your past missed gifts."

"Something like that." Zach closed his eyes wearily. He hoped she never discovered that just because he didn't believe in Christmas didn't mean he'd been stingy in the past.

Ever since Zach had started making good money on the rodeo circuit, he'd given some very nice presents to people. Of course, they were usually checks. Some of them, however, had even been for dollar amounts that would be more than Jenny's roof would take. Never, however, had Zach had as much trouble with anyone accepting a present as he was having with Jenny.

"And you're not expecting to sleep with me in return?" Jenny asked the question crisply. She was just making sure they understood each other.

Zach opened his eyes at that. "Lady, you won't even kiss me. I'm not fool enough to think a roof would get us to where you're thinking."

Zach hoped she'd protest. Hoped she'd say it might at least get him a date. She didn't.

Instead Jenny slowly knotted the gauze on his hand. She didn't even raise her eyes to his but kept her eyes on his burn. "But I don't have anything nearly that expensive to give you in return."

Zach smiled. So it was her pride that was bothering her. He turned his bandaged hand so that he held hers. "At the rate I'm going, maybe you should just give me that ointment in your pocket and a roll of that gauze."

Jenny looked up and smiled back, but she didn't remove her hand. "Cookie baking can be dangerous."

"I never knew kitchen duty could be so hazardous." Zach couldn't control his thumb as it rubbed the back of Jenny's hand.

Jenny had been washing dishes and her hands were still

slightly damp from the water. Even damp, Zach wagered they were smoother than other women's hands.

Jenny's cheeks were pink as she smiled. "If you think this is exciting, wait until tomorrow. You can help me with the ham. And—if you really want a thrill—you can help open the can of yams I'm going to bake."

"It can't be any harder than baking these cookies." Zach settled back into holding Jenny's hand.

Zach couldn't remember ever holding a woman's hand before. He couldn't remember even wanting to hold a woman's hand. He was always too intent on winning a bigger prize. What a fool he'd been, he thought as he squeezed Jenny's hand. He hadn't known what he was missing. He would remember this moment forever.

The warm smell of sugar cookies made the kitchen cozy. Jenny had rolled the dough thin, and Lisa and Andy had used cookie cutters to shape snowmen, angels, bells and trees. Zach had measured the ingredients and helped Andy stir. Everyone had sprinkled colored sugar on the different shapes before Zach slipped the cookie sheets into the oven.

The sky outside was gray, and only a thin light shone through the windows. The electricity was still off but Jenny had lit a candle and set it on the folding table. The glow of the candle cast yellow light all around the kitchen.

Jenny held her breath. She couldn't remember ever having someone sit with her at the end of a day and hold her hand. It should feel innocent, even with the hypnotic feel of Zach's thumb as it traced circles on the back of her hand.

But it didn't feel the least bit innocent. It was one of the most erotic moments she'd ever experienced.

Too bad erotic was a mistake.

"Thanks for helping with everything," Jenny finally said to Zach as she gently removed her hand. "It'll be a wonderful Christmas."

Jenny looked around her kitchen with satisfaction. For the first time, she didn't notice all the things she didn't have. Instead she saw that the folding table still had scraps of tinfoil from the star shapes that Lisa had cut earlier and the kitchen counter was covered with every platter she owned. Each platter was covered with Christmas sugar cookies.

Such a wonderful Christmas merited a wonderful present for the man who had helped make it all possible.

"I can think of a better gift for you than a first-aid kit," Jenny said firmly. She was full of goodwill. Everyone inside her home would have a good Christmas if it was in her power to give them one.

The light coming in from the kitchen window cast shadows around Zach's eyes. "I'm not expecting anything. You don't need to— I mean, the roof doesn't require a present. It's just because—"

"No, I need a present for you." Jenny closed her eyes. How could a cowboy in worn jeans and a towel apron covered with cookie dough look so sexy? Well, it wasn't his fault she couldn't keep her eyes off him. He'd been good to her children and she owed him a Christmas present. She did a mental review of the boxes in her bedroom. "Maybe something of Stephen's—"

"No." The word sounded abrupt even to Zach's ears. Jenny's eyes flew open. To hide his confusion, Zach turned and stole a warm cookie from a platter. "I mean, you should save his things for Andy and Lisa. When they're older they'll want some things to remember him by."

Jenny wondered if her children would remember their father in twenty years. If they did, it wouldn't be because of some sweater or tie.

"He must have been a wonderful father and husband." Zach tried to sound casual as he took a bite out of the cookie.

Zach hated himself for trying to find out more about the man, but the man's very existence bothered him like a scab that wasn't healing right. Maybe someone would let something slip, and Zach could learn the secret that this Stephen had known about being part of a family like this one.

Maybe—Zach didn't dare even hope—but maybe the secret was something Zach could learn if he only had a few pointers. Zach almost choked on the rest of what he had to say, but he said it anyway. "I wish I could have known him. What was he like?"

"Like?" Jenny's voice squeaked. She never talked about Stephen. He was not only a closed chapter in her life, she'd buried the book, as well.

"Yeah. Did he have any hobbies?" Zach supposed the man liked opera. Women always seemed to like opera. Zach preferred a guitar player in a bar anyday. Still, he supposed he could learn to endure opera. "Anything you and he did for special evenings?"

Jenny tried hard to think. She and Stephen hadn't done anything social even in the years before he was sick. Stephen preferred to go out with his male friends rather than stay home with her, and he never wanted to spend the money for a baby-sitter so they could go out together. "We didn't have a lot of money."

"I see." Zach figured that meant they spent a lot of cozy evenings at home putting together jigsaw puzzles and watching videos. The very thought of it depressed him.

Zach would have had a better chance of competing if Jenny had mentioned dinners in fancy restaurants and dancing. He could afford to fly her to Paris for a weekend. It was the home things he wasn't sure he'd ever get right.

The outside light was fading in the kitchen, and the glow of the candle on the table was growing more golden. Zach's face picked up the glow of the candle. He was concentrating on the cookie in his hand with an intensity that reminded Jenny of his picture on the back of that cereal box.

It was the cereal-box picture that gave Jenny the courage to decide to tell Zach the truth about Stephen. She wanted to tell someone. She really did. The words always just seemed to stick in her throat. But if she pretended she was talking to the back of that box, maybe she could get the words out.

"Stephen—" Jenny began and swallowed. She felt almost relieved now that she had decided to tell someone. Even if that someone was just a cowboy who was on the back of a cereal box. "Stephen was, well, it wasn't so much what he was, it's what he— Well, you know I've told you that he wasn't—" Jenny stopped. Zach had turned and was looking at her. All of a sudden, he didn't look anything like his picture on the cereal box.

"Yeah," Zach prompted her.

"I, ah…" Jenny knew it was her chance. She also knew she was a coward. She didn't know what Zach would think of her if she told him about Stephen. Lots of men thought any marital unhappiness was the wife's fault. Maybe Zach would think that, too. "I… we got married awfully young."

Zach almost groaned. No wonder Jenny didn't want to kiss another man. Stephen was probably the only man she'd ever even dated. "You must have been very much in love."

"Uh…" Jenny swallowed. She would try again.

Jenny never got a chance. The quiet giggles from the living room had grown louder and finally they were at the kitchen door.

"Mama, come look," Lisa called as she stood in the doorway.

The house was in shadows.

"Oh, I better get the lantern lit," Jenny said. She'd talk to Zach later. It wasn't that she wouldn't have talked to him, she assured herself. It just wasn't the time yet. She'd tell him all about Stephen. And soon. Just not right this minute. She couldn't risk the children hearing about Stephen.

"Mr. Lightning," Andy called from the living room. "Come see the stars."

Zach followed Jenny into the living room, and the light from the lantern she was carrying made the tin-foil stars reflect a thousand lights. The tree glowed with the reflections.

Zach had unwrapped the Christmas lights from around the reindeer horns that Delores Norris had hung on the postal-truck hood. He'd then clipped the lights to the branches of the Christmas tree. The battery for the lights was nestled on top of the rocks at the bottom of the tree. So far, no one had turned on the lights.

"They're lovely," Jenny said as she put one hand on Lisa's shoulder and smiled at Andy. "I've never seen so many stars."

"Can we turn the lights on now?" Lisa asked. "It's almost dark."

Jenny had told the children earlier that they would turn on the tree lights when it grew dark. Jenny wasn't sure how much power the batteries had left, and she didn't want to run the batteries dry before it even grew dark.

"Let's have some soup first." Jenny looked at her watch. How had the day gone so fast. "It's almost five o'clock. Then we can read the Christmas story before you go off to bed."

"But that will still be too early," Lisa protested. "I wanted to wrap your present."

Zach had hidden the jewelry box the kids had made for their mother earlier this morning. The jewelry box had really been a small wooden toolbox that Zach had kept his leather-working tools inside. Andy had glued some beach shells he'd found in California on top of the box and Lisa had glued a piece of velvet on the inside of the box.

Wrapping presents, Jenny thought in dismay. "But I don't have any paper. Oh, I knew I wasn't ready for Christmas."

"Wrapping paper isn't necessary," Zach said, hoping he was right.

He was wrong.

"Yes, it is," Lisa said, and she looked up at Zach like he was a magician with a hat that still had a few miracles left inside of it.

"I don't have any—oh, wait." Zach remembered. "I do have paper. In the postal truck. Delores carries around a tube of brown postal paper. And tape."

"Brown paper?" Lisa looked skeptical.

"I think there might be some red stamps and some markers." Zach wasn't sure what all Delores kept in her postal bin that ran along the right-top side of the truck.

"We can make Christmas paper," Jenny said in relief. The kids would remember Christmas paper they had made themselves a lot longer than anything she could buy.

"Just remember, you need to go to bed early tonight," Jenny said firmly. "Remember what we said? If you go to bed early, you can get up early tomorrow morning."

And, if they go to bed early, Jenny added to herself, she and Zach would have time to make the presents for the children they'd talked about earlier. Zach had told her his ideas, and she knew the children would love the gifts he had suggested.

"All right," Lisa agreed reluctantly.

"Can I have cereal instead of soup for supper?" Andy asked.

Andy had also asked to have Ranger cereal for lunch when the rest of them had eaten tuna sandwiches. Jenny had given in then. "You've got to eat more than cereal."

"I can have a cookie, too," Andy offered.

Jenny appealed to Zach. "You talk to him."

Zach smiled. He was glad the cereal executives couldn't hear him now. "Real cowboys don't eat cereal for every meal. They need other things, too, to stay healthy. Maybe you should try some soup tonight."

"Are you eating soup?" Andy asked as he walked over and wrapped his arms around Zach's leg.

"I sure am."

"Okay," Andy agreed. "I'll have soup. And crackers?"

"Yeah, we have crackers. And peaches for dessert." Jenny tried to remember everything she had in the cupboards. She was grateful Stephen's uncle had had the good sense to see that the kitchen stove operated off the propane tank like the furnace did. With the electricity still out, they wouldn't be eating anything warm if he hadn't.

Zach left his hand resting on Andy's head. Zach liked the solid weight of the boy as Andy leaned against his leg. "Let's go set the table for your mom."

"I know where the bowls are," Lisa announced as she led the way.

Supper was by candlelight, and Zach was content. He'd eaten candlelight dinners in five-star restaurants at the top of skyscrapers and on cruise ships. At none of those dinners had the conversation lagged or the soup been cold. But he didn't even have to debate the issue. He wouldn't trade this candlelight meal for any one of the others.

"At least the peaches should be all right," Jenny said quietly.

"It was a wonderful meal," Zach assured her. "Wholesome."

"I could heat up some more tomato soup, now that the stove has cooled down." Jenny hadn't realized that using the oven of the stove all afternoon would affect the burners. It meant they wouldn't stay lit for very long.

"I'm content."

Jenny wondered if she should admit to Zach that she was content, too. She wondered at the ease she felt around him. Earlier in the day Jenny had realized she was relaxing around Zach because he didn't criticize her the way she had expected any man would. Zach seemed to be pleased with whatever she had to offer in the way of meals and household comforts.

Zach was a big change from her late husband. Stephen had been visibly unhappy if the laundry wasn't ironed right or the meals weren't to his liking. No wonder she'd been tired all those years when she'd been married, Jenny thought to herself in amazement. She'd been trying to make things perfect for Stephen. And perfection had been hard to maintain when she had two small children to care for as well.

Of course, Jenny told herself, it was easy for Zach to accept things the way they were. He wouldn't be around long and he probably just didn't care.

"I do know how to cook a good meal," she added in self-defense. "It's just the stove and all. I'm learning."

"We're all learning." Zach pushed his chair away from the table. "Let me get the peaches for you."

"After peaches, I want to make wrapping paper," Lisa said.

Jenny rinsed the dishes from supper and left them in the sink. Amazing how liberating that felt. For the second time today she hadn't needed to rush to do the dishes as if she had something to prove to someone. Instead the four of them sat at the folding table and made wrapping paper.

Andy liked to stamp. He'd stamped a red FRAGILE over a length of brown postal paper. The stamp was upside down in some places and sideways in others. Jenny noticed that the confused jumble of it all did manage to look festive.

Lisa was drawing bells with a red pen on another length of brown postal paper.

"I'll need to remember to pay Delores for all this," Jenny said.

"I bet she'd like a picture instead," Zach said as he stood up and walked to the kitchen counter. If he knew anything about Delores, he knew she had a soft spot for these two children. The woman deserved to see them as they concentrated on decorating the postal paper.

"Great idea," Jenny said as she accepted the camera Zach handed to her.

Jenny snapped two pictures and pulled them out to dry. She'd taken a dozen or so pictures of the children over the day. There was one of Andy and Zach cutting out cookies. There was one of Lisa and Zach stringing the lights on the Christmas tree.

Each picture Jenny took, she took two shots. One of the

shots was for herself. The other one was for a Christmas present for Zach. She'd thought about going through the box of Stephen's ties and sweaters.

But, even though Zach wouldn't be wearing either one around Jenny, she didn't like to picture him in anything but the clothes he already had. She didn't want to look at the cowboy and see any reminders of Stephen.

Actually, she thought she might take the whole box of Stephen's things and tie it up tight with some of Delores's postal string before setting it at the back of the large closet in her bedroom. Zach was right. Andy and Lisa might want to see the things someday, but for now, Jenny wanted it tucked away where she didn't have to see it every day.

Jenny couldn't help but wonder, as she listened to her children giggle while they talked with Zach, what her life would have been like if she had married a man like Zach instead of one like Stephen.

Well—she shook herself—that was a pointless thing to wonder about, and on a Christmas Eve.

Chapter Eight

Zach had never heard the Christmas story read to children. Oh, he knew the story. The star. The wise men. The shepherds. The angels. The baby in the manger. But he'd never seen it through the eyes of children.

Zach sat backward on a folding chair with his arms resting on the back. He loved watching Jenny as she sat on the sofa with one child on either side of her and read them the Christmas story.

"And that's why we have peace and goodwill to all on Christmas," Jenny said as she closed the children's book. "Because the baby Jesus was born a long time ago in Bethlehem."

Jenny had moved the lantern into the living room, and it was hanging from a hook she'd rigged up from the ceiling fan. The lantern gave off a yellowish light that bathed the room in a warm glow. The smell of recently baked cookies still filled the air, mingling with the smell of fresh pine from the tree that sat in the bucket of rocks in the middle of the room. A small present was already wrapped and sitting beneath the decorated tree.

"And stars," Lisa sighed. "That's why we have stars."

"Well, we had stars before Christmas," Jenny said softly. She supposed now wasn't the time for a lesson in astronomy. "But none of them were as special as the Christmas star."

"It was the biggest, bestest star ever," Lisa said in satisfaction.

"My star is big, too," Andy said as he pointed to the tree that stood in the center of the living room. "It's that one."

Andy and Lisa had colored their stars. The folded foil stars had been marked with red highlighters and yellow highlighters. Some had flowers drawn on them. One had a horse. They each had a hole poked in their top for a piece of twine so they could be tied to the tree branches.

The stars made the lopsided pine tree sparkle with reflected light from the red and green lights that were twined around the tree branches.

The star Andy pointed to had to be at least four inches across. It was so big it hung crooked on the tree branch. A yellow stick figure had been drawn on it with a big circle around its head.

Zach thought the stick figure must be an angel and the circle a halo.

"It's a beautiful star," Jenny agreed as she shifted the arm she had around the boy and gave him a quick hug.

Andy wiggled down from the sofa and walked over to Zach's chair. "Did you see my star?"

"I sure did," Zach assured the boy. "I think it's the best ever. And that's some angel you drew."

Zach could see Lisa roll her eyes from where she still sat on the sofa. "It's not an angel. It's you."

The girl might as well have thrown a thunderbolt at him. "Me? An angel?"

"It's a cowboy," Lisa said as she stood up and walked over to the tree. She touched the star and then looked at Zach. "See. There's the hat."

"You put me on your star?" Zach repeated stupidly as he looked down at Andy.

The boy was smiling. "I put Thunder, too—on the other one."

Andy went over and touched the star with the horse on it before turning to Zach. "Do you like them?"

"They're the best ever," Zach said as he cleared his throat and then blinked. A bit of smoke from the lantern must have got in his eye. "What a wonderful Christmas surprise."

Andy looked at Lisa and they both giggled.

"That's not your Christmas surprise," Lisa finally said. "We've got that planned for tomorrow morning."

Zach hadn't had the breath knocked out of him this completely since he had been bucked off Black Demon in Fargo last year. He knew his mouth was hanging open, but he couldn't close it.

"We can't tell you what it is," Andy warned. The boy danced in excitement. "It's a surprise."

"Well, I'll be," Zach finally managed to say. "A Christmas surprise for me."

Zach turned to Jenny. He admitted he was a little giddy. Usually the only Christmas gifts he ever got were bottles of booze. "They have a surprise for me."

Jenny had never been prouder of her children. They'd planned a Christmas surprise for a guest in their household without any prompting or guidance from her. Jenny thought about that for a minute, and her pride quickly turned to worry. Her children had planned a Christmas surprise for Zach without her input. That could spell disaster.

Not all men appreciated the same things that children did and Jenny knew that. Granted, Zach had seemed genuinely touched with the stars. But who knew if he'd react as well to some wrinkled tie or cardboard belt buckle.

"I think maybe it's time for bed now," Jenny announced.

Even though both of her children sat with pleased looks on their faces, Jenny was sure one of them would tell her about their planned surprise when she tucked them into bed. If she knew what the big gift was maybe she could straighten a few of the corners or iron it or something. She'd noticed that several of the boxes in the corner of the living room looked as if someone had gone through them this afternoon.

Well, Jenny thought, whatever it was, she would do whatever she could to make it better. If she only knew what it was. Unfortunately, neither one of her children would budge, insisting it was a Christmas-morning surprise and surprises were secrets.

"Well, at least show me before you show it to him. Okay?" Jenny pulled the covers up to Lisa's chin and reminded herself to have her scissors and glue handy in the morning. Maybe she should also get out a needle and thread. "Is the surprise made out of cloth or paper?"

"Mom." Lisa rolled her eyes. "It's a surprise."

"I know, sweetie." Jenny bent down and kissed her daughter on the forehead. "I know."

Zach was in the kitchen, sitting at the table and stamping PRIORITY on a full yard of brown postal paper. He added a few green snowflakes drawn with one marker that still had ink in it. He decided right then that he needed to start carrying a bigger duffel. Either that or he'd have to tell Delores she needed to carry more supplies in her postal bin. He wished he had glitter or velvet or even a red stamp that gave a holiday greeting instead of a postal message. And that was just the stuff at the bottom of his wish list.

Right now, he wished for a whole lot of things. Ever since he'd seen that star, he'd wished he had time to go to Denver or Salt Lake or at least Billings to buy Christmas presents for this little family. He'd like to buy a princess doll and a tiara with real diamonds for Lisa. She could sell it when she wanted to go to college someday—and with a mind like hers she'd definitely want to go.

Then he'd buy a horse for Andy. And if a real horse would be too much trouble, he'd buy one of those electronic ones that they used in bars. He'd find one with a gentle setting. And, if he couldn't find one with a gentle setting, he'd buy the boy a carousel with a dozen horses to chose from.

And for Jenny—Zach stopped stamping and smiled—for Jenny he'd buy a full-length mink coat. Fake, of course, if she was bothered by the real thing. But something warm enough to weather the worst Montana storm her guidebook ever dreamed could hit.

He'd also buy her a tractor.

But Zach knew there was no time to travel and no clear roads even if there was time. There was no way to get to the gifts he wanted to buy. So he'd just have to make do with what he had.

"They're in bed," Jenny announced as she stood in the doorway to the kitchen. She had brought the lantern into the kitchen before putting the children to bed and its yellow light formed a circle around the table and Zach. The Christmas-tree lights had given off enough light for her to see Lisa and Andy to bed. Both children had promised to go to sleep quickly.

"They've had a busy day." Zach didn't know when he'd had a better day himself. He'd certainly never had a better day related to Christmas. He stopped stamping the brown paper and raised it up. "Do you think I should stamp this some more?"

"It looks good." Jenny had never seen a man so taken with Christmas. "I brought the wire hanger you wanted. And the strip of old towel."

Zach admired Jenny standing in the doorway. The red and green lights from the living room backed her silhouette, while the yellow light from the lantern played up the blond highlights in her hair. Her face looked dewy smooth and sculpted. Her eyelashes were thick and he didn't think she was even wearing any mascara. The shadows hid her blue eyes, and they looked like an ocean at midnight.

Zach swallowed and forced himself to think of the presents he still had to make. The night promised to be even longer than the watch on his wrist indicated. "Thanks for bringing everything. I'd better get started."

Zach had taken his duffel into the kitchen. He'd found a few minutes during the day to slip into the laundry room and pound belt holes in the strip of leather he was planning to use in Andy's gift. The rest of the work would be quiet, and he could do it while everyone slept.

"You're sure you want to cut this up?" Jenny walked over to the counter where Zach had laid out the leg garter and picked it up. The lantern light made the rhinestones sparkle quietly. "This had to be expensive."

The black lace and velvet circle studded with rhinestones looked like something out of a classy department store rather than a vending machine. Jenny counted the stones. Fifteen. "Some of these look real."

"The rubies are." Zach rolled the stamped postal paper up. He'd need the whole table for working. "There's only a couple of them. Of course, they're not high quality."

"And you're cutting this up?" Jenny looked at the garter more closely. Those rubies sure did look genuine. "You can't cut this up—not if they're real."

Jenny frowned. She didn't like the fact that Zach had

bought something with actual jewels in it for his girlfriend. A garter was one thing, but jewels! Jewels meant commitment. Maybe Zach's relationship with the showgirl was more serious than he had let on. Of course, he did not owe her any explanations about his relationships with women. Zach and her family were stranded together in a snowstorm. He didn't even want to be here. "I'm sure Patti would want the rubies even if you give them to her after Christmas."

"Ah, well, I don't know when I'll see her now. I mean, she expected me today so—" Zach didn't want to admit to Jenny that he'd lost all appetite for his Vegas vacation.

"Oh, and she won't know what's happened. She'll be worried."

"Not likely."

Jenny felt a little better. "She'll probably see the weather reports about a blizzard here. She'll know your trip might have been interrupted."

"Yeah." Zach didn't want to keep talking about Patti. He knew the showgirl wouldn't worry about him at all. "Do you have that hanger? I think that's the first thing to do— see if I can bend that into a likely shape." Zach looked up at Jenny. "Mind if I use your head to size it?"

"Huh?"

"The tiara." Zach took the metal hanger Jenny handed to him and ran his hands along it. "Good quality."

Jenny sat down at the table.

Zach stood up. This tiara-making business wasn't so bad. He realized he had every excuse in the world to touch

Jenny's head. "Lisa's hair is the same color as yours. Very pretty."

"Thank you." Jenny felt warm—too warm for a night like this. It was thirty degrees below zero outside tonight, and she knew for a fact that she kept the furnace thermometer set at sixty-five. She should be shivering from the cool instead of the heat—she barely felt Zach's hands as they circled the top of her head. Of course, it wasn't his hands that were bothering her. It was him. He was six feet of muscle standing behind her chair. She could feel the heat from his body. She wondered if he could feel her heart racing. "It's been quite a day."

"Mmm, hmm." Zach tried to keep his mind on the tiara instead of the fact that Jenny's hair was soft enough to kiss. And thick—her curls would scatter over a pillow like the petals of a sunflower. And to think he used to prefer long hair on his girlfriends.

What was he thinking? Zach pulled his hand back. Jenny wasn't his girlfriend. She wouldn't even kiss him. Well, he didn't think she'd kiss him. He hadn't asked again since this morning. And she was sitting awfully still in this dimly lit kitchen. He put his hand back, this time on her shoulder, and she didn't pull away. That had to be a good sign.

"Women—they say they can always change their minds, don't they?" Zach asked without thinking.

"Huh?" Jenny turned around to look at him. In the shadows her eyes were deep blue and unreadable.

"Ah…Lisa. You're sure she wants a tiara?" Zach could have kicked himself. He rode bucking horses, for Pete's sake. He was always able to ride out the shoot when the bar was pulled back. He never wavered. He never hesitated. Until now.

Jenny turned back. "Yeah, I'm sure. She's talked about it ever since we moved here. I wish I'd known sooner. I could have found one in a store in Los Angeles and brought it with us."

"Yeah."

Zach told himself a responsible, decent Santa would get on with making Christmas gifts and forget about the woman sitting in front of him. "And what have you wanted for Christmas?"

"Me?" Jenny laughed. "I've been working too hard to think about what I want."

"You need someone to help you."

Jenny leaned back into the man's hands. He was giving her a back rub. It felt wonderful. "I've been thinking of getting a dog."

"A dog?" Zach almost lost his rhythm in the back rub. That certainly put him in his place. He was losing his touch.

"Yeah, someone to chase the rabbits out of the garden come spring."

"You're planting a garden!" Zach had driven through this part of Montana last summer when there wasn't a foot of snow on the ground. "You'll need to put down a layer of topsoil first. The wind blew it all off a couple of years ago."

"The guidebook didn't mention anything about topsoil." Jenny frowned as she turned around to look at Zach. "It said I could grow anything."

"Potatoes might grow," Zach offered. He pressed against Jenny's left shoulder. "They don't take much topsoil."

"But I want snap peas and roses. Sort of an English garden. And some tomatoes."

"Oh." Zach moved over to the right shoulder.

Jenny felt as if her shoulders were putty. Warm, melting putty. Zach was massaging them with the palms of his hands.

Then Zach moved his hands to the base of the back of Jenny's neck.

Jenny held back the moan that purred deep in her throat. "How'd you ever get so good at this?" Jenny regretted the question as soon as she asked it. A single man like Zach only learned to give massages for one reason.

"My horse," Zach answered. Now why had Jenny stiffened up like that? There, that was better. "He had a leg injury."

"Ah, good," Jenny sighed.

"He didn't think so."

"No, I don't suppose he would."

The massage left Jenny relaxed and energized both at the same time. "I should help you with the presents."

"We've got time." Zach had never felt this content in all his life. Not when he'd bought his first horse. Not when he'd first won the Pro-Championship title. Not when he'd signed the contract with the Ranger cereal company. Not ever. "I like being here with you."

Jenny heard the words Zach whispered. Suddenly she didn't care that he was a man who was just traveling through. "I like you, too."

"Like as in like, or…?" Zach didn't want to shatter the quiet of the evening by making a false move.

Jenny stood up and turned to face Zach. There was only three inches between them. Then there was two. Then…

Jenny figured some women lived their whole lives and never had a kiss like this one. It curled her toes and made her breath stop in her throat. She would have swooned, but mothers with two young children did not swoon. "I feel faint."

"Hmm." Zach still had the taste of her lips on his tongue. He was reluctant to let go.

"I think—"

"Don't think."

"I think I need to wrap the Christmas presents."

Ah, Christmas. Christmas had given Zach trouble for years. Strangely enough, for the first time he didn't mind so much. "You can stamp while I finish up on the other presents."

Jenny not only stamped enough brown postal paper to wrap the gifts, she drew red bells on them. So what if the bells grew to look a little like hearts. It was Christmas, after all, and Christmas was a time for wishes and dreams.

It was even, she told herself firmly, a time for dreams that had no hope of ever coming true. She knew Zach "Lightning" Lucas was just passing through. She knew he wished he was in Las Vegas. She knew he hated Christmas and was just being kind to her and her children. But, even knowing all that, she couldn't help smiling when he walked into the unheated laundry room and came back with the mistletoe in his hand. "We could use this for decorations on the packages."

"It's a pity to waste it," Jenny said. She watched the slow smile spread across Zach's face as she added. "After all, it is Christmas Eve."

Jenny floated to bed that night. She'd had one magical night. She'd been kissed. She'd been hugged. She'd been listened to by someone who paid attention.

If she had to keep reminding herself that it wouldn't last forever, that is what she would do. After all, once Christmas was gone, winter would be long and cold. Her heart would have time to mend.

Chapter Nine

Could kisses give anyone a hangover?

Jenny sat in her bed and wondered how she could feel so bad on Christmas morning. Well, technically it wasn't morning yet, she comforted herself as she looked out the window in her bedroom. It was deep gray outside. The wind had stopped blowing. She had a good half hour before she had to get up and pretend everything was well with the world.

It was Merry Christmas time. Hugs and Santa time.

Jenny wanted to crawl into a dark pit and stay there until spring. But—she squinted at the illuminated clock by her bed—in nineteen minutes, she would smile. And she would pretend that everything was wonderful, even if she had to crawl to the Christmas tree on her hands and knees. Christmas was a special time of the year for children, and

Jenny was determined to add to her children's cheer and not take away from it.

It wasn't her children's fault that Jenny had gone crazy last night and thrown caution to the wind. And crazy it was. She'd fallen in love with a man who was only passing through—a man who had not even meant to end up in her house and would have left if the snow had not stranded him. He had only been there to deliver a package, for goodness sake. He was the mailman. And not even the regular mailman. He clearly wanted to spend Christmas with a showgirl instead of a widow and her two young children. What had she been thinking?

Jenny felt around in the semidarkness for the bottle of water she kept by her bed. Now, if she only had an aspirin. Or two. She winced. Make that four.

Zach was miserable. He would never be able to look at another Christmas card again. Or even a postal stamp— Fragile, Return to Sender, Priority—they would all be signals to him to count his shortcomings in the future.

He was a grown man. He should have known he would have to pay the price for those kisses last night. Never before had he so deeply regretted the kind of man he was. If he had any clue as to how to be a family man, he would take a nail and permanently tack that piece of mistletoe to the doorway of this house. And then he'd beg Jenny to marry him.

But he wasn't good at relationships. He didn't even know how much he didn't know. And it wasn't fair to Jenny to pretend otherwise. It certainly wasn't fair to the kids.

Sure, Zach admitted, he'd done all right for a day or two. He'd filled in for Stephen who should have been here with them. Anyone could follow a good act for a few minutes. It was like riding on a bronc that had been winded by the previous rider. It wasn't a fair test. And it wouldn't take long for Jenny to realize he was a fake.

Zach didn't relish seeing the disappointment in her eyes. He would have to leave. But before he left he owed them a merry Christmas. He was, for better or for worse, Santa Claus.

Zach was just snapping his white beard into place when he heard the first whisper. It sounded like Andy. The answer that came sounded like Lisa. Zach hurriedly put the Santa hat on his head. He'd already put the rest of the outfit on— even that belt with the lights.

Speaking of lights—Zach reached for the battery switch to turn on the Christmas-tree lights. The tree glowed in the early-morning light, casting red and green shadows all around the living room.

The tree sat in the middle of the living room, and the lights danced on all four walls. Zach's eyes were drawn to the bulletin board that he'd seen earlier. He'd avoided the pictures on the board yesterday, but now—knowing his hours with this family were limited—he went over to look at the pictures.

He had to smile. There was a photo of Andy dressed as a pumpkin for Halloween. There was Lisa in a frilly white dress and almost no teeth. And the zoo—there must have been four or five pictures of the children at the zoo. Andy by the elephants. Lisa by a giraffe. And the beach—there were so many pictures at the beach. In one of them, Jenny was building a sand castle with Andy. That picture was crooked. Lisa must have snapped it.

Zach wondered how many men's hearts were broken on Christmas morning. He wanted to give so much, and he had so little to give.

"What?" Jenny's voice carried from her bedroom. The children were clearly in with her, and a quiet rumble of whispers followed Jenny's first outburst. Zach couldn't make out any of the words, but he could tell a heated discussion was taking place behind the closed door.

Zach wondered if he was about to get his surprise. It sounded like some surprise. He only hoped the wrapped packages under the tree would be sufficient to repay the children for the amount of convincing they were doing. It sounded like an uphill battle was being fought in there.

He wondered what they were giving him that their mother so clearly disapproved of. It must be something like a knife. Mothers always disapproved of knives—as they should. But that couldn't be it. Jenny wouldn't care if he had a knife.

Maybe—and the thought didn't sit well with him—the children had decided to give him something that had belonged to their father and Jenny couldn't part with it. That made sense. Some favorite shirt or tie. Well, she didn't need to worry about him. He would quietly return anything they gave him that had sentimental value.

The voices went silent and then Zach saw Lisa's head

poke out of the partially opened door. She looked around and saw him.

"You need to go sit on the sofa," the girl directed him, before giving a worried look back into the bedroom. "We're almost ready."

Andy came out first and ran across the room to settle on the sofa next to Zach. Zach put his arm around the boy before he looked down at Andy's hair. A tiny white feather was sitting on top of the boy's head.

"Dum-da-dum," Lisa trumpeted as she stood in the open doorway.

What the…? Zach watched Lisa sneeze. She had a dozen tiny white feathers flying around her. They floated around her before settling to the floor.

Zach decided the children must be giving him a chicken for Christmas. A live chicken. That's all it could be with those feathers. But where had they kept a chicken? There was only one shed on the property and it was so rickety the coyotes would have torn it down long ago if there was a chicken inside. And he didn't hear any squawking. Only a tame chicken would lose its feathers without squawking. Oh, no, Zach thought. The chicken must be a pet.

"Dum-da-dum," Lisa repeated as she stepped to the side of the door and waved her arm for someone to come onstage.

What the…? Zach's first thought was that there must be a truckload of chickens inside Jenny's bedroom. Tiny white feathers floated everywhere as Jenny stood in the doorway in her—Zach took a second look and started to grin—Jenny was in a red-and-white cheerleader's outfit.

"It's a showgirl," Andy whispered.

Zach grinned like a fool. "That it is."

"You told them a showgirl was a cheerleader with feathers in her hair," Jenny accused him as she stood in the doorway to the bedroom. She held a pom-pom in each hand and an exasperated smile on her face. "Lisa even sacrificed her goose-down pillow so they'd have feathers."

"It works for me," Zach said. He couldn't take his eyes off Jenny. She stood there daring him to laugh. Her blue eyes glinted with steel. Her hair was sprayed stiff and covered with feathers. She was absolutely amazing.

"We have a cheer," Lisa announced as she motioned Andy to join her. "A Christmas cheer."

Zach saw Jenny close her eyes in resignation.

"One…two…three," Lisa counted off before she added, "Now."

The three voices blended. They spelled out the words. "M-E-R-R-Y C-H-R-I-S-T-M-A-S—Merry Christmas to you!"

Jenny kicked her leg up and shook her pom-poms. Lisa and Andy just screamed.

"Did you like it?" Andy asked eagerly before anyone else had regained their breath.

"I liked it a lot," Zach answered. Even if he lived to be a hundred, he would never receive a better Christmas surprise than this. "It's the best present ever."

"That's not all," Lisa screeched as she ran to the kitchen and came back with the camera. She handed the camera to Zach before rushing back to the doorway. "You get to take a picture of us, too."

Zach's eyes were blurry and his hands shook. But he snapped two pictures all the same. Now it really was the best Christmas gift possible. He had pictures of Jenny and the kids.

Jenny watched as Zach carefully set the pictures aside to develop. Well, he'd been a good sport about it. Lisa and Andy were still trembling with excitement, although she noticed their attention had moved from Zach to the wrapped packages lying under the tree.

"Did Santa come?" Andy finally asked softly.

Zach swallowed. "Well now, let's see."

It was an hour later before Jenny was able to convince everyone they needed to eat some breakfast. Lisa was pirouetting around the living room, dipping and twirling with her tiara. Andy was proudly strutting with the Stetson hat Zach had given him and the cowboy belt.

Jenny, herself, had been dumbfounded. Zach had given her his sheepskin coat. She shouldn't accept it.

Jenny knew he didn't have another coat with him and that, even though he claimed the Santa suit would keep him warm until he could buy another one, she still shouldn't take his coat.

But she couldn't resist.

It wasn't because the coat was warm and she'd realized winter would be much colder than her guidebook had indicated. No, the reason she couldn't refuse was because when she had the coat around her, she felt like Zach was with her. The coat carried the woodsy smell of him. It just plain comforted her. And she had a feeling she would need some comforting even before the day was gone.

"I need to have cereal for breakfast," Andy said after Jenny mentioned the meal. Andy swung his twine rope around. "I want some of the cereal that real cowboys eat."

"I think I can arrange that," Jenny said. Even though the electricity was out, the milk seemed to have stayed fine in the unheated laundry room. If anything, the room was probably colder than a refrigerator would be.

"But I don't know what princesses eat." Lisa stopped pirouetting. Her tiara tilted on her head, but she managed to look regal. "Andy can have cereal, but what will I have?"

"Peas," Zach answered. He was sitting on the sofa telling himself he'd never known a single moment in his life when he had been happier. Watching the kids play. Seeing Jenny wrapped in his coat. It was a perfect moment in time. "Canned peas."

"What?" Lisa looked as him suspiciously. She even walked over to him and leaned on his knee. "You're teasing me."

Zach brushed a feather out of her hair. "You've heard of the princess and the pea."

"But that wasn't breakfast, silly." Lisa giggled and rolled her eyes. "That was for her mattress."

"Is that right?" Zach watched Lisa laugh and shake her head. Another white feather floated to the floor. "You mean she sleeps on her vegetables?"

The sun had come up and was shining in the windows. The lights were still steadily lit on the Christmas tree, but the sunshine from outside dulled their glow.

"No, she doesn't," Lisa protested. "Nobody sleeps on vegetables."

Zach gave an exaggerated shrug. "I don't know. Kings and queens do strange things sometimes. I figure princesses might, as well."

"You could have toast and jam," Jenny offered. "And I could fix you some tea like the English make it with milk in it."

"I could be an English princess," Lisa agreed, and then leaned even more on Zach's knee as she looked at him. "And you can be my servant."

"Me?" Zach lifted his eyebrows and smiled at the girl. "Well, I guess you're right. A princess does need a servant or two. I would be delighted to serve you breakfast, madame."

"Not madame, it's Princess Lisa."

"Indeed it is, Princess Lisa."

Zach decided to serve everyone breakfast. He put a kitchen towel over his arm and a falsetto tone in his voice. He poured from the right and removed from the left. He made the children laugh and Jenny roll her eyes in merriment.

And then, when Zach almost had his back turned, he saw Jenny twist the cereal box around so she wouldn't have to see his picture on the back of the box.

"A problem with the box? I could remove it from the table if you like." Zach could hear the hurt in his own voice. No wonder men didn't like to be vulnerable—especially over breakfast.

"It's not—" Jenny started to explain. "It's not you. It's me."

"How can it be you and not me? It's my picture on the box." He might be hurt but he wasn't brain-dead. No one here owed him anything. Jenny didn't need to spare his feelings. Still, Zach didn't want his heart to bleed in front of the children. Especially not on Christmas day. He forced himself to smile. "Not that it matters. More toast anyone?"

Jenny took a deep breath and closed her eyes. "I used to talk to your picture."

"What?" Zach had picked up the empty toast plate and now he held it suspended.

Jenny opened her eyes. "I used to talk to your picture on the back of the cereal box."

"Really?"

"I was lonely," Jenny said defensively. "People pick up strange habits when they're lonely. I mean it's not like I knew you then."

"Really?" Zach had never thought of anyone talking to his picture before. "Really?"

"It's not that big of a deal. It's only a cereal box."

Zach started to smile. He almost started to whistle. "No problem. Anyone want more toast?"

Learning that someone made a habit of talking to your picture could boost a man's ego, Zach thought to himself all through the rest of the morning. It made twenty games of rope-the-foot possible with a little cowboy, as the boy learned to twirl his rope. It made ten dances with a princess possible, complete with nine bows and one beheading for displeasing the royal one. It even carried Zach through peeling potatoes and basting the Christmas ham.

It wasn't until Christmas dinner was finished that it occurred to Zach that Jenny would have talked to a box of detergent if it had been sitting on her table when she was so desperate. A woman whose beloved husband was sick would talk to anything rather than confess her worries to her husband.

"I'm sure he was a very special man—your Stephen," Zach said. Christmas, after all, was a time to think of others rather than yourself. Zach wanted her to know she could still talk to him. "It must be hard to have your first Christmas without him."

Zach and Jenny were sitting alone at the table. The children had eaten and fled into the living room to play. The blizzard had ended sometime last night and the sunlight coming inside now was so strong and warm that no candles were needed. The frost had melted on the windows. It was the middle of the afternoon.

Jenny took a deep breath. She owed it to Zach to tell him the truth—the whole miserable lot of it. But where did she start? "Stephen and I would have been married for ten years this coming February."

"What date?"

"Huh?"

"The date. What date did you get married?"

"February 14, Valentine's Day, although I don't see—"

Zach's shoulders slumped. He was right. This Stephen had been a charmer. What woman wouldn't want to get married on Valentine's Day? How was another man ever supposed to compete with that? "You must have had some memorable anniversaries."

"Memorable is right." Jenny hadn't realized for two years that the reason Stephen had been so intent that they marry on Valentine's Day was so that he wouldn't have to remember a separate anniversary date. Even with the added help, he hadn't remembered their anniversary for the past five years. "But that's not what I want to say."

"I know you loved him." The kitchen was warm and smelled good. Sunshine streamed into the room, and Zach could hear the children playing in the living room. He wanted to wrap the memory of this moment around him tight so that he could pull it out on some lonely night in the future and remember the time he'd been part of a family.

There was a soft ticking, and it took a minute before Zach realized what it was—he was hearing the clock. The electricity was back on.

Jenny swallowed. "Love is a complicated thing some-times."

"I'd expect so," Zach lied. He didn't find love compli-cated at all. Painful, yes. Complicated, no.

"It's not always—" Jenny began, and then paused.

The telephone rang.

"Service is back," Zach muttered. He supposed it wasn't fair, but he wouldn't have minded if the electricity stayed off for another week. Especially not if another storm moved in and kept them all stranded together. But he'd known since morning that the snow outside was melting. Sure, the road still had a buildup of snow on it, but he might be able to push his way through in the postal truck this afternoon.

"Hello," Jenny answered the phone. "Oh, hi, Delores. I can't thank you enough for—oh, yes, he's here." Jenny paused, listening. "No, no he hasn't shown up yet. Yes, I'll call you then." Another pause. "No, no, it was no problem. It was good to have him here. Yes, I'll see you tomorrow then."

It didn't take a snowdrift to freeze Zach's heart. He already heard a distant roar coming toward the house.

Jenny hung up and looked at Zach. "Delores sent the county snowplow out to plow our road."

"I didn't think they'd work on Christmas. Isn't that overtime?"

"Double time, but they had to do it. We have the postal truck, and tomorrow is a mail day."

Couldn't the mail just wait for a day, Zach thought. Or maybe a week. Even a month would be okay. "So this is it."

Jenny nodded. "You'll have to drive the postal truck back."

But you can come back then, Jenny thought. There's nothing that says you can't come back. We haven't had nearly enough time to...to what, she asked herself. More time would only add to the heartbreak if he was going to leave anyway.

"I'm going to leave the reindeer horns and the lights," Zach said. He could hardly speak. How did a man leave when every atom of his being wanted to stay? "Delores can pick them up later."

Jenny nodded. "She told me how grateful she was you drove for her that last day."

"No problem."

Zach willed his legs to move. He could hear the snow-plow clearly outside now. There were no more excuses to stay. But he still sat.

"You'll be in Vegas late tomorrow." Jenny twisted a knot in the napkin she held in her hand. Zach had never pretended to be anything other than a cowboy out looking for a good time. Even she knew a widow with two little kids wasn't a good time.

"Yeah," Zach lied. He didn't know where he was going. He didn't care. But he had no appetite anymore for Vegas. A grieving man didn't go to Vegas. He'd rather find a deserted hotel somewhere in the open spaces of Utah and lick his wounds for a few weeks.

A man's boots stomped on the porch before a loud knock came at the kitchen door. "I'm the snowplow man."

There was a moment of silence.

"He'll want a cup of coffee," Jenny finally said as she stood to open the door.

"I'd best say goodbye to the kids." Zach stood, as well. The dream was over.

Chapter Ten

"I hear you were one popular Santa Claus," Delores Norris said as she opened the door to her brother's house for Zach. The warm smell of roasting turkey came floating out into the cold air behind her. "Why, I got calls—"

"Calls?" Zach's heart started to pound. He stopped scraping the snow off his boots and just stood there.

Delores nodded. "Mrs. Goussley left three messages telling me how much the cats missed you already and what a great Santa you were."

"Oh." Zach grunted as he started scraping his boots again. The cats.

Christmas had gotten the best of him again. Next Christmas he wasn't taking any chances. He'd head to a deserted island, maybe someplace off the Alaskan coastline. Or maybe Iceland. No one went to Iceland in the winter.

"And, of course, the candy canes were a hit," the older woman continued as she accepted the bag from Zach that held the Santa costume. "They always are."

Delores was just as Zach had pictured her. She had bouncy gray hair and a mouth that didn't stop chatting. Her bright eyes welcomed him like he belonged.

How was she to know he didn't belong anywhere?

"I suppose Thunder is able to travel," Zach said.

"Well, yes, but you don't want to head out this afternoon. You won't make it to a town with a hotel before dark. Besides, we have a spare room and a whole half a turkey left from dinner. There's nothing like a fresh-turkey sandwich with dressing on the side."

Delores was the picture of hospitality with a red-checked apron hanging over a navy sweatsuit. She had pearl earrings on her ears and tennis shoes on her feet. She was looking at him as if he was a long-lost friend.

Zach forced himself to smile. "Thanks, but I'll be moving on. I might make it into Wyoming before nightfall."

"Well, if you're sure." A tiny frown settled on Delores's forehead. "But I'd like a chance to thank you by giving you a night's stay at least."

"No need to thank me."

"We've got pie, too. Apple and cherry. I've never known a cowboy to turn down a piece of homemade pie."

"That's kind of you, but I'd best be moving on."

"Well, all right then." Delores stepped out onto the porch and crossed her arms. "Let me just go park the postal truck in its spot."

"I can move it if you tell me where it goes."

"It's easier just to show you," Delores said with a wave of her hand as she marched off the porch.

"Your feet will get cold," Zach called after her. Oh, well, Zach thought, if she didn't care, who was he to make a big deal out of it.

Zach followed her back to the postal truck.

"Oh, isn't this nice?" Delores had already opened the door and leaned into the truck. She reached out for the photographs that Zach had laid out on the dash.

Zach winced. He'd taken the pictures out so he could look at them as he bounced along the country roads back into Deep Gulch. "I'll just pack them up. Got my duffel in back, too."

Delores stepped back, holding all four pictures. She squinted in the sunlight as she tilted the photographs up so she could see them better. "Why, aren't those nice?"

"Yeah." Zach swallowed. He didn't know what to say. Not that there was anything to say. A picture was just a picture.

Delores looked closely at each picture. Zach didn't have to see the pictures to know what she saw. A picture of Jenny as his showgirl. A picture of Andy roping Zach's foot. A picture of Zach dancing with Princess Lisa. A picture of Zach and the children dragging the Christmas tree up from the coulee.

"Well," Delores said softly as she lowered the pictures and turned curious eyes toward Zach. "Looks like you had some Christmas."

Zach grunted. "I was just doing what I could to make sure they had a good Christmas."

"I see."

"Anyone would have done the same." Zach held out his hand. He wasn't going anywhere without his pictures. "They're good kids."

"Uh-huh," Delores agreed. She didn't hand over the pictures, though. "I don't think I've ever seen the kids like this—laughing and being silly."

"Well, it's Christmas. You know how kids are at Christmas."

"I suppose." Delores took another hard look at him as she handed him the pictures.

The sun warmed the air considerably, but it was still too cold to stand outside and talk. Zach hoped that encouraged the woman to go back inside. "They're just missing their father."

"The kids?" Delores seemed surprised. "Did they talk about him?"

Zach shuffled. He hadn't meant to get into a conversation about the man. "Well, no, but you gotta figure he was a good father. Good husband, too. They got married on Valentine's Day, you know?"

"No, I didn't know."

Zach knew it was time to go. There was only a couple of hours of daylight left, and he'd like to get closer to the Wyoming border before pulling off the interstate for the night. But his mouth just kept talking.

"Must have been tough when he died," Zach added. What was wrong with him? Then he knew what he wanted to say. He knew the question he wanted to ask someone. "Wonder what made him so special anyway?"

Delores looked him over once again. Zach felt her gaze. But the woman wasn't unkind about it. She was obviously just thinking.

"What makes you think he was special?" Delores finally asked.

"Well…I…" Zach stammered. Of course the man was special. "The kids are such good kids and Jenny, well, Jenny is wonderful."

Delores nodded. "Funny thing, though. Jenny never talks about her late husband."

"Well, no, but…"

"Kids don't, either."

Zach was silent. Come to think of it, the kids didn't talk about their father.

"And did you ever see those pictures she's got hanging on the wall in the living room?"

Zach smiled and nodded. "They liked the zoo."

Delores nodded, too. "Ever wonder why there's no pictures of the father there?"

The silence cracked over Zach's head. Delores was right. There were no pictures of Stephen. "What do you suppose that means?"

Delores shrugged. "I don't know for sure." She looked up at Zach and smiled. "But if I was you I'd go ask Jenny about it before I drove away."

"You think it might not have been—" Zach cleared his throat. "I mean, do you think a man like me could have a chance?"

"I'm not the one you need to ask."

Zach figured there was a silly smile on his face, but he couldn't stop the grin from spreading. "Mind if I borrow the postal truck again? I'll be back in a few hours."

Delores grinned back at him as she handed him the keys. "I don't need it until nine o'clock tomorrow morning."

"Tell Doc I'll pick Thunder up later."

"Don't worry. That old horse of yours will be fine here."

The road back to Jenny's place had just as many bumps as it had the first time Zach had ridden over it. The difference was that this time he grinned a little more at each bump he drove over.

Jenny thought she heard someone drive up to her house, but she wasn't sure. She and the children had been sitting on the sofa with blankets snuggled around them. Jenny had offered to read to them, but they both seemed to just want to sit and be quiet.

"I think someone is here," Jenny said softly as she untangled her arms from the blankets.

"Tell them to go away," Andy muttered. "We don't want nobody."

"This is Montana," Jenny chided her son gently as she stood up. "Neighbors are important and will always be welcome in our house."

"If it's a stranger, you should be careful," Lisa advised glumly. "It's not just snakes you have to watch for around here."

"I'll be careful," Jenny said as she started to walk toward the kitchen. "It's probably just the snowplow guy again."

Jenny had to step around the Christmas tree to get to the kitchen. The batteries had died on the tree lights, and the stars didn't sparkle anymore. Andy's hat sat forgotten beside the tree. Lisa's tiara was next to it.

Christmas this year had been both the best ever and the worst ever for her little family.

The sun had melted most of the frost in the small window of the outside kitchen door. But the afternoon had faded and the light had never been good on that side of the house. She saw a shape, but she could not tell who it was. She squinted, anyway—those shoulders reminded her of— not that it would be him.

Jenny opened the door. What in the world—?

Jenny tried to form a word, but couldn't for a full minute. Then it occurred to her that many things could explain why this particular man was standing on her porch. "Forget something?"

Zach smiled. "I guess I did."

"Let me know where it is and I'll go get it." Jenny knew it was rude to leave someone standing on the porch, but she didn't want her children to know he was here. He'd only break their hearts two minutes later when he left again.

"Well, I don't quite know where it is." Zach tried smiling harder. His smile was often called *charming* by women.

There was no smile in return. "We only have the five rooms."

Zach looked at Jenny. She didn't exactly look welcoming. In fact, she barely looked as if she tolerated his presence. Her eyes were guarded. She wasn't smiling. She hadn't invited him into the house and it was cold outside.

All in all, Zach conceded, it didn't look good. But a man didn't ride wild horses because he believed in taking the safe route. Zach reached up and ran his hands around the side brim of the Stetson hat sitting on his head. It was the same gesture he used when he was ready to start a rodeo ride.

"It's more of a question than anything."

"Oh?"

"When you talked to my face on that cereal box, what did you talk about?"

Jenny could hear Lisa and Andy running toward the kitchen. She didn't have much time. "Is this some market-research question? You think your sponsor would like to know? Maybe they'll find some small demographic niche of women who are crazy enough to talk to cereal boxes."

The footsteps entered the kitchen.

"Mr. Lightning!"

"Santa!"

Two pairs of feet ran to the door and planted themselves beside Jenny.

"You're back!"

"You came!"

Now this was a better welcome, Zach thought as he looked down at the kids. "Hi, there. Mind if I talk to your mom for a minute?"

"Sure," the two voices answered.

But no feet moved. Three pairs of eyes kept looking at him.

"Alone." Zach swallowed.

"Maybe you could go pick out the books you want me to read for you tonight when it's time," Jenny suggested.

"Okay," Lisa said, and started back to the living room. The girl nudged Andy to follow her.

Zach waited until the children were in the living room. "I'm not asking about the cereal box because I care about marketing. I want to know what you were thinking and feeling. I want to know why you don't have any pictures of Stephen on your bulletin board."

"Stephen?" Jenny paused. This was about Stephen?

"Was it because it was too painful for you to have any pictures of him around?"

"No," Jenny answered. "It's just that we didn't have any pictures. Not ones like that. I mean, we have a couple of formal shots—he needed one for a business thing once. But that was taken at a studio."

"Was the man camera shy?"

"Stephen? No."

"Then why don't you have any pictures?"

Jenny suddenly felt very tired. She'd never complained about Stephen. Never complained about him to anyone. She told herself she was protecting him. But now she wondered if she was only protecting herself.

There was such a long pause Zach wondered if Jenny was ever going to answer him.

"Because he was never with us," Jenny finally admitted. She needed to tell someone the truth about her life. "When we went to the zoo, he went fishing with some buddies of his. When we went to the beach, he went to a ball game with some other friends."

"So he wasn't some kind of superfather?"

"Stephen? No. He was barely a father at all."

Zach was beginning to have hope. Maybe he'd do all right as a father. But there was something even more important he needed to know.

"And as a husband? How was he as a husband?"

Jenny looked up at Zach. She saw longing for the children and for her in his eyes. She had never realized until now that Stephen's disinterest in being a husband only added to his disinterest in being a father. The two weren't separate. A man who would make a good husband to her would also make a good father to the children.

Especially, she thought to herself, if it was this man standing before her. She looked at him carefully. She could see the fears in his eyes. The drawn tension around his lips. All pretense was gone from his face. He was letting her see his insecurities and his longings.

Jenny reached up and caressed Zach's cheek briefly. She needed to let him see her as well. All her fears. Her defeats. Her tiredness. "He never loved me."

Jenny closed her eyes. There, she'd said it aloud. Stephen had never loved her.

A moment passed before Jenny realized her fears had not come true. Telling someone the truth about her and Stephen did not cause a crushing blackness in her heart. Instead, her heart felt lighter than it had in years.

Zach reached up and covered Jenny's hand with his. "He was a fool."

"I really tried to make him care." Jenny let Zach draw her into his arms.

"He didn't deserve you," Zach whispered. "You deserve someone better—someone more like, say, me."

Jenny opened her mouth to speak.

"No, don't answer yet. Hear me out." Zach held her quietly and talked in her ear. He'd never had such an important moment in his life. Every word counted. "I grew up in a family of loners. But I can learn how to be a good husband and a good father. If you just give me time."

Jenny opened her mouth again to speak.

"No, that's not all. I want you to know I work hard, too. We can build a farm here or we can do something else. Whatever you and the kids want."

Jenny opened her mouth again to speak.

"No, that's not all, either. I—"

Jenny reached up and put her fingers lightly over his mouth. She didn't intend to ever hide the truth from this man again.

"If you don't stop talking, how can I ever say yes?"

Jenny had seen her share of sunrises. But she had never seen anything as full of brilliant hope as Zach's face.

"Yes?" he asked. "I mean, I know you would want to wait a few months to be sure, but yes, sometime. That's good."

Jenny supposed it was too much to have expected her children to really sit and pick out books to read when Zach was around. She saw them peek around the doorway into the kitchen.

"Is Mr. Lightning staying?" Andy whispered.

Lisa just rolled her eyes and lifted the camera up to take a picture.

Jenny closed her eyes when the flash hit. She kept them closed for the kiss that followed. And for the one after that.

Later that night Zach and Jenny together pinned the picture Lisa had taken on the bulletin board. The picture was a little blurry and tilted sideways. But Jenny knew that, even though they would have many more pictures together over the years, this first picture would always be special.

Epilogue

Zach and Jenny decided that April was a perfect month for a wedding.

Zach had finished the new roof by then, and Jenny had planted the first seeds in her garden. They both had taken time to test their first rush of love and be confident that what they felt for each other was strong enough to last forever.

The four months also gave them time to become part of the community of Deep Gulch. Zach took a job as the relief carrier for Delores and rented a room from the doc. Jenny joined the parents' group at the school and volunteered to staff the refreshment stand for the basketball games.

When the organist started the bridal march at the church, almost everyone in and around Deep Gulch was there to watch the two of them say their vows.

Zach and Jenny had told everyone that wedding gifts weren't needed. But the people of Deep Gulch all brought wrapped packages, anyway. There were pink oblong boxes. White oblong boxes. Gold oblong boxes. Delores was the first to notice that the boxes all looked alike. Since she also held an oblong package in her hand she knew what the presents were—dozens of family photo albums. Everyone knew, by now, that Jenny loved to take pictures of her family.

Not that Jenny looked as though she cared what she received for wedding gifts. Delores decided she'd never seen a more beautiful bride.

Jenny herself was holding Zach's hand so hard she was afraid she'd dent the ring she'd just slipped on his finger.

"You may now kiss the bride," the minister announced.

Jenny didn't even notice the camera flashes as Zach smiled and then bent to kiss her.

*   *   *   *   *

New York Times bestselling author
Linda Lael Miller
is back with a new romance featuring
the heartwarming McKettrick family
from Mills & Boon® Special Edition.

Sierra's Homecoming
by Linda Lael Miller

On sale December 2007

Turn the page for a sneak preview!

Sierra's Homecoming

by

Linda Lael Miller

Soft, smoky music poured into the room.

The next thing she knew, Sierra was in Travis's arms, close against that chest she'd admired earlier, and they were slow dancing.

Why didn't she pull away?

"Relax," he said. His breath was warm in her hair.

She giggled, more nervous than amused. What was the matter with her? She was attracted to Travis, had been from the first, and he was clearly attracted to her. They were both adults. Why not enjoy a little slow dancing in a ranch-house kitchen?

Because slow dancing led to other things. She took a step back and felt the counter flush against her lower back. Travis naturally came with her, since they were holding hands and he had one arm around her waist.

Simple physics.

Then he kissed her.

Physics again—this time, not so simple.

"Yikes," she said, when their mouths parted.

He grinned. "Nobody's ever said that after I kissed them."

She felt the heat and substance of his body pressed against hers. "It's going to happen, isn't it?" she heard herself whisper.

"Yep," Travis answered.

"But not tonight," Sierra said on a sigh.

"Probably not," Travis agreed.

"When, then?"

He chuckled, gave her a slow, nibbling kiss. "Tomorrow morning," he said. "After you drop Liam off at school."

"Isn't that…a little…soon?"

"Not soon enough," Travis answered, his voice husky. "Not nearly soon enough."

* * *

Don't forget
Sierra's Homecoming
is available next month!

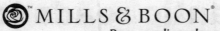
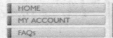

Romantic reads to
Need, Want

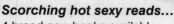

LOOK OUT...

...for this month's special product offer.
It can be found in the envelope containing
your invoice.

**Special offers are exclusively for
Reader Service™ members.**

You will benefit from:

- Free books & discounts
- Free gifts
- Free delivery to your door
- No purchase obligation – 14 day trial
- Free prize draws

THE LIST IS ENDLESS!!

*So what are you waiting for —
take a look* **NOW!**

DM/OFFER